ONE FOR THE ROGUE

Also by Charis Michaels

The Virgin and the Viscount
The Earl Next Door

ONE FOR THE ROGUE

The Bachelor Lords of London

CHARIS MICHAELS

AVONIMPULSE
An Imprint of HarperCollins Publishers

Excerpt from *Along Came Love* copyright © 2016 by Tracey Livesay.
Excerpt from *When a Marquess Loves a Woman* copyright © 2016 by Vivienne Lorret.

EPub Edition DECEMBER 2016 ISBN: 9780062412966

Print Edition ISBN: 9780062412973

Avon, Avon Impulse, and the Avon Impulse logo are trademarks of HarperCollins Publishers.

AM 10 9 8 7 6 5 4 3

For my husband, with gratitude and love,
for the old house and the new house and
the real Rossmore Court.

PROLOGUE

This is the tale of two brothers.

No, allow me to go back. This is the tale of two *half* brothers, a distinction that does not affect the brothers as much as it creates a place for the story to begin.

They were born deep in Wiltshire's Deverill Valley, less than a mile from the River Wylye, in a crumbling manor house called Rossmore Court.

Although the Rainsleigh title was ancient and the family lands entailed, the boys' parents, Lord Franklin "Frankie" Courtland, the Viscount Rainsleigh, and his lady wife, Este, were not held in high esteem—not by their neighbors in Wiltshire nor by members of London's *haute ton*. Instead, they were known mostly for their predilections: recklessness, coarseness, drunkenness, irresponsibility, and deep debt.

Their notoriety did not curtail their fun, however, and they carried on exactly as they pleased. In 1779, the viscountess became pregnant, and Lord and Lady Rainsleigh added "woefully unfit parents" to their list of indiscretions. Their firstborn was called Bryson—the future viscount, Lord

Rainsleigh's heir. Young Bryson was somber and curious, stormy and willful, but also inexplicably just and kind.

In 1785, Este and Frankie welcomed a second son, favored almost immediately by his mother for his sweet nature and easy manner, his angelic face and smiling blue eyes. The viscountess named him Beauregard, known as "Beau."

On the whole, the boys' childhood was not a happy one. Lord Rainsleigh was rarely at home, and when he was, he was rarely sober. He managed the boys with equal parts mockery and scorn. Lady Rainsleigh, in turn, was chronically unhappy, petulant, and needy, and she suffered an insatiable appetite for strapping young men, with a particular preference for broad-shouldered members of staff.

Money was scarce in those years, and schooling was catch-as-catch-can. The brothers relied on each other to get along.

Bryson's hard work and good sense earned them money for new coats and boots each year, for books, and for an old horse that they shared.

Beau employed his good looks and charm to earn them credit in the village shops, to convince foremen to hire them young, and to persuade servants and tenants to stay on when there was no money for salaries or repairs.

And so it went, each of the boys contributing whatever he could to get by, until the summer of 1807, when the old viscount's recklessness caught up with him, and he tripped on a root in a riverbed and died.

With Frankie's death, Bryson, the new viscount, set out to right all the wrongs of his father and cancel the family's debts. He moved to London, where he worked hard, built and sold a boat, and then another, and then another—and then five. And then fifteen. Eventually, he owned a shipyard and became wealthier than his wildest dreams.

Beau, on the other hand…

Well, Beau had no interest in righting wrongs or realizing moneyed dreams—*he* wasn't the Rainsleigh heir, thank God. His only wish was to take his handsome face and winning charm and discover the delights of London and the world beyond.

For a time, he sailed the world as an officer of the Royal Navy. For another time, he imported exotic birds and fish. He spent more than a year with the East India Company, training native soldiers to protect British trade. His life was adventurous and rambling, sunny if he could manage it, and (perhaps most important) entirely on his own terms.

Until, that is, the day the Courtland brothers received, quite unexpectedly, a bit of shocking news that changed both of their lives.

The news, which they learned from a stranger, was this: the boys did not share the same father.

The horrible old viscount—the man who had beaten them and mocked them, who had driven them into debt and allowed their boyhood home to fall into ruin—was not, in fact, *Bryson's* father after all. Bryson's father was another man—a blacksmith's son from the local village with whom their mother had had a heated affair.

Beau, as it turned out, was the only natural-born son of Franklin Courtland.

Beau was the heir.

And just like that, Beauregard Courtland became the Viscount Rainsleigh, the conservator and executor of all his brother had toiled over a great many years to restore and attain.

It made no difference that Beau had no desire to be viscount, that he was repelled by the notion, that the idea of becoming viscount made him a little ill.

In protest, Beau threatened to leave the country; he threatened to change his name; he threatened to commit a crime and endure prison to avoid the bloody title—all to no avail.

He *was* the rightful Viscount Rainsleigh, whether he liked it or not.

His brother, now simply Mr. Bryson Courtland, shipbuilder and merchant, set out on a new quest: to train, coach, and cajole Beau into becoming the responsible, noble, respected viscount that he himself would never be again.

To answer that, Beau seized his own quest: resist. He could not prevent his brother from dropping the bloody title in his lap, but he could refuse to dance to the tune the title played.

He would carry on, he vowed, exactly as he had always done—until…well…

"Until" is where this tale begins.

But perhaps this is not a tale of two brothers or even the tale of two half brothers.

Perhaps it is the story of one brother and how the past he could not change built a future that he, at long last, was willing to claim.

CHAPTER ONE

December 1813
Paddington Lock, London

Emmaline Crumbley, the Dowager Duchess of Ticking, had agreed to a great many things in life that she later lived to regret.

She regretted leaving Liverpool to move to London.

She regretting marrying a decrepit duke, three times her age.

She regretted cutting her hair.

Most recently—that is, most *immediately*—she regretted striding down the wet shoreline of Paddington Lock at seven o'clock in the morning for the purpose of—

Well, she couldn't precisely say what she had agreed to do.

Instruct a full-grown man on the finer points of eating with a fork and knife? On sitting upright? Teach him to smile and say, "How do you do?"

Teach him to dance?

"Good God," she whispered, "I hope not."

Her tacit agreement with Mr. Bryson Courtland, the new viscount's brother, had not been a specific checklist so much as a vague wish to *refine* the new lord. A wistfulness. Mr. Courtland was *wistful* (really, there was no other word) about how perfectly suited Emmaline was to sort out his wayward brother. About how she might, in fact, be his only hope.

And there it was. The reason Emmaline had agreed to do it, despite her mounting regret. There was perhaps no stronger leverage than being anyone's only hope.

And what Emmaline needed right now—more than she needed to stop agreeing to things or even to stop regretting them—was *leverage*. Leverage with the wealthy, shipbuilding Bryson Courtland, no less. If Mr. Courtland wished to see his brother trained in the finer arts of being a gentleman, well, she stood ready to serve.

The shifting gravel crunched loudly beneath her boots, and she walked faster, trying to outpace the sound. She spared another look over her shoulder. The canal was deserted at this hour, something she could not have guessed. Her plan had been to come early but not to find herself alone. In this, she was lucky for the fog. Visibility was no more than five feet. Just enough to make out the name on the last narrow boat in the row.

Trixie's Trove.

A ridiculous name, painted on the hull in ridiculously overwrought script. Everything about the boat was, in fact, ridiculous, from the peeling purple paint to the viscount who lived aboard it.

Certainly the fact that she was broaching its wobbly stern for the third time this month was ridiculous.

Ah, but you agreed to this, she reminded herself. *It is a very small means to a much larger end.*

Squaring her shoulders, Emmaline contemplated the swaying gangplank, a rickety ribbon of loosely wired boards. She'd learned to navigate the moldering plank on her two previous calls to the houseboat and could easily step aboard without snagging the silk of her skirts (even while she felt a small thrill each time the stiff black bombazine caught and tore).

Three more days, she reminded herself, and she could trade full mourning for half. In place of black, she would be permitted to wear…gray. Hardly an improvement, but at least she could get rid of the detestable, vision-blocking veil. And the black. Oh, how she detested the black.

Gulls squawked forebodingly in the distance, and she paused to scan the shoreline. The Duke of Ticking's grooms had never trailed her this early in the morning, but their spying became more prevalent with each passing day. A quiet path was no guarantee of a safe one. At the moment, she saw only the misty shore, an empty bench, and the outline of the buildings lining New Road. Safe and clear. For the moment.

Drawing a resigned breath, she clasped the ropes on either side of the gangplank and teetered onboard.

The viscount's houseboat was strewn with an indistinguishable jumble of provisions and rigging and dead chub. She knew to expect this from previous visits and now picked her way to the door. At one time, it had perhaps been painted red. Orange, maybe. Now it was a dusty, mud-smeared gray. Precisely the color, she hypothesized, of the viscount's pickled liver. Thankful for her gloves, Emmaline took up her skirts to descend the steps that led to the door when—

Crash!

The door swung open and banged against the cabin wall. Emmaline skittered back, silently flailing, until she collided with an overturned barrel. She sat, swallowing a gasp and whipping around to gauge her distance to the side of the boat. Less than a foot, but she was steady, thank God, on the splintered planks of the barrel. She closed her eyes. *Means to an end. A great favor for a great favor.*

Female laughter burst from the door, and she opened her eyes. Three women staggered onto the deck in a chain of wild hair and sagging silk and dragging petticoats. At their feet, a dog pranced and barked.

"Give my regard to Fannie," a man's voice called after them.

"Oh, we'll tell 'er, lovey!" called one of the women. More laughter. The trio linked arms and tripped their way to the gangplank, working together to stay upright. The dog, meanwhile, had caught scent of Emmaline and padded over to sniff the hem of her dress. She watched the dog warily and gestured in a shooing motion to the bustle of women trailing onto the shore. The dog ignored them and plopped her shaggy front paws on Emmaline's skirts.

"Next time, I'll be expecting Fannie," the man's voice called cheerfully again from within.

The viscount, Emmaline guessed. On previous visits, she had not heard him speak. Well, perhaps she had heard him speak but not actual words. He had mumbled something unintelligible. He had snorted. There may have been the occasional gurgling sound. She had come early today in hopes of discovering him in full possession of his faculties, especially speech. In this, she seemed to have succeeded, but she would never have guessed he would not be alone.

Now she heard footsteps. Something fell over with a clatter. There was a muttered curse, more footsteps. Emmaline shoved off the barrel and stood, her eyes wide on the door. The dog dropped from her skirts but remained beside her, and she fought the impulse to sweep her up into her arms. Protection. Ransom. Courage with a wet nose and shaggy tail.

But the dog left her when the man who matched the voice emerged to fill the doorway. Tall, rumpled, untucked, he leaned against the outside wall of the cabin and stared into the mist.

Oh.

She forgot the dog and took a step closer.

Oh.

But he was far younger than she'd thought. Not a boy, of course, but not so much older than her own twenty-three years. Twenty-seven perhaps? Twenty-eight?

And he was so...fit. Well, fitter than she'd guessed he would be. Of course she'd never seen him standing upright. The doorway was small, and he was forced to angle his broad shoulders and stoop to see out. He hooked his large hands casually on the ledge above the door and rested his forehead on a thick bicep. Squinting lazily, he watched the women disappear into the fog.

One of them called back, an unintelligible jumble of hooting laughter and retort, and he huffed, a laugh that didn't fully form.

Emmaline looked too, ever worried about the grooms, but the shoreline was a swirl of cottony mist.

When she swung her gaze back to viscount, he was no longer laughing or squinting. Now, he stared—but not at the shoreline.

The viscount was staring at her.

Bloody, bleeding hell, the blackbird was back.

At the damnable crack of bloody dawn.

Beau Courtland thumbed through his mental guide to making oneself disappear. It was too late to hide or feign unconsciousness, but he could always plunge over the side and into the canal. Limited options, really, but he was highly motivated.

"Lord Rainsleigh?" the woman called, taking a step toward him.

Beau stared.

"Lord Rainsleigh?" she called again, louder this time. As if once hadn't been terrible enough.

His eyes flicked to the side of the boat. The canal would be icy in December, but he was growing less and less particular.

"You have the wrong boat," he called back, beckoning his dog with a snap of his finger. Peach trotted to his side.

"I am the Dowager Duchess of Ticking," she went on. "How do you do?"

Buggered, he thought, *and you?*

And now they both had titles? Brilliant. This ruled out charity crusader, which had been his first guess. Or missionary, which had been his second. She wore enough black fabric to smother a horse and a stiff black veil, which obscured half her face. He couldn't see her eyes.

"I've come at the request of your brother," she continued.

Beau swore. The only thing more tedious than his title was his brother's ambitions for it. His mood spiraled, and he dropped his hands from the door jamb and trudged up the steps to the deck. Useless move, because he still couldn't see her face. Although...nice mouth, for all that. Pink and plump and pursed into a pout.

He knew from the lilt in her voice that she was young. And her posture. Upright and effortless. Her mouth was...

It occurred to him that he'd gotten close enough. In fact, he fought the urge to take a sudden step back.

"I'm here about the tutorials," the veiled woman said.

"What tutorials?"

"Well, guidance—for you, really. As you assume your new role as viscount." She closed the last steps between them and folded the veil back with black-gloved fingers. She turned up her face.

Now he did take a step back.

The face that blinked up at him seemed to burn away the morning fog. Large brown eyes, thick lashes, a dimple on one creamy cheek.

And that mouth.

"Comportment," the mouth was saying, "manners, responsibilities, life at court. I am an acquaintance of your brother, Mr. Bryson Courtland. He has, er, asked me to help you settle in to the expectations of your new role as viscount."

And just like that, their conversation was over. "Good-bye," he said.

Later, he would look back and concede that his brother had played it very well. A shockingly pretty girl—a widow, no less, his favorite. Delicate. Large eyes like a baby owl. The dimple. *The mouth.*

Later, he would curse his decision not to leap over the side and swim for Blackwall.

Instead, he dismissed her. Firmly, with finality and conviction. At his feet, Peach barked once for dramatic effect.

And then he turned on his heel and strode across the deck, clipped down the steps to the door of cabin, and was gone.

CHAPTER TWO

Emmaline stared at the wet spot on the deck where the viscount had been.

A crash sounded from inside the cabin, and she looked to the open door. She picked her way across the deck to the top step. "If you please, Lord Rainsleigh?" She peered into the dim interior. "We haven't yet—"

"If the arrangement was with my brother," he called from inside, "then I suggest you tutor *him* in manners and comportment and life at bloody court."

"On the contrary," Emmaline called down the steps, "your brother feels quite strongly that these are areas in which *you*—"

"How much is he paying you?" He popped his head out of the door.

Emmaline straightened. The sun was up now, and she could see his face more clearly. His eyes were blue. Terribly, *piercingly* blue, like the underpinning of a flame. "I beg your pardon?"

"My brother. How much has he *paid you* to hunt me down and train me to roll over and play dead?"

"Play dead?" she repeated.

"Whatever the sum, I'll double it."

"Sum?" She sounded like a parrot, repeating everything he said, but she hadn't been prepared to tell him the terms of the arrangement with his brother. She hadn't been prepared to tell him anything about herself at all.

Mr. Courtland had suggested that his brother would be "reluctant," but she would pin this more like "opposed." *Aggressively* opposed.

"I've never paid a woman to go away," he said, looking her up and down, "but there's a first time for everything."

Emmaline felt herself blush. She also had not been prepared for him to provoke her. "Oh, but your brother has not paid me, my lord." This was not precisely a lie. "I am a duchess."

"Congratulations." He disappeared inside again, and Emmaline was left staring down at his dog. She heard rustling, the sound of something heavy being slid, pots clanging together.

"I've agreed to help," she called, "because your brother and sister-in-law have done me a great favor, and I am indebted to their kindness." Another not-quite lie. In fact it was very true, indeed. There was more, far more, but surely this was enough to end the discussion of payment in as many words. Even before she was a duchess, Emmaline had never worked in her life.

"No money was exchanged, certainly," she said, just to be perfectly clear. "And my assistance is meant to be quick and discreet. Only the fundamentals—an overview, really. Four sessions. Perhaps five. I'm certain if you would but hear what I propose—"

"Don't care," he called back. His dog padded inside and turned around to stare up at her through the door.

"I am a *dowager* duchess," she went on, "in case you're worried about…about…" She allowed the sentence to trail off, unable to name anything that might worry him. Of course he wouldn't care that she was a duchess, widowed or not. She wasn't prideful about the title, but her strategy had been to catch him off guard and use it to bully him. It wasn't every day a dowager duchess showed up to one's floating rubbish bin and offered to…to…bestow her wisdom, such as it was.

Emmaline closed her eyes. She'd assumed the viscount was too thick or awkward to grasp the manners of a gentleman, that it would be easy to gently guide his simpleton's brain through basic etiquette. But that wasn't the case at all. This person wasn't stupid; this person simply did not care.

"You've no care at all," she confirmed, "about your comportment?"

"None."

"But…why?"

"What difference is it to you?" He poked his head out again. He was wearing a hat—a weathered, tanned-leather hat pulled rakishly low over his vividly blue eyes. "If he's not paying you?"

"Well"—she hesitated only half a second—"he and his wife saved my brother's life."

"Hmm. They're useful in that way." He disappeared again. She heard the rattle of a chain or keys on a ring and the *thunk* of a trunk lid.

"Would you not, at the very least, tell me why you refuse the lessons?"

"No," he called. "I won't. Why not repay my brother himself? You couldn't know this, but he adores balls, garden parties, seats at the opera. The more dukes and duchesses he knows, the better, in his view."

Emmaline shook her head and hurried down another step. "Oh, but my husband is deceased, Lord Rainsleigh. As a dowager duchess, I am less privy to operas and balls and such. And anyway, your broth—"

"Dowager?" he said, appearing again, "as in, grandmother?" Now he wore a sweeping leather overcoat that whirled around his boots like a cape. His hands opened and closed as he fitted them with tight leather gloves. He fastened what appeared to be dagger into a sheath on his belt.

Emmaline blinked. He looked nothing like a viscount, but not for the reasons she had guessed. When she'd called before, she'd considered his slouched, unconscious form to be droopy or atrophied, lazy or faint. That was…inaccurate. He looked like a highwayman, nimble and wild and dangerous.

She stumbled back half a step.

"No, not a grandmother," she said. "My husband has died, and his son from a previous marriage has inherited. The new duke's wife is the duchess. I am the dowager duchess."

The viscount frowned. "How old are you?"

"Of course a gentleman would never demand to know the age of a lady."

For a moment, he seemed to consider this, but then he reached out and grabbed her arm. "Sorry to ruin your morning, sweetheart, but this conversation has run its course. And I'm expected in Newgate." He gave her arm a tug, mounted the steps, and hustled her up to the deck.

The dowager duchess gasped and stared at his hand on her arm. Beau ignored her and kept coming, handing her up, *dragging* her up. Peach leapt and barked at their feet.

"Here is the rub, Lady Tickle," he said.

"I am the Dowager Duchess of *Ticking*," she insisted, trying to yank her arm free.

"Bloody hell, you're a skinny little thing." He said this to keep himself from not saying the half dozen other observances prompted by her sudden proximity. Her reflexes were quick and athletic; her breast against his wrist was small and pert—his preference. The smell of her was clean and bright and like nothing he'd encountered since he'd installed himself on the canal. The hair she tucked so severely beneath her awful hat was blonde—bright gold-streaked blonde, the color of sunshine on the sand.

"This is just the sort of unwelcome comment that I would advise against in my tutorial," she gasped.

"'Unwelcome,' is it?" They reached the top step, and he began to weave her around the coils of rope and piles of rigging to the gangplank. "Allow me to illustrate the meaning of the word 'unwelcome.' My brother abdicated the title to me against my will. It was *unwelcome*." He paused, kicking a buoy out of the way. "I deplore the bloody thing. You may tell my brother, not for the first time, that I will not wear a viscount's costume, or live in a viscount's house, or fill my days with viscount-like pursuits, whatever they are."

"But…*why?*" she asked, scrambling to keep up.

Because I can find plenty of less important ways to fail, all on my own, he thought, *and have a better time doing it.*

"Because the very idea bores me to death," he said. This was also true, of course. There were other reasons, but she would not be privy to them. Even his brother did not know these.

Why Bryson had insisted upon giving up the bloody title, when only five living souls knew his parentage was illegitimate, was a mystery he would never unravel. No one else needed to know he didn't happen to be *blood related* to the viscount's long line of aristocratic rotters.

Except Bryson claimed that he himself would know, and he had too much respect for the ancient-lineage rubbish to deceptively carry on when he had no real claim.

Bollocks.

There was such a thing as being honest to a bloody fault.

And to no good end.

And at the cost of someone else's entire bloody life.

Not that the duchess needed to understand any of this. The duchess needn't understand anything more than "sod off."

They came to the little metal gate that blocked the gangplank, and he kicked it open with his boot. "Get out," he said.

"*Lord Rainsleigh,*" she implored, tugging at her arm.

"*Stop* calling me that."

She opened her mouth to object when the sound of footsteps rose from the pathway beside the water. She whipped her head around.

At their feet, Peach grew very, very still and sniffed the air, letting out a low, ominous growl.

The duchess cocked her head to the side, listening.

The footsteps continued. Closer now—louder. Peach barked once, twice.

Under his hold, her entire body went taut. He studied her face. She was holding her breath.

"What's the matter?" he heard himself ask. He released her arm.

She held up a hand to quiet him, staring wildly at the shore.

The steps on the path trod closer. More than one person. Two sets of boots, maybe three. A stray cough. Peach leapt from the boat and ran down the shore in the direction of the sound, barking into the fog.

The duchess took two steps back. She looked right and left, paused to listen, and then looked again.

"What's the matter?" he asked again. She'd taken on the look of someone who might, at any moment, whip over the side and swim away. She didn't answer, didn't even look at him. She raised her hands to her horrible hat and tugged the veil back over her eyes.

"This isn't finished," she said, gathering up her skirts.

Beau was ready with a retort, to inform her that it was, in fact, finished, but she scrambled around him to the gangplank. He sidestepped to let her pass, and she darted from the boat. In seconds, she was swallowed by the fog. She didn't look back.

Beau watched the hazy spot where she had gone until the approaching footsteps grew loud enough to be shapes in the fog and then men. There were three of them. Liveried grooms. They shuffled along the path beside the water, looking around, mumbling among themselves. Peach trotted behind them importantly, as if she had herded them his way.

They glanced at him and then on down the canal, clearly unimpressed. He had that effect on people. And it was exactly the way he liked it.

CHAPTER THREE

When Emmaline bustled to her carriage, the driver and two of the grooms were gone.

The lone remaining groom stammered an explanation—something about hearing the sound of a child's scream. His colleagues, he claimed, had dashed away to render aid.

Emmaline murmured her concern and climbed into the carriage to wait.

And now there would be screaming children. How creative. She would add this to the list of previous excuses, including ladies robbed at knifepoint, fisticuffs, spooked horses, and overturned carts. Every manner of crisis seemed to follow her carriage and require the pressing attention of at least two of her grooms.

Bollycock.

The servants were away because they had been *following* her. The Duke of Ticking made certain of that. If she managed to give them the slip (as on this foggy morning), she returned to an unattended vehicle. More often than not, she beat them back.

She'd already endured eighteen months of mourning, long enough by far to venture outside the house. She was careful to only make church or charity calls (as far as anyone knew). And yet Ticking had her followed everywhere. What a pity his spies were not clever enough to determine how she evaded them. In the front door of any given church and out the back—that was how she did it. From the rear alley, she could go wherever she pleased. In Paddington Lock and beyond, if she was careful.

Oh, but she'd cut it very close today. She could not fathom the punishment for being discovered on a canal narrow boat with…well, with a viscount who looked more like a brigand than a gentleman. Ticking already tightened his restrictions on nearly a weekly basis. More spies more of the time. It had become increasingly difficult to weave together the many elaborate strings of her plan. She could not endure more surveillance. She must redouble her stealth. Accomplish more in less time with each precious trip outside the house. Most of all, she must pin down the viscount and make him agree.

When the absent grooms finally returned, they offered precious few details about the alleged child and his alleged screams, and Emmaline smiled serenely and pretended to read her Bible for the journey home. Better to bore them to death, she'd learned, than take care with what she said.

"Master Teddy is in the Green Room, Your Grace," her butler, Dyson, informed her when she arrived at her tidy dower house in the rear garden of the new duke's townhome mansion. "Only one visit this morning from His Grace," he added.

"Thank you, Dyson," she said, smiling a sad, knowing smile. The butler had relocated with her from Liverpool when she'd married the old duke. He'd suffered a demotion and wage cut to remain in her service, but he was loyal and grand-fatherly, and Emmaline wasn't quite sure how she would have survived the move—or the Duke of Ticking—without him. She'd made him butler as soon as the duke was dead.

The Green Room was so named for the color of the ceil-ing, but the towering floor-to-ceiling alcove window that looked out over the lush dower-house garden offered a view equally verdant. It was one of her brother's favorite rooms, and she was gratified by every small thing that brought him joy. When their parents had set sail on their ill-fated Atlantic crossing, Teddy had come to live with her and the duke in the ducal townhome. He'd not wanted to be left behind, but then to learn of the shipwreck? He had been steeped in sad-ness, mourning in his own way, unsettled and afraid. The cold marble, dark wood, and stained glass of the four-hundred-year-old townhouse had not aided matters. There were days when it had been difficult to coax him from his room. But the dower house was small and snug, just two levels and a cellar, six bedrooms, a dining room, a parlor, and the Green Room. It was smaller than their childhood home by leagues, but it had a door that closed and a garden with a wall. Until Emma-line could enact her plan and escape the duke altogether, it was vastly preferred. It was home.

Now she paused at the door to the Green Room, listening for her brother. The voices inside were low and reasonable, not unpleasant. God help her, they almost sounded…happy.

"Have I missed breakfast?" she said brightly, walking in.

On a settee by the window, her brother, Teddy, hunched over a large colorful book spread across his lap. Miss Jocelyn

Breedlowe, his new caretaker, sat beside him, pointing at what appeared to be an illustration of a tree filled with tropical birds.

Teddy looked up. "Malie," he said, referring to her by the name he'd called her since boyhood. He'd been late to speak and later still to call anyone by name.

Her heart clenched when she saw him now—his handsome face sharpening into manhood more every day. On the outside, he looked every bit the young, handsome heir to their father's great fortune. Nineteen years old. Tall, broadshouldered, always smartly dressed by Mr. Broom, the valet he'd had all of his life.

Only his brain had been left behind—stunted, somehow, since birth. In his mind, he was forever aged four or five. He could memorize the Latin names of an aviary of birds in one afternoon but still struggled to make simple conversation or find his way to the park and back.

"And what do we have here?" Emmaline asked.

Miss Breedlowe looked up and smiled gently. "Parrots," she said. "Teddy has memorized the scientific names of all of these lovely birds."

"This I believe," said Emmaline, coming to stop in front of the book. "Which is your favorite, Teddy?"

Without looking up, he pointed to the colorful illustration of a robust, spectral-hued bird. "Parrot." He rattled off a glossary of one-word facts about the habitat and feeding of a rainbow parrot. "Get one, Malie?"

"Take on a parrot? I'm not sure the animal you described would be comfortable in London, would he?"

Teddy appeared to think about this, staring at the illustration.

"But perhaps we can locate a few more books about him," said Miss Breedlowe. "We might even try our hand at sketching him, you and I."

Teddy did not answer, his attention still on the book, and Emmaline winked at Jocelyn.

"I had the maids build a second fire in the opposite grate," Jocelyn said, stepping away. "He prefers this room above all others, but I worry about the chill that seeps through the glass."

"Yes, please," said Emmaline. "Do what you can to be comfortable. I've suggested to His Grace that the room would benefit from velvet curtains to stave off the cold, but I won't hold my breath."

They chatted a moment more about Teddy's morning. Not since her parents perished on their voyage to America had Emmaline had a confidant with whom she could discuss her brother. In this way—in every way—meeting Jocelyn Breedlowe had been a godsend. Jocelyn was compassionate and measured with Teddy, not to mention helpful and inventive. Emmaline had wept with relief and gratitude after their first session.

Ironically, it was Emmaline's own failure to her brother that brought Miss Breedlowe to them. Teddy had gone missing in October—two harrowing days and a sleepless night with no trace of him—until charity workers employed by a woman named Elisabeth Courtland had stumbled upon him and brought him in from the streets, thank God.

Along with the return of Teddy, Emmaline had gained two new friends—Elisabeth Courtland and one of her volunteers, Jocelyn Breedlowe. When Emmaline learned that Jocelyn was a professional caretaker, she hired her immediately to help Emmaline do better at looking after Teddy. Jocelyn was another set of hands and pair of eyes but also support and respite for Emmaline.

Most of all, Jocelyn allowed Emmaline to slip out of the house to pull together the intricate plan that would, she hoped, earn her and her brother's freedom from the Duke of Ticking.

In the weeks that followed Teddy's rescue, Jocelyn Breedlowe had become so much more than a caretaker; she'd become a new friend. Emmaline had no idea how badly she needed friends until she met Elisabeth and Jocelyn. Sometimes she felt Jocelyn was as essential to her own sanity as she was to Teddy's care.

"Your errand went well, I hope," Jocelyn said casually.

Went well? Emmaline repeated in her head, thinking of the viscount—of his obstinacy and his flippancy, of his immediate rejection for the harmless, mutually beneficial thing she had offered him.

Inexplicably, she also thought of his blue eyes, easily the least useful detail to remember.

She snapped her head up. "Quite well. There's more work to be done still, but it was another step."

The agreement she'd made with Bryson Courtland had been vague and casual at best, and Emmaline had not shared the specifics of it with anyone, not even Jocelyn. She'd told her only that she was making plans for her and Teddy's financial independence, that it was terribly important business, and that Teddy's inheritance was at stake. For now, that was enough. Until she'd managed to gain control of any one of the five or six spinning plates in her wild scheme, she would keep the specifics close.

Now, she told Jocelyn, "Dyson said the duke called while I was out."

Her friend nodded into the dying fire. "He did, I'm afraid. Not thirty minutes after you'd gone."

"Heavens, I left at dawn. His staff must watch us at all hours. What reason did he give?"

"Oh," Jocelyn said with a sad chuckle, "the usual things. He wished to know when you were due to return, where'd you'd gone."

"None too subtle, is he?" Emmaline let out a tired breath and raised her hands to her hair to fish for the nagging pins that held her hat in place. Before she was free of it, Dyson appeared in the doorway and cleared his throat.

"His Grace the Duke of Ticking to see you, Your Grace," the butler said pointedly. Dyson was proficient at announcing the new duke and warning Emmaline in the same breath.

Emmaline made a face and worked more diligently on the hat. "Thank you, Dyson, I shall meet His Grace in the drawing room. Can you show him in—"

"Do not bother, Emma," said the duke as he strode past the butler. He glanced around proprietarily, as if he had immediate designs on every corner of the room. He was a short, ruddy man, purposeful to the point of doggedness. His face was perpetually creased with a look of unspecified determination. *I shall*, it always seemed to say. He made the simple act of selecting a chair and taking a seat seem like a scheduled event. *His* schedule, of course, *his* event.

Emmaline snatched the hat from her head and smoothed her hair.

The Duke of Ticking went on. "I won't linger. I just came to bid you good morning and make certain you returned safely home."

"I am quite safe, Your Grace," Emmaline said.

"One can never be too cautious—a young woman alone, especially so early…" The duke allowed the sentence to trail off. He raised his eyebrows at her, allowing his deep curiosity to show. "Where did you say you'd gone?"

"Oh, I'll not bore you with my charity errands."

"The church employs clergy, as I'm sure you're aware, to carry out the Lord's good work."

She smiled vaguely and studied her hat. If he wished to explicitly restrict her movements, she would make him say it in as many words. She waited.

"I only mention this," he went on, "because Marie, Bella, and Dora had a mind to call on the dressmaker's later this morning, but I will need our family carriage. I thought to send them in yours, but I couldn't say for certain when you would return."

"Quite," Emmaline said.

Marie, Bella, and Dora were three of the duke's oldest children. Or three of his middle children. There were so many of them, she struggled to keep them straight. None of them rose before eleven o'clock in the morning—this she knew—and it was only now nine thirty.

"I should think you might enjoy a shopping trip with the girls," Ticking mused, "considering your proximity in age.

They quarrel with their mother, but you may have a calming influence on them, just as you did on their grandfather."

The duke never failed to mention Emmaline's age in relation to both his own young daughters and his dead father.

"Forgive me, Your Grace, but I was under the impression that the smaller, older carriage was mine to use exclusively, as dowager duchess," Emmaline said. "When I assumed residency in the dower house, I was told the carriage came with it."

"It is my preference that we *share* the vehicles in this family," Ticking said, speaking to the ceiling as if conjuring up a high ideal.

"I see. If you're in need of my carriage for your children, you need only tell me in advance. I can rearrange my schedule."

He pivoted in a half circle. "Is it truly *your* carriage, Emma?"

Yes, it is, actually, she thought, anger and frustration simmering. *The carriage is mine. The dower house is mine. Even your carriage and the grand townhouse in which you live are mine—salvaged from the auction block with the dowry my father paid to marry me to yours.*

Instead, she said carefully, "I understand your concern about the carriages." She'd overheard her father say this to business associates many times. *I understand.* When there was nothing more to be said, this statement neither agreed nor disagreed, but it got in a word.

And it wasn't even a lie; she did understand all too well.

She understood that her husband had fallen from his horse and died before he'd bothered to include her in his will, binding her to the miserly new duke as dependent and tenant and hostage.

She understood that her parents' ill-fated trip to America had taken their lives before they'd determined how to pass down their prosperous family business and tidy fortune to Teddy. As male heir, he was entitled to it, but his mental state meant he could not manage any of it.

Most of all, she understood that her own gender entitled her nothing—not her parents' money and not even the dowager stipend, if the Duke of Ticking did not wish to dole it out.

She'd spent the last year and a half trying to challenge this understanding from every possible angle, freeing herself and Teddy from the legal trap and social prison that fate had so cruelly landed in their laps.

Across the room, the duke ran a hand over the smooth, pomaded surface of his hair. "Very good, then. Will you require use of the carriage tomorrow?"

She looked at him. This was none of his business, and he knew it. "I may send it to fetch Miss Breedlowe," she said.

"Ah, yes. The new nurse. How are you getting along, Miss Breedlowe?" He squinted at Jocelyn.

"Very well, Your Grace," Jocelyn said, "but I should not take credit for being a proper nurse. I am merely a companion to Teddy."

"A companion, yes…" His voice always spiked when he spoke of Teddy—louder still when he spoke to the boy.

He ambled closer and bent at the waist, his face two feet from where Teddy sat with his book. "I say! Teddy? How do you like your new nurse?"

Teddy looked up at the duke and then to his sister, his eyes uncertain. Teddy was not accustomed to bellowing, and he'd never liked Ticking, but Emmaline had warned him repeatedly against rudeness to the duke. She held her breath and nodded slowly to him.

"That's right, Teddy," she urged. "Can you bid His Grace a good morning?"

Teddy's gaze swung back to the duke.

"Are you sure he does not require a doctor's care?" asked Ticking, studying him as he would an animal in a zoo.

"Quite sure," Emmaline said in a clipped tone. Her simmering patience had rolled to an angry boil. "Say hello to His Grace, Teddy."

Miss Breedlowe moved silently to the boy and slipped the book from his hands.

"Quite fond of that book of yours, Teddy?" said the duke.

"Parrots," said Teddy.

"Parrots?" the duke repeated. "And what need might we have for parrots in England? Planning a journey to the tropics, are you?"

"Teddy is a student of the life sciences," Emmaline said.

"I asked the boy," snapped the duke.

"Parrots," Teddy repeated. Emmaline felt his tenseness mounting like a string being pulled back from a bow. He couldn't tolerate being hemmed in, especially by someone with a booming voice whose morbid expression was at odds with the interest he showed.

"Shall I take Teddy out to break the ice on the fountain, Your Grace?" asked Jocelyn, God bless her. She put a calming hand on the boy's shoulder. "This is something he and I had planned to do for thirsty birds in want of a drink."

"That sounds lovely, Miss Breedlowe. Thank you," said Emmaline. "Off you go."

Miss Breedlowe leaned to whisper something in Teddy's ear and, miraculously, he nodded. Ticking watched their exit with a keen, calculating eye.

"If that will be all, Your Grace," Emmaline said, "I hoped to join Teddy in the garden before Miss Breedlowe leaves." She smoothed one of the feathers on her hat.

The duke lowered fleshy lids over pale eyes. "I would bid you not to fret, Emma, over the money you've spent to have your brother looked after. This expenditure does not trouble me."

Not fret over the money? Emmaline had not used the modest allowance Ticking allotted her to pay for Miss Breedlowe's service. Her parents left her money to care for Teddy when they set sail on their doomed journey. She paid Jocelyn from this account. But she dare not make specific remarks on any of Teddy's finances to the duke. The less the duke knew about Teddy's money—before their parents' drowning and after—the better.

"I understand," she said again.

"Now that you have such a capable caretaker for the boy," he went on, "you may wish to spend more time in the company of *my* children. My father adored them, you know."

Well, that was a lie. The late duke had been appalled that his son and daughter-in-law had willfully reproduced seventeen times (and counting), and he was never so annoyed as when his son brought any fraction of the wheedling grandchildren for what always proved to be a raucous and destructive visit.

But now Ticking would expect some general commitment. This was his way. He made disagreeable statements and waited, daring her to oppose him.

He watched her speculatively.

Emmaline cleared her throat. "My plan has been for Miss Breedlowe to allow me a few hours outside the house for charity pursuits. Otherwise, Teddy and I enjoy each other's company. We always have."

Ticking nodded with feeling. "You are a devoted sister," he said, pity in his voice. In his mind, Teddy was a burden. Well, a burden or a bag of money.

"Thank you."

"The duchess and I had hoped you would be a devoted grandmama too," he went on. "Furthermore, the company of children is a perfect diversion for a lady in deep mourning. Far more acceptable, some might say, than charity work outside the house. Before sunrise."

"Oh, but I'm only in full mourning for three more days, Your Grace. And I'm afraid I might find myself entirely out of my depth amid *seventeen* children."

"Nonsense," he said. "Your many years with Teddy will serve you well. Intelligent, capable children may prove a relief to you after looking after a boy who struggles so."

Now, Emmaline could but stare.

"Think on it, Emma," he instructed, turning on her to stride to the door. "Think about your background and what you bring to this family. Here is a way to contribute."

And there it is, she thought. *The real "burden" to the dukedom has always been me—the common merchant's daughter whose dowry sustains them even while my breeding makes them look the other way.*

Chapter Four

Beau grappled with the memory of the veiled woman for two days after she'd gone, a new and unwelcome distraction. Women, in his view, were largely interchangeable, not to mention abundant, and it wasn't like him to spend more than ten minutes cogitating over one in particular.

She wasn't special, he told himself, she was more like…cautionary.

If he must think of her, he should do so in terms of wariness. *Extreme* wariness. If he meant to avoid her, it was better to understand her.

For example, he wondered about her age. Not more than twenty-five, an honest guess. Possibly as young as nineteen. Far too young to be shrouded in widow's weeds.

And why, he wondered, had she returned to hector him? Two—now three times? The third time, it had taken real work to get her off the bloody boat. He'd all but pitched her into the canal. When she *had* gone, it had been in a sudden, fraught sort of mad dash—a flight, if he was being honest.

Like she had been spooked. Something to do with liveried grooms on the shore. Why?

When he wasn't asking himself *why,* he asked *what.*

What could any of these details matter, when she'd managed to string together all the words he hated most in the world and then repeated them, again and again.

Rainsleigh.

Viscount.

My lord.

Expectations.

Manners, manners, manners.

A description of the conditions inside Newgate Prison would have been more welcome.

Newgate was a ready comparison, as Beau stood adjacent to it now, eating an apple and watching an unmarked door across Creed Lane. He'd posted himself against a lamppost since dawn and planned to stay another hour at least, taking note of who came and who left. It was boring work, although essential for the raid he would lead later in the week.

The raid.

When he wasn't thinking about the duchess, he was thinking about the raid.

His sister-in-law, Elisabeth, ran a charity that rescued young girls from brothels and retrained them for honest work and a new life. Through a series of small, seemingly harmless favors, Beau had somehow become the group's de facto muscle and chief brothel raider.

It had seemed like a good idea the first time he'd done it—dangerous and clandestine, and best of all, so very unlike a viscount. Sixteen months later, and he was still leading the raids, although he promised himself after each one that it would be the last.

He took another bite of apple and spun it in his hand. "I should leave Britain," he told his dog. She lay at his feet, lazily watching as horses and pedestrians plodded down Creed Lane toward Cripplegate.

"It tortures Bryson that I remain to fail, each and every day, at being what he expects me to be. Bollocks, it tortures *me*."

The dog lifted her head from her paws and cocked her head, listening for the five or six words that she understood.

"We could go to Africa. Cape Town." He shook open the broadsheet newspaper in his hand. "The Dutch have gone toes up, and the Crown is playing guard dog against the French. There's money to be made. Ships sail every week."

He took a final bite of the apple and tossed the core. "Next month," he told the dog. "After the raid. Not before—but after. Most likely."

The next raid would infiltrate a particularly nefarious prostitution ring that, Beau had discovered, changed locations every few weeks. From his surveillance, they had learned there were girls on the inside as young as nine. He'd worked with Elisabeth and the raiding team to plan a covert raid for the early morning hours, in and out very quickly, rescuing as many as a dozen girls, if they were lucky. The door he watched now was a suspected third way in, but "suspected" wasn't good enough. He must know for sure. Two back doors were useful, but three would be even better.

"Let's take a walk, Peach," Beau told the dog, watching an old woman slip from the door with a marketing basket.

Peach gave a noncommittal yawn and stretched. Beau shoved off the lamppost, tucking the paper under his arm, starting to whistle.

"Ah, there you are, Lord Rainsleigh."

His whistle died in his throat.

Surely not.

Peach deserted him immediately and trotted to the source of the voice, wagging her tail.

His brain spun through every conceivable scenario that allowed him to have misheard.

Not her. Not *here*. Not again.

The voice spoke again. "You are not an easy gentleman to find."

And there it was. No one in his acquaintance dared refer to him as a gentleman, except his brother. And this was not the voice of his brother. This was not the voice of any man.

This was the voice of the duchess.

She stood beside his lamppost with her voluminous black bombazine shining in the morning sun like wet feathers.

"You. Cannot. Be. Serious," he said lowly, checking around to see who on the street might have noticed. The answer was everyone, of course. It was impossible not to notice a woman dressed in head-to-toe ink-blot black, the spines of her elaborate hat spiking toward the sky.

"You'll forgive the intrusion," she began.

"No. I will not forgive the intrusion. What in God's name are you doing here?"

"Elisabeth Courtland suggested I might find you in the vicinity of Newgate."

"Elisabeth has no particular notion of where I may be at any given moment in time. Try again." She opened her mouth to answer, but he spoke over her. "What do you know of Elisabeth?" His sister-in-law shared none of Bryson's ambition for the title. She had no reason to set this woman on him.

"I am a volunteer in her charity office," the duchess said. "We are friends, she and I. She told me you would be preparing for the raid."

Beau narrowed his eyes, studying her through the damnable veil. If anyone could guess his location, it would be Elisabeth, but she, more than anyone, understood the incredibly covert nature of surveillance. They would discuss this the next time he saw her.

"I have no wish to detain you or interrupt whatever you are endeavoring to accomplish here," the duchess went on, "but I should like to speak with you again. About the lessons. If you'll but hear my offer, I shall leave you to your business."

"You shall leave me, regardless. Better yet," he said, looking around for some place to conceal himself from the brothel door, "I'll leave you. We will not have this conversation again."

"Wait, Lord Rainsleigh—"

He cringed at the sound of the title and summoned the dog with a low whistle.

"I'm prepared to tell you why," she called to his back.

He hesitated half a second, responding to some note of urgency in her voice, but moved on. He could be urgent too. *Urgently*, he opposed aristocratic practices of lordly duplicity and petty tyranny, and he wanted nothing to do with any of it. His brother thought he eschewed the title because he was lazy. Quite the opposite. He'd witnessed the abuse and advantage of some of the country's most "noble" gentlemen; as a result, he'd sworn he would never be a party to anything like their unearned entitlement, and he meant it. Even if he found himself a viscount. This woman could explain herself to the lane, or the lamppost, or the walls of Newgate Prison for all he cared, but not to him.

He crossed the verge behind him and slipped around the edge of a building into a narrow alley. The gutter ran with a trickle of rancid water, and he kept to the side, his back against the wall, balancing on the border stones that formed a small ledge.

"I can't remember the last time someone has turned his back on me and walked away," said the duchess's voice from the mouth of the alley.

Beau looked back. She'd hovered in the entrance, the voluminous black bell of her skirts puffing into the slim opening. "Are you mad?" he rasped.

"Possibly." She studied the murky water and gathered her skirts in thick handfuls.

"If you step one foot in this alley," he warned her, "you'll disprove all your elevated claims of propriety. It's a sewer, madam, make no mistake."

"Don't be silly," she said, taking one careful step, and then another, and then another. "This is not impropriety. This is…*thoroughness*."

"You *are* mad," he said, marveling at her dexterity as much as her gall. She was picking her way to him.

"I…I know you must feel rather pursued." She came to balance directly across from him on the opposite ledge. They were separated only by three feet of dim alley and the cold, dirty water at their feet.

"'Pursued'? Try 'hunted.'"

She answered this with a nod. Beau watched her, hating the veil for blocking her eyes. He waited, anticipating…what? He could not say. She drew one deep breath and then another. She raised her chin. Would she now scream? Cry? Launch herself at him? It was a rare moment, indeed, when he could not read the intent of any given female. But he'd never met such a young widow before, nor any high-born lady who would chase him into an alley.

He was just about to suggest that she find her way back out into the street when she reached to her veil and rolled it away.

Just like that, the dismissal died on his lips.

Beau stopped breathing and watched. Her nose appeared first, small and pert. It wrinkled from the rank smell of the alley.

Next, her eyes. He could only make out their shape beneath the veil, but now they shone with warm, brown color.

"I've struck a deal with your brother," she told him next. "You might as well know. The two of you are said to be very close. He would have told you about our bargain soon enough."

"Bryson and I rarely speak," Beau admitted carefully. "What *deal*?"

"Well," she began, "I am in urgent need of passage to America."

"Aren't we all," Beau said. "Why?"

She ignored this question and said, "Your brother has promised to accommodate me if I can…educate you."

"Why do you require passage to America?" he repeated. "Americans hold duchesses in even lower esteem than I do, or so I hear."

"I am not at liberty to discuss my…business in America. I can only reveal that your brother has promised to grant me passage on one of his ships if I can teach you anything. Anything at all."

"You told me Bryson rescued your cousin," he said.

"Not a cousin. He rescued my *brother*. Teddy. Well, his wife's charity rescued him, and then Mr. Courtland located me and delivered Teddy back into my safekeeping. This is how I met both Elisabeth and Mr. Courtland."

"If your brother was lost, why aren't your parents making some compensation to Bryson?"

"Oh," she said, "my parents are dead. Lost at sea, I'm afraid."

Beau scoffed. "Of course they are."

"Surely I don't have to point out that this is another entirely inappropriate response."

Oh, I am the master of inappropriate, he thought, but he said, "Forgive me. I am marveling that my brother managed to dispatch both a widow *and* an orphan to me in the same woman."

"I am not meant to be pitiful, my lord," she said. "I am meant to be useful."

"What you *are* is in my way."

"When I learned that your brother was the owner of a shipyard," she pressed on, "I became determined to both repay him for the great favor of rescuing Teddy *and* earn my passage on one of his ships. This is when he offered me the arrangement. *Your* training for *my* passage."

Beau whistled. "Quite a bargain." Why Bryson would strike such a deal with a young widow was inconceivable, but he was loath to invite any more of the story than strictly pertinent to *him*. "And what am I meant to get?"

"Well, the knowledge of how to carry on decorously, I suppose. Confidence in every situation. An air of nobility. Proper address, to the right sort of people, at the correct hour, in all the most important places."

"So nothing, effectively speaking."

"If it's my qualifications that give you pause," she said, "please remember that I managed to marry a duke."

"Right. The dead duke. And what if I've set my cap for a prince?" He cocked an eyebrow.

She laughed at this, a light, magical jingle that seemed to surprise them both, like she may not have laughed in a very long time. Something very male and very needy inside him responded to this, and he instantly scrambled to say something to make her laugh again. He wondered if she knew what came next—after the next joke, and the next.

She raised a gloved hand to her face, touching her pretty mouth with delicate fingers. It was a gesture he'd elicited a thousand times by hundreds of girls, but he'd never seen it done quite so naturally or without pretense.

It occurred to him suddenly, forcefully, that perhaps he had approached this woman in all the wrong ways. He'd been defensive and dismissive to her—his natural responses to the title and the threat of rules and manners and "training." But this was hardly his natural response to a beautiful woman. His natural response to beautiful women (really to any woman) had been to flirt and charm. It was what he did best. Why in God's name hadn't he come back with that? He'd seduced every female from whom he wanted anything for as long as he remembered. Rarely, if ever, did he fail.

Blithely, without really thinking, he stepped off the ledge and sloshed through the water to the spot where she balanced on the opposite wall. He stared at her openly, hotly, eye to eye. He lifted his hat, ran a hand through his hair, and then dropped his hat back on his head, propping the brim rakishly back. He raised one reliable brow.

As if on cue, her cheeks shot pink and her eyes grew. Her hands felt for the bricks behind her. She began to inch sideways.

He propped one hand on the wall to stop her. "Careful," he said.

She narrowed her eyes. "You're very clever, you know. If we were having this conversation over tea instead of…" She looked right and left.

"In the gutter?" he offered.

Another laugh, and Beau felt the familiar hum of blood pumping through his own veins.

She clarified, "I was going to say out of doors, but I suppose that is more to the point."

She started again, "If we were having this conversation over tea, that would be a perfectly diverting thing to say. Setting your cap for a prince." Her eyes were still smiling, a very good sign indeed.

Beau leaned down, just a little. "Despite what my brother believes," he said, "I require no instruction on how to make conversation with a pretty girl." She was more than pretty, he thought objectively. In fact, saying the words out loud seemed to emphasize that she was, more to the point, beautiful. Thin, willowy, with brown eyes that seemed lit with a sort of amber glow. He dare not clarify this, however. There was value in understatement.

She cleared her throat and looked beside her at his hand on the wall. Her gaze traveled back, following his arm, over his shoulder, and up to his face. She licked her lips and swallowed hard. Beau stared at those lips. He knew this dance well.

"I didn't set my cap for anyone," she volunteered softly, "not even a duke. The title was my parents' dream."

"Do tell," he said, inching closer. He could see her tightly swept-back blonde hair. He could see her eyelashes. He could see one particularly lovely freckle beside her small nose.

"In particular, my mother wanted a title for me," she went on. "She was very ambitious. My father worked hard to be a great success, but he came from nothing. I wasn't even raised in London. I left my home in Liverpool to marry the duke. I was not a traditional debutante."

"We have that in common," he said, and she laughed again. The more she laughed, the more he wanted to hear it. He stared down at her with an expression that rarely let him down.

"To make up for all of this," she said, speaking faster, "my comportment had to be perfect. My knowledge of the accepted customs of a lady or gentleman was—*is*—exhaustive, taught from birth. My manners had to be impeccable if I wanted to catch the attention of a duke."

"Your big brown eyes couldn't hurt." He gave a half smile.

Another laugh. "I think it was more like my father's golden piles of money." She looked away, offering him her delicate profile and the curve of her neck. Now it was his turn to melt, which shouldn't really be the plan, should it? He saw the pulse jump in her throat, and his own heartbeat kicked up. He told himself that no seduction would play out authentically if he didn't feel it too.

They were so close now. Close enough that he could smell the scent of her skin, even in the dank alley. She was warm beneath the layers and layers of black, and he could feel that too.

"Regardless of my…er, resources," she said, "I would not have been a serious prospect for the Duke of Ticking, or any gentleman, if I had not been taught to behave properly. You'll not find a more qualified teacher than I."

She turned her head and met his eyes. They locked gazes. Beau's body, which had been stirring and buzzing, now hardened with awareness.

She licked her lips, and Beau doubled down. "You know, *Your Grace*, I could be persuaded to explore your offer if…you consented to make it more interesting." He craned back just enough to sweep her body with a predatory gaze. "When you speak of lessons and a capable teacher and an attentive pupil, certain subjects do spring to mind. Quite the opposite of why you've been sent, but I'm doubtful you'd find fault with my version of education."

She blinked once, thick lashes closing over rich brown eyes. Her perfect mouth puckered into a surprised O. She bit her top lip and slid it slowly free. He watched with rapt attention, surprised to realize he was holding his own breath. How utterly stupid it had been not to lead with seduction. Not only was it effective, but there would be a delectable reward for him too.

"This is the opposite of what your brother had in mind."

She was trying to invoke authority, but she looked impossibly young. And flushed. And...*curious?*

Beau swallowed hard and moved closer. His coat grazed her skirts. Their faces shared the space beneath the brim of his hat. The closeness suddenly wanted *more* closeness, and he fought the urge to move all the way in, until her back was pressed against the wall, and he was pressed against her.

"My brother's not an idiot," he said, speaking almost into her ear. "I think we can all agree that he did not send an *ugly* woman to whip me into form. Perhaps we can strike our own bargain, you and I? Learn a little and play a little?" His voice was just above a whisper.

She answered with a small, low intake of breath, one of Beau's very favorite sounds. She tipped her head up just a little, the universal gesture of invitation. Beau locked eyes on her mouth. He bent toward her, hovering just inches away. He was a heartbeat from the heaven of her mouth when was seized by the unfamiliar choke of restraint. He blinked and raised up, just an inch. If and when he seduced her, he thought, it must be a conscientious, measured sort of thing. He mustn't take more advantage than his brother was already taking. He might be a rogue, but he was not a debaucher of desperate widows. In alley ways. Even so, his concentration was rapidly slipping. Measure and conscience were hardly his strong suits under the best of circumstances.

By some miracle, she spoke again, breaking the spell. "No," she said softly, "I am quite determined to honor your brother's original intent."

She lowered her chin and stared at the collar of his shirt. Beau knew a flash of disappointment so deep it registered as anger. He also knew just what to say to change her mind. The pretty words were on the tip of his tongue.

But now she fidgeted. She cleared her throat. Despite his position looming over her, she began to slide away. She yanked her skirts from the grip of the rough wall. She staggered a little but managed to stay out of the wet. While he watched, she picked her way back to the street.

He'd done it; he'd scared her away. Regret seemed to fill the space where she'd been, but regret of what? What he'd done or what he had not?

"Everything about this exchange has been an example of what a gentleman would never, ever do," she was saying, almost to herself.

"Oh, I've only scratched the surface," he warned smoothly. This was the truth.

"Today we've learned how *not* to behave." She was reciting now. Her voice was too loud, and it echoed on the stone walls. "Next time we'll do it my way."

He hopped out of the gutter and balanced on the ledge. This was a threat, and he knew he should reply in kind. He thought for a moment, willing his brain to do its job despite the residual desire swirling in his head.

"If you value your virtue," he finally called, "there won't be a next time."

There, he'd said it. She'd been forewarned. If she turned up again, he would not put her off. If she turned up again, he would do the opposite.

But she gave no guarantees. She stumbled from the alley, smoothed her skirts, her gloves, the ridiculous hat on her head. Without looking back at him, she turned and strode away.

CHAPTER FIVE

Emmaline fought the memory of her assignation in the alley for the next five days. It was the week of the new duchess's birthday, and she told herself that any memory would be an improvement over the hours she spent celebrating inside the ducal townhome.

"I should like for you and Teddy—if he is able," the duke had informed Emmaline on Sunday, "to pass the coming week with the family. The duchess will celebrate her birthday on Friday, and we've a lovely party planned. The children are excited to celebrate with their mother, and your help would allow Her Grace to enjoy the day without the full burden of their deafening joy. It is the least we can offer the duchess on her special day. She does love the children, but she and I should also like some time alone, as I'm sure you can imagine."

Whenever Emmaline imagined the duke and duchess alone, she saw the conception of yet another child. In the spirit of the duchess's birthday, she wondered when the duchess would reach an age that biologically disqualified her from procreating. Seventeen was a lot of children, even by the most fruitful standards.

"What, exactly, do you mean, Your Grace," Emmaline asked, "by passing the week with the family?"

His tone made it clear she was being ordered rather than requested, but she refused to *guess* how much family time would qualify.

Ticking licked his ruddy lips. "Why not simply begin with us after breakfast, hmm? See how the festive days unfold. The children's nannies and governesses and tutors do not seem to coalesce in an organized manner until ten o'clock. The duchess struggles, before then, to keep everyone in line. After that, there are sure to be three or four children who are not at lessons or naps or diversions at any given moment. They would delight in your company. Stay through supper, if you like."

"You would have me stay *all day*, Your Grace?" Emmaline asked. She'd barely managed to keep the frustration from her voice. "For how many days would you have me arrive for breakfast and remain through supper?"

Every day. She'd already known the answer. He'd hinted at this arrangement often enough.

The duke shoved up from his desk. "Forgive me if I believe that your attention *inside* the ducal household is more appropriate for a widow of your station than these unaccounted errands with which you occupy yourself around town. Shall I remind you that you are still in mourning, madam?"

Emmaline's face grew hot. She did not relish confrontation, but she would not be falsely accused. "I am in *half* mourning, Your Grace," she said. "Your father has been gone for eighteen months, may God rest his soul."

"Quite so," blustered the duke.

They stared at one another. It would only complicate her plans to make him truly angry, and perhaps some time away would dilute her repeated thoughts of Beau Courtland.

She said, "I should be happy to celebrate the duchess's birthday on Friday."

"The celebrations begin *tomorrow*," he countered.

"Monday, then."

"And bring your brother, if he is able."

This will not happen, she thought, but she said, "I understand."

The days that followed were a weary slog of wailing infants, fighting boys, and pouting girls. Mealtimes were a whirl of chaos and mild, flavorless food. She passed afternoons listening to the older girls prattle on about their prospects for marriage or the boys' plans for travel and horses. When the maids were stretched thin (which they always seemed to be), Emmaline cleaned porridge from the rug, swept broken lanterns from the tiles, and picked at torn pillows that blew feathers to every corner of the room. She changed nappies. She tied bows. She removed shoes and buckled them back on again. She endured pokes, prods, climbing, clinging, and the painful pulling of her hair, strand by strand, from beneath her hat.

It was tedious and exhausting, and (worst of all) it did nothing to satisfy her thoughts of the viscount. One idle memory from the alley could set her cheeks aflame. His words echoed in her head. She saw him leaning over her against the alley wall. She saw his hand beside her face and his mouth when he'd dared her to allow him to teach her instead.

She could, with alarming clarity, recall the position of every part of her and every part of him. She blamed this on her inexperience with closeness, in general, and touching, in particular. Her parents, God rest them, had not been affectionate, and Teddy became agitated by anything more than a quick hug. For the short time she'd been married to the duke, he endeavored to touch her only in her bed under the cover of darkness, and even then, the effort had ended in a scratchy, slobbery sort of misery that, to this day, left her stomach in a knot and her skin cold.

But Beau's—er, Lord Rainsleigh's—proximity had not elicited stomach knots or coldness of any kind. Quite the contrary. Beau Courtland had caused her stomach to fill with a swarm of moths' wings that beat in unison and her skin to grow first warm, then hot, then tingle.

In reality, he'd hardly touched her at all. In fact, lengthy retrospection revealed he had, in fact, not touched her in the alley. He'd done something far worse instead; he had planted the seed of *wanting* his touch. In the alley or anywhere else for that matter. It was a compulsion that made absolutely no sense, as she couldn't remember the last time she felt even the slightest stirring of interest in a man. Furthermore, the interest in *this* man of all men made no sense at all, because he'd done nothing but foil her attempts to repay his brother, and he was rude, and outspoken, and (on two occasions) unconscious from drink. If her marriage to the duke taught her nothing else, it was that she wanted nothing to do with drunkards ever again.

But he hadn't been drunk in the alley. In the alley, he seemed in total command of not only his faculties but hers as well.

The only thing more striking than the memory of Rainsleigh that endless week was Ticking's gall. With increasing frequency, the duke appeared to hover over her shoulder (stopping just short of lending a hand, of course) and hound her with not-so-subtle questions about the hundreds of thousands of pounds that her parents left behind when their ship went down.

Who ran the company since her father's death? he wanted to know. *How would Teddy's inheritance be managed? Were there any other beneficiaries? Did Emmaline have access to the money?*

Emmaline had bit her tongue to keep from shouting, "The money has nothing to do with you!"

But the reality of his control was becoming more obvious every day. *This* was why he had tried to curtail her movements. *This* was why he did not wish for her to contact anyone outside of his family or his staff. The more freely she moved around London, the more carefully she could arrange safeguards for Teddy and herself.

The converse was also true. The more he hemmed her in, the more she became dependent on him (or so he assumed).

On Friday evening, when the last piece of cake had been eaten and the final toddler ripped screaming from her skirts, Emmaline trudged across the garden to her dower house and collapsed on a fainting couch while Teddy and Jocelyn Breedlowe looked on in concern.

After five minutes of staring at the wall in blessed silence, Dyson bade the footmen roll in the tea cart. There were biscuits, and tea, and sherry, and Emmaline's favorite luxury—*ice*. She crunched on a piece and picked up a note that Dyson informed her had arrived earlier in the day.

"Oh, 'tis from Elisabeth Courtland," Emmaline said, sitting up and breaking the seal. "She's looking for you, Jocelyn, no doubt. I keep you from your work at her foundation when you mind Teddy for me, day after day. But I could not subject my brother to the madness in Ticking's nursery for five days. I could not."

Jocelyn chuckled a dismissal and helped Teddy select biscuits from the trolley while Emmaline scanned the note.

Dear Emmaline,

We have missed you this week at the foundation. Jocelyn assures me that you have duties to the duke, which I completely (albeit sympathetically) understand. If your schedule opens, however, I should like to invite you to tea tomorrow afternoon in Henrietta Place. A few other neighbors may also be there—lovely women that you will enjoy. Nothing formal or fussy, mind you. Please bring Teddy if he can be persuaded. He is always welcome, and Bryson should like to say hello. My hope is that Jocelyn will also come.

We have some news, Bryson and I, and I want to share it among close friends. It would mean ever so much if you were there.

Warmly,
Elisabeth

"They must be expecting," speculated Emmaline after she read the letter aloud to Jocelyn.

"It's possible," Jocelyn said, "although she hasn't said anything to me. Would you like me to stay behind with Teddy?"

Emmaline shook her head. "By no means. You should not forgo the diversion so that I may go. I will either take her at her word and bring Teddy or send my regrets."

She looked over at Teddy, happily eating biscuits and poring over yet another bird encyclopedia. "Would you like to go out tomorrow, Teddy?"

Her brother looked up, munching.

"Mrs. Courtland has invited us to her house to enjoy a lovely tea. You'll remember that Mr. and Mrs. Courtland have the grand library with thousands of books. There'll be one or two on birds, I'd wager."

"Books," Teddy said, staring at his biscuit. "You will go, Malie?"

"That's right. We shall both go. Miss Breedlowe too. It's all settled, then." She smiled tiredly at Jocelyn. "After the week I've endured, I could use some time out of the house. I'll tell the duke there's a revival at Holy Trinity. Surely after five days of forced confinement, he cannot restrict me now."

Chapter Six

Beau had not called on his brother's townhouse in Henrietta Place since he'd bought the boat and settled in Paddington Lock. The move had angered Bryson, and Beau's choice of a dilapidated boat on a murky canal only riled him more. A deliberate thumb in the eye. But Beau preferred the water, and he never intended to remain in London for long. Leaving Henrietta Place had put an end to the daily barbs and jabs, and it gave their once-strong bond a fighting chance.

But now it was December, and this meant that two former brothel raiders, Joseph Chance and Jon Stoker, were home from university until after the New Year. The young men eagerly rejoined the brothel-raiding team whenever they were in London, and Beau could certainly use them for his current target. But they were university men now, and Elisabeth and Lady Falcondale next door kept proper family rooms for them in their homes. If Beau wished to brief them, he had little choice but to seek them out in Henrietta Place. Bryson would be at home, naturally, but Beau's plan was to enter quietly through the kitchen, convene with Joe and Stoker in the mews, and ride back to Paddington before he ever encountered his brother.

"*Beau?*" called a familiar voice in the hallway, not five minutes after he'd slipped inside the kitchen door.

Beau tensed at the sound. Slowly, he turned.

"You're here." Bryson walked slowly to him.

"Indeed," said Beau. "Stoker and Joseph can be found in the vicinity, or so I've heard."

Bryson nodded, studying him. Beau wore buckskins, tall boots, and a long duster, his usual attire. His brother hated his lack of formality.

"I'll not stay long," Beau told him. "I did not intend to disturb you."

"No disturbance," Bryson said. "We are glad to see you. We—I have missed you."

"Better to miss me than resent me," Beau said.

"I never resented you, Beauregard. I merely wanted you to—"

"Bryse, don't. I've not come for a lecture. I will see the boys and go. But perhaps I should call at the foundation office?"

"No, no," Bryson said, catching up, "please don't go. The boys are here. And Elisabeth would be crushed to miss you—as would her guests."

"Guests?"

"You're in luck. Elisabeth is in the drawing room taking tea with the neighbors."

"Which neighbors?"

"Oh, the expected assemblage. Jocelyn Breedlowe, Lady Falcondale, Miss Baker, Miss Lucy Eads…" The names were familiar; women Beau had genuinely missed since he'd moved away from Henrietta Place.

His brother finished, "And, of course, Lady Frinfrock."

Beau laughed. "Well perhaps I could pop in for a quick hello."

The Marchioness of Frinfrock was an eighty-five-year-old widow who presided over the street like a ruthless schoolmistress. She maintained a pretense of aloof detachment and claimed she preferred plants to people. But when she saw value (or rather, when she saw the opportunity for *improved* value), she drove her personal stake into the lives of others, whether they desired her intrusion or not. She was opinionated and crotchety, and she employed biting rudeness, designed to weed out the weak or insecure. Oh, but for those courageous souls who could see beyond her crusty exterior, she was generous, and indulgent, and wise.

Beau Courtland she adored, although she did her best to disguise it as outrage and shock. Beau devoured the attention. There were few reactions he valued more than adoration, outrage, and shock.

"Oh, and there is one more guest," Bryson said, turning down the great hall to the drawing room. "A new friend of Elisabeth's. A young widowed duchess. Lady Ticking."

Beau stopped and stared at his brother's back. "Lady Ticking is here?" His heart rate inexplicably kicked up. "Why?"

Bryson glanced back. "She's become very friendly with Elisabeth. I'm happy to introduce you, actually. Lovely woman. Please be on your best behavior." Beau hadn't moved, and his brother paused. "What is it?"

"You're rubbish at pranks, and you know it."

"What does that mean? What prank? It's an honest request—please be pleasant."

Beau laughed. "Far too late for that."

Bryson was shaking his head. "What's gotten into you? Since when have you balked at meeting a pretty girl?"

"Well, at least you admit that much."

"Admit what? I've no idea what you're talking about."

"I'm talking about my previous acquaintance with Lady Ticking. My *multiple* previous acquaintances. You act as if I'm about to clap eyes on her for the first time."

"Are you saying you already know the dowager duchess?"

"Hilarious, Bryse. Don't forget that I am the clever one."

"I have no idea what you're talking about," Bryson repeated. He sounded truly concerned. "How could you possibly know any duchess? *What* do you know about her?"

Beau put his hands on his hips. "Well...I know you're holding an Atlantic crossing over her head. I know you've enlisted her to train me like a monkey. She told me all of it, Bryson." His brother stared, and Beau said, "Your relentlessness about the bleeding title is a marvel, really it is. But to go so far as to tell a desperate widow that she may earn passage on one of your precious boats if she can take me in hand? You've all but extorted her."

"Extortion?" Bryson sounded horrified. "I haven't held anything over her head. She's Elisabeth's friend. I barely know her. What do you mean, take you in hand?"

With exaggerated patience, Beau told his brother about her visits to his boat and their encounter in the alley.

"Good God," marveled Bryson, "she took me at my word."

"And what the bloody hell does that mean? *Everyone* takes you at your word. You're Lord Immaculate, remember?"

Bryson cocked an eyebrow. "Not anymore."

The casual tone with which Bryson could discuss the loss of his title had taken months to cultivate, and Beau tried to remind himself of all that his brother had given up. He'd had Elisabeth by then, of course, which was the *only* reason he'd survived the loss of the title, but it had taken months for him to discuss the whole affair with such nonchalance.

Now Bryson shook his head. "I'm not surprised she believed what I suggested, but there was no actual 'agreement,' Beau. No 'deal'—not in a formal sense. She was our guest to dinner, and I was simply making conversation, and idly so, about you and the title. About how much I felt you could bring to the viscountcy, if only you would apply yourself."

Beau made a growling noise.

"Come now—surely you know I discuss this on occasion. It's no secret how I feel."

Beau glowered at him, but Bryson kept talking. "She was telling us about her childhood and how much comportment and elocution and etiquette training she had endured. I commented how convenient it would be for her to school you in this, her area of expertise."

"How *convenient* that she is also blonde and brown-eyed. And a widow. All my favorites."

"Well, I'm not blind. But I thought of her because of the copious free time she might have, now that she's been widowed and moved into the dower house. She'll have fewer obligations with the old duke's son carrying on as lord and master."

Beau shook his head in disgust. "And you idly suggested that she use this newly discovered free time to train me? After you bandied about my gross social ineptitude, of course."

A servant passed, trimming candles, and Bryson pulled Beau to the wall and said lowly, "If you want to know what happened, here it is: we discussed her proficiency in society life and my desire for you to take some interest. I joked that she could serve as your tutor. She then asserted that she had less spare time than ever before, because she is determined to carry out her late father's dream of exporting his business to America."

"She's determined to what?" This was the last thing Beau expected to hear.

Bryson repeated, "Carry on her father's dream of exporting his business to America. Her father and mother died when their ship went down on the way to New York. Did you know it?"

"She made cryptic reference to a shipwreck. But I really don't know anything about her except that she follows me around and harangues me with your misplaced desire to see me bound up and gagged with a satin bow."

This wasn't entirely true. She'd revealed more in the alley. About her parents selling her, for all practical purposes, into the aristocracy. He'd thought about it far too often in the last week.

Bryson continued. "So you don't know who her father was, do you?"

"I cannot say it enough: I know almost nothing about her."

"Theodore Holt," Bryson said. "This was her father."

Beau smirked, and Bryson explained, "The publishing giant from Liverpool. She's Holt's only daughter. He made a fortune printing and selling cheap, salacious novels—you know the ones, Holt's Fireside Adventures? Provocative, rollicking stories for the masses. Brigands, and pirates, damsels, and duels."

"Never heard of him." This was another half-truth. Beau had read the runaway best seller, *A Proper Scandal*, the summer before, along with everyone else in London. He'd paid no mind to the publisher, but he knew the book to be part of the popular Fireside Adventures series. He'd read several, in fact.

"Theodore Holt was as rich as King George and set to grow richer, apparently, reselling his previously published adventures to Americans. Of course, they'll be all new to the colonials. According to the dowager, she intends to realize her father's dream. She told us that night that she'd arranged every detail of her father's plan to sell books in New York, *except* for the shipping of the first lot."

"Quite a big detail to leave unanswered."

"I suppose that was her motivation to take me at my word," Bryson said, "even if I was merely thinking wishfully out loud. I promise it never crossed my mind that she would take my offer seriously. I chuckled at her ambition and told her—*as a mere joke*, mind you—that if she could teach you anything—anything at all—*I* would convey her tawdry novels to New York in trade. But I was speaking hypothetically. We all laughed at the notion and began talking about something else entirely. I never thought she'd do it. And to seek you out herself? Egad. I cannot believe she ventured as far as Paddington Lock." He made a disgusted face.

Beau studied him, considering this. "What care would a wealthy dowager duchess have for plying trade in America— peddling books or anything else?"

Bryson shrugged. "She was more discreet when it came to this. I didn't press because—and you must believe me—I truly thought it was a joke." He drew nearer to Beau. "But what of your meetings with her? Please tell me you were not rude or abrasive or, God forbid, indecent. She's all of twenty-three years old, and I cannot say for sure, but I believe the new duke may not be altogether gracious to her. I would truly regret it if you caused her any distress."

"Then why did you launch her at me with a bloody incentive of hustling books to Americans?" Beau shoved off the wall and strode down the hall, his mind spinning.

She intends to realize her father's dream.

Sell the books in New York.

The new duke may not be altogether gracious to her.

Behind him, Bryson called to his back, "Stoker and Joseph are with Falcondale and me in the library. There is more to discuss, Beau. Please don't leave before you and I speak."

"The ladies are in the drawing room, you say?" Beau called over his shoulder. To his way of thinking, his brother had said enough already.

[faded text from previous page showing through]

CHAPTER SEVEN

Emmaline couldn't remember the last time she'd enjoyed herself more. How lovely Elisabeth Courtland's friends were. Well, perhaps "lovely" was not the precise term for one neighbor in particular; but Lady Frinfrock was bitingly clever, and the other women did not seem to take offense at her strident opinions or unsolicited advice. Elisabeth had just delivered the most exciting news to the group, and the marchioness was challenging her around bites of cake.

"But of course you will not move away before summer," Lady Frinfrock demanded of Elisabeth. "Your furniture will be ruined, piled into carts in the rain, with the roads in the worst condition of the year. If you must go, wait until the weather is mild, when—"

A knock at the door interrupted her, and Elisabeth looked relieved. The Courtlands' butler, Sewell, stepped into the room and intoned, "Lord Rainsleigh to see you, Mrs. Courtland."

"Beau?" said Elisabeth.

Emmaline's teacup froze halfway to her lips.

Lord Rainsleigh swept in on a whirl of long coat and the wave of his hat. "I beg your pardon," he said, winking at Elisabeth, "I was told this was a meeting of the Milkmaid *Chastity* Society. Sewell, you've misled me again."

Silence reigned for a beat, and then the women erupted into a fit of laughter. Emmaline laughed too, but really what she felt was breathless. Beau Courtland worked to be clever, and he excelled at it, but he was dashing without even trying. He was rakish and irreverent; overtly, intriguingly masculine in way that Emmaline had never known a true gentleman to be.

"Ah, refreshment *and* a show," said Lady Frinfrock. "But why have you come, Rainsleigh? I was told you'd moved away and set up camp beneath a bridge. Have the river dwellers evicted you already?"

"No, in fact, we've all become fast friends, the river people and I. And I've spoken so highly of Henrietta Place, and of you, in particular, Lady Frinfrock, that a certain unwashed contingent of them plans to abandon canal life and relocate here. Your garden could house a dozen of them at least. It's charming, really, how unconcerned they are with the notion of crowding. Or bathing. You'll marvel at how quickly one becomes accustomed to the smell." He strode up to the old woman and bowed over her hand.

"Do not threaten me with displaced river people when you cannot even be bothered to visit your brother and sister-in-law for months on end. Miss Baker and I have counted the days. Your neglect is an abomination, and that says nothing of your infrequent calls to me."

More laughter, and the viscount looked with deep (and deeply counterfeit) regret. "Counted the days, have you? Why, my lady, I've underestimated how very much you care."

The women laughed again, and he glanced around the room, taking stock of the adoring faces. Miss Breedlowe. Miss Baker. A young woman introduced as a family friend, Miss Lucy Eads. Another neighbor, Lady Falcondale, who balanced a toddler on her knee. And finally…

Emmaline held her breath, waiting for him to pivot to her. When he did, their gazes locked, and he raised one eyebrow. Emmaline blinked but did not look away.

"Oh, but allow me to introduce my friend, the Dowager Duchess of Ticking," called Elisabeth behind him.

"The duchess and I are already acquainted," Beau said. His blue eyes did not leave hers, and she forgot, for the moment, to breathe.

"Oh, that's right," said Elisabeth. "She volunteers at the foundation, and we have discussed your role in rescuing my girls."

"Yes," Beau said, "and it occurs to me that you and I might review the meaning of the word 'covert' before I risk monitoring another brothel."

"Do not tempt me with insubordination," Elisabeth said, laughing. "Stoker is in town and would unseat you as raid captain, given half the chance."

"Would that we were all so lucky," said Beau. "But it's Stoker and Joseph I came to see, actually."

"You'll not distract from the progress these boys have made in school, Rainsleigh," ordered the marchioness. "They are university men now and properly so. But this does not safeguard them against your nightly procession of spirits and loose women."

"Nightly procession?" He made a whistling sound, and the women chuckled. "Well, I must occupy myself somehow until I recover from your repeated rejections."

"Clever as always," said Lady Frinfrock, "but perhaps you'll become serious long enough to announce your intended move back to Henrietta Place."

"Not likely. I've told you I'll not return until you acknowledge our secret love, my lady. Not a moment before."

The old woman harrumphed. "One can only assume this means that you did not know that Elisabeth has just announced that she and Mr. Courtland will abandon this house to your care, God save us, because they've a mind to move away."

Emmaline saw the flash of panic shoot across the viscount's face before he asked coolly, "I beg your pardon?" He paused in his selection of a biscuit from the cart and looked at Elisabeth.

"Bryson had plans to seek you out this week," Elisabeth told him. Now she stood, scrambling to her feet to meet his hard gaze. Carefully, she set her teacup on the tray. "We would have told you sooner, but the reasons for our move had not been public. That is, up until ten minutes ago."

"So you *do* know the meaning of covert," he said lightly, but Emmaline saw his tenseness. For the first time since he'd swept in, he appeared unsettled. Confined. He glanced around at the interested faces beaming up at him and then back at Elisabeth.

She chuckled. "We were only secretive out of an abundance of caution. I...we are expecting a baby, Beau." She touched a hand to her belly, and joy broke through the seriousness on her face. "But because of my advanced age..."

"Yes, you are an old crone at thirty-two," he said with a terse smile.

"We wanted to be sure the baby and I were healthy before we shared the news. I am nearly three months along now, and the doctor believes things look very promising, indeed. Meanwhile, Bryson and I have had time to consider how we wish to raise our family. I should like to continue my work at the foundation after the baby is born, and it would be easier if we lived closer to my office."

"Of course."

Elisabeth added, "In Bryson's mind, it was inevitable that we would leave this house. In his mind, you are the rightful owner."

She said this softly, almost regretfully, as if she was sympathetic to his obvious shock and distaste. Even so, Emmaline was indignant on his behalf. Had it been strictly necessary to announce more than her impending motherhood? When she announced the baby to the other women, only the marchioness had lingered on the topic of the Courtlands' move and the future of the house. Clearly the viscount didn't wish to discuss it. Even more clear was the fact that he did not wish to live in Henrietta Place. He'd stolen away to a rotting houseboat to escape it, and apparently he had not been back for months.

His expression had gone cold and agitated, and Emmaline looked away.

"Congratulations," he finally said. "I shall be thrilled to meet my niece or nephew. I have waited a lifetime to be an irreverent uncle. Any child of Bryson's will desperately require such a figure in his life."

"Bryson will speak to you about the house," Elisabeth persisted. "I...I'm so incredibly glad you have come. He has missed you."

"Not enough to inform me before the neighbors that I'm to become an uncle. But I've already seen Bryson, actually. When I came in."

Emmaline's head snapped up.

If the viscount had already seen Mr. Courtland, then they would both know about her.

Her heart leapt into a triple-time patter, and she fought the urge to bolt to her feet and assure him that she had not misled him, not entirely, and not on purpose.

"Doubtless I'll have to run the gauntlet of his expectations again when I seek out Stoker and Joseph—which I should do straightaway." He leaned in to kiss Elisabeth on the cheek. "Ladies," he said, flashing a smile at the room. To Lady Frinfrock, he said, "My love. Until we meet again."

"You are a scoundrel and a rogue, Rainsleigh, and I *do* know the difference," said Lady Frinfrock, waving him away with her hand.

With that (not inaccurate) pronouncement, Beau bowed deeply, swept his hat before him, and then strode to the door.

The last thing Emmaline saw before he ducked into the hall was his glance in her direction—one quick, enigmatic look, and then he was gone.

CHAPTER EIGHT

Inside Bryson's library, Beau found his brother's neighbor, Trevor Rheese, Lord Falcondale, reclined in the chair behind the desk, his boots propped up on the blotter, puffing on a cheroot. Joseph and Stoker were kneeling on either side of a marble chessboard, their hands locked and their faces nearly purple, struggling at an arm-wrestling match. Another young man watched from a chair by the window. Bryson pored over papers at the corner of his desk.

"Would you believe the ladies are arm-wrestling too?" Beau asked, giving Stoker a light nudge to the hip with the toe of his boot. The boy lost his edge and toppled. "Falcondale's infant has almost beaten Miss Baker."

Joseph laughed, stretching his arm, and Stoker bolted up, swearing under his breath.

Jon Stoker was a former street boy in whom Elisabeth had seen potential. (Elisabeth couldn't toss a rock without hitting something or someone she felt had potential.) She'd taken Jon in, seen him tutored, and, for two years now, financed his education at a university in Yorkshire.

Joseph was the former serving boy of Lord Falcondale, although the two had survived many adventures together and were far more like family than master and servant. When the Courtlands sent Stoker to school, Falcondale had followed suit with Joseph. The boys had known each other in Henrietta Place, and their unique mix of humble beginnings and sponsored education had only strengthened their friendship at university.

They'd both grown since the summer, more men now than boys. They wore proper trousers and shirtsleeves, waistcoats, and boots. They were cleanly shaven, with haircuts and watch chains. When Beau spoke to them, they looked him in the eye.

It did not escape Beau's attention that some elevated, princely version of this metamorphosis was exactly what Bryson expected of him. But Beau had been to university. Eton too. He'd been a horrible student, naturally; a behavior problem prone to truancy and pranks. But he'd graduated to spite his father and because it had been important to Bryson. It was the least he could do, considering Bryson had paid his tuition.

But now? Now his father was thankfully dead, and Beau had been financially independent since he'd taken a commission in the navy. He owed Bryson nothing, and he owed less than nothing to the bloody viscountcy. He might be unreliable, carousing, or drunk, but he was not (and never would be) an aristocrat—not in manner or practice. Not after all that he'd seen.

Falcondale stood up behind the desk and reached to shake hands. "He lives. Good to see you, old man. The boys have been asking for you, but I told them you'd drowned."

"Touching," Beau said. "How is school, lads?"

Joseph was quick to rattle off his enthusiasm for classes and sport and mates and local girls and the climate in Yorkshire, while Stoker simply shrugged. "It's all right," he said.

"And who is your friend?" Beau nodded to the young man in the window chair.

"Oh, that's Teddy Holt, the Dowager Duchess of Ticking's brother. We were demonstrating my superior strength to him, weren't we, mate?" Joseph said, pantomiming a roundhouse punch to Stoker's bicep.

Falcondale said, "Teddy is keeping a very stern eye on us while the ladies gossip. He's a quiet one, which is a pleasant switch from this lot."

Bryson looked up from his paperwork. "Mind the vases, boys. They look breakable because they *are*."

To Beau, Bryson said, "You'll remember Teddy Holt— you picked him up wandering the docks alone one night on a raid. This is how we met the dowager duchess. Teddy has been known to go on an unscheduled ramble and frighten his sister, although less now that they've invoked Miss Breedlowe to assist with his care."

"Miss Breedlowe," said Teddy, responding to the familiar name.

"Lovely woman, isn't she, Teddy?" said Falcondale. "And every minute she spends with you relieves her of time spent with Lady Frinfrock."

Beau watched the boy. Stoker and Joseph had opened the face of Bryson's grandfather clock and were tinkering with the inner workings. The boy watched them, transfixed.

"Mind if we correct your clock, Mr. Courtland?" Joseph called, his head deep inside the body of the thing.

"Clock," Teddy repeated.

"Only if you promise not to make it worse," said Bryson.

"Clock," Teddy said again.

"And if you include Teddy in whatever you are doing. There is a strong chance he knows more about it than you do."

The young men summoned Teddy, and he watched closely as they explored the gears and springs and interlocking mechanisms.

Thinking back, Beau did remember this boy. He'd picked up so many young people—girls, certainly, but also other lost souls they happened to encounter as they went through the nocturnal work of planning or executed raids. Teddy had looked more lost and forlorn than most, cold and wet, wandering the docks in Southwark. Beau had first assumed he was drunk, but they'd just rescued a girl who claimed she'd seen the boy walking in circles among the gulls on the boardwalk for the last day and a half. Beau had almost left him, but he'd circled back at the last minute and rounded him up. He'd handed him over to Elisabeth with seven young prostitutes, an African serving boy, and three starving cats. Elisabeth, for better or for worse, never turned anyone away.

But the irony of this memory was that the duchess owed *Beau* for Teddy's rescue, not Bryson. *He'd* gone back for the boy; *he'd* delivered him to Elisabeth.

Beau was just about to point out this fact, when there was a knock on the door.

"Her Grace the Dowager Duchess of Ticking," said the butler importantly, swinging the door wide.

Falcondale whipped his feet off the desk and snuffed the cheroot. Stoker and Joseph turned away from the clock and dipped their heads.

"Malie," said Teddy Holt.

The duchess stepped tentatively inside, with Miss Breedlowe behind her.

"Your Grace," said Bryson, dropping his paperwork, "is anything the matter?"

She'd worn gray today. This was the first time Beau had seen her out of the suffocating black. Half mourning, he assumed. The veil was gone, thank God, but she was wearing another one of her awful hats—now in matching gray. It depressed him to know that so many hideous hats existed in the world, and she owned all of them.

The gray and the hat did nothing to diminish her beauty, and every man in the room stared. Beau looked away, irritated with himself. He enjoyed pretty women. Hell, he even enjoyed plain women. But there was something about *this* woman. She caused him to reverse his first instinct and do the opposite. He wanted to stare, but he wouldn't allow it. He wanted to flirt with her, or tease her, or tell her she was lovely, but he hadn't even choked out a greeting.

"Forgive the intrusion, Mr. Courtland," she told Bryson. "My brother and I cannot linger. The duke will expect us back to Portman Square before long, and our carriage is due." She looked to Teddy. "Time to go, Teddy Holt. What can we say to Mr. Courtland and his friends?"

"Clock," said Teddy.

"Oh yes, it's lovely." She smiled at Stoker and Joseph. "Thank you, gentlemen, for entertaining Teddy. The opportunity to dismantle a clock is one he won't soon forget. Come now, Teddy, say your good-byes."

"Clock," Teddy said again, turning back to the open face.

"*Teddy*," the duchess said, her voice firmer, "you know how the Duke of Ticking, er, worries when we are away too long."

The boy tensed at the sound of the duke's name, and he plodded to his sister.

"There's a good boy. Perhaps the young men could be convinced to pay a call to look inside our grandfather clock."

The boys agreed, and Miss Breedlowe stepped forward to lead Teddy out the door.

The duchess said, "Thank you again, Mr. Courtland, for a lovely afternoon."

"You are welcome any time," Bryson said. "Elisabeth enjoys it, to be sure. And now that I've learned you've made the acquaintance of my brother..." He let the sentence trail off.

Beau finally looked at her, *really* looked at her.

If he thought she'd blanch or deny their association, he was wrong.

She said, "Oh yes, quite so," and smiled warmly.

Bryson stepped up and held out his arm. "I'll walk you out." She slid her gloved hand on his brother's bicep, and Beau looked away.

Bryson called back to him, "Beau, do not leave."

"I wouldn't dream of it, *Papa*," Beau said.

Chapter Nine

Emmaline fixed her face with what she hoped was a pleasant expression and allowed Mr. Courtland to guide her into the hall. What choice did she have?

They know.

While she walked, while she smiled, while she stared at Teddy and Miss Breedlowe in front of them, she heard a resounding chorus of, *They know, they know, they know.*

Bryson Courtland knew that she had been trying to instruct his brother, doggedly so. She'd been doing it whether he remembered asking her to do it or not. Whether he *wanted* her to do it or not.

And the viscount knew that his brother hadn't specifically—not contractually, not *really*—promised her an Atlantic crossing, if she did it.

Everyone knew. Doubtless, Elisabeth and Jocelyn would soon know. There was little to be done but explain her motivation and then asked to be excused. Forever. Back to her dower house, where she would remain, trapped under

Ticking's rule, with Teddy and his money at the duke's avaricious mercy. Also forever.

Emmaline squeezed her eyes shut, struggling to remember the logic she'd employed when she'd hatched the idea. It was but a loose plan—one of many loose plans that she hoped to weave together to form a net that would rescue her and Teddy from the Duke of Ticking's grip.

It had all begun so innocently. Bryson Courtland had mentioned his desire for his brother to undergo some of what he called "comportment training"—a review of working manners to get his brother through a fancy dinner, some advice on who was who in society.

Emmaline remembered thinking at the time, *My God, these are quite literally the only things I know how to do.*

How could she not put the otherwise inane knowledge to good use?

And so she had laughingly, gratefully agreed.

So what if the offer, such that it was, came off as casual and undefined? So what if she hadn't realized the extreme challenge that the new viscount posed? In theory, it had been a conceivably attainable means to an end.

"You might be my only hope," Mr. Courtland had said.

In fact, the opposite was true. If he could convey Emmaline and Teddy and two hundred crates of books to New York City, *he* was *her* only hope.

But how to relate that to Mr. Courtland as they traversed his great hall in strained silence?

Truthfully and earnestly, Emmaline thought.

And then apologize profusely, and flee.

But first, she would congratulate him on his impending fatherhood. She had opened her mouth to say this when Bryson Courtland turned to her and said, "Whatever you're doing, keep doing it."

"I...I beg your pardon?" Emmaline stammered. She missed a step.

"Obviously, you took our discussion about my brother and his abominable manners to heart."

"Obviously," she managed, her heart pounding.

"I hope you'll believe me when I say"—he glanced back over his shoulder—"that never in my wildest dreams did I think you'd agree to such an arrangement. And certainly not that you would track him down yourself. I shudder to think what you've witnessed in Paddington. Even I have not called to the canal."

"I believe you," she said, hoping it was the right thing to say.

"Please tell me that my brother has not offended or inconvenienced you." He looked earnestly concerned.

An image flashed in her mind of the viscount bent over her, and she felt her traitorous cheeks go pink. "I am unharmed," she said.

"Taking him in hand is hardly the work of a duchess. I...I am shocked but undyingly grateful."

With this, Emmaline felt herself breathe for the first time since the viscount had strolled into the drawing room.

Mr. Courtland was grateful.

She was doing him an earnest favor.

The plan was working.

The bloody plan just might work.

In consideration of his candor, Emmaline followed suit. "I am undyingly motivated to see my father's books sold to Americans," she said. "But I can only pay you for the shipping *after* I've made the sales in New York. Until then, this work with your brother is quite literally the only thing I have to offer."

Bryson was shaking his head. "Please do not concern yourself with the shipment. Elisabeth would garrote me if she knew I demanded anything in trade to transport your books. I will be happy to convey the crates to New York, even without attention to my brother. You need only ask."

"Oh, but I would never—"

He held up a hand. "Consider it done. We sail to America every month at least. It is my pleasure to assist you. But this other…" Again, he let the sentence trail off.

"Consider it done," she repeated. "It is my pleasure to assist you." She gave a small smile.

He closed his eyes and pinched the bridge of his nose and then looked in the direction of the drawing room where the ladies were taking tea. "There is a chance that Elisabeth will garrote me anyway," he admitted. "She values your friendship, and this is no small thing to ask a friend. Still, if anyone loves my brother as much as I do, it is she. We both want him to succeed."

"She speaks very highly of him."

They resumed their walk down the hall, and Emmaline asked, "Is there anything in particular I should tell Lord Rainsleigh about my role in the, er, lessons? Clearly, he is opposed to the very idea. Doubtless, he told you this."

Bryson glanced at the library and then back at her. "But this is why I confide in you, don't you see?" He dropped his voice to a whisper. "My brother has *complained* about me. He doesn't enjoy my talking about him when he isn't present to defend himself. And he's *complained* about your badgering him. And he's questioned your motivation. But he has not asked for you to stop." He raised his eyebrows.

Emmaline blinked. Something light and ticklish flipped in her belly. She worked to control her expression. "Very good, then," she said.

"Repeat whatever you already told him about your reasons," he went on. "Paint me the villain. If he was really opposed to your presence, he would have told me, in no uncertain terms, and left London on the next boat. Instead, he simply protested, albeit a bit too much. He is typically full of conditions or ultimatums. In this, there was none." He glanced behind them. "Ah, and will you look at that? I've just caught him watching us from my library door."

This bit of news brought on another stomach flip, and Emmaline glanced behind her. The doorway was empty.

"To that end," said Bryson, his tone becoming formal and detached, "I am wondering if you would excuse me? I worry that Elisabeth is in need of me."

"Oh, but do you think that she is—"

"Just a calculated guess." He winked. "If you don't mind, I should like to have my brother see you out in my stead."

Before she could answer, he looked over her shoulder and called, "Beau?" He beckoned with his hand.

To Emmaline, he whispered, "I pray you will tell me if I take advantage by pressing for this…this…arrangement. Or if my brother becomes too difficult. I know it to be a very odd and likely taxing thing for woman of your station."

It'll be worth it, she thought, but she said, "It's the least I can do."

"It's a generosity I won't soon forget," he said, and she thought, *I'm counting on it.*

But now she heard footsteps, and the viscount was beside her.

"What's happened?" Lord Rainsleigh asked cautiously.

"Elisabeth requires my attention," said Bryson.

"She's not unwell, I hope."

"Only fatigued, I'm sure," said Bryson. "She has limited reserves of energy where Lady Frinfrock is concerned. This was true even before she became pregnant."

"Lady Frinfrock has that effect on all of us," said the viscount. "Should I offer to see the marchioness home?"

Bryson shook his head. "I will go to Elisabeth. But please, escort the Duchess to the door."

CHAPTER TEN

The duchess held her arm out to him, and Beau stared at it. Everything about this moment felt like a trap. Her presence in his brother's house. His brother's denial of an arrangement with her. Her necessity for an escort down a perfectly safe and comfortable hallway.

Beau knew when he was being managed, and he didn't like it. He wondered what would happen if he left her standing with her graceful, gray-sheathed wing outstretched.

But he would not leave her, of course. Bryson had begun to back away, and Beau took her arm.

"Lose your way to the door, did you?" he asked, gesturing to the very obvious door. Her brother and Miss Breedlowe could be seen ahead, watching maids string a doorway with evergreen garland.

"Hello again to you too," she said, falling into step beside him. "I might add that 'hello' would be one of many polite greetings you could extend to a lady when you are burdened with her company."

"Back to this, are we?" he said.

"But of course. I've just assured your brother that our lessons have commenced. We need only set up a time and place. Surely you're not surprised at this."

"I am surprised, in fact. Why would you tell him this, if it is not true?"

"Well, it could be true."

"But it's not."

"You could make it true."

"I could also marry Lady Frinfrock and be knighted for courage and sacrifice, but this also will not happen." He stopped walking and looked down at her. "Why did you pretend to have an arrangement with my brother? He's told me what actually happened, obviously."

She chewed her bottom lip. His concentration slipped, just a notch. He heard himself ask another question: "What happened to the widow's weeds?"

"I am in half mourning now," she said. "My husband has been dead for a year and a half. On Wednesday."

"May God rest him," he said sardonically, although he had no idea why. For all he knew, the late Duke of Ticking may have been the great love of her life. Her mourning might be entirely authentic. The thought irritated him for some reason, and he pulled her along again.

He asked a third question, "Do you miss the veil?"

She shook her head. "It would be difficult to miss something less. I wonder, Lord Rainsleigh...as I see it, you suffer from only one true obstacle to propriety."

"Please don't call me that. And while you're at it, please don't elaborate on my obstacles."

"It's your forthrightness. You say whatever you think. You pay no mind to whether you will shock, or offend, or insult someone. You don't care if you make people uncomfortable."

He dipped his head closer and said in a low voice, "Do I make you uncomfortable, Your Grace?"

She missed a step. He hustled her closer on his arm.

"You've just said my name properly, Lord Rainsleigh."

"Oh, would that you could do the same," he said. They were nearing the door, and he stopped again. "But I digress. Bryson has told me that he never asked you to…educate me."

She nodded, seemingly more to herself than him. "Well, perhaps he did not in as many words. He is a gentleman, so of course he would never ask this outright."

"Because gentlemen operate on vague innuendo, do they?"

"Because, as a lady, I'm sure he never thought I would consider such a thing."

"But you have and with an unladylike tenacity. Why?"

She opened her mouth to answer him, and he said, "And don't say you owe him for rescuing your brother, because *I*, madam, rescued your brother. When I saw him, I was reminded that Teddy and I originally met on the pier outside of a brothel in Southwark. If it hadn't been for me, he might still be there, feeding the seagulls." He watched her reaction and then added, "If he was very lucky."

She blinked up at him. Her hand slid from his sleeve. "So it was you?" she whispered.

"Yes, it was me, and please don't change the subject. Just bear in mind that if you owe anyone for your brother's safekeeping, 'tis *me*."

"Elisabeth didn't say exactly how Teddy came to be discovered," she said. Her face took on a faraway expression, and she glanced at her brother beneath the garland and then back at him. Beau saw a glimpse of the fear and worry she must have felt when he'd gone missing.

"Thank you," she said with great feeling. "Thank you so very much."

Now her expression was grateful, and he wished he hadn't told her. In his experience, gratefulness was one step away from expectation. "It was nothing," he said.

"You rescue all of the girls who come to the foundation, don't you? That's how they are delivered to Elisabeth—by you?"

And there it was: expectation. Next came disappointment.

He said, "At the moment." Before he could stop himself, he reached out and replaced her hand on his arm.

"Are you afraid that you cannot carry on as a proper viscount in the light of day if you rescue these girls in the night?" she asked. "Because I believe that you can."

"What I'm afraid of," he said, speaking low, "is that you care too much about my future as a *proper viscount* and for no good reason. You still haven't told me why you've misrepresented the alleged arrangement with my brother."

Sewell chose that moment to sweep in with her belongings, and she smiled and presented her back to the butler so that he could whirl a gray cloak around her shoulders.

"I bade the grooms to summon your carriage, Your Grace," Sewell said, "but they tell me you arrived on foot."

She smiled at the butler. "That is correct, Sewell. We will walk, but thank you."

Beau furrowed his brow. "Arrived on foot? In this weather? Where do you live?"

"Portman Square. My dower house is behind the duke's townhome."

"That's ten blocks from here. You cannot walk ten blocks in the snow."

"Oh, I have my carriage; it simply isn't here. I've left the rig and grooms outside Holy Trinity Church," she said. "It's not far. Down the street and around the corner."

Beau looked out the window at the cold, heavy grayness of the afternoon. "Why not ride door to door?" She made no sense.

"If I come and go through a church, there is less hassle at home."

"What kind of hassle?"

She paused in the act of settling her cloak and looked at him. "My stepson holds a very limited view of my personal freedom."

"You have a *son*?"

She shook her head. "The Duke of Ticking is my *stepson*. My late husband had several children by his first wife. His oldest son inherited the dukedom, naturally. He is twenty years older than I am, at least, but I was married to his father."

"Twenty years older? My God, how old was your husband?"

"When he died?" she asked.

"When he took a nineteen-year-old girl as his wife."

"How did you know I was nineteen when I married?"

"Lucky guess."

She looked away. "He was sixty-four when we married."

Beau blinked, allowing a moment for the gross injustice of this to settle in. What a bloody waste, bridling youth and energy with decrepitude and fatigue. It also bordered on perverse. Her lithe, firm beauty offered to someone soft and sagging, doubtless with yellow teeth and hair in his ears.

Beau could feel himself scowling down at her. "So now that he's cocked up his toes, his son makes you trudge through the snow?"

"His Grace has been very adamant in adhering to the appropriate mourning period, I'm afraid. I am only permitted to leave my house to attend church or call on charities. This is how I am able to see Elisabeth at the foundation. He does not know the nature of her work, obviously. My excuse for this afternoon was prayers at Holy Trinity."

"So how have you turned up to call on me in Paddington? *Three* times?" But he remembered the footsteps on the shore and her subsequent flight from the boat.

"Oh, I have discovered ways to call on people and places, as long as the servants only see me leave the carriage and go into a church. Luckily, there are many churches in London, and a widow may come and go quite freely at all hours. Holy Trinity is particularly convenient to Henrietta Place, because it has a side door that is obscured from the street."

Beau glanced again out the window. "It's snowing," he said. "I will walk you."

She shook her head. "If we were seen walking together, it would make my life far more difficult than a little cold and snow could ever do."

Beau became vaguely aware that he was grinding his teeth. He detested petty tyranny. It was the primary reason he had no wish to be viscount. He'd rather die than join the overbred, unfeeling ranks of those who wielded arbitrary dominion because they'd been told from birth it was their God-given right. He'd seen the face of this entitlement before, and at painfully close range. He'd sworn then to never be party to the ruling class.

He watched her fuss with her cloak, straightening the collar and buttoning four buttons beneath her chin. He wondered what else, besides restricting her movements, this new duke felt was his God-given right. He couldn't stop himself from asking, "Jealous, is he? The new duke?"

She shook her head. "No, he is piously committed to his wife. They have seventeen children."

"Seventeen! Bloody hell—*why?*"

She shrugged, smoothing graceful fingers over skin-tight gloves. "I've come to believe he continues to conceive the children in order to give me something to do." She chuckled to herself. "His punishment for perceived indiscretions is to assign me to their care."

"All of them?"

"Honestly, once there are more than four or five, it makes no difference how many there are. They are legion."

She drifted to the door, and Sewell materialized again, sweeping it open with a bow.

Beau grabbed the top of the door and pushed it closed. He dismissed the butler with a jerk of his head. "So our conversation in the alley," he said lowly, "was motivated by secrecy. You hide from this…person? The Duke of Ticking?"

She looked up at him. "Our conversation in the alley was motivated by extreme necessity." Her eyes flashed with a conviction he had not seen before. He could not look away.

"What do you mean?"

"Necessity, Lord Rainsleigh," she repeated. The playful, lecturing tone was gone. Her voice was frank. "I understand why the notion confuses you. Your needs are so few, you run from the abundance. In this, we are not the same."

Behind them, Miss Breedlowe and Teddy began to crowd toward the door, and Emmaline waved them back to the garland. She continued. "You wanted to know why I care so much about your behavior? Well, the truth is that I don't. For the most part, you and your habits are immaterial. I don't care if you succeed as a viscount or fail. I don't care if you ignore the title or become prime minister. Your brother has offered me a way to earn my own way, independent of the new duke, and I mean to seize it. My father is dead. My husband is dead. Neither of them provided for me before they left this earth, so I cannot *pay* Mr. Courtland for this kindness in advance. But I can offer work in trade. You, my lord, are that work, whether either of us likes it or not."

Beau cocked his head, considering this. If what she said was to be believed, his brother had not been desperate to see him trained. Quite the contrary, *she* was desperate to do his brother a favor. Perhaps this was why Bryson was so surprised.

He opened his mouth to clarify this, but a different question came out. "So the new Duke of Ticking does not have lecherous designs on you?"

She shook her head and gestured to Miss Breedlowe and Teddy, calling them to the door. "I don't even think His Grace enjoys my company."

"But what else could he want?"

"If I had to guess, I'd say he wants the same thing that I do. My father's money."

"And the solution is to keep you under lock and key?"

"I believe he thinks it's the most prudent way to insinuate himself into my life and Teddy's life and establish that he is guardian over us."

"But you are a grown woman, and a widow to boot. Do you require a guardian? And he's not related to Teddy at all."

"I am a twenty-three-year-old female with no obvious male to oversee my affairs. His Grace would gladly rise to the occasion. Especially if Teddy is in my care. My brother's mental challenges will mean he is the ward of *someone* all of his days. If I am that person—which I am determined to be—Ticking is naturally motivated to see himself as my guardian. In this, who do you think will control all of Teddy's money?"

"No." Beau marveled at the thought. "He wouldn't."

She turned the knob on the door and opened it. They were hit with a gust of cold, damp wind. Miss Breedlowe and Teddy trundled out into the fog and down the steps. "He would and he is," she said. "But not if I can leave the country and make my own money first."

"The books. My brother told me you intend to open your father's publishing company in America."

"Well, I don't know about all that. One step at a time. I've come upon a heap of my father's old books. The titles have sold all they ever will in England, but I believe I can sell the remaining lot in New York."

"Quite an ambitious first step."

"The first ones always are, I've discovered." With those words she smiled, a sad, earnest smile, and descended the front steps into the icy December afternoon.

CHAPTER ELEVEN

The first official etiquette lesson took place one week later, on Beau's boat, while he fished off the bow.

Emmaline had arranged the session through Miss Breed-lowe, who had informed the viscount of the time and date when she next saw him in the street in Henrietta Place. To Emmaline's relief, he had not objected (nor had he consented, according to Jocelyn), and she was uncertain that he would cooperate until she found him on the deck of his boat at the appointed time, making repairs.

"Good day, Lord Rainsleigh," she called. Her cheerfulness sounded forced, and she bit the inside of her mouth. *Keep calm. Deliver the tutorial. Be on your way.* This was a transaction, and nothing more. It made no difference what she thought of the viscount—good or bad, attractive or unsavory.

It only mattered that she paid this debt to his brother.

He looked up from his work on the deck. "Duchess," he said. Not a greeting so much as an identification. He returned his attention to his work.

"Perhaps a review of greetings and polite conversation should be our first order of business," she called back purposefully. In her head, she thanked God that he hadn't said, "Bugger off."

Still, he was hardly ushering her on board. In fact, he had not even stood.

She waited.

His dog plodded over to sniff her hem and wag her tail. Emmaline looked right and left. As before, there were few people on the canal path. Two boys batted a rock with a stick beneath a tree. An old man on the next boat smoked his pipe and read the newspaper.

It occurred to her that perhaps the viscount chose the canal for privacy. This, she understood. Even now, after easily giving her grooms the slip, she was wary of discovery. She would not be safe for long, standing on the deck in open view of the path.

With no more greeting or invitation forthcoming, Emmaline patted the dog and picked her way to the spot where the viscount knelt with his tools. He was dressed in buckskins and tall boots, the sleeves of his shirt rolled up his thick, tanned arms. With powerful, efficient movements, he shoved an iron rod deep into a crack on the boat's deck.

Emmaline ventured, "Do you intend to…make repairs to your boat while we review?"

The viscount tossed down the iron with a clatter. "No. I intend to fish."

"Oh," she said, watching him shove to his feet and wipe his hands on his trousers.

He asked, "Do you intend to instruct me while I fish?"

"I suppose that could be made to work." She harbored no illusions that he had transformed into an eager student since they'd last met. His consent to abide her was…enough.

She wondered if he regarded their interaction only as something to "abide." He had not been suggestive with her in the Courtlands' hallway—not like he had in the alley—but she thought she'd felt an awareness…a watchful attention to her face as she spoke, to her hands in her gloves. She had felt him watch her from the window long after they'd trudged down the street.

Now he seemed determined not to look at her. He led the way to the bow of the boat over a thin strip of deck between the cabin and the railing. The area was so small that Emmaline was forced to hold in her skirts to scoot by.

"Can you manage?" he called back.

"A gentleman would extend his hand and kindly offer to assist me," she said. She was not helpless, but it occurred to her to pack as many kernels of information into this session as she could.

Teetering only a little, she edged onto the small triangle of a foredeck and dropped her skirts. They immediately expanded to dominate the already small space, and she made a noise of frustration and gathered them up again. "His Grace was adamant that our mourning clothes be as ostentatious as they are dark," she said.

"The duke selects your clothing?"

"He commissioned all of our dresses for full mourning and for half," she said.

"All of who?"

"He has ten daughters, plus his wife and me. Hundreds of pounds in black and gray garments, if you can imagine. I should add here that a gentleman might issue a mild, unspecific compliment to a lady's appearance but never demand to know who bought her dress."

"A mild, unspecific compliment," he repeated, shaking his head. "And this is effective? Do you enjoy mild, unspecific compliments, Duchess? Because this has not been my experience." He bent to a tangle of what appeared to be fishing line, poles, and a bucket of bait.

"Well, I should think I appreciate any well-intentioned compliment." The back of his shirt pulled across his shoulders as he stretched and untangled the wire. He could not see her, and she allowed herself to watch the play of muscles through the fabric.

"My experience is that the more specific and vivid a compliment, the more effective. For example…" He stood up and propped a pole and line against the railing. "What if I were to say, Why, Duchess, I see you've worn another gray frock. You know, I consider these a vast improvement over the black. But both colors beg the question: what colors do you really favor? When you can wear whatever you want?"

"That is a not a compliment," she said.

"I'm not finished. I would further ask: Do you prefer the whimsy of lace, I wonder? Or the richness of unadorned fabric? Do you favor gold and purple, which would bring out the hazel undertones in your brown eyes, or burgundy and moss green to make your skin glow? Would you choose layers and layers of petticoats or just enough to be decent?" He glanced at her skirt and then took up the hook on the end of the line.

Emmaline's mouth fell open just a little. It took a moment for her to formulate a response. "A gentleman would never, ever mention a lady's petticoats."

"Well, that depends on his intended result, doesn't it?"

"No. Not if the result is to be simple pleasantness. As it should be." She cleared her throat. She remembered the late Duke of Ticking's first compliment to her. *I thought you'd be bigger,* he had said.

The viscount told her, "I cannot imagine a single instance when my intention for a compliment was to be pleasant."

"What is your intention?"

"Well, that depends, doesn't it?" He reached into the bucket and pulled out a piece of bait and worked it on the hook. "Sometimes it's to charm. Sometimes to delight. Sometimes it's to get something I want very badly indeed." His voice had gone soft and gravely. "Sometimes it is to distract. Many times, it is to…compel."

What has been your intention for me? The words were on the tip of her tongue, and she barely managed to contain them. Her heart pounded. He was watching her again. His blue eyes casually were on her face as his hands tested the weight of the pole.

"Lord Rainsleigh," she managed to say, "are you aware that a viscount may embody the title in many ways?" When she'd organized topics for the lesson, she'd planned to begin with this.

He sighed and muttered under his breath, "And we're off."

She went on. "You need not be a humorless sort of paragon, or a leader of society, or whatever it is you find distasteful.

You may compliment ladies, albeit respectfully. You may fish for sport. You may be a gentleman farmer. Or a traveler who sails the world, like Lord Falcondale. A scholar. A crusader, even."

"A sodden lay-about?"

She chuckled, and before she could stop herself, she said, "Well, my late husband was certainly that."

He looked up. She had not organized any personal insights. But he appeared to be listening for once, so she added, "Ticking was believed to be a perfectly respectable duke. But he drank to excess."

He turned back to his pole. "Did your parents know he was a drunk before they married you to him?"

"I cannot say." She turned away. After the wedding, when she'd discovered the extent of Ticking's drinking and carrying on, she had wondered this herself. Had her parents understood the union into which they had, for all practical purposes, *sold* her? Marriage to a man who drank so much he soiled his clothes?

She glanced at the viscount. "Would your title be more palatable to you if, er, sobriety was not expected? Because truly, it has more to do with the way you behave in front of certain people, in certain places, at certain times of day. Outside of these expectations, you may do whatever you wish. This is how Ticking carried on." She thought a moment more. "I believe this…this duplicity is what my parents did not know. Certainly, it came as a shock to me."

He raised his eyebrows, acknowledging what she said, and then cast his fishing line into the canal. They watched the hook and bait sink into the black-green water. After a moment, the viscount said, "I have no wish to behave one way in front of some people and another way for others. There is only one way I can be."

Emmaline felt a small, unexpected pulse of admiration at this. Her eyes snapped to his profile. It occurred to her that of course manners did not necessarily equal integrity. Such a simple truth—and one that had become so painfully obvious in the last three years.

"Good manners do not necessarily mean you are a good person," she recited. "Rather, bad manners may distract from good qualities. My late husband could charm the doublet off the bishop in church and be falling down drunk by Sunday tea."

The viscount pulled his line from the water and grimaced at the bare hook. He pierced a fresh grub and tossed it out again. "Took you to church, did he? Where else did he take you?"

"I beg your pardon?"

"Your late husband. *The duke.* I wonder what a man fifty years your senior could possibly have in common with a girl from Liverpool. Where did your interests meet? The theatre? Parties? Opera? Balls?"

She paused.

Nowhere, she thought. *We had nothing in common.*

But it was not a good use of their time to discuss her arduous marriage to the duke. In fact the abject misery of her marriage was an argument *against* aristocratic life, which likely the viscount already knew. "The Duke of Ticking has been dead almost as long as we were married. Honestly, I don't remember."

This lie was accompanied by a strong tug on his fishing line. The pole bent, and the viscount widened his stance and yanked, jerking the hook and a small perch from the water. Emmaline sucked in a breath at the sight of the flapping, fighting fish. He swung the line and caught it in his hand, splashing both of them with water. Emmaline laughed and clapped her hands, genuinely impressed. Without thinking, she hopped up to get a closer look. He smiled at her, showing off the shiny, squirming creature, and then he worked the hook from its mouth and tossed it back into the canal.

"Too small," he said. "We'll let him fatten up, and then I'll try him again in the spring."

Emmaline watched the fish arc through the air and then plop into the water.

"He swam away," she said.

Just like I will do. I've been cut loose, and now I will swim away.

"Lord Rainsleigh," she said, turning to him, "would you mind terribly if, while we worked on your manners, you taught me how to fish?"

CHAPTER TWELVE

It occurred to Beau that perhaps Bryson had enlisted this girl not so much to *teach* him but to *test* him.

Would you mind if you taught me to fish?

As if the fishing ploy hadn't been the first thing that crossed his mind when she'd settled on the bow of the boat and watched him bait his hook with those big, brown fascinated eyes.

Instructing any female on the art of practically anything was a tried-and-true method for seduction, one he'd employed countless times.

Allow me show you how to mount this horse…or shoot this rifle…or drive this carriage…or smoke this cheroot. The opportunities were endless, really, as were his personal conquests as a result. He'd never taught a woman to fish, but it took no imagination to fully comprehend the opportunities—*Hold the pole just so; lean into me; cast like this; we'll work together to pull him in, shall we?*—and the subsequent reward.

But for once in his life, the goal was not his own reward. He'd consented to the lessons because he felt sorry for her.

Orphaned and widowed and responsible for a sick brother and battling a mercenary duke? Beau might be careless and selfish, but his heart wasn't made of ice. On the contrary. He was the very soul of chivalry; everyone said so.

He'd also asked himself what harm, really, her instruction could do? He'd been angered by his meddlesome brother, not the pretty girl with her book of pretty rules. With the correct attitude, he'd thought, he could endure the lessons while leaving the duchess to feel as if she'd honored her obligation (real or imagined) to Bryson. She wouldn't actually change his behavior, not really, but it would allow him to look at her, and flirt with her, and enjoy her company. It wasn't as if he could deny that he wanted to look and flirt and enjoy her. And if they wound up in bed? Well, he would not be stricken with a fit of conscience as he had been in the alley. She was a widow, after all. And she wasn't as desperate and helpless as he'd first thought. Well, perhaps she was desperate, but she was quite capable. Tenacious and ambitious and very clever. Making love to her would not take advantage so much as...entertain her. He'd make devilishly sure of that.

After he'd accepted this, Beau had enjoyed his first real peace in days—weeks, in fact. He looked down at her now, enjoying the glow of her amber-brown eyes in the winter sun.

"Learn to fish?" he asked.

She nodded. "Not every nuanced thing about it. If you could teach me only the basics, it would be like a trade, in a way. Your expertise for mine."

Beau thought of all the areas of expertise on which he would rather barter, but he said nothing.

"I should like to know how to fish," she was saying. "I've made a commitment to educate myself on any skill that I might one day find useful."

His expression must have said, *Useful for what?* because she added, "To be less at the mercy of others. The depth and breadth of my...well, my helplessness came as quite shock to me when I found myself widowed, with no parents. I was ill equipped to provide for myself and for Teddy. But no longer. I am determined to take advantage of any opportunity I have to educate myself. I shan't be helpless again."

Beau tried to imagine her fishing for food in order to survive. It was a far-fetched image, but he could respect her desire to be self-sufficient. Most women in her position would have thrown themselves headlong into the business of marrying again. She'd done the opposite, far more difficult thing.

He held the fishing pole to her. "All right," he said and explained where to grip the pole, how to keep the tip out of the water, and the motion of casting. She listened carefully, nodding only when she truly understood. Her questions were thoughtful rather than coy. She earnestly wished to learn to fish.

Through sheer force of will, Beau leaned in only every now and then. It was, perhaps, the first time he had ever endeavored to touch a woman less instead of more. But seducing her was a possibility, not a guarantee. If it came to that, he would not sprint to capitulation; he would savor, meander. Allow her own desire to reveal itself in time. Already, she was satisfyingly flushed. She laughed at every other thing he said. It was a sweet sort of torture, holding himself back—almost as much effort as finding excuses to touch her.

As for the actual fishing, she caught on quickly, and Beau found himself enjoying the simple pleasure of a morning spent on the cold canal with a beautiful woman. After their hooks were baited and dropped into the water, they fished for a time in silence. When she spoke again, he thought she might comment on the landscape, which was brittle and barren in winter but starkly beautiful in his view.

Instead, she said, "I don't mind telling you, Lord Rainsleigh, that your manners do not seem glaringly out of line. It's more that it's your...bearing."

"Ah." He frowned at the view. "This again."

"It was meant to be a compliment."

"You said compliments were to be unspecific and pleasant."

"Exactly, which mine was. I will now veer from that rule in order to further instruct you." She spoke to the canal, her pretty profile pale against the black-green water. "It's not as if you spit when you talk. Or speak out of turn. In fact, your banter with Lady Frinfrock on Saturday bordered on witty and charming. But your attire is wrong, I'm afraid." She glanced at him, up and then down. He raised one eyebrow. She looked away.

"The way you hold yourself calls too much attention to your...form." She cleared her throat. "You lean rather than stand and sprawl rather than sit. Yet when you walk, you carry yourself with a strident sort of"—she rolled her shoulder—"disregard for who might be in your way. And you look others in the eye a moment too long. It unnerves them, I'm afraid."

She glanced at him again. "This is what I have observed."

He nodded to her fishing line. "Move your bait." There were worse things, he realized, than hearing her observations.

"And you are too forward," she went on. "And blunt. You aren't discerning in what you say." She glanced again. He realized it unsettled her to say this. He smiled.

"There, I've said it," she finished. "Your bearing. That's the worst of it. If you make the slightest effort to refine these superficial things"—she looked down the canal—"you will be well on your way."

"That bad, am I?"

"Your choice of dwelling would go a long way toward appeasing your brother. This boat, I hope you don't mind my saying, is in terrible repair. It's filthy and piled with nets and rigging and God knows what. Short of a seagoing expedition, you could not possibly require these items. When I first discovered you, I couldn't believe any man would willingly reside here, let alone a gentleman."

Ah, but isn't that the point? he thought.

"If the house in Henrietta Place is not to your liking," she went on, "why not sell it and take a house that suits you? Something on the water, if you like. If you must be on a boat, why not a respectable yacht on the Thames? You cannot be comfortable here. You cannot."

"And you're comfortable where you live? The dower house in Portman Square?"

"I *do* notice when you answer all of my questions with your own questions. Please tell me you know this."

"Yes, but do you take my point? You've trotted yourself out as the authority on high society, and now you're trying to sell me a bill of goods about it. I'm merely asking if your experience in this world has been worth the effort."

"Well. It's better than here."

"Certain of that, are you? You're making quite an effort to leave that esteemed address."

"I'm trying to leave my situation under Ticking's authority," she said. "The dower house itself is perfectly lovely."

"So you say. But if the new duke is so oppressive, why didn't you return to your childhood home after your husband died?"

"Oh, my childhood home has been sold."

He stared at her. "*Sold?* To whom?"

"The highest bidder, I assume. I wasn't consulted."

"Why not?"

She raised an eyebrow at him. "Everyone in Liverpool assumes that I am a fixture of the dukedom now—and what a lucky girl. What interest have I in my childhood home? I'm a duchess now. The house was the first thing my father's board of trustees sold after he drowned. Their primary interest was the survival of the company, not his personal assets."

Beau set down his pole. "What of your brother? Was he not living there?"

"Teddy was staying with the duke and me the summer that my parents intended to travel to America. They never came back, of course, and he has been with me ever since."

"But surely *some* family member was consulted before they went so far as to sell your parents' house."

"They sought permission from the new duke. Naturally. My husband was dead by then."

"Because if there's a duke in the vicinity, he must be the authority."

She nodded. "In the absence of other male relations—yes. From what I gather, my father's trustees assured His Grace that the money from the sale of the house would be put into Teddy's trust with the rest of his inheritance."

"Oh, I see. And Teddy became a golden goose."

"The irony is that I don't even think Ticking realized Teddy's potential for wealth until he'd been told about the sale of the Liverpool mansion. He had been openly hostile to me since his father and I married. I am so very *common* in his eyes, don't you see? Never mind that my dowry saved the entire family from bankruptcy. He was loath to even allow me to inhabit the dower house."

"But now he keeps you under lock and key."

She nodded. "Now he is terrified that I might discover a way to provide for myself."

"Ah, yes, which you have done. The books. Soon to be in great demand in America."

"God willing."

"How have you managed to get your hands on your father's books, if his trustees go about selling houses out from under you?"

"Oh, these are old books, best sellers from years ago. Papa printed too many copies, and they were piling up in his various warehouses. His goal had always been to sell them to a new audience. He thought France or Bavaria initially, but the books are written in English, after all. America is an obvious market."

"And the Liverpool trustees support this venture?"

"They are focused on publishing new books by new authors in England. This was how my father made his fortune, and they are less willing to try new things now that he is gone. Selling old books in a new market is a risk."

"One you are willing to take."

"What choice do I have? If I can make a go of the American book buyers, then I shall have my own money, and we won't have to worry if or when Teddy's inheritance will be doled out."

"And these trustees, they just gave you the old books?"

She cleared her throat and looked down at her pole. "In a manner, yes. I wrote to them and asked if Teddy and I might have them. I did not say why, to be honest, and they didn't care. They were happy to have the free space in the warehouse, I believe. They are my books now, mine and Teddy's. We are the children of Theodore Holt. Really, they always belonged to us."

Beau hissed between his teeth. "You've balanced it all on the head of a pin, haven't you, Duchess?"

"The plan has been many months in the making. I have found a young lawyer who is willing to help me without alerting the duke. I found your brother and a means to ship the books. You see now why I have been so motivated to train you?"

"That I will never see."

"It was the only thing your brother wanted and the only thing I had to offer."

"I will concede that I am impressed with your wherewithal. Very impressed, indeed."

She nodded and opened her mouth to say more when her fishing pole quivered from sudden tension beneath the water. She gasped slightly and looked up, her expression a mix of excitement and uncertainty. He paused, struck by the sheer hopefulness in her face. When had he ever seen a woman with less guile? She charmed him without even trying.

He stepped behind her, placing his hand on hers, holding the pole steady from around her body. It was a simple gesture, practical and necessary and brotherly. If he hadn't done it, she would have dropped his pole in the canal. Still, the contact of his skin with the warm softness of her glove felt like the first correct thing he'd done all day. After that, it was easy to hold tighter, to edge closer. His chest bumped the back of her shoulders, and his legs were lost in her skirts.

"Careful," he said, very close to her small, white ear. "You've got a bite."

"Oh, but I think I can do it," she said. She grasped the pole with both hands, and Beau widened his stance, allowing her to lean into him for balance.

"He…he must be a whale," she said, straining against the pressure on the end of her line. She staggered a step, pulling harder, but then the line went suddenly slack. She stumbled and fell back against him.

Beau reacted but not fast enough. Before he could move, one of the sharp, decorative flourishes on her hat gouged him in the eye.

"*Oof*," he said and released the pole to grab his eye.

In the same moment, the line and pole went taut again, more sharply this time. The duchess held on tighter with one hand and reached her sagging hat with the other.

Beau shouted again, dodging another glancing blow by her hat. He darted from behind her to take the pole. "Let me have it." He grunted the words in the exact moment the great beast on the end of her line gave another forceful yank. The duchess shouted, clung, and tipped. While he watched in horror, she flailed and fell, hat-first, into the freezing water of Paddington Lock.

CHAPTER THIRTEEN

After the heart-in-her-throat sensation of dropping through open air, Emmaline felt the hard *thwack* of cold water against the side of her face. The slap was loud and painful, a jolt that she heard and felt in the same stunning moment.

Next, breathtaking coldness swallowed every part of her body, sucking down arms and legs, chin and scalp. It rushed into the tightest area beneath her corset, the arch of her foot inside her shoe, the back of her neck. It froze the scream in her throat. She gasped instead, taking in a mouthful of rancid water. She spit and coughed, gulping for breath, all the while, bubbles—hundreds and hundreds of bubbles—rose through the layers of her dress and petticoats, belching on the surface of the water as it pulled her down, down, down.

Almost too late, it occurred to Emmaline to kick.

She flailed against the water and threw her head back, pointing her mouth to the sky. Her winter boots were worthless under the surface, slicing through the water like rocks tied to her feet. Kicking only served to twine the wet fabric of her skirts—now heavy and bunched—around her legs.

Suddenly, there was more water—a great, rising splash—and she had the panicked thought that whatever canal-dwelling creature had pulled her in was now lumbering forth to devour her.

But then she saw a white shirt plastered across tanned muscle, she saw blond hair, sopping wet, thrown back with a whip of his head.

Rainsleigh. He burst from below the surface and darted to her, scooping the water in great, muscled strokes.

"You're all right," he barked over her gasps and thrashing. "You're all right. Careful. Stop kicking. There's a good girl. Breathe. *Breathe*, Duchess, breathe."

She made an indistinguishable sound of fear and disbelief, and he clamped his arm around her waist and tugged her against him. He was warm and strong and inexplicably buoyant.

"Your bloody skirts weigh ten stone," he grunted, hauling her more securely against him. "Stop struggling, Duchess. Can you go limp? This will be easier if I'm not made to fight you."

She nodded but did the opposite. It was a reflex to tense. Going limp felt like giving up. And the coldness. Her arms and legs were rapidly going numb. If she relaxed, she would lose control altogether.

"No, *loose*, Duchess," he said, breathing hard into her ear. "I've got you. I cannot pull you to shore if you're as rigid as a plank. Allow your body to go soft. Move with the water, not against it."

With stilted movement, teeth chattering, Emmaline nodded and tried again to unlock her freezing muscles.

"I...I'm...it..." Her thoughts were a jumble of terror and the overwhelming sensation of numbing cold.

"You're all right," he said again. Above them, his dog barked furiously from the side of the boat. "Peach!" he yelled. "Quiet!"

To Emmaline, he said, "Keep your mouth closed. Canal water will make you sick for a month."

He'd been furiously treading water, his legs in constant motion against her skirts, his free arm massaging the surface, but now he gave one strong kick and stretched out, dropping his shoulder into the water and shifting her, tucking her against his side.

She scrambled, clasping her own freezing hands on top of the arm banded around her waist. He spoke softly into her ear, assuring her with inconsequential praise. Now they were tilted, lying sideways in the water but somehow more afloat. In a matter of strokes and kicks, they were nearly to his boat.

"H-how will I climb to the shore?" she stuttered, teeth chattering. "My skirts. Too wet for me to pull up. And I...I cannot be seen. Especially now."

"Well, you can't remain in the water. No one swims in this canal, Duchess. It's just not done."

Emmaline ignored his joke and darted her gaze from water to boats to shoreline. She saw only the old man on the next boat and the two boys. The man watched placidly from his deck, smoking his pipe. The two boys had left their game to run to the shore, excitedly pointing and exclaiming at their progress.

When they reached stern, the viscount's stroke changed to sharp thrusts that bobbed them around the edge of the boat to the wall. He lunged, catching the barnacle-frothed ledge with his hand. His legs, which had been kicking smoothly beneath her, now scrambled for purchase against the side. Emmaline reached out too, straining, but the wall was too slick to catch hold, especially in wet gloves.

"Wait," he said, breathing heavily. "Give us a moment. I have you. Catch your breath."

Emmaline shrank back, panting.

"Put your arm around my neck," he said.

She hesitated only a second and then looped herself to him, bringing them almost cheek to cheek. Their breath mingled, his labored and strong, hers hissing through chattering teeth. Her body was suctioned to his side, and he held them both aloft in the water. She could not remember a time she had been so intimately and confidently held. Her parents or nannies must have carried her as a child, but she had no memory of it, and Ticking never embraced her, thank God.

His body against hers felt hard but also completely alive. Muscles strained, his chest pumped for breath. The arm at her waist was as unyielding as an iron manacle. He was warm and solid. She had the illogical urge to burrow into his side. She wanted to never let go.

"Are you all right?" he asked, craning back to look at her. "Were you hurt? Do you feel a cut or gash?"

She shook her head, and she felt her hair hanging wet and heavy down her neck, fanning out around her shoulders on the surface of the water. She reached up to her head. "My hat," she said.

"On the bottom, if we're lucky. It nearly put my eye out. You fell because I was fighting that bloody hat."

She winced and tried again to look behind her. She had survived. She was frozen, and submerged, and hardly on dry land, but she had not drowned. She had not been devoured by marine life. But how would she return to her carriage? What of dry clothes and dry hair? How would she explain the loss of her hat? Ticking prized the hats above all other mourning attire. His valet distributed them daily among the women in his household from the duke's private collection.

"I'll go back for it if I must," sighed Rainsleigh, watching her, "but I won't like it."

She shook her head. The very last thing she wanted him to do was leave her. She looked around again. The rancid smell was more pronounced here, and a foamy gray residue slid in around them, catching on the wet sleeve of her gown.

Above them, the two watchful boys burst between the boats and dropped to their hands and knees to marvel over the fall and rescue. The dog leapt to the stern of the boat and started barking anew.

"Peach, quiet!" Rainsleigh shouted. To the boys, he said, "Give us room, lads. Better yet, make yourselves useful. There's a guinea for each of you if you'll stand on the path and keep watch. But do it casually, without calling attention. I am well aware of your proficiency for feigning innocence."

The boys exclaimed at being enlisted and darted to do his bidding.

Now he looked at her. "Right. Out you go. Try again to catch hold of the side."

She looked at the slimy black wall, swallowed, and released the arm around his neck to slowly extend it.

"Bloody gloves," he mumbled, watching. "Will they come off?"

Emmaline endeavored to peel back the sopping leather from one trembling hand. It wouldn't budge. Her fingers were numb. The wet leather was unyielding. It terrified her to hold to nothing, and she wrapped her right arm around his neck and tried again, struggling with the glove beside his ear.

"Leave them," he said, edging her up to the wall. "Try the wall again, and use your feet. Go slowly and feel for the grooves between the stones. Dig in for leverage." He guided one wrist and connected her hand with the lip of the wall. "Hold on. There you are. Brilliant. Other hand too. Squeeze, Duchess. Force your fingers to work."

When she clung to the side, he released her waist. She gasped and reached back for him.

"No, don't let go—and don't kick. You cannot swim in boots and a bloody dress. Here, I'll lift you." He closed in behind her again and wrapped his hands around her waist, hoisting her up. She threw her elbow onto the top of the wall. "That's it," he called.

She followed with her shoulder, her chin. She clung with all of her might, her heart hammering.

"What…what will you do?" she said, barely able to talk with her chin lodged against the top of the wall.

"Climb out and pull you up by the arms. Do not let go of that wall. I'm strong, but not strong enough to hoist you up from behind while I tread water. Can you hold tightly until I'm out?"

Emmaline nodded, despite her serious doubt. She squeezed her eyes, determined not to drop from the wall.

When she felt his warm solidness leave her, she squeezed tighter. She heard a splash. When she opened her eyes, he was surging up, his palms planted on the ledge and his leg thrown on solid ground. He surged again and vaulted entirely out, dousing her with water and scrambling to his feet. Before she could blink, he spun and dropped before her. Fetid canal water dripped into her eyes, and she blinked and looked down. His feet were level with her face, bare and almost blue from the cold.

"Well done, Duchess," he said. "Ready to bid farewell to Paddington Lock?"

Emmaline nodded, hunching against the wall with renewed strength. She took a deep breath. Before she'd exhaled, he slid his hands to her forearms, heaved, and pulled her out.

He landed on his backside with a wet *thwack*, and she sprawled helplessly on top of him, her hair covering them both like a wet, tangled net.

"Well done," he said again.

Before she could swipe the wet hair from her face, he collected her beneath the arms and bounded up, tossing her over his shoulder.

She said "*Oof*" and opened her eyes to see his wet shirt stuck to the corded muscles of his back. Her arms flailed, numb hands ineffectual, scrambling to find a handhold at his waist. His dog scampered below her, barking anew.

"Where are you taking me?" she asked to his back.

"Inside the cabin on my boat," he said, kicking the gate on his gangplank and striding on board. "We have to get you out of those wet clothes."

CHAPTER FOURTEEN

So much for savoring and meandering, Beau thought, sloshing onto the deck of his boat with the shivering, dripping, traumatized duchess thrown over his shoulder. He clipped down the steps to the cabin, stooping to duck through the door.

"Careful, Duchess," he said, squatting to roll her off of his shoulder. "Use your legs. There you are. Don't worry; it only feels like you'll never be warm again."

She stood, thank God for small favors. He'd worried she'd be too hysterical for her legs to hold her. The truth was, she wasn't hysterical at all. She simply huddled, pooling water on the floor, darting her gaze around in breathless, shuddering jerks.

"I'll…I'll need dry clothes," she said. Her breath was choppy and shallow. "Where will I get dry clothes? And my hair. It takes hours to dry. Hours."

Beau lunged for the stove and stoked the coals before stabbing four logs into the orange glow. He crossed back to the door, shooed the dog out, and slammed it to trap what little heat remained.

"First things first," he told her, plucking a blanket from his bed and dropping it on her shoulders, "we must get you dry to get you warm. Give me a moment to change myself, and then we'll get you sorted."

She winced under the blanket and reached to free clumps of her long, tangled hair.

Beau watched her as he unbuttoned his shirt. "I had no idea your hair was so long."

She glanced at him, and he raised an eyebrow. "What?" he asked. "It is a crime, hiding all of that hair."

When he whipped his wet shirt off his shoulders, she froze, a clump of wet hair extended in one hand. Her eyes grew huge and then returned to her hair with diligent attention, piling it over her shoulder to shield her face.

"You will change here?" she asked through the wet blonde veil. "In front of me? You cannot mean for *me* to change in this cabin with you?" She sounded scandalized even through chattering teeth.

"What I mean," he said, "is to get dry. We are both at risk until we are out of the wet clothes and our body temperatures return to normal." He shoved into a fresh shirt.

Her hair was free now, hanging down one shoulder nearly to her waist, adding to the pool of water at her feet. He took a rag from the basin and shoved it at her. "Take this and soak up the water for your hair. The blanket does no good if it's sopping wet. You've brought half of the canal inside."

She reached for the fabric with her eyes averted.

"My breeches are the next to go. Consider yourself warned."

She made a sound of distress and pivoted, turning away as if the sight of him would turn her to salt.

He chuckled, peeling off his dripping buckskins and pulling on a dry pair. "Desperate times call for desperate measures; isn't that what they say? Don't blame me. I wasn't the one who decided to dive into the canal."

"I didn't dive; I fell," she said to the wall. "As you well know. Thank you, by the way, for saving me." She turned when she said this and caught sight of him sliding his buckskins over his hips.

Beau paused, watching the shock and then curiosity play across her face. Their eyes met, and the cabin suddenly felt as small as a closet. She dropped one corner of the blanket.

"This is entirely inappropriate," she whispered. An observation, not a warning. She was sounding less scandalized by the minute.

Beau cleared his throat and fastened his breeches. "Have you ever undressed yourself, Duchess?"

"I beg your pardon?"

"Your dress? Your stockings or boots? I'm guessing you've always undressed with the help of a maid?"

"Well, I've certainly never been undressed by a man."

He stopped breathing for a moment, allowing this statement to settle in. Beau had spent a lifetime ripping various offending garments off various thrilled women for the sheer drama and titillation of doing it. And now here he was, compelled by necessity to enact the same ripping for the purpose of her safekeeping, and he was doddering. And holding his breath. And *talking about it*. It ruined the effect—not to mention risking her health—to hesitate, but his brain was hung on whatever Ticking may or may not have done to her inside their strange, mismatched union.

He shook his head and crossed the small cabin to her. She watched him, catching the fallen edge of blanket and rising up to her full height. She raised her hand to brush back her hair, and he reached out and caught it.

"Gloves first," he said, pulling back the soggy leather. It rolled off her fingers with a sucking sound, and he dropped it to the floor.

"Yes, of course." She began working on the other glove, but she fumbled, still too cold and numb.

Beau seized her hand and rolled back the second glove. "Let's table the conversation of men undressing you," he said, taking up her bare hands together, massaging them in his own, working them back to life. Her skin was gray-blue beneath his fingers. He felt the pulse in her wrist, strong and fast, racing along with his own.

"Is Miss Breedlowe with your brother?" he asked.

She nodded.

"Good. She will help us. I'll send a note by way of the boys outside. Could Jocelyn and Teddy be seen leaving your dower house in a Rainsleigh carriage? Would this raise suspicion?"

"No, not likely. Ticking mostly monitors me." Her eyes were locked on their joined hands. "Jocelyn will lose all respect for me after this," she said. "She will refuse to care for Teddy."

"Don't jump to conclusions. Jocelyn Breedlowe has seen quite a lot in her time in Henrietta Place. If this is the worst of it, I'll eat my hat."

She laughed then, the desired effect, and he felt her fingertips begin to fold over his own. *Yes*, he thought, and he laced their fingers together, squeezing.

She allowed this, looking into his eyes. "How will Jocelyn and Teddy know what to do when your carriage arrives? Wait." She pulled her hands away. "What carriage? You have no carriage."

"The vehicles in the mews in Henrietta Place are mine," he said. "Or so I'm told. Does the duke know your handwriting?"

"No, he shouldn't. I'm doubtful he believes I can read or write."

Beau snickered and leaned away, taking up parchment and a quill from his desk beside the bed. He scratched out four or five lines and read them to her:

Dear Miss Breedlowe,

Slight change of plans for today, if you please. The St. Peter's chapel choir has detained me with their rehearsals. The imposition will make me terribly late for an alteration I have at Madame Dupree's. This is the fitting for the dress I'll wear to the Duke's…

He paused and looked at her.

"Christmas breakfast," she provided.

He raised his eyebrows, impressed with her collaboration, and scribbled it in.

He continued:

…to the Duke's Christmas breakfast. I find myself at a loss for how to fetch the dress to Madame's studio unless I impose on you to assist me. Could I persuade you and Teddy to meet me at her studio with the dress in question? Madame's direction is below. The slippers too, as I'll want

the hem to be accurate. My friend Mrs. Courtland has agreed to fetch you in her carriage for this errand.

He looked up. "Will your maid know which dress?"

She nodded, and he returned to the note, signed it, and dusted it with sand. Next he wrote a second letter to the head groom in his brother's stable, ordering one of the carriages to Portman Square and then on to his boat in Paddington. Discretion, he stressed, was essential.

He cracked the door to the cabin and whistled for Jason and Benjamin, the boys he'd paid to watch the path. After an urgent exchange, he dismissed them with all the importance of a secret mission and a morning in London with his horse.

When they'd gone, he turned back to her. "Sorry. I know you are uncomfortable. That summons may take an hour or more. The sooner we invoke Miss Breedlowe's help, the sooner she will arrive. In the meantime, you cannot wait in wet clothing."

She looked down at her wet dress and then back up at him.

He pointed to the bed behind her. "Sit," he commanded, "and let us undo your boots."

CHAPTER FIFTEEN

"I can wait for Miss Breedlowe," Emmaline assured him, her lips trembling.

"But I cannot," he said. "Perhaps you have grown accustomed to the smell of canal water but not I. And you're dripping on my floor. Most urgently of all, your lips are turning blue."

She touched a hand to her lips.

"And wet boots will blister your feet, if you do not succumb to frostbite first."

There was no argument for this, and she knew it. Her body quaked with shivers, she was almost too cold to properly breathe. She could not remember being more miserably uncomfortable. She sat unsteadily on the bed behind her, cringing at the feel of layers and layers of wet silk and wool.

"I can unlace my boots." She reached for her foot.

"Hold up your skirts." He knelt before her.

"I can do it."

He cocked one perfect eyebrow. "You would prefer that *I* hold up your skirts?"

"I can do both," she assured him, but when she bent at the waist, rivulets of green water squeezed from her skirts onto his bed.

She snapped up. Perhaps she could not do both.

He simply waited, and she hitched up her skirts and slid a miserable, leather-clad foot in his direction. "Why are you being so nice to me?" she said, but she thought, *Please don't stop.*

If his ministrations to her feet felt anything like the attention he'd given her hands, she would freely extend every body part to him for the same treatment. She held her breath.

"I'm nice to everyone," he said, plucking at the laces with detachment.

"You have not been nice to me, not always."

"Hmm. Perhaps you weren't wet enough." He wiggled the boot, jostling her foot from the stiff, wet leather. The looseness registered as a burn, a colder version of cold. Numbness gave way to thousands of pinpricks. She was powerless to move her foot this way or that to work the boot free, and he put his hand on her ankle and moved it for her.

"Careful," he said, sliding the boot off. When her foot was finally free, he wrapped his large hand beneath her arch and began to massage. Emmaline bit down on her lip to keep from moaning.

"Waggle your toes," he said, his voice strangely hoarse. "Force the blood to circulate."

She stifled another moan and did as he bade. She resisted the urge to offer up her right foot only because she would not have him leave her left. This was another first. No one had ever massaged her foot before.

"You will warm up more quickly without the stockings," he said.

Absolutely not. The correct words sprang to her lips, but they would not come out of her mouth. She was so miserably cold and wet, and the thought of his warm hand on the bare skin of her foot was too enticing. She wanted to say, *Absolutely, yes,* but she settled with, "I'll do it," and she bent at the waist to lift her skirt and unfasten her garters. He pulled back, allowing her room, and her hair fell around her face, shielding her from his view. Did he watch her? She dare not check, but she felt flagrantly exposed, fishing up the hem of her skirt to her thigh. Her heart pounded in her ears and behind her eyes.

"Can you manage?" he asked hoarsely.

She nodded, but in truth the second hook was hung. She tried again and again.

"Let me," he said.

"The fastener is hung," she said.

"Right." His voice was calm and matter-of-fact, as if he relieved women of their wet stockings every day—and perhaps he did. But she could not look at him, and she kept her eyes on his hand as he gently set her dripping hair aside and lifted the hem of her skirts. Gently, fleetingly, she felt his hand skim her leg, then her knee. Each glide of his fingers was warm and purposeful on her wet skin. She bit her bottom lip.

Now she felt his palm, flat on the side of her knee. She felt nimble fingers make startlingly quick work of the fasteners. Wet wool went slack and sagged, and he pushed the drooping fabric over her knee and down her leg. It was off her foot in the next moment, and he dropped the fabric to the floor with a *swack*.

Now he wrapped his hand around her bare foot, and she gasped out loud, powerless to stifle her reaction. She could but breathe in and out, in and out. She breathed as if she'd just run a great distance, like she'd swum the length of the canal instead of being carried out in his arms.

"I told you this would feel better," he said. He tugged the corner of the blanket on which she sat and dried her foot, her ankle, and higher still, up her leg. Emmaline said nothing, and she allowed herself not to care. She'd been conditioned to say exactly the right thing at precisely the right time, but were there words, she wondered, for this?

"Are you all right?" he whispered. It came out as a rasp, and he cleared his throat and asked again. "Duchess?"

She nodded, even though nothing was all right. Her clothes were ruined, it was unlikely she could make it home without discovery, and no part of her plan to compensate Mr. Courtland was being realized. They were realizing quite the opposite, in fact. Her would-be pupil knelt at her feet and put his hands on her, and she absolutely did not want him to stop.

"I'm curious," the viscount said, taking up her other foot and starting in on the boot. "His Grace never undressed you?"

"What?" The only thing this situation needed was a frank discussion about who had or had not undressed her.

"You said no man had ever undressed you. And that"—he worked the wet boot off her foot—"is a crime against nature. You were married, for God's sake. Was the duke an invalid?"

Another unneeded discussion but far less provocative than his last question. She conceded. "No, not an invalid, but also not…youthful."

"He would have to have been very old indeed to pass up the opportunity to do what I'm doing right now." He looked up, enclosing her foot with his left hand and reaching up to draw down her stocking with his right.

Emmaline closed her eyes. "He was quite old," she murmured.

The viscount cleared his throat again. "He would have to have been dead."

The garter gave way in an instant, and he slicked the wet stocking from her foot and took up both feet and massaged them together.

"Thank God he is dead," she said quietly. She looked up suddenly. "I've never before said that out loud."

His hands stopped abruptly. "He was cruel to you, Emmaline?"

She blinked, surprised to hear him use her given name.

He stared, his hands still immobile. He raised his eyebrows.

"Not cruel. Simply…" Her voice tapered off. She was disinclined to describe the nature of her marriage, which vacillated between loneliness and disgust. She would not waste this moment talking about the Duke of Ticking.

"Old?" he provided.

She chuckled. "Well, yes, he was that. The duke had no interest in me. My dowry was a means to an end for his debts. He was lost to drink—had been for many years, I believe. I was immaterial to his daily life."

"And his nightly life?"

Emmaline shrugged. What could she say?

He nodded and set her bare feet carefully on the dusty boards of the cabin floor. He shoved to his feet and then took her by the wrists and pulled her up. "You've already said he did not undress you."

"I don't know what you're asking," she whispered.

"I don't either."

He'd whispered this, but it was an irritated whisper, and she was confused. "No one has ever asked me so much about him, dead or alive. All that mattered to anyone else was that he was a duke."

"All that matters to me is his treatment of you. And it matters too much."

Emmaline studied his face. "What do you mean?"

"Nothing," he said, still irritable. "I mean nothing. I mean that if we don't get you out of this dress, you'll catch pneumonia and die, and I'll be blamed. Turn around." He made a spinning motion with his finger.

Her heart stopped for two beats. She heard herself say, "Shoes are one thing. But the dress? I cannot. If Miss Breedlowe is coming, I will wait for her." There, she'd said it.

"You cannot be comfortable."

"More comfortable than I would be naked."

He made a growling noise and said, "I will give you a nightshirt. And you may wrap in the blanket."

"Yes. You have a solution for everything."

"No, that's my brother. He has a solution for everything." He opened a trunk and rummaged inside. "He solves problems; I fix them." He produced a wad of white linen and tossed it on the bed.

Emmaline stared at it. "How did my lessons on propriety devolve into the most scandalous encounter I can imagine?"

"Everything about me is scandalous, Duchess," he whispered, taking her by the shoulders and spinning her. Gently, he gathered her hair and dropped it over one shoulder. "I tried to warn you," he said softly, unfastening the first taut hook at the top of her spine. "I tried to send you on your way, or scare you off, or reverse what my brother offered. But no, you would have none of it. And now here we are. Make any claim you want about my improper etiquette or rubbish manners, but the burden of good behavior is about to now fall entirely on my avaricious shoulders, and I can honestly say that I don't know what will happen. I've told you that I don't believe in pretending to be something that I am not."

She was trembling now. The bodice of her gown hung slack at the neck. She said, "But you could still be a gentleman if we...if I—"

"I *am* being a gentleman, Duchess," he said, sounding strangled. He blew out a heavy breath. The bodice of her gown felt looser with each pluck of a hook. "If I weren't being a gentleman, you would already be naked."

CHAPTER SIXTEEN

Beau wondered idly, his brain fogged with lust, how many women's bodies had been laid bare to him in his life. Five hundred? A thousand? In all of those years, with all of those women, he could honestly say that no woman—not the first saucy chambermaid, ten years his senior, or his favorite Parisian courtesan—had ever filled him with such a pounding, heady rush of desire as this woman. And he couldn't even see her body.

Well, he could see part of her body—but none of the parts that he usually found interesting. He saw the line of her neck, graceful and long. He saw the point of her shoulder, round and smooth and so proudly upright. He saw the whorl of her ear, the baby curls at her hairline. The more he saw, the more he wanted.

Please, his mind and body seemed to shout in unison. *Please, please, please.*

But please *what*? Possibly for the first time ever, Beau found himself torn between lust and protectiveness. He wanted to make love to her, but he also would not scandalize her with his raging lust. He wanted to rip the dress from her body, but he was terrified that she would bloody well freeze to death.

She turned her face slightly to look over her shoulder, accentuating the provocative view of her drooping gown, now open down her back. It was unintentional, of course, which made it all the more provocative, and his world shrank to the widening V that exposed her back. He channeled every bit of willpower he possessed to keep his hands on the line of hooks.

When he released the last one, he moved to her shoulders and peeled off the heavy wool, edging it down her arms. She'd tipped forward just a bit, a rote move she likely affected every day when her maid unfastened her dress. The pop of her bottom and the arch of her back nearly shattered his self-control. He swallowed a groan. The sleeves were at her elbows now, and she affected an eye-popping little shimmy that slid the heavy, dripping fabric to her wrists. He rested each side of the open back against her skirts, and she pulled her arms out, allowing it to hang from her hips like a wet apron.

"There you are," he heard himself say, his voice raw. "We'll push it down over your petticoats. Does your maid typically take it off over your head?"

She nodded.

"Right. But it's too wet and heavy for that now. Can it go unaccounted for?"

"Do you mean will they notice if it comes home in a wet, reeking tangle on the carriage seat?"

"I mean will anyone care if I toss it into the canal?"

"No," she laughed. "My maid is discreet, and we can make up a tale for the laundress."

"Good. Are you ready?"

"Yes."

She was shivering violently now—quaking—yet he hesitated again. Was she truly ready? Could she want this?

He said, "I'm sorry for the indelicacy, but you know the dress has to go, and it's too bloody complicated to remove yourself."

"Yes." More shaking.

"If old Lady Frinfrock had fallen into the canal, I would insist upon disrobing her as well. I hope you know that."

Again, "Yes."

But she's not Lady Frinfrock, is she? Beau thought, taking hold of the bunched fabric at her waist. On the contrary, she was a young woman who, if he was being totally honest, he'd wanted since the first moment he'd seen her. And each moment spent with her made him want her more.

Forget seduction, he thought—*she* was seducing *him*. And why not, for a bloody change? Let her drive whatever intimate interlude would develop between them. He was too selfish to vow that it wouldn't happen—*God, please let it happen*—but *she* should propel it. It must be her choice.

But now she had taken matters into her own hands and begun to wiggle and shove the dress down. He was spurred to action, tugging from the back, sliding the dress past her hips. It fell with a sucking sound to her feet, and he took what he thought of as a very gentlemanly position at her elbows, steadying her as she stepped out of it.

And then they'd done it. She stood before him in her shift, corset, and petticoats. She wrapped her arms around herself, still cold. She rolled her shoulders and shook her head, sliding several locks of long, blonde hair swinging down her back to brush the base of her spine.

He smothered a growl. "I'll throw the dress out then," he said. "It's too wet to burn."

"What if Miss Breedlowe doesn't come with another dress? What if the boys cannot reach her?"

"The boys have been promised enough sweets to last them until spring, not to mention my undying gratitude. And Miss Breedlowe is nothing if not resourceful."

She nodded, and he took up the blanket again and dropped it on her shoulders before scooping up the dripping gray dress and pitching it out a window onto his deck. A proper navy burial would come later. Now…her corset.

He opened and closed his hands at his sides. He cleared his throat. "Listen, Duchess. We've reached a crossroads. It's one thing to take off the outermost layer but quite another to strip you bare."

He looked down at her, bracing himself to see the scandalized expression for which he'd been waiting.

She fluttered her eyelashes and licked her lips, looking back at him with perhaps the least scandalized expression he'd ever seen. She appeared in no way scandalized. She did not even appear particularly cold.

His gaze dipped to her mouth. She licked her lips again.

"What do you want, Duchess?" he asked hoarsely.

"I want to kiss you," she said. "That is what I want."

He blinked and took a half step back, uncertain he'd heard correctly.

"I beg your pardon?" he rasped.

Her eyes grew wide, and her cheeks glowed pink. She opened her mouth to speak but hesitated. He stared, waiting, willing her to say it again. He had to be sure.

But she did not say it again. She squeezed her eyes shut and looked away. He'd hesitated, and she'd lost her nerve.

Bloody hell, Beau thought, reaching out. *What's happened to me?*

In hindsight, it was a valid, telltale question, but he did not wait to answer himself. He scooped her against him— *sweet relief, yes*—and dropped his lips on hers.

She made a little gasping sound—surprise and uncertainty and pleasure; truly one of his favorite sounds—and he kissed her.

$\ast$ $\ast$ $\ast$

Years later, long after the resolution of the things that began that day, Emmaline would think back and marvel at the rare mix of courage and impulsiveness that precipitated her bald-faced request for a kiss.

Well, perhaps she would not marvel at the courage, because she'd come to know courage since Ticking had died. Courage had been her steadfast companion as she made the plans that would free her from his son. Courage allowed her to seek out the viscount in the first place, to make good on a promise to Mr. Courtland that wasn't even really a promise. Courage had not been long in her life, but she was well suited for it, she discovered, and the more she employed it, the more she could conjure it out of thin air.

And today, the air seemed to swim with it.

While Beau had issued simple commands to lift, or bend, or step out of the wet clothes, she'd been fantasizing about spinning around, tipping her head up, and tasting him. Just once. Well, perhaps more than once.

There was so much more, of course. She'd wanted to feel his arms around her and feel the rasp of his beard against her cheek. She wanted to put her hands on all the dips and swells and planes she'd seen beneath the wet shirt on his back. She wanted to crawl up his body and coil around it. She wanted and wanted and *wanted*. After a year spent needing to do things simply so she and Teddy could survive, she was exhilarated by the impulse to do something out of pure desire.

And oh, what desire.

They were new, these impulses, and she wasn't entirely sure what to do with them except to…ask for them.

The moment his lips had touched hers, the conscious world hung in suspended stillness. Like being pitched over the side of the boat again. But instead of the cold slap of water, his mouth was warm, and his big hand anchored her against him at the waist.

She tried to breathe but forgot how; she tried to turn her head, but so did he. She turned the other way, and he did too. She felt herself floundering, but she didn't care. She could do little more than hang on.

"Careful, Duchess," he said gently, pulling back. "Are you all right?"

She nodded, and he dipped his head. Again she felt the indescribable sensation of his lips on her lips, his breath with her breath, her eyelashes batting up against his cheek.

His mouth nibbled and nicked, and she tried to follow along. Her hands left his chest and wrapped around his neck to get a better grip. The blanket sagged, and she let it go.

He pulled back again. "Emmaline? Emmaline, sweeting—wait."

She opened her eyes.

He stared down at her; his beautiful blue eyes narrowed. "You *have* kissed a man before me, haven't you? Some beau before you were married? The old duke himself, no matter how decrepit?"

She felt heat rush to her cheeks. "Well…" she began. She was winded, and it made it difficult to speak. "I was not allowed to court men before the duke. And the duke was not given to…er, kissing. Not me, at least." *Thank God*, she added in her head.

She watched his expression. It had not occurred to her that she might *fail* at kissing. Especially with Beau Courtland, who seemed put on this earth for the sole purpose of flirting and kissing and whatever else came next.

"Am I terrible at it?" she asked.

"No," he said carefully, "by no means…" He looked so incredibly adorable in that moment, unguarded and perplexed, that she could not resist rising up on her tiptoes and kissing him again. One quick peck on his lips. He caught her and kissed her back, longer, smoother, *better*.

He made a moaning sound and gathered her closer, his hands roaming from her shoulders down to her waist, grazing the swell of her bottom. She shivered, rising on her toes again to better reach his lips. His hands left her bottom, and he cradled either side of her head and pulled back, just resting his forehead on hers.

"Try this, Duchess," he said between heavy breaths. "Lips together to begin. One quick brush"—he brushed his lips across hers—"then the other way. Then back again." He demonstrated again. "When you can no longer resist the movement of brushing, we'll settle together, your lips on mine. Then, we nibble." He demonstrated this too.

Emmaline loved all of it. She loved it so much, and he demonstrated it so gently but also with such heat, as if he could barely wait to gobble her up, that she forgot to feel abashed. And oh, how he was right. Everything he suggested, in fact, did make it better.

The second time he pulled away and rested his forehead on hers, breathing hard, her eyes were closed. She was lost to the sensation, savoring the feeling of being held and the strange, strumming awakening in her body.

"Do I have it?" she asked, opening her eyes.

He laughed, a painful, choked sound. "Yes, Duchess, you have it. You are a natural. And the old duke was a fool." He kissed her again. "But I'm worried, because you're actually still wet. Despite my best efforts." He let out a pained laugh. "What should we do about the shift, and corset, and the petticoats?"

Take them off, said a voice in her head. But even in a fog of desire, she knew it was one thing to ask for a kiss and quite another to be stripped bare.

"I can wear them until Miss Breedlowe arrives," she said.

"Or you could take them off, and you could enjoy a proper kiss without being miserable and wet and rank at the same time," he said. "Here is what I suggest…"

The explanation was lengthy, and it took him away from her. He swiped up the nightshirt on the bed and waved it in front of her. She would slip this on first, he told her, *over* the wet undergarment. When she was covered, he would reach beneath it and unlace them. The shift could be rent in two. Then all of them would fall to the floor, and she could step out of them as she had the others. When they were gone, only the dry nightshirt would remain.

It was a reasonable solution—well, reasonable in the upside-down, unreasonable world inside the cabin of his boat, where she allowed him to undress her and invited him to kiss her. In *that* world it sounded reasonable.

Emmaline nodded and held up her arms to receive the nightshirt over her head. After that, she stood perfectly still, holding her breath, as the viscount lifted the tail of the shirt, reached up from behind, and unlaced her corset beneath.

When the wet corset fell—a sweet relief she would not soon forget—he reached beneath the shirt again and untied her petticoats at the waist. When they were loose, he stepped back, and she pushed them down—more relief—and stepped free. They mounded on the floor like a wet sail, limp on the deck after a storm.

Before either of them lost heart, he steadied her and reached beneath the nightshirt again. The sound of ripping linen came next—she heard it before she felt it—but then there it was, a swift, controlled jerk, and her shift hung in two pieces. With minimal maneuvering, she shouldered from it, and it shed to the floor.

"Now," he said, stepping to her again, "we'll use the shirt to dry all the wet places that remain."

And while she stood before him, trembling, heart pounding, he pressed his hands to the voluminous fabric of the nightshirt and gently swabbed the skin beneath, working in small circles to soak up the residual moisture.

It had the potential to be as breathtaking as his removal of her shoes and stockings, but he was businesslike and efficient—at first. With every circle, his movements grew slower and more lingering. She swayed, entranced by the sensation, and he brought his free hand to her waist and held her steady. His eyes grew dark blue and half-lidded. He let his head fall forward. She felt his breath on her skin.

After he'd rubbed her back through the shirt, he applied his ministrations to her belly, then lower, to the side of her hip, then her legs. Emmaline's knees threatened to give way, and she grabbed his shoulder for support.

"I believe that is enough of that," he rasped, and his eyes slid to her lips.

This time, she did not bother to ask him. She tipped her face up. He understood and scooped her to him, gathering fistfuls of the nightshirt, clinging, his lips sealed to her lips.

They bypassed the brushing and the nibbling altogether now, and he pounced on her mouth. She grabbed his shoulders and held on. He chuckled, pulling back only to suck in breath and nuzzle his cheek against her ear.

"How much time do you think we have until Miss Breedlowe and Teddy arrive?" Emmaline asked.

"Enough," he breathed, and he took two steps to the side and collided with the bed. He fell, pulling her down on top of him.

CHAPTER SEVENTEEN

Beau hit the bed with a satisfying *thump* and tightened his arms around her, collecting himself against her.

"Careful, Duchess," he mumbled, trying to arrange her on top of him. She wiggled. She jostled. She was unsettled and jittery. He couldn't remember ever being in bed with a woman quite so jittery or jostle-y. It felt good—everything about her felt good—but it did not go unnoticed, and faintly, regretfully, he began to hear something that sounded like an alarm bell in the back of his head.

"Careful," he repeated, more cautiously this time. He held her secure with a hand to her hip. "You're all right. Are you comfortable?"

"Sorry," she said, laughing, her hair falling all around them. She dipped her head to kiss him, but the bells were louder now, outringing the roar of blood in his ears. Deftly, he scooted to the side.

"You want this, Duchess, right?" he said. "You want us to—"

"I want you to kiss me," she said thoughtfully, and her eagerness sent another jolt of desire straight to his groin. He closed his eyes.

When he spoke again, his voice was hoarse. "Forgive me, but I may have failed to clarify one small detail." His voice broke like a youth's, and he cleared his throat. "When I asked you about the kissing, I did not specifically ask you if the old goat had taken you to bed. If he had consummated the marriage and performed his duties as, er, husband."

He opened his eyes narrowly and regarded her. When she said nothing, he pressed, "Is this true, Emmaline? You are not a... Ticking took..." He searched her face.

She ducked her head. "I don't wish to talk about the Duke of Ticking," she said.

"Neither do I; believe me." He sat all the way up. "But Emmaline, this is very important. I must know."

"How could he consummate the marriage if he had not kissed me?" She still would not look at him.

"It can be done. Or... so I've heard," he said lowly. Silently, he added, *But I hoped it had not happened to you.*

He stared at the ceiling. Oh God, if she was a virgin, this could not happen. Not even the kissing. If she was a virgin, he could not touch her at all.

She sighed and shrugged her shoulders. She placed a shaky hand over her eyes, breathed in and out, and then let her hand fall. She looked away when she spoke. "The duke came to... er, my bed only rarely. Maybe a dozen times? Fifteen? He was always drunk, every time. He did not kiss me. He endeavored to... touch me, but it was..." She took a deep breath. "He usually became entangled in my dressing gown or could not work the buckles on his trousers. Once, he fell from the bed. Several times, he passed out, and I slipped from beneath him to sleep on the chair beside my fire." She looked back at him. "So the answer is no, I'm afraid. Being intimate in this way was not a…feature of our marriage."

Beau stared at her, seeing now a newer, younger, entirely innocent girl wrapped in a blanket on his bed.

A virgin.

A virgin whom he had undressed and pulled down on top of him.

Whom he had kissed senseless and been prepared to do so very much more.

Swearing softly, he dropped his head between his knees and stared at the rumpled sheets. He was a great many rotten things—a scoundrel and a rogue, just as Lady Frinfrock had said—but he was not a despoiler of virgins.

Even if she was a widow.

Even if she did kneel beside him in his bed, wearing only his nightshirt and a deliciously curious expression.

Even if she had driven him to delirium and back with her beautiful body and hungry mouth and—why hadn't he seen it?—innocence.

Beau made a noise of frustration and swung his feet off the side of the bed. "Please tell me that I don't have to explain what happens, Duchess, when a man and a woman fall into bed on a kiss, as we have done. Please tell me you know what comes next, even if they are kissing for the very first time." He laughed bitterly. "*Especially* if it is for the first time." He glanced at her. Her expression suggested that she might not, in fact, know what happens. He groaned and pushed out of bed.

"Well," she began, speaking to his back, "unlike you, I can be taught—"

"*That* will not happen." He laughed coarsely, dropping onto a trunk and reaching for his boots.

For a moment, she was silent. He thought of how she must feel—rejected and embarrassed—and he cursed. He raised his head to make some excuse that blamed himself, but she cut him off.

"Like so many things since I left home," she said, "I am learning a revisionist version of the real world. My mother was not honest with me." She looked down at her hands. "She was determined that I learn everything exactly, precisely right and behave accordingly. If I was to learn so much correctness—day and night, *for years*—why were so many things misrepresented?" She shook her head and then looked up again.

"Why would she suggest that men prized innocence above all things?" she demanded. "Clearly, it is *not* prized by all men. Not by you. I have bored you with my inexperience." There was no manipulation in her words; she wasn't trying to wheedle him. She was trying to sort it all out.

"Do I appear bored to you, Duchess?" he said.

"Well, you are…away."

"Yes, I am away, but at the cost of my personal comfort and with an exhausting test to my self-control. I am not bored, Duchess. I am trying to protect you from my…lack of boredom. It is a lack of boredom so great that I would have had you on your back, helpless to pleasure, in less than a minute.

Your mother was not misrepresenting the value of innocence. For better or worse, innocence in a female *is* prized above all else. I did not make the rules, Duchess, but I won't break them with you. The untimely loss of your innocence can, as you've surely been told, bloody ruin your bloody life. Of all the wrong I may have done in my life, I've always taken care not to corrupt anyone else on my way down. And that goes for you too." He closed his eyes and pinched the bridge of his nose. "No matter how exquisite the wrong might have been."

"But all I wished for was another kiss," she said, laughing a little. She kneed off the bed and stood beside it.

Beau was shaking his head. "You know, I actually believe you." He threw open his wardrobe to rummage for his hat and coat. "Another kiss would be lovely, wouldn't it? But if we've learned nothing else today, Duchess, we've learned this: rarely, if ever, is it simply 'another kiss.'" He found his hat and jammed it on his head. "One leads to two, two leads to four, and then we are lost. And after that, well..." He jerked his duster from the hook. "Trust me; I never would have touched you if I'd known we would never get to the 'after that.' I don't deal in virgins—never have, never will."

"It was only a kiss," she said, more to herself than to him. She'd backed against the wall.

"Are you not hearing me? Men do not stop with 'only a kiss.' *I* do not stop."

"But you have stopped," she told him. "You leapt from the bed and began storming around, lecturing me."

"Better than what I want to do," he snarled. He glanced at her, saw the spark of interest in her eyes, and before he could stop himself, he dropped the coat, strode across the cabin, and trapped her against the wall. If he could not make her see, he thought, he would scare her.

And yet she did not appear scared. Her eyes were huge; her mouth was parted and smiling, just a little. Her hands went immediately to his shoulders, latching on.

Dipping down, growling into her ear, he whispered, "You don't want to know what I would do to you if I could."

She gasped and fell into him. He growled again and kissed his way from her ear to her mouth, catching her lips in a searing kiss. He filled his hands with swaths of the loose fabric of his shirt and squeezed, trying to resist the lithe, subtle curves beneath it. She whimpered and kissed him back, trying to keep up.

When he could stand it no more, when he was a fraction of a second from lifting her back to the bed and falling on top of her, he tore his mouth away and took two big steps back.

"Stay away from me, Duchess," he said, breathing hard. He willed his legs to take two more backward steps. "I'm warning you. I've used up a lifetime of restraint in one bloody morning, and I cannot be counted upon to do it again."

And with that, he snatched up his jacket, whirled around, and strode from the cabin.

CHAPTER EIGHTEEN

Jocelyn Breedlowe told Teddy they were going on an adventure, an adventure so secret even Jocelyn had not been told why or where. She told him that Emmaline had gone ahead of them, and the demands of the adventure had required that they follow in a second carriage and bring along a change of dress for his sister.

This narrative, she found, was the only way to get Teddy out the door. Teddy (not unlike Jocelyn) was suspicious of change and of unexpected carriages and vague-but-urgent missives that required either of them to play along with a fiction riddled with considerable gaps.

But the vague urgency of Emmaline's note could not be denied, nor could the Rainsleigh carriage waiting outside the dower house.

When they were safely four or five blocks from Portman Square, out of sight of the duke's suspicion, Jocelyn slid the glass aside in the carriage window and asked the groom to name their actual destination. If nothing else, she could prepare Teddy, not to mention herself.

"Paddington Lock," came the reply. "Lord Rainsleigh's summons."

"You mean Mr. Courtland's order," Jocelyn said, shouting to be heard over the noise of Oxford Street. On occasion veteran members of staff still reversed the title of the former viscount with the new.

The groom shook his head. "No, ma'am. The viscount himself asked that we collect the pair of you and deliver you to him."

Jocelyn nodded and sat back in the carriage seat, her mind a whirl of possibilities and second guesses about the duchess, and Rainsleigh, and the dress that swayed bumpily from a hook beside her head.

Twenty minutes later, the carriage rolled to a stop along a canal lined with bobbing narrow boats. The sunlight was bright for December, and they squinted as they stepped out on the gravel path, looking carefully around, wondering how they could possibly know what they were expected to do next.

Jocelyn spoke gently to Teddy about the canal and the boats and the possibility that they would see gulls and perhaps even jumping fish.

"Miss Breedlowe, thank God," said a voice behind them, and they turned to see Beau Courtland, Viscount Rainsleigh, striding up, a dog at his heels.

"Lord Rainsleigh," she said, shading her face with her hand.

"Hello, Teddy," he said to the boy. "How grateful your sister will be that you've come to her rescue. She's gotten herself into quite a scrape."

"Is the dowager duchess quite all right?" Jocelyn asked lowly. She would not alarm the boy.

The viscount nodded—one curt nod—and then he looked away. "Now that you're here."

He looked at the water. "May I take the boy to the canal and show him the lock where they control the water level? While we are occupied, it is my hope that you might…see to Her Grace. Did you bring the change of dress?"

Jocelyn nodded, studying him. She had spent far less time with the viscount than any of the other gentlemen in Henrietta Place, but she knew him well enough to know he was, at the moment, rankled, which was very rare indeed.

"Is she…" Jocelyn began, hoping to learn at least something of the duchess's state.

"She fell into the canal," the viscount said, too low for Teddy to hear.

Jocelyn stifled a gasp, but the viscount held up a hand.

"She is unharmed," he said. "Soaked through and without the necessary dry clothing to reach home. She's waiting in the cabin of my boat." He pointed. "More than anything, she is worried about raising the suspicion of the duke. Did he see you and the boy leave?"

"Not as far as I know. We were ready when the coach arrived, and we rolled away within minutes. Your staff is discreet and capable."

The viscount looked to the grooms, horses, and carriage parked beside the path as if seeing them for the very first time. Likely, he was.

"Aren't we lucky in that?" He gestured to the water and smiled at Teddy. "Shall we explore Paddington Lock, Teddy?

Your sister will want to know what you've seen. And I don't believe you've met my dog?"

"Adventure," said Teddy, going easily with the viscount.

Jocelyn let him go and walked resolutely to the dingy, peeling narrow boat, second to the last on the end of the canal.

Emmaline heard the knock on the door and stood, clutching the viscount's nightshirt around her.

"Your Grace?" came Jocelyn's tentative voice.

Emmaline could have wept with relief. "Yes, thank God. Please come in. Mind the trunk and the rifles and the rusty whatever-it-is on the floor." She rushed to assist her, reaching for the boxes that Jocelyn balanced in one hand while she hoisted the dress high in the other. "Oh, bless you—you've brought it all. But how is Teddy?"

"Quite well, actually. The viscount has taken him to see the lock. I've told him we are all on an adventure."

Emmaline toppled the boxes on the bed. "An adventure. That is one way of putting it."

In her head, Emmaline had rehearsed a long speech. She had constructed both justification for her actions and blame. She had released Jocelyn of all future association with her, citing the outrageousness of today. But now, looking at her friend, moving from box to box, pulling out shoes and petticoats and, thank God, a hairbrush, all she could say was, "Oh, Jocelyn. You will not believe what I've done."

Jocelyn turned from the dress and considered her. "Well, I have been told that you fell into the canal."

"Yes," said Emmaline, "that too."

Jocelyn held out stockings, and Emmaline rolled one on, trying not to think of how the previous stockings had been removed.

"You were not harmed, I hope."

She shook her head. "The viscount, he…he jumped in after me and fished me out. He swam with me to safety."

"I have heard he can be very resourceful."

"I came here to tutor him in manners and decorum. His brother, Mr. Courtland, and I worked out a trade for this service." She told her briefly about her charge to teach the viscount to be a gentleman.

"Mr. Courtland is known as an inventive businessman, I think," Jocelyn said, holding out two shoes. Her voice was neither disbelieving nor accusatory. She sounded…pleased.

Emmaline nodded and stepped into her shoes, closing her eyes at the feel of the warm, dry barrier between her still-cold feet and the dusty floorboards. "I'm sorry I did not tell you about it in detail—" She stopped herself and started again. "I'm sorry I did not tell you."

"Perhaps it's better that I did not know." Jocelyn laughed a little, and Emmaline laughed too. Jocelyn continued. "Elisabeth had not mentioned this arrangement. I can assume Mr. Courtland believes it is better that his wife not yet know. Can you go without a corset, madam, just until you get home? I did not bring one."

Emmaline nodded, and she pulled a simple petticoat from a box and gave it a shake. "Honestly, even Mr. Courtland did not know I'd taken his offer seriously until the viscount complained to him. I am highly motivated to get my father's books to America, and my resources are limited. The duke watches every move I make, as you know. As plans go, it was improbable but working. It was actually almost working. Until today."

She stepped into the petticoats and pulled them to her waist.

"Well, surely you did not fall into the canal on purpose," her friend said.

"No. Not the canal."

Jocelyn reached for the dress, another overwrought gray winter gown, too formal for daytime, but it had been the easiest excuse for the summons. They sat on the bed and laid it across their laps, working together to unfasten hooks at the back.

"He undressed me, Jocelyn," Emmaline whispered, not looking up from the hooks. "He gave me this nightshirt. He dried me. He wrapped me in a blanket." Her cheeks burned as she said this, but when she said the words out loud, she found that she could not—would not—regret it.

Jocelyn's hands paused over the hooks. "Did he take advantage of you, madam? Have you been…overcome?"

"Oh, no. 'Twas nothing like that. There was…" Emmaline looked to the window, as if she might suddenly see him outside. "We shared a kiss. I asked him to do it, and he did. But that is all. He…he refused to do more, and when he learned of my vast, er, inexperience, he regretted the kiss. He is regretful."

She looked back to Jocelyn. "I came here to teach him to be a gentleman, and I asked him to kiss me instead. I've no regrets; honestly, I do not. But I wonder…" She stood up and paced to the window. "I wonder what Mr. Courtland will think of our bargain now? And I also wonder what you will think of me." She dared a quick look at her friend. Her cheeks, already raw and chapped from the cold water, burned.

Jocelyn smiled gently and gave the open dress a shake. She held it out. Emmaline paused, still uncertain of her friend's generosity, but then accepted it.

Jocelyn watched her pull it on, reaching to pull and fluff as she went. "I think...that if you came here to teach the viscount the ways of a gentleman, and he saved you from drowning. And then he undressed you but refrained from imposing anything more than a kiss...well, I'd say that you have given his gentlemanly tendencies a rigorous training indeed. I'd say that you have more than kept your promise to Mr. Courtland." She crossed her arms and stepped away. "That is what I'd say."

"Oh," said Emmaline, smoothing the sleeves of the dress over her arms. "Oh." Her mind spun. Is that what they'd done? Reinforced gentlemanly behavior? Could this arrangement be salvaged?

"As for me," Jocelyn continued, stepping around to do up the back of the dress, "I have seen far more colorful interludes in service to both Mrs. Courtland and Lady Falcondale, so do not worry about my judgment."

"I...you are gracious, Jocelyn. How lucky I am to have such a gracious friend."

"Yes, well, that said, perhaps we should consider some joint arrangement for Teddy and you and me. Perhaps I can care for Teddy *and* offer my services to you as something like a chaperone. Assuming your tutorials with the viscount will continue."

Emmaline shut her eyes. "I shall never be able to repay you. But do you think he would consent to more lessons?"

Jocelyn made a discreet coughing noise. "This would be my guess."

"I like the idea of a chaperone, if you could be so disposed. Would you do it, Jocelyn?"

"Considering the circumstances," Jocelyn said, stepping away and folding the viscount's nightshirt, "I think it might be best."

Chapter Nineteen

After Miss Breedlowe and Teddy were sent home in the Rainsleigh carriage, Beau followed the duchess to the church, where she'd left her own carriage nearly four hours ago. From a distance, he watched as she was bundled safely inside it and rolled away. Then he returned to his boat to pack. Given the circumstances, he saw little choice but to leave London. Immediately.

He wouldn't leave England—not yet. He still had at least one brothel to raid for Elisabeth and business to attend. Any long-distance journey would have to wait, but he should leave the city of London before he did something colossally stupid, such as call on the Dowager Duchess of Ticking. For any reason whatsoever.

But especially for another tutorial.

Beau stomped around the cabin of his boat to pack, dodging Peach, trying not to relive the memory of his and Emmaline's time together.

This was impossible, he discovered, because...what else was there? Her body was gone but the very feel of her seemed to linger in the small cabin. He could still smell the wetness of her hair. He could make out the imprint of their embrace in the tangled bed. He heard her voice in his head and tasted her on his lips. Briefly, he considered dunking himself in the canal again for good measure.

What if he never recovered from the unrequited desire of kissing her but not…doing anything else to her? What if he never again looked at her face without remembering her expression when he taught her how to kiss?

But this was why he had to go.

He'd somehow managed to disentangle himself from her, although he had no idea how. Disentangling from anything as lovely as her was not like him at all.

In contrast, it was absolutely like him to ride to Essex, where he was long overdue. If his eventual plan was to sail from England altogether, he should go to Essex and remain until the New Year.

A virgin. A bloody beautiful, lithe, responsive, eager…virgin.

Beau looked again at the cold water of the canal, stripped off his boots, and jumped.

Thirty minutes later, dry again but still shivering, he rolled a large stone from the shore and wrapped the duchess's still-wet gown and petticoats around it. It hit the water with a *thwack* and sank. The vision of murky water swallowing the bundle brought back the vivid memory of her fall, the moment of shock and fear when he'd realized she was no longer standing on his deck beside him but was sailing through the air. Never had he stripped himself of his coat and boots so quickly. Never had he been so grateful that no one of consequence had witnessed it.

The acknowledgment of this, in particular, reminded him of the one-hundredth reason he had no wish to be viscount. Men who were *not* viscounts rarely had to worry if anyone of consequence was watching.

After the duchess's clothes were given a proper water burial, and he ran the boys Benjamin and Jason to ground, he fed and brushed his horse and called on the local public house for his own meal. Then, because he could see no peace until he took some action, he called the boys back.

After negotiating an extortionist sum, the boys agreed to deliver the following note:

> *Your Grace, the Duchess of Ticking,*
>
> *I am writing to inform you that I leave London for Essex at first light. I should be gone from the city for an undetermined time. In light of what's happened, I think this is best. I hope you are well. If you should require me for some reason related to today's events, you may write me care of Ned and Ethel Barnes, Dunningham Road, Hockley, Essex.*
>
> *Beauregard Courtland*
>
> *PS: By my request, the Barnes family does not regard me as viscount, so I implore you not to invoke the title if you must write.*

* * *

Dear Lord Rainsleigh,

> *I hope it is appropriate to use the correct form of address on the inside of this letter, as I have followed your directive*

*to invoke your given name on the outside. Regardless, if
this reaches you, I wish to thank you for your note and
the forwarding address. Whether you will admit it or not,
gestures such as these are proof that you are halfway to
proper manners just as you are. Naturally, I will take credit
when I report your progress to your brother.*

*Which brings me to my purpose for writing. Although
you specified that I not contact you unless there were
repercussions from the canal, I have other pressing news.
Your brother and I have determined that I shall sail for New
York, along with Teddy and the books, in a months' time.
Mr. Courtland has been, and continues to be, the very soul
of generosity. Considering this, it is my great hope that you
will return to London before my departure so that we might
complete at least two or three more tutorials. It is the least I
can do to settle my debt to your brother.*

*I am assured of your reluctance to do this, and of course
you owe me nothing. Your consent to do the lessons at all has
been a kindness. I should also like to add that Miss Breedlowe
has agreed to be present at all future sessions between us. All
lessons learned without her attentive company have, I feel
certain, already been thoroughly explored.*

Sincerely,

Emmaline Crumbley

*PS: I cannot hide my curiosity: Who, pray, are the
Barneses, and why have you called on them in Essex?*

Beau was so surprised that she'd written him, he accused
Ethel Barnes of teasing him when she'd returned from the

village with news of a letter. But there the folded parchment sat atop her marketing basket, and just a week after he'd arrived.

He'd known it was from the duchess, of course. No one knew of his connection to the Barneses, not even Bryson, and he'd all but invited her to write him before he'd left. Still, he experienced a jolt of unnamed...something when he'd popped the seal and skipped to the closing to read her name. Then, heart pounding, he'd returned to the salutation and read the entire letter four times.

He would read it again later, he knew, in the privacy of the small room he shared with the Barneses' sons. Until then, he had countless hours to determine how he would reply.

His first inclination was to not reply at all. Allow his silence to speak for him. Of course they would *not* meet again, not for lessons or any other reason.

She had emerged in his mind as the strangest combination of thudding, mouth-watering temptation and threat-of-death restrictions, and both unsettled him in a way to which he was not only unaccustomed but that he did not care for at all.

He knew his limits, especially where temptation was concerned, and he could not—should not—go near her.

Not even with Miss Breedlowe present. Not even to pay her perceived debt to his brother.

But how to say it? Or not to say it, as was his first inclination.

For two days, he left the letter unanswered as he helped Ned Barnes around his farm, as he played with the Barnes children, and sat, reading or talking with the oldest boy, Lewis. Finally, on the third day, Polly, the Barneses' daughter, had asked him very plainly at breakfast from who the letter had come.

His policy with all the Barneses had been honesty from the start, and without thinking, he told her that the letter had come from a woman, a lady, who lived in London. Polly had been approving but concerned. Why hadn't he written in return to the London lady, she wanted to know. Did he realize she was likely watching her post every day, waiting patiently for his letter in reply? Was he not aware that the post could take a week or more to make its way to London? She remedied this by offering to share her own paper and pen—supplies he had bought her, she reminded him, so of course he should help himself.

And so Beau allowed himself to think that it was Polly Barnes, aged fourteen, who had pressed him into replying to the duchess. This made it easier somehow. And when he wrote, he did not mince words or overstate. He scrawled out six lines from Polly's stationery kit and posted it himself on the third day.

> *Duchess,*
>
> *The lessons are finished, as I'm sure you know. My brother requires no compensation, as I'm sure you also know. The only thing worse than sitting for lessons on my own ineptitude would be sitting for the lessons with Miss Breedlowe looking on. This will not happen.*
>
> *I am in Essex looking after a family in whose great debt I have been for many years. This is a bit of personal history that I would ask you not to share. I reveal it only because you have revealed so much yourself.*
>
> *Sincerely,*
>
> *Beau*

Dear Lord Rainsleigh,

Thank you for your reply. Honestly, I did not expect one. What a pleasant surprise. Yet another gentlemanly skill you already possess: timely correspondent.

I can only guess that you did not expect this, another missive from me, and I admit that writing to you again borders on just the sort of aggressiveness that has, in the past, made you feel hunted (by me). I risk this to gently suggest two things.

First (and most aggressively of all), please reconsider your willingness for a few additional tutorials. If Miss Breedlowe is not a good solution, then we could meet either in a bustling public place that the duke and his spies are not prone to visit, or we could include Teddy—or both.

Second, I would like your permission to intercede with your brother on the topic of your alleged "refinement" (for lack of a better word). To be honest, it is unclear to me exactly why Mr. Courtland sees you as unfit. At the risk of overstating things, I have discovered you to be perhaps a bit rough…to be beholden only to yourself…but also to be honorable and fair, civil and even charming (when the mood strikes). There are so many examples I could cite, both specifically (such as a rapport with Lady Frinfrock and your easy kindness to Teddy) and in general (whatever benevolence you bestow on this family in the country).

But of course I will say nothing to him unless I hear from you. And I will not press you again about the lessons if the answer remains no. I only ask again because my debt to your brother grows ever greater. Only now, as the date of our sailing rapidly approaches, have I come to comprehend the myriad details involved in transporting these books. Where I have been remiss, your brother has so kindly stepped in to make arrangements…tariffs, means of unloading the books in New York, proper packing to prevent damage, travel papers for both Teddy and me.

Of course I had only conceived of a way to escape the duke, my most immediate threat, yet I have much more to learn. Your brother has done (and will do) so much more than simply convey us across the sea. I should like to repay him, and working with you was his request. But of course I can only impart what you are willing to hear. I will not become a scold simply to assuage my own feeling of indebtedness.

Moving on, I should add that the young men on your raiding team, Jon Stoker and Joseph Chance, have discovered new information about the next brothel you intend to raid, and they are positively champing at the bit to move forward. Elisabeth is holding them off until you return, but she has asked me if I might know where you've gone and when you'll return. You have been very clear about your discretion with the Essex trip, and I assure you, so have I. But I thought you would like to know.

Yours,

Emma

This is what happened, Beau told himself, staring down at her latest letter, when a man engaged the affections of an innocent *virgin* and then broke one of the very few rules he had for himself and kissed her.

She sought the man out in the country with long correspondence that referred to him as honorable, fair, civil, and *charming* and offered to advocate on his behalf to his brother. She signed her letters with "Yours" and then the incredibly intimate shortened version of her Christian name, "Emma."

Emma.

Although he read the letter at least a dozen times the day it came, it was the one line that he studied for days to come.

"Emma" was, he thought, quite the perfect name for her. "The Duchess of Ticking" was too ridiculous, "Dowager Duchess" was too infirm, "Emmaline" was too...heavy.

Emma.

For some reason unknown to him, his brain tried, repeatedly, to add the pronoun "my" before it.

"*My Emma.*"

This confused him as much as it irritated him, but he came to regard it as he did other irrational thoughts, like the wild notion he'd had when he'd first walked the cliffs of Dover: *What if I just stepped right over the edge?* he'd thought. He would not, of course, but that did not stop the mad thought from darting through his mind.

And what had he done? He'd taken five prudent steps away from the soaring face of the cliff and enjoyed the view from there.

And now he should do the same. He was *trying* to do the same, but she'd continued to send these letters, which he continued to read and reread by the light of the Essex moon.

Five prudent paces back, he told himself a week after the last letter had come. He would find the correct words and send a terse reply that would put a stop to all dialogue between them.

Dear Duchess... began his first attempt.

~~We cannot continue to correspond because, well, perhaps I didn't make myself clear, but I do not deal in virgins. The reason I do not deal in virgins is because, in my view, any woman not blood-related to me is either a conquest or a mutually beneficial lark, and virgins cannot survive either designation without lasting damage.~~

After tossing that effort into the fire, he began again.

~~Dear Emmaline,~~

~~You are too beholden to my brother's favors and too generous with your impression of me. Please disabuse yourself of both. You cannot see beyond your own elaborate plans now, but eventually you will escape the Duke of Ticking and remarry—hopefully someone closer to you in age this time—and the last thing you need as part of your new marriage is any memory of me.~~

~~I am aware that your requests to meet do not invite "memories," but I also know myself, and if we convene again for any reason, I fear it would be a meeting neither of us would soon forget...~~

A third time, he began,

~~Dear Duchess,~~

~~I am a scoundrel and a rogue and you're too green to know the difference.~~

A fourth time...

Dear Duchess,

~~*Keep away from me, for God's sake.*~~

After four or five additional failed attempts, Beau gave up and fell into a fitful sleep. The next day, when Ned Barnes set out to do some early winter pruning to his small apple orchard, Beau joined him. The Barneses asked nothing of him, as always, but they would not turn help away if he offered it. Since the night of the fire, Beau had made it his practice to offer it whenever he could.

Today, he would collect the discarded apple tree limbs that Ned clipped and drag them to a heap at the end of each row.

It was mindless work but satisfying and necessary to the success of the trees. Most of all, Beau knew that Ned's son Lewis would be doing the work if his burns had not hobbled him for life.

Beau trudged back and forth from the pile of clippings a dozen times, hoping they would finish before the threatening rain. The older man paused, and from the top of the ladder, he said, "Polly tells us you've quite a flurry of correspondence coming and going from London."

Beau stilled momentarily over the cut branches, not accustomed to personal chattiness from Ned Barnes. He looked up the ladder at him. "Aye," he ventured.

Ned pruned a few more branches and then said, "A young lady, is it?"

Again, Beau went still. " 'Tis a dowager duchess. The lady is a widow."

There was almost nothing Beau would not give to the Barneses if he could, but a discussion on this topic was one of those unavailable things.

"A widow, *ohhh*," said Ned. "You are too charming for your own good, I suppose. Too handsome, too. 'Tis a chore to keep the widows and wives of wayward husbands at bay, no doubt." He chuckled.

At any other time, this statement would be true. But it was not true here, and it grated on Beau not to correct Ned. But he was determined not to encourage this line of questioning, and so he said nothing. He trudged to the pile with another armful of clippings.

"This one must be quite smitten to hunt you down all the way in Essex," Ned said when Beau returned.

Beau neither affirmed nor denied this and pulled another bundle of brush to the heap.

When he returned again, Ned's assumption still hung in the air, erroneous but uncorrected. Like the sticks and twigs at the base of the tree that Beau had failed to collect.

Beau cleared his throat. "This widow is not...like the other women. She is young." Why he had named this, of all things, Beau had no idea. It seemed essential to the explanation. "She was married only a short time to an old man who died within years of their marriage." He paused, searching the ground for more errant sticks. He didn't know when enough was enough.

"God bless her," said Ned mildly, "a widow so young."

"She is in a spot of trouble, I'm afraid, and I have...well, I cannot really say what I have done." Without thinking, he added, "Hopefully I have not made her troubles worse."

"Careful with the giving of aid to widows," said Ned Barnes, tromping down from his ladder and dragging it to the next tree.

"Needy, are they?" Beau chuckled, thinking perhaps they had returned to idle small talk.

"Oh, no," said Ned, climbing the ladder, "I meant that reputation of yours, as a scoundrel. You'll have trouble keeping it up if you start giving aid to widows. It's one thing to help a poor farm family in the country. No one is the wiser. But a young widow in London? Word is bound to get out."

Beau watched the pruned limbs fall from the apple tree. "I want her to stop writing me."

"This is because you don't know what it feels like when the letters stop." He chuckled to himself. "Fancy her, do you?"

So much for the idle chatter. "She is not available to me."

Ned thought of this for a moment, studying the canopy of the tree. "This widow certainly writes a lot of letters to a man who is…unavailable. Certain, are you, that she knows this?"

Now Beau was mildly annoyed. Ned was not simply making conversation; he was meddling. "I am trying to find the words to communicate this very thing, in fact," Beau told him, and then he added, "so any suggestions you may have on the topic would be welcome."

Ned laughed at his tone. Beau was rarely anything but deferential to the Barneses, and his annoyance was clear.

The older man said, "Well what is this reason? The *real* reason?" He stopped pruning and looked at Beau.

"She is an innocent," he told Ned, quite possibly just to shut him up. "She is young and innocent and, although floundering a bit at the moment, she will set herself to rights and have a proper life with a new husband, a home, children—all of it. Wrangling with me will only postpone that, not to mention spoil it a little. Or a lot. It was no small thing to leave her first marriage as an innocent. She should begin her new life without me to muck it up."

Ned thought about this for a moment and then nodded, returning to his pruning. Before he descended his ladder to drag it to the next tree, he said, "No possibility of you offering her that new life? With you? The house and children?"

"No," answered Beau immediately, now actively wishing it would rain. "No possibility."

Ned climbed up the ladder into the next tree. "Why not?"

"Well, because…I cannot abide legal constructs. Marriage is among the worst of these, in my view. Another determination of the way I interact with others. Bound to this one, restricted from all others. When I consider the fire and your family's pain, these are the same reasons I have no wish to be a bloody viscount. I do not relish *the law* telling me how to regard you, or my brother, or anyone else for that matter. I…I don't like people telling me what to do."

Now Ned laughed out loud, a rare sound. "Well then, you certainly don't need a wife."

Exactly, Beau thought, still irritated, and an image of the duchess flashed in his mind, sitting on the bow of his boat, informing him that he strode around too purposefully and looked people in the eye too aggressively, and he wanted to laugh too.

"I am wrong for her," he said instead. "And she is not pursuing me, not in a romantic way. She has ambitions for her future as a woman of business in America. And she is far too refined to give chase. But I am not refined, as you know, and if I give her too much regard, well... I feel responsible for safeguarding her innocence. I see no other way to effectively do this but to stay away."

"Another blow to your reputation as a scoundrel, I'm afraid. You feel very responsible all 'round."

"I don't care about my reputation," Beau said. "I care about hers."

To this, Ned Barnes had no answer, thank God, and they worked together in companionable silence until Polly Barnes came running to the orchard with a telltale folded letter in her hands.

Cheerfully, she extended it to Beau. "Another letter came just now. I thought you would like to see right away."

Beau refused to look at Ned as he nodded to Polly and took the letter, his heart suddenly pounding in his chest. Trying not to appear as eager as he felt, he broke the seal.

Dear Beau,

I'm sorry to entreat you in this manner, but I am frantic with worry. Teddy has gone missing again, and we are all desperate to find him. You discovered him before. May I impose upon you to return and do it again?

Emma

This letter, he only read once. After he read it, he folded it, tucked it into his pocket, and ran from the orchard. A quarter hour later, after he'd declined dinner and refused to wait out the threatening rain, he had saddled his horse, bolted to the road to London, and was gone.

CHAPTER TWENTY

Tears of relief stung Emmaline's eyes when the viscount blew into her dower house with a cold blast of icy rain. He was mud-splattered and wind-whipped, soaked from the storm. His brother stood by the fire and called out to him, scolding him for dripping on the rug and wearing his hat indoors, but Beau ignored him and strode to Emmaline, coming to a stop before her and jerking off his hat. His blue eyes were creased with worry and something else, something starkly different from the regard of every other friend or stranger who'd turned up to help search. *Resolve.*

Not anguish, not hopelessness—resolve.

For the first time since Teddy had disappeared, Emmaline felt like someone looked beyond her alleged nerves or supposed hysterics and would get down to the business of simply finding her brother.

"What's happened?" the viscount said lowly.

"Beau?" called his brother from behind him. "Don't crowd her, for God's sake. What are you doing here?"

Rainsleigh ignored him. His eyes were locked on Emmaline's. He raised his eyebrows.

"Two nights ago," she told him. "His Grace had called on us after dinner with six or seven of his children. One of the girls had prepared a song on the pianoforte, and the duke thought I would enjoy a listen. While the child played, the duke's sons filed out into the garden, and they coaxed Teddy to follow. They were gone only minutes before I escaped to check on them. By then, one of the boys had opened the garden gate and Teddy, apparently...wandered out." She paused, struggling for composure. "The boys claim they did not know how long he'd been gone or what direction he went."

"So the duke knows he gone?"

Emmaline nodded. "Oh, he knows. And he is making a show of his deep concern. He volunteered to call personally to Bow Street for help, but he did not return with an officer for hours. Meanwhile, I searched up and down the intersecting streets surrounding Portman Square and Baker Street. I called his name. I knocked on doors in the dark. Out of desperation, I sent for your brother, who came with Joseph and Stoker, and they searched the park nearly all night. But we found nothing." Her voice broke, and she gulped in a breath. "Not a trace. It's as if he's vanished into thin air. And now it's been days. And it's so cold, especially at night. By some miracle, he was wearing his coat, but..."

Her voice broke again, and the viscount bit off his glove and reached for her, closing his fingers around her arm.

"Take heart," he said lowly, stepping closer. "Emma, stop. Do not cry. I will find him." The certainty of his words bolstered her as much as the touch of his hand. She nodded, composing herself, trying not to lean into him. She glanced at his brother, who hovered nearby, listening to their exchange.

To her dismay, the tears in her eyes began to fall in earnest, jumping down her cheeks even while she blinked and blinked, breathing hard, trying not to give in to the threatening despair.

The viscount sighed and bit off his second glove, scuffing the teardrops with his knuckles. "I found him the first time, didn't I?" he whispered. "And I wasn't even looking."

She chuckled, raising her chin, refusing to give in to the hysterics for which they'd all been waiting. The viscount squeezed her arm and held it. She topped his hand with her own.

"Beau?" said Mr. Courtland, stepping up. "I worry that you're not giving the dowager duchess enough—"

"And I worry that you," shot back Beau, "could not find sand if you fell from a bloody camel." He squeezed her arm again before stepping away. "Where are Stoker and Joseph?" he asked his brother, tugging his gloves back on and reseating his hat.

"They've been out for two hours, searching the park again," Mr. Courtland answered cautiously. He stared at the viscount with something akin to astonishment. "But Beau, take care. You lead these raids to collect Elisabeth's girls, I know. And you've seen God knows what kind of adventure on your travels. But the Duke of Ticking has been very involved in the search, going so far as to muster Bow Street himself. He's not present at the moment, but I feel—"

The viscount cut him off. "I don't care about the duke or Bow Street. Will Falcondale help?"

Mr. Courtland opened his mouth to oppose him, but his wife was suddenly beside him, yanking him to her height and whispering feverishly in his ear. Emmaline could not hear the words, but Elisabeth's expression dared him to contradict her.

When he spoke again, Mr. Courtland was contrite. "Elisabeth wishes to vouch for your leadership." He coughed. "And of course I trust you. Forgive me. Tensions are high. No one is gladder that you've come than I."

I am, thought Emmaline. *I am gladder.* She looked back and forth between the two brothers.

Mr. Courtland continued. "Falcondale and I were making inquiries on the other side of the park, but only I returned. I came in at sunset to encourage Elisabeth to go home." Now it was his turn to cast a threatening look on his wife. "Miss Breedlowe will wait with the dowager duchess."

Rainsleigh nodded. "Elisabeth, go home and rest. You bring extra worry for all of us, not to mention fresh guilt for the dowager duchess if you overextend yourself or the baby."

He didn't wait for her to reply but turned back to Emmaline. "I'll spend thirty minutes changing horses and walking the length of the garden myself. I'll examine the gate by which Teddy allegedly left. When Joseph and Stoker return"—he looked at his brother—"we'll make a plan for our next move based on anything they may have discovered. It is lucky the boys have not yet returned to school. Bryson, have you slept? Can you ride?"

Mr. Courtland nodded slowly, watching his brother. "Yes. I can ride."

"Can your stables provide me with a fresh mount?"

"Yes, of course. They're your bloody horses."

Rainsleigh scowled, and Emmaline stepped up. "I've asked the kitchen to bring whatever they can for you and the other searchers."

When he looked at her—really looked at her—she wanted to go to him so badly, she ached with it.

"Thank you," he said, and then he winked at her. It was exactly the right gesture, and her heart lurched.

"Which way to the garden?" he asked. "I'll need two grooms with lanterns outside so I can bloody see in the bloody dark."

When he was gone, Emmaline raced to the kitchen to check on a meal and then to her desk to write a list of the events of the night as best she remembered, with times and the names and ages of the duke's sons from the garden. She added her hasty impression of each boy, just to be thorough. If she had to guess, she knew which one had opened the gate, and she made a note of this too.

How good it felt to write this down, she thought, her pen racing across the paper, to give it to someone who would read it, who might bloody *use* it. Mr. Courtland had been concerned and helpful, but he deferred to the Duke of Ticking. And His Grace?

The duke had responded to Teddy's disappearance with pompous bluster but fractional sincerity. He'd taken a very high-handed, almost saintly role in the ensuing search. With escalating volume, he'd lamented the danger the boy was in while also tsking over the *daily* risk Teddy posed as a "dim-witted imbecile" who would be "better served by confinement" under the safety of lock and key.

Emmaline had failed at civility every time the duke called, despite his obvious displeasure. On a normal day, he would never stand for such rudeness, but he was too busy making a lordly impression on the various officers to scold her. The more they "Your Grace'd" him and bent and stooped, the less he seemed to notice Emmaline's failed reverence. The search for Teddy was clearly an afterthought.

If it had not been for her friends, she would have no effective help at all.

Through it all, Emmaline held her tongue. Teddy *would be* found, she told herself—she forced herself to believe. After that, her plan to leave London and seek her fortune in New York would commence. The more she rankled Ticking, even now, the more difficult it would be to make this escape. So she endured his false worry and ineffective lordly intervention, and she relied on her friends. And she paced. And she prayed.

And then the viscount had come, and now the real work of finding Teddy was underway.

Just after dawn on the morning of the third day, not long after the Duke of Ticking had called on the dower house to check on the progress of the Bow Street Runners, Emmaline had her first flicker of an answered prayer.

She'd been enduring the ruminations of the duke, refilling his coffee and calling for more cake, when Rainsleigh, followed by Mr. Courtland, Lord Falcondale, Stoker, and Joseph crowded into her breakfast room. She gasped, her heart lodging in her throat, and scrambled around the table.

Please, please, please, she thought, seeking out the viscount.

He stood near the back, wetter and more mud-streaked than the others. Their gazes locked, and he did not look away.

His brother, meanwhile, had seen the duke and stepped forward.

"Your Grace, good morning. Forgive this disruption to your breakfast."

"The duke is not breakfasting," Emmaline cut in. "Please, tell me what you've found. Anything?"

Mr. Courtland held out a hand, gesturing...*what*? His gesture was beyond interpretation. She was desperate for an earnest answer. She looked frantically between Mr. Courtland and the viscount.

Mr. Courtland continued, still addressing the duke. "We've come straight from searching through the night, and we do have a small piece of news."

Emmaline gasped again and clasped the back of the nearest chair.

"At the risk of misleading you, I am happy to report that we have happened on a clue."

Now Emmaline clapped a hand over her mouth to contain a sob. She looked to the viscount again. He was watching her, and he gave a slow, measured nod. He eyed the duke, looked annoyed, and then looked at her again. He waited for his brother to continue.

"Two ballet dancers leaving Covent Garden after a performance last night," continued Mr. Courtland, "claimed to have seen a boy matching Teddy's description sitting on a bench beneath a lamplight, eating something—a piece of fruit or a potato, perhaps."

"Was he wearing his coat and hat?" Emmaline interjected. She'd lain awake every night, imagining him freezing to death in an alley.

"They did not mention a hat," Mr. Courtland said. "But they did see his coat. Distinctive, you'd said. Red."

Emmaline reached out for the next chair back, then the next. "Did they speak to him?"

"No, unfortunately, but they claim he was talking to someone else. An old man. This man approached the boy, and they said he looked like a priest or some member of clergy. They were under the impression he was giving the boy some kind of aid, perhaps taking him in."

Emmaline considered this, clutching the chair tightly enough to fracture the back. If only Teddy could recite his address. She and Miss Breedlowe had worked with him on this for hours. He could easily memorize the direction; it was just a matter of getting him to say the words.

She asked, "But how can we find this clergyman? Did the women know his church?"

Now the duke was making belligerent snorting noises, shoving away from the table and throwing his napkin with a flourish. He stumped to Emmaline and stood beside her, taking full measure of the men, their wet clothing, and red eyes, bleary from no sleep. Only Mr. Courtland was dressed like a true gentleman, and his coat and boots were smeared with mud. They all smelled like damp horse and frost.

Before Mr. Courtland could answer her question, the duke cut in, "I beg your pardon, Courtland, this is all very colorful and dramatic, and look how you have distressed the dowager duchess. If this was your goal, you've certainly achieved it. But let me assure you that I have applied to the Runners of Bow Street on this matter, and I have every confidence that their *official* search will produce the errant boy in due time. The officer assigned to the incident calls on me with regular briefings, and I can assure you that I've heard no such thing about ballet dancers, or red coats, or men in the night."

Mr. Courtland cleared his throat. "Quite so, sir…" He revealed the first twinge of annoyance but remained cordial. "Since the boy has been missing, I've worked—"

From behind him, the viscount cut his brother off. "Bryson, please. The duchess asked a bloody question. Her sanity hangs in the balance."

Mr. Courtland hesitated, looking from the viscount to Emmaline to the duke. The viscount swore under his breath and shoved his way to the front. Ignoring the duke, he said to Emmaline, "The dancers have seen the man in Covent Garden before. He ministers to drunks and street boys, apparently. They could not give us his name or direction, but they felt sure he would be a friend to your brother, not a threat."

"Yes, right," murmured Emmaline, making sense of this.

The viscount continued. "You'll remember that ministries such as these are your friend Elisabeth's bread and butter. Her foundation would not operate without the network of charitable-minded parsons, vicars, rabbis, and priests that inform her and give her patrons aid. She knows every open door and hot meal in the city. She will help us discover this man."

"Yes, of course." Emmaline nodded, blinking back tears. Her heart raced. She felt spent and exhilarated at the same time. The viscount was right. If the man really was a clergyman, Elisabeth's connections could provide a place for them to start.

Rainsleigh went on. "But I'll need you to work with her to draw up a clear list. When we know on which doors to knock, we can return to the streets with a little direction."

"*Work?*" blustered the duke beside Emmaline. "Perhaps you were not aware, sir, but the dowager duchess is in mourning. There is no place for her dealing personally in this search. And certainly not on the hearsay of…ballet dancers or men who prowl Covent Garden at night."

Emmaline ignored the duke. "I can do it," she said. She signaled for Dyson to bring her coat.

To the duke, she said, "It's no fool's errand, Your Grace. It is the only lead we have."

The duke's eyes narrowed as he considered this. He glanced back and forth between the group of men and Emmaline. She went on, invoking a new tone. "Please understand, I *will* assist them. In any way I can."

The viscount looked at Emmaline. "If your carriage is available, Your Grace, *I'll* see you to Henrietta Place."

Emmaline nodded, but the duke stopped them cold, exploding with an indignant sound of outrage and denial. "And who, sir, do you believe that *you* are?"

The duke's hands were clenched into fists at his sides, and his neck seemed to extend, red and bulging, from his cravat. His eyes bored into Rainsleigh's.

Oh, no. Emmaline looked at the viscount, holding her breath.

Mr. Courtland opened his mouth to speak and then closed it. He too looked at his brother.

Stoker and Joseph shuffled back.

Lord Falcondale stood shoulder to shoulder with Rainsleigh, slowly shaking his head.

To his credit, the viscount did not swell up or shout. He stared levelly at the smaller man. After a long moment, he used a gloved hand to tip his hat from his head. He stepped easily around his brother.

"Who am I?" he repeated calmly. "I'm Beauregard Courtland, Viscount Rainsleigh. Who the bloody hell are you?"

CHAPTER TWENTY-ONE

Beau's heart pounded like the toll of a bell. Emmaline's carriage waited, steps away, and he forced himself to take long, measured strides instead of a blind sprint.

I've said it. I've survived it.

I've said it, and the world did not end.

He'd tossed out his full name and the title like a weapon, as ineffective as it felt. Now it seemed stuck in his gut, rapidly bleeding him to death. He was freezing; he'd been freezing all night, but now he was also sweating.

He glanced back at Emmaline, but she was whispering last-minute orders to the butler. Her problems were far greater, of course. What was his bloody torment over the title when compared to a missing boy?

He held his breath for two beats and then exhaled heavily. He'd said the name only once, after all. Likely, it hardly registered. His brother had heard. And Falcondale. But they were allies.

Of course, he'd wanted the duke to hear his title, easily the first time he'd ever wanted this. But it was a means to an end. Put off the duke. Protect Emma. Earn himself a place in the search.

The butler was nodding now, ducking back inside and closing the door behind him. Emmaline embarked on the icy steps, and Beau took her elbow.

"Careful," he said, his voice miraculously calm. A groom whipped open the carriage door, and he stepped back so she could climb inside.

I've said it, he thought again. *And I still draw breath.*

It was only a name. A string of letters. It meant less to him than possibly to any man, ever. Saying it did not make it his identity.

Emmaline settled on the carriage seat and watched him with worried, cautious eyes. She knew the title haunted him. She knew, and now she would ask him about it.

The only thing he wanted less than identifying himself as viscount was explaining why he detested it.

He looked away and collapsed on the opposite seat, rapping twice on the ceiling to signal the coachman to drive.

"Would it be cliché to thank you again?" she asked. The carriage rounded the corner of Portman Square. "Surely you know how—"

"Yes," he said softly. "It would be cliché. And yes, I know. I wish I had been in London the night he'd gone. I wish I could do more." *I wish I could touch you.* The thought rose, unbidden, in his mind. He shifted in his seat.

The dowager carriage was cramped and tattered. With the windows closed against the morning cold, the pervasive smell of him—horse and boot sludge—permeated the small space. He'd folded his height inside what felt like a rolling cupboard.

Beau hunched, making an effort to, at the very least, approximate distance, but it was no use. They were knee to knee.

Emmaline balanced on the opposite bench, fully contained with artful grace. Not even a whisper of skirt brushed his knees.

She told him, "You're the only one who has done anything at all. I shall never be able to repay you for racing here. You took over, didn't you? The only one. Even if we never—" She stopped and looked out the window.

He ached to reach for her, but he squeezed his fingers into a fist. "No suppositions. We will follow every lead until one of them takes us to him."

She nodded.

Despite her poise, she looked fragile. Tired and fraught and on the precipice of a very high peak. She looked as if she were bracing for the devil around the next turn. This frailty was either new or newly revealed. The resiliency she'd shown the night he'd arrived in London had surprised him. He could not remember ever having been so impressed. She'd forgone the expected hysterics or useless sequestered vigil and carried on like a working partner in the search. Anyone else would have run mad, but she had been self-reliant and tough, and her nerve bolstered everyone else. His respect for her, already so great, had soared.

Respect. He smirked at the irony of the word, looking at her now, *relishing* the sight of her, finally alone with him. Respect for Emmaline had been the last thing on his mind during his time in Essex. He'd called up the memory of undressing her after he'd fished her from the canal, fantasizing about all the different paths that could have taken. There were so many delicious things to teach her. He did respect her, of course, but was it respect that caused his heart to thud and his hands to itch to reach for her?

The roads of London were wet and slick and crowded this morning, and the carriage rolled on in halting jerks. It became work to balance on the seat. She braced herself with her hands on either side, rocking with the motion.

It occurred to him that he knew at least a hundred tricks for disarming a lady in a moving carriage. What irony that now he would not employ a single one. He watched her instead, wishing he could say the thing that would give her even five minutes of peace.

She turned back from the window. "I failed Teddy by not forcing him to learn the name of our street and number of the dower house. If he could but recite it, this man from Covent Garden could bring him home today. If he knew where he lived, he might already be home."

"How did Bryson bring him home when I came upon him in September?"

"I usually put a card in his pocket with my name and address, just in case. But there was no time for the card. He went with the duke's boys to the garden unexpectedly. It's a miracle he even took his coat."

"This is your fatigue talking. All of us are running on too little sleep. You are not to blame." He sighed and sat forward. His hat flopped into her lap, and she laid it on the seat beside her. Their knees brushed.

"You've slept least of all..." She touched his knee when she said this, her gloved fingertips just grazing the fabric of his buckskins.

Beau blinked, trying not to watch her hand. He wanted her, even now. He was a cad. A rogue and a scoundrel, just as Lady Frinfrock had said.

She went on. "Luckily, His Grace has not made the leap. If he knew Teddy could not tell a stranger that he lived in Portman Square, the duke would have more fuel to his fire for guardianship."

Beau nodded, trying to keep up. The soft thrum of finger-tips on his knee slowly unraveled him. "I don't care about the duke," he said.

"Yes, well, Ticking certainly cared about you. I thought he might burst with shock at the sight. You crowded in and reported the only real progress we've had." She studied him. "He believed you to be my friends from church. And then you stepped forward and properly introduced yourself."

Beau recalled the duke's expression in that moment. The designation of "viscount" had transformed him from Invisible to Relevant. Or more to the point, from Invisible to *Threat.* The regard was night and day, and it had gratified him, just a little.

"He will not set you to the margins of this search or of your life," Beau said.

"We'll see about that. But I thank you for standing up to him. I know…I know it troubles you to invoke the title. It was a sacrifice."

"I don't want to talk about the title," he said.

His voice was harsh, too harsh, and her hand froze above his knee. She pulled her hand back. "Forgive me."

"You've too many problems of your own to take on my complicated resentments."

"I should like to help you." Her voice was a whisper. "In any way I can."

His mind was a whirl of all the ways she could help him, so many ways in this carriage alone. Instead, he said, "Help yourself by working with Elisabeth on this list of clergy. When you get down to business, you'll find her knowledge to be exhaustive, but she struggles to organize her thoughts concisely. Being succinct is not her most ready skill, God love her, not in the way it is for you."

The duchess smiled at this—a real smile, despite the clawing worry—and he wondered if he'd ever charmed a woman by simply telling her she was capable.

She returned her gloved hands to his knees, first one and then the other. He stared at the tight gray leather.

"Your notes," he went on, clearing his throat, "the ones you gave me from the night that Teddy was lost, were impeccable, by the way. Very useful. Elisabeth is smart and thorough, but she can become distracted and overdo. I've seen your notations, not to mention borne witness to your list of my own faults and shortcomings. I've faith that you'll keep her on task." He looked at her. "Try to produce the best list in the shortest amount of time. I don't have to tell you that time is of the essence."

"Thank you for giving me some purpose and allowing me to contribute. I'm not sure I could bear any more sitting and waiting."

"Well, my goal is not to distract you, if that is what you think. You're very organized. I've no doubt you'll make a fine bookseller when you reach New York."

She made a noise of frustration. She squeezed her eyes shut. "New York is the last thing I can think about." She made the noise again and dropped forward, laying her head on his knees.

Beau went still, staring down at the back of her head and the embellishments on her hat. He held his breath. It had been a long time since a beautiful woman had collapsed across his lap. It was an innocent gesture, not meant for him. She was overwhelmed.

Even so, he thought he could ride through the night with her laid out across his lap.

When she didn't move for five beats, six, an eternity, he settled one hand on her back. Carefully. Gently. A comforting, brotherly gesture. It was his first time to touch her, to really touch her, since the day she'd fallen into the canal.

"You cannot let this defeat you," he managed to say. His heart beat as if he'd never been alone with a pretty girl in a carriage before.

She turned her head to the side. "If you find him—"

"*When* we find him."

"*When* you find him, Ticking will restrict our freedom all the more." She sat up suddenly, and Beau jerked his hand away.

"But perhaps I should be restricted," she said. "I cannot believe I've allowed this to happen twice."

"Stop," he said. "Your devotion to Teddy is without question. Just look at the grand scheme you've devised to get the two of you all the way to New York. If you blame yourself, then the duke has already won. Do not fall prey to his rhetoric; it's nonsense."

She swiped away a tear and nodded. "Thank you," she whispered again. Two simple words, easily said and heard a thousand times a day, but something about the way she said it, deeply felt, deeply personal, made his throat constrict. For a moment, it was hard to breathe. Her hands were still on his knees, and she gave them a little squeeze. He looked down at them and then up at her. She stared back with a slow, shy, unmistakable look. Invitation.

Beau's heart stopped. He checked their location out the window. Two blocks from Henrietta Place. He swore in his head. He'd almost made it. Almost. Now the restraint felt like the most grievous waste of time.

"Emma," he whispered, and he scooped her hands from his knees and brought them to his lips. He kissed her knuckles through the leather and then tugged, one swift movement—*come*.

She went, slipping her hands free, and encircled his neck. She fell against his chest. Her hat gouged him immediately, a faux ivy sprig to the throat. *Penance*, he thought.

She chuckled and reached up, unpinning it and tossing it on the seat beside his own. When she returned to him, he locked his arms around her, pulling her tight. He closed his eyes and reveled in the spare-but-solid weight of her, the smell of her, the particular softness of her cheek against his throat.

"Oh, Duchess," he sighed. To speak now would only betray himself, but he could not *not* say the words. "I'm so sorry this has happened. I wish I could make it all go away."

"I wish I did not have to trouble you. I feel horrible for pulling you away from your business in Essex."

He shook his head, rubbing his lips across her hair.

She raised her face up, her lips dangerously close to his own, and he willed himself not to respond. It wasn't *that* kind of embrace, but he had spent all of its adult years not knowing of another kind. His body throbbed, and he pressed one chaste kiss on the top of her hair. And then another. And then one more, slow and lingering, not chaste at all.

She pulled away and tipped her head up, raising her lips to him. Beau stared at her mouth—easily the favorite feature of a face filled with favorite features—and he whispered again, "Emma."

She closed her eyes and resistance was futile. He lowered his lips gently to hers.

The kiss surprised him. It was nothing like before, on his boat. Not better or worse, simply different. He gently nibbled, and her lips moved just as softly. Almost at once, they both seemed to need a harder, more fortifying union, and he cradled the back of her head and went deeper. For one long moment in time, they were fused, holding and being held. Beau, usually so ready for the next pleasurable thing, willed the world to stop, just for a moment, to prolong it.

But the feel of the road beneath the carriage changed. The jostle of the road turned to the jiggle of cobblestones. They'd turned into Cavendish Square. Henrietta Place would be next. Only a minute more.

Beau dragged his face away, stringing kisses across her cheek until he could plant another on her lips. She scrambled to keep up, trying to catch his mouth and kiss him back, and they laughed a little.

He squeezed her once more, and she squeezed him in return, and then he lifted her, bodily, from his lap and settled her on the opposite seat. She patted her hair and reached for her hat. He watched her repin it, reveling in the efficient grace with which she wielded the awful thing. She smiled up beneath the brim, a sad, resigned smile.

Beau smiled too, realizing, perhaps for the first time ever, that there were other types of embraces. Sweet and tender, intimate or soul-feeding. Restorative. Necessary. He saw how these could be just as potent as the hot and seductive type.

Some of these might, he thought, even be more potent.

Chapter Twenty-Two

The viscount did not linger in Henrietta Place. He explained to Elisabeth and Emmaline how the list of possible clergymen would be the most useful, and then he took a horse from the stable and left.

On another day, she thought, she would have the time and energy and space in her heart to consider the sight of him leaping onto a horse and riding away. She would have, perhaps, hours or days to relive the kiss in the carriage, or the look on his face when he'd finally done it, the sound of his voice when he'd said her name.

But not today.

Today, her brother was missing in the bitter cold of winter, and the Duke of Ticking was outraged that she'd defied him by taking the carriage and leaving with another man. Today, there was work to be done. The only time and energy and space in her heart was for Teddy, and for fear, and for hope.

They set to work on the lists immediately, with Elisabeth rattling off names of pastors and vicars, priests and rabbis at random. Emmaline took down their names and locations and asked for a map of the city. Next, she organized the list based on proximity to where the dancers had supposedly seen her brother in Covent Garden. After she'd put down all the benevolent-minded churches close to Covent Garden, she made lists of all the other churches, arranging them in easy-to-follow routes that ran from Covent Garden outward. Taken together, the list missed no possible houses of worship, from the central most to the most far-flung. Luckily, Emmaline knew many of the churches from her own comings and goings to evade the duke, an unexpected resource. All the while, Elisabeth stood ready to help, marveling encouragingly at Emmaline's acumen and speed.

"I cannot say how much of a contribution it will be," Emmaline told her, "but I am grateful for something to do besides wring my hands and receive the duke at regular intervals."

"Yes, Beau was clever to task you with this," Elisabeth said thoughtfully. "He is a far more proficient leader than anyone gives himself credit."

"Oh, he is very clever," said Emmaline, perhaps a little too quickly. Her friend stared with interest, and she added, "That is, his recklessness need not overshadow his other useful talents."

"Indeed." Elisabeth watched her. "Your enthusiasm for him is…refreshing."

Emmaline was not sure how to respond to this. She did not feel refreshed or enthusiastic. She felt distracted and distressed and grateful. But anyone who bore witness to his leadership in Teddy's search could tell that she and Rainsleigh had *some* rapport. But it was a rapport born of necessity and crisis.

They were hardly sweethearts. Outside of Teddy's disappear-ance, the viscount was a consummate Lothario who drank too much and lived on a canal by choice. She was soon to be an expatriate in America, and her surprise virginity had sent him bolting to the door. Really, they couldn't be less suited.

And the embrace of today?

Well, the embrace of today was meant only to be a comfort.

And Emmaline was a widow in half mourning who should know better.

"Did Beau say when he would come back for the list?" Elisabeth asked, watching her copy the last of it.

"Two hours," Emmaline said.

Elisabeth nodded. "That gives you forty-five minutes to lie down before he comes."

Emmaline protested, but Elisabeth would not hear of it. "When Beau finds Teddy, you will be no comfort to him at all if you do not rest. You haven't slept in days. Sleep now to keep up your strength. I will awaken you if we hear anything. Anything at all."

It was the mention of Teddy's comfort that convinced her. He would be sick and wet and terrified after all this time. And she was so very tired. So very numb and tired and heartsick. She scarcely remembered the walk to a guest room, and she was fast asleep before she'd even settled her head on the pillow.

"Your Grace? Your Grace?" Miss Breedlowe's face, tight with urgency, hovered above Emmaline as she swam through a fitful sleep to wobbly consciousness. "Emmaline, will you awaken?" Miss Breedlowe repeated insistently, as if they were both late for something very important. It was unlike her, Emmaline thought groggily. Always so calm, Jocelyn. She got on with Teddy because of her calmness.

Teddy! Wakefulness returned like a bucket of cold water, and Emmaline bolted upright in bed.

"Teddy," she said, throwing off the covers and swinging her feet to the floor. Her vision blurred and the room tilted, but she blinked, willing herself awake. "How long did I sleep?" she asked, searching the floor beside the bed for her shoes. Daylight shone through the windows. Afternoon light? Oh God, the next morning? It felt as if she'd sleep for a week. "Teddy," she said again, her only coherent thought.

"Malie," came the answer from across the room.

Emmaline froze. Breath left her lungs, and she gasped. She knew that voice. But did she dream it?

She spun and saw her brother, her wind-whipped, matted-haired, slightly thinner, very-much-alive *brother* standing at the foot of the bed.

"*Teddy!*" she sobbed, scrambling to grab him and clutch him to her. "Oh, Teddy, my brave brother"—she pulled away now and stared through tears at his face—"where have you been, Teddy? I've been sick with worry! We've been looking for you for days!"

Not waiting for an answer, she pulled him against her, hugging him as if their lives depended upon it. She clutched the back of his head so tightly he cried out and began to squirm.

She loosened her hold, and he repeated, "Malie." Gently, contritely. He leaned awkwardly against her, raising one limp arm to pat her on the elbow. "Lost, Malie."

She nodded against him, too tearful to speak. He squirmed again, and she let him go, sitting back on her haunches on the still-made bed.

"Oh, Teddy," she said, smiling through her tears. "I'm so sorry I did not look after you more carefully. This has been my fault. Can you forgive me? I will do better in the future. I promise. We will put the note in your coat with our direction and never take it out."

"Lost," he said again, and he looked very young, despite his adult man's body and five days' worth of fuzzy beard on his face.

Emmaline nodded and looked away, wiping the tears from her eyes, seeing the room for the first time. Jocelyn Breedlowe stood by the window, looking out.

In the doorway, she saw the viscount, watching, with his head ducked. When he caught her gaze, he made a small salute—his hand to his hat—and then he pushed off the wall and slipped away, disappearing down the hall.

"Rainsleigh, wait!" she called, sliding from the bed. But when she reached the doorway, he was gone.

She turned to Jocelyn.

"I don't believe Lord Rainsleigh has slept or eaten since he returned to London," Jocelyn said. "Perhaps it's best to let him go. He insisted upon personally seeing Teddy safely to you."

"Yes, of course," said Emmaline, still a little confused by sleep, overwhelmed with the return of her brother. She looked at the empty doorway, feeling helpless. She looked back at her brother, feeling elated.

"I'm so very glad you are home, Teddy," she said gently. She reached for him again. "Let us fetch Mr. Broom to get you into dry clothes, shall we? Wash your hair. Find something warm to eat. Then perhaps we can talk about how you will never, ever wander out of an open garden gate, ever again."

"Lost," said Teddy, his voice still very childlike, and Emmaline nodded, took his hand, kissed it, and led him from the room.

CHAPTER TWENTY-THREE

The full weight of four days with virtually no sleep burned behind Beau's eyelids. He stepped outside, staggered two steps, and squinted against the cold December sun. He was tough, but he also knew his limits, and he'd fall off his horse if he tried to ride for the Paddington in this state.

Perhaps just one night in any of the twenty lavish beds in his brother's house, he thought. With the delicious bounty of Bryson's well-paid chef. And a hot bath, and clean clothes, and servants to wait on him.

He'd slip in the kitchen door and not be noticed, he thought. He had no wish to intrude on Emma's reunion with her brother and even less desire to hear her thank him again. Her gratitude was not in question; it would not be prudent for either of them to test how far that gratefulness extended.

Beau trudged up the kitchen steps and, for once, did not quibble with his brother's butler. "Bath, then bed," he told Sewell. "Immediately. In twelve hours, food. The more the better."

"Very good, my lord," the butler said, drawing off his muddy coat and taking his hat and gloves. Beau staggered to his old room without looking back. By the time he'd peeled off his clothes, a tub in the corner had been filled with steaming water. He made quick work of a bath and then dropped into bed, naked and still wet, and was asleep in five minutes.

"Beau, wake up. *Wake up*." Bryson's voice cut through the deep fog of subversive sleep and jolted him awake. He blinked at the canopy above his head.

I'm starving. His first useful thought.

"Put on some clothes, for God's sake," his brother said.

Emmaline. His second.

"Is the duchess's brother unharmed?" Beau asked, his voice like gravel in a bucket.

"Teddy Holt has a sore throat and a cough but is expected to recover. The duchess, however, is overwhelmed with every emotion from relief to guilt. I understand she would see you as soon as you are able. She wishes to express her gratitude."

"That won't happen." He sat up.

"Why bloody not? She has been sick with worry and nearly as sick with relief. You torture her by not allowing her to express her thanks. It's rude and ungracious."

"Yes, well, no surprise there. You hired her to remedy that very affliction. The failure is all mine, by the way. My rudeness is ingrained, apparently. Pity."

"I didn't *hire her*. We casually discussed something that she required and I wanted. I left the discussion and didn't give it a second thought, while she took every word to heart. I'm sorry if you were caught in the middle."

I'm not sorry. Beau thought of the kiss in the carriage. He thought about the look on her face when she'd seen him in the hallway after he'd delivered Teddy Holt. "Tell Her Grace she may thank me via letter." He fell back in bed. "I could sleep another week, at least."

"At the moment, you're needed downstairs," Bryson said. "Two street boys who claim to be in your acquaintance are at the kitchen door. With a dog. Sewell tells me they refuse to leave until they speak with you."

Beau grunted, rubbing his jaw. "Mercenary little bastards. I left them money to feed and water my dog until I returned from Essex. I'm sure they've spent the lot."

"What were you doing in Essex?"

Of course his brother would not allow the comment to go unnoticed.

"Tell the boys to wait in the mews," Beau said, ignoring the question. "I need ten minutes to get dressed." His clothes had been freshly laundered and folded on a chest nearby, and he plodded to them.

His brother did not leave.

"Your dog is welcome here, obviously," Bryson said. "And so are you."

"Thank you."

"I could learn the nature of your business in Essex if I wanted to. I hope you know this."

Beau pulled on his boots without an answer. The unexplained trips to Essex had tortured his brother for years, but not as much as Beau's history with the Barnes family would do, if he knew about the fire.

Bryson said, "I have wanted to respect your privacy."

"Thank you," Beau repeated. He was dressed now, balancing the endurance of this conversation with the extreme demands of his stomach. He had hoped to eat before he left. "What time is it?" he asked.

"Nearly one o'clock. You've just missed luncheon, but Sewell will see it laid out again if you are hungry."

Beau frowned. "I only slept five hours?"

"Nearly one o'clock on *Thursday*. You slept a day and a half. I instructed the staff not to disturb you. God knows you needed your sleep. I only awakened you now—"

"To sort out my dog," Beau finished, but he thought, *to wheedle me with questions.*

"I don't care about the dog. The grooms will mind her if you like—although the river boys must go or make themselves useful." He paused a moment. "If you must know, I awakened you because the Duchess of Ticking is due here at a quarter past one to discuss her journey to New York. Forgive me if I presume too much, but I thought for some reason that you would like to know."

Beau froze for half a beat. *Right,* he thought. *No meal.* He forced himself to move again, faster now. The knife slid into the leather sheath on his belt, and he ran a hand through his hair. He needed a shave, but it would have to wait. Before he could stop himself, he asked, "What about the journey to New York?"

"Something about the duke. Her situation under the care of the Duke of Ticking is far direr than I allowed myself to believe. Her brother's disappearance only made matters worse."

"In what way?" Beau followed Bryson into the hall.

"The Duke of Ticking was livid when Emmaline returned to Portman Square with Teddy. He didn't even feign relief that the boy had been found. He threw a tantrum worthy of a two-year-old. Elisabeth and I accompanied them there, and I was honestly afraid to leave her."

"Well I hope you did not. She was exhausted, and the boy was frozen through. The last thing either of them needed was the temper fit of a bloody...vulture...prince."

Bryson had gone on walking, but now he turned. "We weren't given much choice, were we? I'd had cross words with the duke the day before. You'd spirited the dowager duchess away without a backward glance, remember?"

Beau opened his mouth to protest, but Bryson stopped him. "I realize you were given little choice, but my relationship with the dowager duchess can only be described in the most convoluted terms—and yours can't be explained at all. The Duke of Ticking is her guardian, for all practical purposes. It is his right to know where she goes or who minds her brother."

"How is it his right? Who has given him this right?"

"She is a young woman with no husband or father. His Grace sees it as his duty to look after his father's widow—a view that I believe would be shared by most of the civilized world. The fact that she is so young, not to mention of common birth, only increases his control."

"Common birth?" scoffed Beau. "She was rich enough to buy herself a duke for a husband, and her brother is sitting on a pile of money."

"*Precisely.* More motivation for the Duke of Ticking to lock her in and never let her go. As a duke, his influence is vast."

Beau was seized by anger. It doused him like a bucket of water had been dumped over his head. "Naturally, you're just the man to defer to that sort of thinking."

His brother stepped up until they were almost nose to nose. Anger flashed in his eyes, and his voice was deadly quiet. "No," Bryson said, "*I'm* the man who is stealing her away to another country to escape from it all. In doing so, I risk what very little is left of my reputation, not to mention legal action, my company, and my family. The real question, *Lord Rainsleigh,* is what are *you* going to do for her?"

For this, Beau had no answer, and his anger grew. He'd opened his mouth to shout some inane curse when Sewell stepped through the door and intoned, "Her Grace the Dowager Duchess of Ticking to see you, sir."

"In the ballroom, Sewell," snapped Bryson. "I'll be there shortly."

Beau blinked and took a step back. "The ballroom? Why receive her in the bloody ballroom?"

"Because," Bryson said, grinding out the words and turning away, "it's proven the only room big enough to store two hundred crates of her bloody books."

CHAPTER TWENTY-FOUR

Emmaline had not expected to encounter Lord Rainsleigh in Mr. Courtland's ballroom. She'd been standing on a stool, peering into an open crate of books when they came in. The sight of him caused her to go perfectly still. At the same time, she fought the strange urge to give a small jump. What she really wished to do was run to him, but this was easier to curtail. She could not run to him. His brother was there, and servants bustled in and out. It was imprudent to look at him at all, really. One glance and then away, she vowed.

In that glance, she'd seen enough to set her heart racing. He wore clean, pressed clothes but his hair was tousled, and he had not yet shaved. Seeing him, she thought, was a little like turning the bend on the Ainsdale road in Lancaster and catching the first glimpse of the Irish Sea. It took your breath away.

But of course he was not the Irish Sea, and she was not in Lancashire. He was merely a man, and she was in London with her mind on the moon when it should have been on evading the Duke of Ticking and starting a new life an ocean away.

Of all the times to turn fanciful and heartsick, she thought. Now she could see why her mother had kept her so protected as a girl. Awareness and attraction and heart-racing desire were a potent combination. If allowed to bloom, it could easily become, well…*all*.

She took a deep breath and squared her shoulders. She barely had the time or energy for *some*. *All* was entirely out of the question.

But now she was standing behind the crate like a spy, and she stepped down from the stool and cleared her throat. The men looked up, and Mr. Courtland smiled and signaled to her. The viscount did not smile. His look was hard and urgent and inscrutable. He appeared neither happy nor sad to see her but rather intensely *aware* of her. The large sun-washed room seemed suddenly more vivid in the thrall of that look—the floor shinier, the colors of drapes brighter. Emmaline held her breath. He was the first to look away.

I am too inexperienced and green for him, Emmaline reminded herself, walking to them. *He does not feel the same way I do.* She glanced at him again, but he'd turned away, studying a crate of her books. *He is a philanderer and a flirt, and he loves all women, even old Lady Frinfrock, even me perhaps, but not in…*

Not in my way.

I should know better, she finished, stopping in front of Mr. Courtland. Perhaps she would do better not to look at him at all. Not even one glance.

"Good afternoon, Your Grace," Mr. Courtland said. "We were pleased to get your note. We have been anxious for word on Teddy's recovery."

Thank God, she thought, *for Mr. Courtland's reliable manners and concern.*

"Teddy is nearly his old self again," she said. "Thank you so much for asking. I hope you'll forgive my intrusion, but I saw the chance to slip away this afternoon, and I seized it. There has been a troubling development. I worry it may complicate our plans." From the corner of her eye, she saw Rainsleigh pivot in her direction.

"What's happened?" the viscount snapped.

"Good morning to you too, my lord," Emmaline said, examining the button on her glove.

"Forgive my brother," said Mr. Courtland. "He slept through luncheon."

"Forgive me," she said, "for not impressing upon him how to say a proper hello."

"You are aware that I'm standing right here?" asked the viscount. "*What* troubling development?"

Emmaline told Mr. Courtland, "The Duke of Ticking feels it is best if Teddy and I vacate the dower house and move into the family townhome with him and the duchess and their children." It knotted her stomach to say the words.

"*What?*" demanded the viscount. Now he was beside her. "Tell him no. Tell him not a bloody *chance.* Tell him you have no wish to move into his overpopulated and undersupervised brat factory. He cannot force you."

"In fact, he can," said Emmaline, finally looking at him. "If I am to enjoy any freedom, any at all, I must consent to the things about which he is most adamant. And he is very adamant about having us out of the dower house. In the wake of Teddy's disappearance, he feels our life there is not secure enough to keep Teddy safe."

Beau hissed out a breath.

His brother glared at him. "Beau, please." To Emmaline, Mr. Courtland said, "Your Grace, did you suggest a larger staff in the dower house to assist you in Teddy's care?"

Emmaline shook her head. "He denied my request for more staff, even before Teddy went missing. In fact…" She looked away now, tears forming in her eyes. "In fact, he wishes to let go of Teddy's valet, Mr. Broom, a man who has carefully tended Teddy since he was a boy. His Grace plans to assign one of his own footmen to wash and dress him."

She took a deep breath, reaching for composure. "I'm not sure what we'll do without dear Mr. Broom. Teddy will be devastated to lose him. We all will. If I can argue only one point, it will be this. I am prepared to, quite literally, beg the duke to allow us to retain the man. I'll promise anything."

Beau turned away now, swearing again, and she allowed herself to watch. He made no effort to hide his outrage. How good it felt to see someone was as angry as she was.

Emmaline went on. "I am telling you this simply to reiterate my determination to sail as soon as your ship can be made ready. I will do whatever it takes to steal away, even if it means that Teddy and I climb out the window in the middle of the night and run through the streets of London to Southwark."

Mr. Courtland opened his mouth to speak, but she rushed to finish. "Until then, I may not have the freedom to meet with your or even to send word by letter. His Grace is highly suspicious of my relationship with Elisabeth and you and"— she looked at the viscount—"Lord Rainsleigh. But please do not take my silence for lack of heart. We *will* make our way to New York. I will sell these books. I will repay you for your kindness and the passage." Cringing, she glanced at the viscount. He was just as rough and untamed as when she'd first met him. She looked back to Mr. Courtland. "In actual money, that is."

"You cleared your debt when you took my brother on," said Mr. Courtland. "He is impossible to teach—even the king's own herald could not have done better—and I blame myself for suggesting it."

"Well, I do not," she said, her voice going suddenly serious and urgent. She would say this now. "In fact, I could not be more grateful. He restored my brother to me, finding a helpless boy in all of teeming London." She glanced at the viscount's averted profile. "If I had not worked with him on the…er, lessons, then he would not have known. I would have never met him at all."

"Yes, I will give him that," said Mr. Courtland. "He is handy in a fight—or a rescue, if you will. There are worse things."

"We owe our lives to the viscount," Emmaline said, her voice tearful. She'd been given no opportunity to thank him, a breach that never left her mind, despite her relief and every other pressing concern. How strange it felt now, strange and insufficient, to say the words in relay, telling his brother while he stood not three feet apart. But he would not look at her.

But perhaps it was for the best, she thought, because deep down, she worried the thank-you was merely an excuse. She *was* grateful, but her compulsion to express it was all tangled up with her compulsion to simply see him again. To touch him, if she could.

Was she grateful, or was she falling in love?

Would she have wanted so badly to kiss him if he hadn't saved Teddy's life?

Well, that's a stupid question, she thought. *I've wanted to kiss him since I followed him into the alley.*

And especially since he saved Teddy's life.

Thank God, Mr. Courtland was here. She'd said the words, Rainsleigh had heard them, and the strange, intoxicating little dance between them was not allowed even the first steps. After today, they would likely never drift into that dance again, and good riddance. For her sanity, and her future, and the burgeoning stirrings in her naïve little heart.

"Well, you may tell him what you wish," said Mr. Courtland now, "because I'm due in a meeting with Dunhip. Try not to worry about the voyage, Your Grace. I trust you to handle the Duke of Ticking in a manner most advantageous to your eventual departure but also to your daily survival. We will see you on the boat with the books. On this, you can rely."

He glanced at his brother. "Have Sewell show the duchess out, will you, Beau? You know how Dunhip frets when I am detained."

And then, while she watched, he turned and strode from the ballroom, closing the door behind him.

Emmaline blinked, held her breath, and turned to look at Lord Rainsleigh. They were alone together again.

CHAPTER TWENTY-FIVE

Beau turned his head at the sound of the ballroom door clicking shut. His brother had trapped him in a closed room with a woman so brimming with displaced gratitude her voice broke with the sound of it.

He'd done this on purpose, but why?

To torture him? Likely. Bryson viewed it as a brotherly obligation to torture him whenever the opportunity presented itself.

Only with Bryson, it was never torture for torture's sake. There was always some sort of truth to be gleaned, a lesson learned, or a comeuppance to be taken between the eyes. And in this situation, with *this* woman, the possibilities for self-improvement were legion.

Beau already knew his brother thought he should grant the duchess her tearful gratefulness. He'd said as much. *And* his brother thought Beau should embark on the next heroic gesture to aid and abet her.

Do as I would do, was what Bryson really wanted. Be a man—be *that* man who stands up to the Duke of Ticking and his demands on her living arrangements or Teddy Holt's sacked valet or any of the rest of it.

Sorry, Bryson, Beau thought, exhaling, *it would take a lot more than being trapped alone in the ballroom to accomplish all of that.*

Or any of it.

However, there were other ways to occupy oneself in a closed ballroom with a beautiful woman.

Beau glanced at her. This was unnecessary, considering he could bloody well *feel* every move she made. The rustle of her silks. The slide of her gloved hand across the wooden crates. He'd become somehow intimately attuned to her; his senses leapt with every blink and sigh.

"You've slept," she said to his profile.

"Like the dead. And you?"

She nodded, paused a beat, and then said, "Lord Rainsleigh—"

"Please stop calling me that," he said. "Not only do I detest the name, you and I are"—he leaned back against the crate of books behind him—"more personally acquainted, don't you think?" He raised an eyebrow.

When all else failed, he could count on the tried and true. He had no wish to seduce her—no, that was wildly inaccurate; he had every wish to seduce her, but he could not, would not touch her. Still, some habits were ingrained. Especially when he was unsettled. And she, like no woman before her, unsettled him.

He finished, "Call me Beau, I beg."

She laughed a little. "All right. Beau." She looked at the floor and then back at him. "Elisabeth told me how you found Teddy. The priory in Hampstead."

Beau shrugged. "And she told me how quickly and proficiently you laid out our map of prospects."

"It was your tenacity that found him. You discovered the dancers who set you on the right path. He would have never been found otherwise—"

"Perhaps, but he would have had a very nice life as a papist in Hampstead."

"I wanted him home with me, and you were the only one who understood my desperation. You did this."

"My brother and Falcondale would have run him to ground eventually. You have a useful partner in Bryson—for all things. When he says he will get you and your books safely to New York, he will do it. Managing this is the larger, more complicated task. Save your gratitude for him. He actually revels in that sort of thing, the needy bastard."

"Do not diminish what you have done for us." She took a step toward him. He was torn between rolling from the crate and staying right where he was, leaning back, propping his arms wide on either side. He looked her up and down, another old habit, and she watched his perusal.

She took another step.

Beau's heart began to pound.

"What I have done," he told her, spreading his arms on the crate, "is nothing compared to what Elisabeth and Bryson will do. Please don't confuse the two. Bryson is the solver of great problems. I am…I am…"

She was upon him now, just a step away. His eyes locked on her lips, and he lost his train of thought.

"You are the one," she said softly, closing the last step, "who came when I called."

She leaned in. "You are the one who tore off into the night."

She raised up on her toes. "You found him. And I *will* tell you thank you."

And then she kissed him. One small, sweet swipe of her lips against his, just like he'd taught her. Beau held perfectly still, not taking his eyes from hers, even as she rose up to kiss him a second time, even as his vision swam with her closeness.

The last time, he kissed her back—no amount of control could prevent this—and she made a small noise, a little sound of triumph and relief. Her eyelids fluttered closed, and she kissed him again, longer, slower, far more than a peck. How had she become so proficient at kissing quite so fast?

He'd kept his arms outstretched on the crate behind him, but now she stumbled, swaying on her tiptoes to reach him, and his hand shot out to steady her. Her own hands fell to his biceps, latching on, clinging to the muscle beneath the fabric of his shirt.

"*We can't*, Duchess," he breathed between kisses, his hands squeezing her arms to keep from hauling her against him.

"You…you do not want me," she whispered back. She nodded a little, just to herself. This is what she believed, he realized. She actually believed this.

"No, Duchess. It's the opposite." He laughed, a hoarse, strangled sound, and shook his head. "I want you too much."

Her head shot up. "Well, that makes no sense. You 'want me too much.'"

Her hands slid from his arms, and she reached up to pull the pins from her hat. "Honestly, Rainsleigh—"

"Beau," he corrected, staring at her mouth.

"*Beau*," she said. "Either you enjoy me or you don't, but I think I deserve more than the fraught, empty excuses with which you ply your other conquests. If my inexperience is unappealing to you, say it. I understand—"

He groaned and yanked her to him. She dropped her hat. "Your inexperience," he hissed, "is bloody irresistible to me. Stop talking for five seconds and feel the evidence of how much I want you." He kissed hard. "Even through the layers of that terrible gray skirt—"

"Your repeated insults of my attire are as rude as they are unnecessary. I've told you I have no choice in the mat—"

He cut her off with a roll of his hips, one quick, meaningful thrust, and she gasped. Her eyes flew to his face.

"Do not tell me I don't want you, Emma," he said quietly into her ear. "I have wanted you since the first time you lifted that bloody veil and blinked at me with those big brown eyes. I lie awake at night, fantasizing about all the ways I might possibly contrive to have you." He rolled his hips again, and she sucked in a breath.

He swallowed hard. "You are wrong about the other women. I'll tell you, and freely so, that I love everything about the way you look and feel. Your hair, your mouth, your eyes. But I have known beautiful women before. With you, Emma...with you, there is *more*." He paused, breathing in the scent of her hair. It smelled like vanilla and lemons and *her*.

She made a whimpering sound, and he dragged his beard across her jaw and kissed her again. When he came up for breath, he continued, forcing out the words. "I am not put off by your innocence. I am struggling to protect it."

She opened her mouth to object, but he held up a hand. "Wait, listen. Your life is very complicated at the moment. You are consumed with the journey to New York, and with the Duke of Ticking, and these books—the whole lot. It is an enormous undertaking, steeped in worry, and your entire future hangs in the balance."

She nodded and looked away. "And I should focus on it wholly. With no distractions."

"No—hardly. By my count, you could stand for *more* distractions in your life, not fewer. I'm amazed you have not collapsed under the pressure of it. Your courage and foresight are staggering to me, Duchess—truly."

"And I thought you only noticed my hair and mouth and body."

It was a joke, but he was reminded again that Emmaline was not like other girls. Praising her beauty would not carry the same weight as praise for her proficiency at life in general. This was the girl who'd asked to be taught to fish.

"Those are lovely too," he said, giving her a quick, appreciative kiss, "but what I intended to say was that your life will not always be so full of struggle and strife and risk. Eventually, you will sell the books and earn the money to make your own way, just as you've said. Eventually, you will wish to marry again. I will not take the innocence that belongs to you and your future"—he struggled for the word—"life."

"But I am a widow," she said, "and no one expects me to be inno—"

He cut her off, "It's not what will happen with our bodies, Emma. It's what will happen to your heart."

She laughed again, an explosion of sound with a bitter edge. "What about your heart?"

"Oh, Duchess. I have no heart."

She squinted and pushed back from him, straining against his arms. "Congratulations," she said, "you've managed to say something stupider than *wanting me too much*."

"Joke if you will," he said sadly, "but I have seen the whole world, several times over. We are playing with fire, Duchess, and God help you, the burden for keeping you unscathed has fallen to me. Remember…remember when you wanted me to kiss you? You did not wheedle or manipulate; you plainly asked me to do it. When you needed help finding your brother, you wrote to me and asked for it. Even now, you refuse to be put off with your bloody gratitude, despite my surliness. Do you see how open and honest you are? This is no small thing, Emma. Openness and honesty are rare and wonderful, but they veritably *spell* innocence. *This* is what I mean to protect by keeping myself as far away as possible.

"A passionate affair—and believe me, any affair between us could be no other kind—a passionate affair would gobble you up and then spit you out on the other side. Your heart would be left harder, less trusting. Do you see?"

She turned her eyes away and bit her lip. He could almost hear the wheels of thought turning in her head.

Carefully, he kissed the tip of her nose. "Perhaps I'm heartless, and perhaps I'm not. But whatever I am, I am not the type of man to use up innocent women and then leave them. For all of my failings to Bryson, he brought me up to be more than this."

Emmaline breathed in deeply and then let it out, a resigned sigh. She looked up. "But I didn't ask you for a passionate affair," she said softly. "I...I only wanted a kiss."

He squeezed his eyes shut and drew her to him, kissing the top of her head. "Oh, Duchess. It's never only a kiss. Not with you, love. Not with you."

He felt her burrow against his throat, and he squeezed her, breathing in. He brushed slow, tender kisses against her hair, again and again, until she raised her head, tilting her face to him.

He looked down at her, an eyebrow raised—*Did you hear anything I've just said?*—and she smiled. She rose up on her toes to kiss him.

The new position fitted their lower bodies more tightly together, tongue and groove, and he swallowed another groan. Almost too late, she realized this and wiggled again—a small, tentative bop of her own hips, just as he had done. Pleasure and need exploded behind Beau's eyes.

"Hold still, Duchess, or I swear to God, you will lose the very innocence in contention right here on this cold, hard ballroom floor."

She tried to laugh, but it came out more like a gasp.

He chuckled and kissed her back, running his hands from her back to her bottom, kissing her properly, kissing her as if this would be the last time, as if his life depended on it. She wrapped her arms around his neck and held on, matching fervor. He cupped her bottom and pressed her into his need, just once more, and she made the most intoxicating sound of pleasure and assent.

The vast ballroom shrunk to the fusion of her and him and the solid crate on which they leaned. He widened his stance, allowing her to fall even closer, and she sighed and worked her fingers at the collar of his shirt.

He was lost to the sensation and to her. He wanted to memorize the dips and swells of her body so he would not forget for a lifetime.

He had just begun to wind the fingers of his right hand into the thick fabric of her skirt, inching it up her leg, when he heard the faint sound of a dog barking in the distance. He ignored it and was walking his fingers down her leg, praying the silk would soon end and give way to stocking beneath, when he heard it again, louder this time. Barking. The clatter of claws on parquet floor. His hand went still. He forced himself to open his eyes.

Yes, there it was again. Barking, claws on wood, and now he felt urgent paws on his legs, whimpers, a large wet tongue.

Peach.

Beau blinked and tried to end the kiss. Behind them, he heard the distinctive sound of a female voice insistently clearing her throat.

Beau coughed and pulled away, drawing Emma's face against his throat.

"Forgive the intrusion," said a female voice, "but this dog would not be put off."

Elisabeth.

Beau breathed a sigh of relief and looked at the ceiling.

"Sorry to intrude," Elisabeth continued, "but Bryson was insistent that we learn your intentions for this animal. She has eaten a raw steak from the cook's counter and relieved herself on the drawing room rug. Bryse is not amused."

Beau cursed and thanked God in the same breath. He nodded to the ceiling.

Emmaline had gone stiff and breathless in his arms, and he leaned down to press a chaste kiss on her head. " 'Tis only Elisabeth," he whispered, "and she will not judge."

Peach continued to jump and claw at his leg, whining now, and Beau snapped, "Down, Peach, you infernal dog." He squinted at Elisabeth and ran a hand through his hair. "Apologies."

" 'Tis nothing," she assured him, keeping her voice light, "but you know how Bryson is. Especially about the rugs."

To the duchess, Elisabeth said, "Would you come with me, Emmaline? Oh, I see you've lost your hat. I'm rubbish with millinery but perhaps more useful than Beau." She glared at her brother-in-law. "You did mention when you arrived that it would be imprudent to stay too long."

"Imprudent," repeated Emmaline, turning to follow her, sweeping up her hat. "Yes. That is accurate."

CHAPTER TWENTY-SIX

Jocelyn Breedlowe hurried home through Lady Frinfrock's garden gate, anxious to outpace the threatening rain and reach the warm parlor before teatime. Teddy Holt had been a challenge today, distracted and listless, and only her most creative diversions had served to draw him out.

When the dowager duchess had returned, she was more fraught and harried than usual and in dire need of a friendly ear. Of course, Jocelyn could not leave until she had obliged her.

She felt a responsibility, perhaps misplaced, to the duchess's very complicated situation with the new viscount. Everyone adored Beau Courtland, but until Emmaline, no one had dared to *love* him.

Jocelyn felt more uncertain and worried for Emmaline than ever she had for Piety or Elisabeth. It was one thing to fall in love with a man who had no room for a woman in his life but quite another to fall in love with a man whose life had too many women already. But perhaps the viscount only wished everyone to believe he had too many women. Lord Rainsleigh, for the most part, was an enigma to Jocelyn—a lord who had no wish to be a lord, a skirt-chasing drunk who always seemed to be sober and alone.

She'd said nothing to the dowager duchess, save assurances, and certainly she did not suggest that Emmaline had fallen in love with the viscount. This was, after all, mere conjecture on Jocelyn's part. Only when Emmaline was composed and able to face an afternoon of Teddy's parrots (and even worse, an afternoon of the Duke of Ticking), Jocelyn bade her good-bye and finally hurried home.

She'd just rounded the corner to Lady Frinfrock's garden door when she spotted Elisabeth Courtland pacing back and forth beneath the willow tree that shaded a stone bench.

"Oh, Jocelyn, thank God," Elisabeth said, looking up. "I thought you'd never come home."

"What's wrong?" Jocelyn paused, immediately concerned. "Is it the ba—?"

"No, no, it's nothing to do with me." She stopped pacing and held out her hands, palms up. "I'm worried about Emmaline."

"Because of the Duke of Ticking?" Jocelyn asked carefully.

Elisabeth waved her hands. "Of course His Grace is intolerable. But that is a separate worry. Because of my brother-in-law, Beau."

"Oh, Lord Rainsleigh." Jocelyn checked the darkening sky. This could take some time. "What of him?"

The story that followed was the same one she'd just heard from the duchess, albeit from a different point of view.

Jocelyn listened and then admitted, "I'm grateful that you finally know of their…friendship, because I am also worried for her."

Elisabeth's grabbed her wrist. "You *knew*?"

Jocelyn made a guilty expression and nodded to the bench. They sat beneath the drooping willow. "Well, some of it, I'm afraid."

"Has Emmaline suggested that she is unhappy? God forbid, is she *frightened* of his advances?"

"No. If she is unhappy, it is not from his advances, more like his...withdrawals."

Elisabeth slapped her hands on her knees. "Of course she is." She shook her head. "Beau Courtland cannot meet a woman without charming her, bewitching her, and then deserting her to moon over him for a year. I've asked Bryson about it, and he refuses to discuss it." She shoved up from the bench. "'Let nature take its course,' he said. He seems to have every belief that his brother will behave honorably with her. *Ha*. Where he got this notion, I have no idea. Bryson is too blinded by the love of his brother to see the risk to Emmaline's heart."

"Or," countered Jocelyn, "Mr. Courtland loves his brother enough to see the *potential*."

"You believe Bryson has been matchmaking?"

"They have been very much thrown together, I'm afraid. The rescue of Teddy. The lessons..."

"*What* lessons?"

"Perhaps that is a better question for Mr. Courtland."

"That *jackal*," Elisabeth said on a breath. "He's been playing Cupid all along and failed to inform me."

"Well, you work very closely with his lordship and Her Grace at the foundation," said Jocelyn. "The contrivance might have been too great—if you knew of his plan, that is."

"Regardless, he should have told me."

"And what would you have done?"

"Well, forbidden it, for one." Elisabeth returned to the bench. "I...I will be so angry if he breaks her heart."

"Is it possible Mr. Courtland designed it the other way around?"

"What do you mean?"

"Instead of breaking the duchess's heart, is it possible that she will mend the viscount's?"

There was a pause. "*Ohhh*. But could it be? To be honest, it makes perfect sense. How exactly like Bryson in every way." She thought a moment more. "No wonder he sent *me* in with the dog. He was afraid of what he might find."

"Oh yes, the dog. She told me."

"I embarrassed her with my intrusion. I did try gainfully to put her at ease, but...they were rather preoccupied."

"He's told her they should not really see each other again after today."

"What? He kissed her as if they could not bear to be apart."

"Of this I have no doubt. And yet he is very determined to stay away. He threatened to leave the country."

"Good God, not this again. He cannot go now. I need him for at least two more raids before Stoker and Joseph return to school. I've yet to find a replacement for him." She paused again. "I never thought I would say this, but...I worry we may need to help them along."

"You're joking," said Jocelyn, laughing now. "These are rare words, coming from you. You mean 'help them,' as your aunt helped you with your husband? If only Lady Banning could hear you say it."

"Perhaps Lady Banning should have thought of this before she moved to a tropical island halfway around the world. But let us think. What *would* Aunt Lillian do if she were here?"

"She would fall in love with the gardener," said a voice behind them, "and we'd be left with no one to care for the greenhouse through winter."

The women spun to see Lady Frinfrock rounding the corner, with cane and pruning shears. Behind her, a footman carried a bundle of dead trimmings.

"Lady Frinfrock," said Jocelyn, jumping up. "We didn't hear you there."

"Well, I've heard you, plainly as day. 'Tis my garden, after all."

"Quite so," Jocelyn chuckled. "Elisabeth just caught me as I returned home from the Duchess of Ticking's dower house."

"Oh, yes, *the dowager duchess*," said the marchioness. "I've had an earful about her, haven't I? Cannot say I'm surprised, to be honest. Common girl, really. Married above her reach. Carrying on in the ballroom and God knows where else. Really, Miss Breedlowe, I expect more from you."

"Emmaline is lovely," Miss Breedlowe scolded. "You've said so yourself. And anyway, I have not been charged with chaperoning her. 'Tis her brother I look after."

The marchioness waved the notion away. "Who can keep up with your myriad occupations, Miss Breedlowe, I ask you? No, no, do not answer. And *you*"—she turned to

Elisabeth—"what is it about that house of yours? It veritably begs for inappropriate behavior; nay, it breeds it."

Elisabeth made a scoffing noise. "Beau requires no special setting in which to behave inappropriately. He's shameless, and you know it. And now"—she rubbed two fingers over her forehead—"and now my friend has fallen prey."

"*Now* she's fallen?" the marchioness spat. "Well, you're blind, if this is what you think. Their affection was plainly obvious at the tea when you announced your baby. Their prolonged gazes very nearly scorched the drapes from the windows."

There was a time when Jocelyn had trembled at the very sound of the old woman's voice, but she was braver now. Her time spent in the company of Piety Falcondale and Elisabeth Courtland taught her gumption. Now she could ignore the marchioness's bluster and listen for what she really meant.

"My lady," Jocelyn began curiously, "do *you* believe Her Grace to be a good match for Lord Rainsleigh?"

"Don't be ridiculous, Miss Breedlowe," said the marchioness. "I haven't the time or inclination to consider such things. *A good match.* What care have I if they suit or if they do not, so long as they aren't permitted to carry on indecorously in my street."

Jocelyn nodded thoughtfully and looked at her boots. "Pity, that, because Elisabeth and I were hopeful for them. But now Lord Rainsleigh refuses to see her…"

She allowed the sentence to trail off. Thunder clapped in the distance, and the footman standing stoically behind the marchioness coughed.

Lady Frinfrock raised her cane at him.

"But of course he refuses to see her," Lady Frinfrock said after a moment. "She's made herself too available. Summoning him to rescue her brother, and I can only guess how she's conveyed her gratefulness." The marchioness huffed. "As if there was any doubt that Rainsleigh could locate the boy."

Jocelyn hid a smile. "Quite. But how would you achieve it, my lady, if you wished to nudge them together? That is, without causing the duchess to appear 'too available'?"

"Well, I should think it would be very obvious. I would host a ball."

Elisabeth made a face. "A ball?"

"But of course. It worked in my day, and for good reason. The duchess is a pretty little thing, despite her horrible gray dresses. Pretty enough to invite the interest of other men, certainly. If the viscount could be made to attend, his reaction to her popularity would be very telling indeed. Either he will declare himself or he will not."

Elisabeth was shaking her head. "I hardly think anything as frivolous as a ball would—"

"Better than what's been achieved so far," cut in Lady Frinfrock, "rescuing brothers and learning manners or whatever schemes the lot of you has concocted."

Jocelyn crinkled up her nose, "Who told you about—"

In the same moment Elisabeth exclaimed, "*You* also knew?"

Lady Frinfrock continued, talking over them. "At least a proper ball is decent. With appropriate chaperones— watchful ladies and gentleman of a certain age. It may take some contrivance to ensure she attends. She is in mourning, for God's sake. Let me think on this. And the viscount will resist it, naturally, but if bad comes to worse, then I will speak to him."

Elisabeth raised a hand. "Wait, wait. Who among us is meant to host a ball? I don't know the first thing about it, nor do I wish to."

Lady Frinfrock turned and thrust the pruning shears at the footman behind her. "The Countess of Falcondale will do it. She's been pining to host a ball for an age, and her house is finally complete. The timing is perfect."

"I'm not sure," hedged Elisabeth. "It seems too simple. There is no guarantee that Beau would attend. He hardly responds well to a summons."

"Leave the guest list to me," said the marchioness, already stumping away. "Of course you haven't bothered to learn this about me, but I was born on the eve of the New Year nearly a hundred years ago. Perhaps this year, I am in the mood to celebrate."

CHAPTER TWENTY-SEVEN

After he was discovered in the ballroom with Emmaline, Beau made a point to stay away for a week. The first of many weeks away, he told himself. Christmas came and went, and Beau passed it alone on the canal with his dog. For the first time, he considered the irony that *people* made one lonesome, not the lack thereof.

He'd spent countless Christmases alone without a care in the world, but now that he knew Emmaline and was at odds with his brother, loneliness threatened to overwhelm him.

But he would not allow himself to see Emmaline because he could not give her the devotion she deserved. And he would not see his brother because he did want to tell him why he would never be viscount. Beau could not feign laziness or invoke his hatred of establishment forever. Not after he'd essentially played along with the title in front of the Duke of Ticking. Bryson would never allow him to go back.

So Beau had stayed away, miserable on his boat with Peach, with the occasional visit from Benjamin and Jason.

Finally, on Boxing Day, Beau decided to embark on the final brothel raid before Stoker and Joseph returned to school.

He'd never intended to raid brothels indefinitely, but he could finish what he began with their current target, the truly abhorrent brothel he'd been scouting for months. He could enjoy the boys' cocksure, youthful competence and set up Elisabeth with at least a dozen girls before he decided what he would do and where he would go next.

They devoted two more days to surveillance and then set upon the brothel in the early morning hours. The night was cold and clear, with a bright moon that illuminated the patches of ice on the roads. He ambled casually inside as a customer, one of his favorite ruses. Meanwhile, the raiding team disarmed guards and slipped into back doors and windows. Twenty minutes later, they hustled out with fifteen girls, a deaf stable boy, and a forty-year-old woman who wished to consider a new life.

The thrill of success never failed to exhilarate him, but when the raid had come and gone, he could see nothing for his current misery but to make some real plan to go away. All the way *away*. Farther than Paddington or Essex or even Europe. She was going to America, he knew, so the most prudent thing to do was to go in exactly the opposite way.

He was studying a map of the world when the invitation came. A ball, hosted by Lord and Lady Falcondale, to celebrate New Year's Eve.

He tossed it into the fire.

He did not think of the invitation again until the personal entreaties began. First, Bryson, who sought him out in his favorite pub in Southwark. His brother actually ordered a drink and hunched over the bar. He ate chestnuts. After five minutes of meaningless chatter, he got to the heart of the matter.

"You've called to Falcondale's home on numerous occasions," Bryson said. "You like the man. Don't you see? This ball is the rare opportunity to turn up at an elevated function as a proper member of society *and* be comfortable, all at the same time. And why not mark the coming of the New Year at a gay party? Be a civilized member of this family for once in your life."

Beau had chuckled sadly, paid for his drink, inquired after Elisabeth's health, and said *no*.

Next, Elisabeth had approached him at the foundation. Her request had been a subtler, more casual, *oh-what-could-it-hurt* sort of thing, but then she'd made the mistake of suggesting he do it as a favor to Bryson. Beau said no.

Finally, Lady Frinfrock had come. All the way to Paddington. Her carriage had trundled off the road and rolled nearly to the bank of the canal. Her footmen and a very concerned-looking Miss Breedlowe had handed her down to the very water's edge.

"Beauregard Courtland," she had called, shading her eyes with her hand, "you cannot mean to have abandoned Henrietta Place to take up residence in this sewer."

"Good morning, Lady Frinfrock," he'd said. "In fact, I have done." He'd been untangling rigging on the deck—strenuous, dirty work—and he'd stood in buckskins, tall boots, and an open shirt with the sleeves rolled back, and a coil of rope over his left shoulder. He hadn't bothered with a hat, and the cold December wind had whipped his hair wildly away from his face. Despite the physical nature of this task, experience suggested this was not an altogether unappealing picture for her ladyship. He'd affected a mock bow.

"But just look at the sight of you!" she had called. "Have you no servants to do the work of restoring this...this vessel?"

" 'Tis only me, my lady—and you, if you've finally consented to steal away with me."

"Clever as always, despite your inhuman dwelling. But where do you take your meals or wash?"

"I've a cook stove in the cabin. It lacks only your loving care to provide nightly hot meals of porridge or gruel for us. And I bathe in the canal, obviously." This reference had been made with a discreet wink at Miss Breedlowe.

" 'Tis no wonder your brother worries so for your future. You'll either drown or rot, eking out a wretched existence here. I had hoped for an invitation to take tea, but I cannot risk my health to remain, even for ten minutes. I've come only to deliver a message, and then I will away before Miss Breedlowe and I catch our death."

"Message?" Beau had hopped onto the shore.

"My neighbor, the Countess of Falcondale, will host a ball in honor of my birthday in four days hence. I would that you were there."

Beau had expected this, and he'd said, "You couldn't know this, my lady, but I have sworn off balls until—"

"I've not dragged myself or my vehicle to this godforsaken corner to hear excuses, Rainsleigh. To show your face, even for an hour, will not do you any great harm, despite what you think. It is my only birthday wish."

He'd laughed. "Now this I cannot believe."

"Believe? You *believe* that you accomplish something important by relegating yourself to this ditch, far from proper home and hearth, but I am here to inform you that you are very wrong. This canal proves nothing but your obstinacy. But you are diverting and handsome, and the ball shall be an interminable bore if you do not attend. I demand it."

Beau had opened his mouth to offer up yet another denial, but the marchioness had affected a small cough, then two, then four. They'd been weak, pitiful things, and even Miss Breedlowe had stared at her with incredulity.

"Are you quite all right?" Beau had asked, hiding a smile.

"And what if I am not? Perhaps I am old and ill and will expire in the cold, hard winter we are sure to suffer when January comes. Perhaps I will never see another springtime. Perhaps this will be my very *last* birthday in this earthly coil."

Beau had looked at Miss Breedlowe, who'd shrugged resignedly, and then back at the marchioness. "Are you suggesting I should attend your birthday celebration at the risk of your sudden death?"

"No one knows when life's very breath will be yanked from our lungs, my dear boy. I know this better than most people and certainly better than you. You would not risk yourself in these conditions if you understood the fleeting nature of good health. We must seize opportunities when they arise, which is why I consented to the ball in the first place, and why I have ventured into the wilds of Paddington to insist that you attend me there."

"Well, if you insist..." Beau had said. How could he say no, when she had threatened to die to compel him? Although really, it had been the compliment—"diverting and handsome," was it?—that had convinced him. He knew the old bat enjoyed him, but this was high praise indeed.

"Very well, it's all settled," she had said, waving away any opportunity for him to oppose her again. And then she had turned to go, sending her footman scrambling to hoist her into her carriage while Miss Breedlowe had held her cane and the train of her skirts. "Proper dress and an attitude of openness as well, Rainsleigh!" she had called from inside the carriage. Before Beau could say, *Don't count on it*, she had rolled away.

And now here he was, trudging to Falcondale's front stoop amid a swirl of ball-goers, his head bent behind the upturned collar of his evening jacket, his boots shined, his gold watch—which he would check repeatedly, marking sixty minutes—in his pocket.

Falcondale's wife had hired a butler called Bevins, and, wisely, the man had swallowed his request to announce Beau. There would be no announcement, no footman to lead him to the hosts, and Beau would not linger for the midnight buffet. The hosts would be lucky if he waved as he sailed out the door in one hour's time.

He clipped down the steps to the ballroom, keeping close to the wall, and veered straight for the drinks table. After he'd downed first one drink and then the next, he ordered a third and glanced around the ballroom, taking note of who had come, how reliably far they stood from him, and, most important, if anyone had noticed he'd arrived. If he was very lucky, no one would notice at all.

Falcondale's wealthy American wife had spared no expense in restoring the house, which she'd bought four years ago when she'd moved to London. Beau searched for her now, sipping his drink, welcoming the warm, loosening sensation the spirits released in his bloodstream. He located Lord and Lady Falcondale, standing beneath a heavy swag of garland that hung from a set of towering double doors. Lady Falcondale smiled and extended her hands to the next trussed-up couple who waited in line to greet them. Falcondale stood stoically beside her with a grim expression of measured endurance.

Poor sod, he thought, turning his attention to the other guests, hoping to spot Lady Frinfrock. When he'd devoted ten minutes to her entertainment, he'd be that much closer to the door.

He had just shoved off the drinks table to amble to the windows when he saw her. Emmaline. Here at the holiday ball. But why? He stopped walking and stared. He'd not seen her since his brother's ballroom. She'd occupied nearly his every waking thought since that time and all of his dreams.

But why was she here?

She wore another of her oppressive gray dresses, and she was seated among women two and three times her age, many of them also dressed in gray or black. In her arms, she held an infant, squalling and red-faced. Beside her sat another woman in gray, presumably the new Duchess of Ticking, judging from her lordly expression and—oh hell, it was just a guess. Behind them both stood the Duke of Ticking, staring out at the dancers with an assessing scowl, as if he had been named judge of the dancers, and he found them all lacking.

And then—Beau blinked, not believing his eyes—there was Emmaline's brother, Teddy. Teddy was here at the bloody ball. He stood half-beside, half-behind the Duke of Ticking, his hair combed back and a dark suit bunching at every joint and juncture on his lanky frame. His face was tight with an expression of quiet terror. His Grace clasped Teddy by the shoulder, one pale hand holding him still.

But why had they come? Moreover, why had they been invited? Lord Falcondale had helped to search for Teddy Holt, and he knew well of the duke's unfair control of Emmaline and the boy. If, for some reason, he did not remember, or Lady Falcondale did not know, then Bryson and Elisabeth knew it all too well.

And yet here was Emmaline, clearly miserable, minding a baby while her brother suffered four feet away. She looked trapped and frantic at the same time. Her eyes darted from her brother, down at the baby, and then out at the crowd again.

Beau began to walk, weaving his way through the dancers, around a small forest of potted ferns, through more dancers. Men exclaimed and women gasped as he shouldered them out of the way. He was nearly to her when his brother, Bryson, along with Elisabeth, Joseph, and Stoker intercepted him.

"Beau, wait," said Bryson. He put his hand on Beau's shoulder.

Beau paused, grateful for a preliminary repository for his anger. "Bryson, do not," he said, staring at the hand.

"For God's sake," his brother said in his ear, "the last thing she needs is a scene. Grant me two minutes before you go charging in. We've been trying to help her since she arrived, but if handled wrongly, the duke and duchess could pose a considerably greater obstacle in the days to come. We must remember the final goal is to get her out of the country, as planned."

Beau relented long enough for Bryson and Elisabeth to shuffle him out of the path of the dancers, but he craned his head, not wanting to let her out of view. "Why is she here?" he snapped.

Elisabeth said, "Piety invited the Duke and Duchess of Ticking and their elder children—Piety invited all of London, I'm afraid—but we never thought they'd attend."

"Who invited *her brother*?" Beau said, grinding out the words. "Crowds unsettle and confuse him. She's worried sick about him—just look at her."

Elisabeth said, "Teddy was not invited, but apparently His Grace has taken to dragging him everywhere in an effort to show how devoted he is to the boy's care." She glanced at the duke. "And to demonstrate to the world how Teddy struggles."

Beau swore. "But why would any of them come? I only consented myself because I assumed the guest list included no one of consequence. I had no idea they'd be here."

Elisabeth made a scoffing sound, and Bryson cut in, "Lady Frinfrock sent a special invitation to Her Royal Highness Princess Charlotte. When word came down that she intended to come, the guest list doubled."

Beau started. "Princess Charlotte is coming here?"

"Apparently." Bryson straightened his lapels. "It would seem that she shares an interest in gardening and has become friendly with Lady Frinfrock from meetings of the Royal Society of Horticulture. Naturally, all of London has turned out to see Her Royal Highness. Including the Duke of Ticking and his family."

"But why has he brought an *infant?*" hissed Beau, watching the baby grab hold of one of Emmaline's earrings and pull.

"God only knows," said Elisabeth. To her credit, she looked nearly as worried as Beau felt. "Emmaline has been charged with minding the baby all night while the duke and duchess watch their older girls dance."

As if on cue, three young women filtered from the dance floor to crowd around the Duke and Duchess of Ticking. They wore gray, like Emmaline, but in shades more akin to lavender or fawn or silver. Only Emmaline wore a dress the color of wet ash. Beau gritted his teeth, watching as the girls milled around their parents, paying absolutely no mind to Emmaline or Teddy. They preened and fanned themselves, casting appraising glances at the other dancers and whispering.

One of them cackled, a high, whooping sound that rang out above the music, and Beau saw Teddy jolt, stagger back, and squirm under Ticking's hold. The duke gave him a harsh look and a shake, and the boy stilled. The girls laughed again, while Emmaline bit her lip and squeezed her eyes shut.

"We must get them away from here," Beau said, his anger strumming through his veins. "Teddy may bolt at any moment, and I wouldn't blame him."

"True," said Bryson, "but, as I've said, we only complicate the dowager duchess's situation by making demands or acting rashly now. All of London is watching, Beau—just as His Grace designed it."

Beau ignored Bryson and stepped around him, signaling for Stoker and Joseph. The boys fell in behind him without question.

"Take care, Beau," Bryson said. "I understand your haste, but please be aware the situation is very precarious."

Beau could barely hear his brother over the sound of the music and laughter and the blood roaring in his own ears. He strode up to Emmaline and stopped. He had no clear notion of what he intended to say or do, save helping her.

At first, she did not see him. The baby cried, and she shushed and bobbed him in her arms. But gradually, awareness dawned, and she looked up. When her eyes registered him, she sucked in a little breath.

The jolt of her eyes looking up nearly propelled Beau to reach down, take her up, and haul her through the ballroom and out the door.

"Hello," he said steadily, not taking his eyes from her.

"Lord Rainsleigh," she managed in a whisper.

Before he could speak again, the duke's daughters took notice of him, and he and Joseph and Stoker were suddenly surrounded by their fluttering and sidling and simpering.

"Why, Grandmama," trilled one of the girls, a top-heavy blonde with small eyes and unfortunate teeth, "won't you introduce us to your friends?"

Emmaline's expression did not change. She held Beau's gaze for a long moment and then looked to the girl. "The Lady Dora Crumbley, the Lady Marie Crumbley, and the Lady Bella Crumbley, please make the acquaintance of"— she swung her gaze back to Beau, and he gave the slightest nod—"the Viscount Rainsleigh and his friends Mr. Jon Stoker and Mr. Joseph Chance."

At the mention of the title, the trilling and fanning intensified. He might hate the title, but they would not, despite it being less elevated their father's. Regardless, he was very much at home with captivated females. He winked discreetly to Emmaline and then turned his most rakish, golden smile on the girls.

"How do you do? What a pleasure. Tell me your names again, so I may discern one beauty from the next..."

With the expected enthusiasm, the young women's eyes grew wide, and they affected small, breathless little gasps and descended. Fans fluttered, hands were raised for a kiss, and eyelashes batted. They were a swarm of locusts that had been waiting for little more than to gobble him up.

CHAPTER TWENTY-EIGHT

Emmaline hadn't seen the viscount for ten days.

He had not written or called when she and her brother had been forced to leave the dower house and take rooms on the top floor of the duke's townhome. She had not seen him during any of the brief, clandestine meetings she'd had with Elisabeth and Bryson to finalize the arrangements for her sailing to New York.

She had managed the last-minute details on her own, exactly as she had taught herself to do. She actually had assumed Lord Rainsleigh had left the country, just as he said he would.

After a year of painful changes and realizations, having him simply go was a new and different kind of hurt, almost physical in nature, like a wound somewhere between her heart and her throat.

Despite how much she wished that she were mistaken, that he would suddenly appear, she found that she resented him a little more every day. As if her current obstacles weren't enough, now she would be charmed and kissed and helped by him, only to have him leave her behind without a proper good-bye or even a good reason.

She could solve her other problems—not easily, but she was determined to solve them—while Beau Courtland could not be solved by anyone.

He was simply *lost* from her.

Gone.

The new feeling of this man, whom she enjoyed very much (almost more than anyone else, if she were being honest), had been there for a time. But now...he was not.

Lost.

An unplugged hole in her day and in her heart.

Except now he wasn't lost. Or he wasn't in this moment—this miserable, precarious, wretched moment, possibly the worst one since her brother had gone missing. He'd appeared in all of his golden, handsome, blue-eyed glory to stand before her in a fine evening suit with a folded cravat, snowy white against his tan face, and polished boots. And then he raised one irresistible eyebrow. She could not remember ever having seen him so cleanly shaven and properly turned out.

And to think, she marveled in spite of herself, she had assumed he could never look more handsome than he had in his long coat and buckskins.

She swallowed, trying to control whatever expression was borne of her reaction to him. The other females in his orbit made no such effort, and even the Duchess of Ticking sat up a little straighter, pulling her cloying, obsessive attention away from the duke for perhaps the first time ever.

Dora, Marie, and Bella were shamelessly affected, crowding around him as if he were Father Christmas. The girls were so delighted by his attention that even the Duke of Ticking, who must have remembered the viscount from the search for Teddy, said nothing and watched with bemused detachment.

Oh, and the viscount entertained them. He asked sly, provocative questions, listened intently to their answers, and simply *presided* (for there was no better word) over their corner of the ballroom. His attention was so controlled, almost predatory, the entirety of the swirling ballroom behind him seemed to fade away.

It was as dashing as any iteration Emmaline had ever seen of him. His smile was sincere and held just a hint of provocation; his gaze was direct and intimate. He made some inappropriately specific compliment (just as she had bade him not to do) about each of the Duke of Ticking's daughters' hats, or the diminutive size of their delicate hands, or the unique color of their satin dancing slippers.

He was so intoxicating, in fact, that for one breathless, heartbreaking moment, Emmaline thought he had come to flirt with them in earnest. But then he gestured to Teddy and said, "Ladies, you'll forgive me, but I must be introduced to this strapping young man behind us. Pray, who can do me the honor?"

Collectively, the girls scrunched up their noses, confused by any interest whatsoever in Teddy. But they were nothing if not urgently eager to please the handsome, effusive viscount, and Lady Dora piped up immediately, her voice a conspiratorial whisper, "Oh, you cannot mean Teddy. But Teddy is a dolt. Do you see how Father must take him by the shoulder to keep him from running mad through the ballroom? The music unsettles him. And the crowds. Really, I believe everything unsettles him but books and birds and being locked alone in his room."

The other two girls giggled their approval of this statement, flapping their fans and nodding so vigorously the feathers in their headpieces threatened to molt to the floor.

Tears of hot rage shot to Emmaline's eyes, and she squeezed little Henrick in her arms. The baby let out a squawk, and she looked down at him, grateful for anywhere to look beyond the mean-spirited delight in Dora's face.

"Books and birds and his room?" she heard Beau repeat, his voice echoing their laughter.

Emmaline looked up, confused at his purpose. His smile was relaxed, his eyes laughing, but there was a hardness around the corners of his mouth, and his grip on the goblet in his hand looked very tight, threateningly tight, like he might snap the crystal just as easily as he laughed. He was angry at their coarseness, even if only she could see it. But why call attention to her brother? Emmaline didn't understand.

He went on. "But I do believe I *know* this young man. *Teddy Holt*...why, yes, I do. We all know him, don't we, Stoker? Joseph?"

The young men had each sidled up to one of the duke's daughters while Beau honed in on Dora. They laughed and nodded now too.

"He looks like he could do with a bit of fresh air," Beau suggested, a note of conspiracy in his voice.

He leaned very close to Lady Dora and winked. "Do you think, my lady, that Teddy Holt"—he chuckled again— "would allow my friends Joseph and Stoker to take him for a turn around the terrace while I made a special appeal to your father, man to man? You'll forgive my formality, but I am old-fashioned, and His Grace's reputation precedes him. I'll not presume any liberties without His Grace's express permission."

Lady Dora paused in her fluttering for half a beat, allowing the suggestions of his request to permeate her brain, and she then flung herself in the direction of her father. Here, she fluttered and bobbed, pointing at Teddy with an overburdened frown. The orchestra had embarked on a particularly rousing anthem, and the volume drowned out her words, but her mother heard, and now she was engaged. The Duchess of Ticking turned to her husband and pointed at Teddy with her closed fan, the undeniable gesture of *out*.

The duke protested mildly, not understanding what they wished or why. This prompted the duchess to rise from her chair and take Teddy by the hand. With a scowl on her face, she wrenched the boy free. Emmaline held her breath. How Teddy hated to be pulled and constrained. And he was already so frightened.

But Beau was ready, and he gestured to Stoker and Joseph, and, God love them, the two young men inserted themselves smoothly amid Lady Dora and the duchess, patting Teddy on the back and whispering in his ear.

Teddy recognized them at once—they'd been there the night he'd been recovered—and he went easily to them. A minute later, they shuffled him away, Joseph's arm around Teddy's shoulder like they were old friends. Stoker cut a line through the crowd to the terrace, leading the way, and they were gone.

Emmaline looked at Beau. He glanced back, one quick look, so fast that surely only she saw, and then he stepped up to the duke and duchess, winking at their daughters, who now crowded around him in breathless anticipation.

"Good evening, Your Graces," Beau said, bowing slightly to the duke and duchess. "Please forgive the interruption, but I should like to ask your permission to dance with"—the duke frowned at him, while his daughters and wife held their collective breath—"your stepmother, the Dowager Duchess of Ticking."

"*What?*" hissed Lady Dora, the first to grasp the unexpected and insulting direction of his request. The duke and duchess were still struggling to hear what he'd said.

Meanwhile, Beau pivoted a half turn and scooped the twitching, fussy baby Henrick from Emmaline's arms. "I know you must be the beloved sister of this dear child," he said to Lady Dora, "because you share the vivid sapphire color of your eyes."

And before she could respond, he deposited the infant in her arms with such force and finality that she was given no choice but to accept him or let him drop into her skirts.

When the baby was gone, Beau turned again, grabbed Emmaline by the hand, and tugged her up.

In the next breath, he whisked her away from the stunned ducal family in one deft, seamless movement.

They were at the edge of the dance floor two beats later, and then the music rose, and Beau moved again, a sort of fluid lunge, and she found herself pulled into a waltz.

"Smile," Beau commanded, and he fixed his own face with a gentle smile.

Emmaline did not smile. She could only guess that her expression was something akin to a gape. How could she smile and behave as if it was perfectly natural to be seated in the corner one moment and whirling around the dance floor in the next? Especially when she believed the dance partner to be half an ocean away?

He was the first to speak. "What are you doing here?" His voice was flat and demanding.

What are you doing here? she thought, but she answered him because it was the polite thing to do. "I was minding the duke and duchess's infant and praying my brother would survive the night." Gradually, her wits were returning. She added, "What are you doing here?"

"Dancing," he said simply.

The music swelled again, and he spun her. On a different night, under different circumstances, she might have laughed in delight at the proficiency of his dancing and the almost flying feel of gliding around the dance floor in his arms.

The combination of seeing him, and seeing such a dazzling version of him, and now being held by him—even within the confines of the stiff, formal dance—set off a heady sort of buzzing inside her head and her belly. She existed for a moment in a dream. The moment would not—could not—be real or governed by the laws of time and space.

She would not describe her reaction as happiness so much as…*not* reality.

Slowly, she felt her expression soften into a sort of mystified skepticism, as if someone had dosed her with an elixir of which she did not trust the effects.

He finished. "Against my better judgment."

"Better judgment in what?" she said, laughing. Surely he would not go to the bother of flirting with Lady Dora and extracting Teddy, only to say he now he regretted it.

He said, "My better judgment in anything at all to do with you."

Or perhaps he would say it. The dreamlike nature of the moment dissolved, and she went rigid, dancing the steps but barely touching his hand in hers. She cleared her throat. "It's lovely to see you, Rainsleigh, really it is, but I've quite enough trouble in my life without the worry that you'll turn up and put yourself out by...how did you say it? Doing 'anything at all to do with' me. If you must complain about coming to my aid, then why come at all?"

"I was tricked," he said. "Lady Frinfrock." He rolled his shoulders, gathering her more closely against him— scandalously close. She could not help but touch him. "She actually came to the canal and suggested that she would expire if I did not attend. I had no idea you would be here."

Emmaline narrowed her eyes at him, feeling her own irritation double with every turn of the waltz. "Are you suggesting that you would not have come if you'd known? Good God, Rainsleigh, I see now why your brother wished to hire me. I don't care how dashing you are; you truly are unfit for decent company."

"My brother did not hire you to teach me bollocks," he said, spinning her again. The ballroom was a blur of jewel-toned silk, evergreen, and candlelight. "I see that now. He was matchmaking. He tossed us together intentionally, because he'd happened upon a girl who appeared to be the perfect combination of temptation and a good bloody influence."

Emmaline opened her mouth to suggest, perhaps, that he simply stop talking so they could enjoy the dance without saying anything more that either of them would regret, but he lifted her up on the next spin, just a little scoop, and her feet left the floor, her skirts whirled around her ankles, and she veritably sailed around the corner of the ballroom in a way that took her breath away.

He made a small, irresistible noise of exertion and set her down without missing a step. They came to the next corner, and they whirled again. Their dancing had become sweeping and athletic, and she was forced to hold tightly to his muscled shoulder and squeeze his hand to keep up. All the while, he continued in that low, flat tone. "You were meant to bewitch me. I would be resentful if I did not enjoy you so bloody much."

High praise, she wanted to say, but the dancing took all of her concentration. She was breathless with the effort and exhilaration.

"I would also resent *Bryson* if he didn't assume, clearly, that I could possibly, remotely, be suitable for a woman like you. Only my brother, blinded by his love for me, would know my every fault and still see me as a suitable match."

Between the complicated dancing and his flat, unreadable tone, Emmaline could scarcely understand what the devil he meant. It sounded as if he'd just paid her a marginal compliment. As if he was revealing that he...enjoyed her company.

She looked up at him, studying his face. Her irritation began to warm into something more like frustrated confusion.

Beau went on. "As always, he aspires too much. For me, that is."

She was not sure how to answer. She tried. "I thought he genuinely wished for me to teach you something. I thought he wanted me to instruct you on basic good manners."

"He wanted you to captivate me. The manners were an added benefit, I'm sure."

Emmaline thought about this. How bad it must feel, whether real or imagined, that he'd been manipulated, even for his own good end. She had some idea of this. Her mother had done that very same thing when she'd married her off at age nineteen.

Beau said, "This song will soon end. I'm not finished. We'll dance again. To the next song, whatever it is."

Emmaline tried to look around, but the room still spun. "It would never do to dance two songs in succession. People will talk. The duke and duchess will be already irate." She thought of Lady Dora. "This does not bode well for my brother. I…I cannot dance again, Beau. I must find him."

"Joseph and Stoker have Teddy in a safe place until we're finished. And we're not finished."

Just as he predicted, the music softened to silence. Beau glided two more steps and then went still. For two beats, he released her, took a small step back, and bowed. Just as the music began again, he took up her hand and waist and pulled her into new steps.

She was powerless to resist him. "I hope you do not believe that I meant to"—she searched for the correct word—"entrap you in some way."

"No," he said, looking over her shoulder at the route they'd cut across the floor, "not you. Only my brother. And Elisabeth, the traitor. And now bloody Lady Frinfrock. It doesn't matter. For some reason, they look at me and see only potential, not risk. As if you did not already have enough problems."

It occurred to her that he was saying these words to her, but the conversation was actually with himself alone. He was coming to terms with his brother's meddling. Why he wrangled with it here and now, she could not guess. But she listened, trying to understand why he suffered some sort of internal turmoil each time he looked at her.

"You are an excellent dancer," she finally said. The truth. These were certainly the most exciting dances of her sheltered life. "I would not have guessed that you enjoyed dancing."

"Viscounts are expected to dance, aren't they? Naturally, this would mean I should hate it. But I wasn't always a viscount, was I? Before you knew me, I enjoyed dancing very much." An afterthought. He wasn't really listening. He stared at the Duke of Ticking's party as they danced past.

"Who brings an infant to a bloody New Year's ball?" he asked.

Emmaline cringed, thinking of tired, fussy baby Henrick. "The duke and duchess have taken to bringing their youngest child with us whenever the family ventures out. I think His Grace wishes to make a show of my role as grandmama. And to keep others away. Nothing discourages conversation like a crying baby."

Beau nodded. "And Teddy? Why subject him to a ball?"

Emmaline squeezed her eyes shut, thinking of her brother. "Yes, why indeed. Teddy has been dragged out repeatedly at the duke's side. I believe the message is, Teddy is very much in his keeping, an invalid, unfit to be left alone, even for a moment. And of course, I am unfit to mind him. Ticking moved us from the dower house the day after I saw you in the ballroom."

"Is it terrible?"

"Well, I mind the children, I suffer constant supervision with no freedom, and my brother endures the repeated torture of family outings, regardless of how the chaos upsets him. It is killing us both, but I hold to the hope of our escape to New York. The new life that will allow us to forget this time. It is the only thing that gets me through."

"Emmaline," he said, not looking at her, "you know that if you were to marry, His Grace would have no control over you. You would not have to forge a new life in another country if you did not care to do. You would not have to do anything at all but walk away from the Ticking dukedom, and good riddance."

Emmaline was so stunned by this statement that she almost stopped dancing. In fact, she did miss a step, but he easily propelled her around.

"Marry?" She could barely form the word. She tried to laugh and failed. "Whom, I ask you, am I meant to marry?" And now she did laugh, a sad, bitter sound. "My dowry was taken by the previous Duke of Ticking. The current duke does his best to present me to the world as a nanny, smothered in hideous gray and perpetually carrying a baby. I have a brother who will require special care for the rest of his life. Before I was a duchess, I was the daughter of a merchant—a rich merchant, yes, but a merchant who came from nothing, just the same." She laughed again. "Who, I ask you, would marry me?"

To this, Beau had no answer, but he effected another of the swooping, airy turns, lifting her around the corner of the room.

She landed with a little gasp. It was impossible to dance in his arms and not be breathless. She tried to find the words to tell him that she had no wish to be married again. That she had a plan about which she was excited and intended to see through, achieving something on her own terms for once in her life. The music swelled to a final, soaring note, ending the song with the pure, joyful blast, and Beau held her until she was steady on her feet.

She caught her breath just as the music faded to wild applause, and before she could tell him anything more, he looked at her and said, "Well, you could marry me."

CHAPTER TWENTY-NINE

Beau had known he would propose marriage to her from the moment he'd seen her sitting across the ballroom with the ducal family, holding a crying baby and enduring her brother's misery.

He'd known this in the same way he'd always known what he would do with any woman. When to tease, when to compliment, when to crowd against the wall for a kiss. It surprised him to learn that his proficiency extended to "when to propose marriage," and he was grateful he'd not been struck with the impulse before tonight.

But perhaps it boiled down to, *what bloody choice did he have?*

He could not toss her over his shoulder and steal away with her; he could not launch himself at the duke and stab him in the thigh with his dagger. But also, he could not see her so incredibly abused.

Were there other ways to remove her from this situation? Beau could not think of one. He also could not think of (or would not allow himself to think of) all the ways marriage had been unfathomable to him before this moment.

He would not think of the conventional marriage Emmaline deserved.

He would not think of his patent unsuitability as a husband.

He absolutely would not think of the high value he put on his own personal freedom.

Most of all, he would not think of how marriage would expand the bloody viscountcy, resulting in not one titled lord, but a lord and his lady. He didn't even want one Rainsleigh, and now there would be two.

But anything was better than bloody, bleeding Dowager Duchess of Ticking.

Whether in denial or simply because he refused to dwell, Beau thought of none of these. Instead, he thought only of her.

The song had ended, and members of the orchestra had chosen that moment to leave their instruments for refreshment and respite. The applause died around them, and in his peripheral vision, he saw couples filtering from the floor. They had but seconds. Standing there in the silence that threatened, looking down at the shock on her face, Beau had the fleeting thought that he might, for the first time ever, pass out cold on the floor.

"I beg your pardon?" she said, blinking up at him.

Of course she would make him repeat it. "If you feel no one else will have you, then why not marry me?" His mouth was dry. He had no idea how he'd said the words without a break in his voice. Without sounding like a quivery, high-pitched version of himself, which was exactly how he now felt.

"Beau," she began, shaking her head, "you honor me with this suggestion, but I cannot allow you to martyr yourself, not for me. Consider the magnitude of what you offer. You detest convention and contractual dealings and being tied down. These are the very definition of marriage. It would make my own situation more miserable to know I'd bound you in such a way, especially when you did it out of some misplaced sense of honor toward me."

It was a pretty speech, and it came out in a gush, almost as if she'd rehearsed it—which, oddly, made it worse. It had been a very long time, indeed, since any woman had denied him anything at all.

Still, she had not rejected him yet, not in as many words, and he was gripped with an unfamiliar sort of determination that would not allow him to look away from her. He raised an eyebrow.

She took a breath and went on. "I know I appear helpless and wretched at the moment, but I've only to survive a few weeks more. My plan is a complicated one, I know—risky and with no guarantee—but it's been many careful months in the making, and I am determined to give it a go. If it works, I'll not only set Teddy and myself free from this…this *family*, but it will allow me to realize the dream of my own."

"I have every belief that you will. I should like to help you."

"So in this marriage you propose, we should go to New York together?"

"Yes, of course. And how lucky you are that I am the sort of fellow who embraces travel to foreign ports and wild schemes."

"Yes, lucky," she repeated, but she did not appear to feel lucky. The head shaking continued, although her expression was conflicted and jittery and flushed. Beau looked right and left. They were very nearly the last couple remaining in the center of the ballroom. The Duke and Duchess of Ticking watched them from the sidelines, looking every bit as if they had been shot by a bolt of lightning, eyes bulging. Their golden goose was being stolen, right before their very eyes, and they knew it. It was just the boost Beau needed.

Beau returned his attention to Emmaline, winked, and took her by the arm. While she stared at him, he half led, half dragged her to the opposite side of the room and stopped on the far side of a fat marble pillar.

"Teddy and I will pay for the dances and this conversation," she said, looking over her shoulder.

"His Grace cannot stop a young widow from dancing with an attentive suitor, and he knows it." He propped an arm on the pillar above her head and looked down at her. She fell back against the cool marble and tilted her head up.

"Perhaps," she said, "but our existence inside his house can be made very nearly unlivable because of it. Every infraction will make it more and more difficult for us to steal away when the time comes."

"I don't want you in an unlivable situation, even for a day."

"And I don't want to marry a man who does not love me. I've done it once already, and it was misery."

This startled him into silence. He blinked and forced himself to close his mouth.

Love?

She was the last person he expected to press him for something quite so personal and intimate and emotional as love. Hadn't she first hounded him about polite detachment in all things? Wasn't that the proper way?

She waited, watching him. It was her turn to cock an eyebrow.

Finally, he said, "You see now why I endeavored to stay away from you. I told you that your heart was open and trusting; that someone like me had the potential to do it great harm."

"And yet now, here you are, proposing marriage. Quite a change of tune. What if I told you that, against all better judgment, I already love you? What say you then?"

Another shock. He forced himself to keep the reaction from his face. "I would say we've only known each other for a month."

She laughed. "Very well, then. I ask you the same thing about marriage. How could you propose marriage after you've only known me for a month?"

He opened his mouth to answer, but she held up a hand. "Stop. I've just watched Lady Dora embarrass herself at the mere suggestion of one dance with you. Women fall in love with you all the time, as we both know."

"That's different," he insisted. "Women like the Lady Dora fall into the kind of love that compels them to sneak out of their bedroom windows, or throw vases at walls, or eat nothing but chocolate for a week." He cleared his throat. "Or so I've been told. Not the kind of—" He looked away and then back again. "Not what you mean."

"Oh my God," she said, shaking her head at the bough of evergreen above their heads, "I am one of those women."

"Stop," he said, almost laughing. "Look, I've not considered marriage before—to you or anyone else—because I'm restless and easily distracted. These hardly are desirable traits for a proper husband. And the example I saw in my own parents' marriage was meaningless—no, it was worse than meaningless. Theirs was actively destructive. As a result, or perhaps as an homage, I've never considered faithfulness to any one woman, let alone marriage."

"Are you trying to convince me or repel me?" she asked.

He continued. "When I, er, discovered how truly innocent you are, I did try to repel you, Duchess, remember? What manner of man would I be if I did not try to protect you from me?"

"The manner of man who would *not* be proposing to me now."

"I'm proposing to you," he said, his voice lower now, serious—urgently serious, "because against all odds, you're in dire need of protection from something worse than I am. God save you, I feel compelled to provide it."

"You feel compelled?" She shoved off the pillar. Her breath came in deep little huffs. "You feel *compelled*? Let us stop talking, here and now, shall we?" She took a step. "I'd rather carry on with no one at all than with someone who *feels compelled*. My late husband felt compelled to marry me to line his own pockets, and I still suffer for that mistake."

"Yes," said Beau, "but he didn't want you, not as I do."

She looked up when he said this, her eyes growing wide, and he felt himself on more familiar, almost solid ground.

He reclaimed the step she'd taken. "Look, Emma. I cannot account for love, because I'm not entirely sure what it means, but I'm very, very sure what it means to *want*. And I want you, Duchess, very much. The size and nature of that want is crystal clear in my mind." He took another step closer and lowered his lips to her ear, speaking in a low, rumbling whisper. "I wasn't going to bring it up, considering your penchant for all things proper, but I would be telling a very great lie if I didn't admit that the appeal of knowing you as a husband knows a wife crosses my mind at least a hundred times a day."

She dropped her head back and stared at him. "So it is to be that kind of union?" Her voice was soft, and the look on her face swamped him with exactly the type of need he'd just described.

He ducked his head again, deliberately bussing her ear with his lips. "Of this you may have no doubts," he rasped.

Emmaline inhaled sharply and looked away, but he saw the flush rise on her cheeks. She swallowed and licked her lips. Beau stayed intimately close—close enough to feel the heat of her body. Close enough to smell her. He waited.

After a moment, she said, "The duke is on his way to us. I cannot hide in the shadows with you all night. Where have the boys taken Teddy?"

He looked up. The duke wound his way through the crowd like a man retrieving a dropped handkerchief. A very important, very *valuable* handkerchief. They watched him stump toward them.

Beau said, "Tomorrow I will apply for a special license." He held his breath.

She was silent, and he breathed again. Silence was not *no*.

"Evasion is converse to my usual way of doing things," he said, "but I believe we will be better served by apologizing to the duke tonight. Tell him we lost count of the songs. Feign idiocy. You'll bear the brunt of his outrage, I'm afraid. Will you be all right? I'll fetch Teddy."

"What choice do I have?" she said.

"Right." He gritted his teeth. He hated to leave her, but he'd exhibited enough rashness tonight to last a lifetime—and that was saying a lot, considering he was Beau Courtland. Still, he could not resist one parting shot, and he leaned down, in plain view of anyone occupying the shadowy space between the pillars and windows, and kissed her—one soft, sweet, slow kiss to her cheek. He lingered there, so close he could see the small hairs at the base of her neck, pulling from the horrible hat on top of her head.

He whispered, "I cannot promise that marriage to me will be proper or easy, but, Duchess"—he breathed in the scent of her—"surely it will be better than what you now endure. I promise it will be better than that."

He kissed her a second time on the cheek, and then he rose to stand behind her, one arm on her shoulder, another on her right hand. They faced the duke together, with Beau willing himself to be patient and genuinely surprised and contrite.

CHAPTER THIRTY

Emmaline would not allow herself to believe that the viscount's proposal was real until she actually saw him appear, in living flesh, in the home of the duke to extract her. In the meantime, she would carry on as if the ball had never happened.

He'd been vague and evasive with the Duke of Ticking after the dancing. Certainly, he made no allusion to a proposal or matrimony. He enthused only about his delight in Emmaline's company and meeting his daughters and what a "winning chap" Teddy had always been.

Whether Beau's silence on the matter was a predictive omission or cunning strategy, Emmaline could not know. It had been six days since the ball, and she'd had no word from him. He could be stealthily procuring a special license or halfway to Spain, for all she knew. Considering this, Emmaline was given little choice but to carry on as if he hadn't exploded into her little corner of misery and promised her the moon. Certainly there was endless work to be done: Meetings with her lawyer about her ownership of the books; calls to the bank for the withdrawal of the last of the generous-but-dwindling allowance her parents had left for Teddy's care before they'd sailed. This money would have to last them until the books began to sell in America. There were provisions to buy and letters to post ahead to shop owners in New York and the landlord of the house she would let. The list was long and varied and, worst of all, must now be achieved under the rash restrictions of the duke's fresh anger and his white-knuckled possessiveness.

It felt like a miracle, really, the myriad things she had accomplished in the week after the ball. But it wasn't a miracle, not really, nor was it courage or confidence, and certainly it was not the misguided hope that Beau would sweep in and rescue her. She did it all because she had no choice, first and foremost, and second, because she'd fallen in love. Being in love, she discovered, used up all the time and energy she would otherwise have devoted to being unsure, of cowering before the bellowing duke, or resenting the copious Ticking children.

Who could have guessed that her preoccupation with loving Beau Courtland would make her doubt less and risk more? Love, she realized, trumped bankers and lawyers and even the Duke of Ticking in the throes of a temper fit.

It was wrong to love him, she was sure. Ill-timed and short-lived, a one-way journey to certain heartbreak, but she'd decided to embrace it, if for no other reason than thinking about Beau twelve hours a day and dreaming about him all night kept all the other anxieties at bay.

Perhaps it would not have happened if she'd known more of love, if she'd ever before been tempted, even a little, to toss in her lot—heart, mind, body—with any man.

But she did not know more than this; in fact, she could not imagine anything quite so distinctive, and singular, and *essential* as the love for Beau she now felt—as if she really had no choice in the matter but to love him and certainly to marry him (if, indeed, he ever turned up to see through his genuinely unique and wholly endearing proposal).

It was a love so great, a love that had grown so quickly and unexpectedly from perhaps the first time she'd ever seen him slouching on his boat, she knew that if he did not come for her, or if he came for her but did not stay, there was a chance that she might never recover.

Oh, life would go on. She would eventually succeed enough to provide for herself. Her brother would be made safe, and she would probably even marry again. But the love that she now felt was so abstract yet also concrete, so urgent yet also spread so subtly beneath everything she did and felt that she knew she would be forever changed.

It felt as necessary as any other part of her, and she could not have stopped it if she had tried. It was a torrent, propelling her as much as pelting her in place. She marveled in the force of it and wondered how she'd managed to keep this love at bay.

And all of this, with not seeing him for six days.

And then, on the seventh day, he came, and the torrent raged in earnest.

He turned up just after breakfast. She and Teddy were seated in the drawing room with the seven or eight of the duke's children who were too old for a morning nap, yet too young for lessons. It had become the new routine to wait here daily, assisting various nannies and nursemaids, until the duke and duchess gave some indication of their plans for the day. After that, she would slip in or out of the house, based on whatever she could glean from staff about when the duke and duchess would go out, or nap, or receive callers.

Beau walked right in with no introduction from the butler, no elaborate whip of the door or ring of a bell for tea. In fact, he veritably *ambled* into the room, as if he too was a resident of the ducal household and thought he might have breakfast with eight or nine children that day.

If he hadn't been so good-looking, so golden-headed and blue-eyed and broad-shouldered, she was quite sure the nannies and maids would have sounded an alarm. But he was all of those things and more, dressed like a gentleman, albeit a little rumpled—exactly the right amount, a streak of mud on his boot, his waistcoat unbuttoned and loose—and the nursemaids paused in their work with the children and looked up, eyes open wide, breath caught.

"Hello," he said sardonically, speaking to the room.

Emmaline's head shot up. Their gazes locked. She drew what was surely her first real breath in seven days. Fireworks exploded in her chest.

He said casually, "There you are. This house is a warren of tiny rooms and crooked hallways. I thought I would never find you."

Emmaline opened her mouth to answer him but realized too late that tears would thicken her voice. She ducked her head instead and shut her eyes. While every other female in the room, children included, gaped at him, Emmaline said a prayer of thanksgiving and listened to the sound of her own thudding heart.

He'd come.

Tears wet her lashes, and she squeezed her eyes more tightly shut.

He'd come.

Against all odds, just as he'd said, he'd come.

The bittersweet distraction of him these last days felt suddenly inconsequential in the face of the real him, tall and confident and standing in the doorway.

He'd come.

From the chair beside her, Teddy said, "Beau."

"Hello, Teddy," he answered, his voice gentle and strong and a little bit ironical. "I'd hoped to find you here. Egad, look at the children. There must be ten of them if there is one. However do you manage them all? Most children, in my experience, are prone to *bite*. Is this a particularly feral lot?"

Little Eleanor, the duke's third-youngest daughter, answered him right away. "Teddy cannot talk, sir, but I can. I should be happy to tell you the names of all my brothers and sisters who are biters."

He knelt to the little girl's level and squinted at her playfully. "You have the look of a biter yourself, madam. I hope you don't mind my saying. Can I count on you to protect me if the mood in this room turns savage?"

"But I don't know what *savage* means," Eleanor informed him, devouring his attention. Other children began to close in on him, crawling to pull up on his knee or grab his waistcoat or smear butter on his boot. The nursemaids fluttered forth, whispering apologies and casting furtive glances at him while they endeavored to pull the children back. He assured them they were no bother and reached out to pat the children's heads or extend an index finger for the smallest one to grab.

Just when Emmaline thought her love for him had stopped her heart, it beat again and felt a little larger each time. For him. All for him.

He looked up at her, and he caught her gaze. The force of that look made her feel as if the two of them shared all the secrets of the world, past and present. That they were one, they *knew*, and that everything would be all right.

But now she heard footsteps in the hallway, and a glance, however forceful, did little to alleviate the impending confrontation, whatever it may be. They both rose—Teddy too— with Beau shoving up from the floor.

A shout echoed in the hallway. "He was warned, Your Grace. Wait in the front hall, I told him, until I learned your preference." This was Neils, the butler.

Next came scrambling footfalls, the sight of a footman dashing past the open doors, and the indiscernible bluster of the Duke of Ticking, already in a full-blown rage from one floor above.

Teddy tensed at the sound, and Emmaline asked the kindest and most reasonable of the nursemaids, Becky, if she might take Teddy and the older children to the garden.

"I've brought Miss Breedlowe in the carriage," Beau told her instead. "Teddy only need reach her in the entryway. She's disappointed me, I must say, by refusing to wander the halls without the duke's or duchess's 'express invitation' or some such. I was given no choice but to abandon her by the door."

"Oh, thank God," whispered Emmaline, and she entreated Becky to take Teddy to Jocelyn, just three rooms away. The girl nodded and quickly gathered up the youngest of the Crumbley children, beckoned to Teddy, and slipped with them from the room.

When Teddy was safely gone, she looked at Beau.

"Sorry for the delay, Duchess," he told her with a wink, "but special licenses are not as easy to procure as one would think. Took some doing, but I have it." He patted his lapel. "It all came together in the eleventh hour. One of Elisabeth's vicars has agreed to manage the thing this afternoon, if you can believe it."

Emmaline took a small step forward, trying to comprehend what he'd said. "*Today?*"

The footsteps in the hallway grew louder, and Beau leaned from the door to look. "Unless you have other plans." He glanced around the toy- and child-filled room.

"But...but whatever can we say to the duke and duchess?"

Surely it would not be this easy. Surely he could not simply wave a paper and free her and Teddy from the duke's avaricious clutches.

"The less, the better, I think," he said, "under the circumstances. Although it sounds as if he might be keen for some word."

"Quite so." She took another step forward. "But how will we—"

"To be honest," he said, cutting her off, "I don't relish the idea of speaking plainly to him or anyone. The longer we linger, the greater chance that I will muck it up. We can send for your and Teddy's things, or you can run up and fetch them now. Either way, make haste. I'd rather not stand around and pretend I'm equipped to debate a bloody duke."

Now the butler's voice rang down the hall. "You, sir, have not been admitted to the family rooms of this house!"

She winced and took another step toward him. "But is it real?" she whispered.

"Quite real, Duchess," he said, but he made a gesture of *hurry up, hurry up.* "God help you, it is real." His blue eyes bore straight into her heart. "Will you come with me?"

Emmaline allowed only two seconds for the words to sink in, and then she nodded, backed away from him, and ran for her and Teddy's rooms at the very top of the stairs.

After the stabbing fear of Emmaline's potential rejection, Beau needed only to manage his anxiety about confronting the bloody Duke of Ticking. Beau wasn't afraid of the man, certainly, but he could hardly fight him hand to hand, here in his own home. Here, he'd be expected to argue with him. He'd played dumb at the ball and slipped away but not now. Now he should say something strident and lasting and authoritative.

His brother had tried to advise him on how to respectfully but firmly appeal to the duke, beginning with a purposeful stride into Ticking's foyer, and ending in an imposing pose behind the closed door of Ticking's library.

Bollocks. Beau's nightmares rolled out in exactly this fashion, and he would not relive the scene in the light of day with a living, breathing tyrant like the Duke of Ticking.

Instead, Beau had approached the ducal townhome in much the same way he approached a brothel he targeted for a raid—make no warning, explain nothing, don't linger. In and out before they fully grasped that they'd been hit.

It was unrealistic, he'd predicted, to expect to make no excuse to the duke, but he'd be damned if he would sit politely across from him in a bloody library and beg his bloody pardon. Beau had a special license—the acquisition of which was easily the most official and binding thing he'd ever bothered to do—and Bryson's solicitor assured him he was on solid ground, marrying her. She was a widow, and her late husband had not imposed a legal guardian over her. All the heavy-handed control had been the presumption of the duke.

Beau had intended to tell this to His Grace in as few words as possible and then be gone. Hopefully, Emmaline would not linger. Certainly the fewer gray or black garments she elected to bring along, the better.

But now the moment of reckoning was upon him, and an incensed butler had intercepted him as he slipped from the drawing door to herd him, with the help of a contingent of footmen, to the front door. The Duke of Ticking stomped down a grand staircase at the same time, still tugging on a brocade morning jacket. A harried valet fussed behind him like a moth.

"What is the meaning of this, sir?" bellowed Ticking. "Charging into my home uninvited and demanding an audience with a widow in deep mourning? After the spectacle you made at the ball on New Year's Eve?"

Beau decided this was more of a rhetorical question, and he elected not to answer. He allowed the duke's outrage to reach center stage instead. The older man marched up to him with his chest puffed out like one of Teddy's birds.

"You will leave at once," the duke hissed.

"Careful," Beau warned, standing his ground.

"How dare you come into my home without so much as a word to me?"

"Oh, I've asked to come in." Beau kept an eye on the stairs. *Come on, Emma; come on, Emma...*

"The hell you have," said Ticking. "I'd never heard of you in my life, and then you turn up at that bloody ball and dupe my wife and daughters into believing you are a gentleman."

"I see the confusion," said Beau. "You mean, how dare I not ask *you?* This point is well taken. I didn't ask you."

The duke was turning an odd shade of purple. *"Whom did you ask?"*

Beau chuckled, dropping his hat on his head. "Why, Teddy Holt, of course."

"The idiot Teddy Holt?" bellowed Ticking. "He gave you permission to call on my home?"

Beau glanced at the staircase again and saw Emmaline, thank God. He stepped to the side to extend a hand to her. She hurried down the staircase with two bags and a case.

"No, not that," Beau answered. "Of course I'd never bother Teddy with a permission to call. I asked Teddy for his sister's hand in marriage."

Emmaline was upon them now, her hand outstretched. Beau took the largest bag, lodged it beneath his arm, and then grabbed hold of her hand. She looked more determined than afraid, and Beau was bolstered by her courage.

The duke shouted, *"Marry her?* Absolutely not! That's preposterous! And indecent! I forbid it."

Beau dropped Emmaline's hand long enough to pull a copy of the special license from his coat pocket. He slapped it flat against the duke's brocade morning jacket. "Not yours to forbid, Your Grace. I would thank you for these last eighteen months of her life in your care, but thinly veiled captivity did not really suit her."

And while the duke scrambled to unseal the license, Beau reclaimed Emmaline's hand, reached for the door handle, told the butler, "Stand aside, or you will regret it," and pulled the two of them through the door.

They were gone in the next moment. He gestured to Miss Breedlowe and Teddy and whistled to his brother's coachman. The carriage door shut behind them, the team of horses lurched forward, and they clattered from Portman Square before the Duke of Ticking—the copy of the marriage license trembling in his hands—had even read the first line.

CHAPTER THIRTY-ONE

The notion of getting married with only two hours' notice had never occurred to Emmaline, nor had a Thursday afternoon wedding, in the near-empty sanctuary of a modest church in Watford.

She'd been married to the late Duke of Ticking in St. Paul's, of course, in front of three hundred guests, in a ceremony that had taken her mother nearly a year to plan. The cost of her wedding gown alone had exceeded fifty pounds, with semiprecious stones sewn into the neckline and a coronet on her head that twinkled with real diamonds.

How ironic that she had never felt more beautiful than she did for the surprise marriage to Beau Courtland. She'd escaped the Ticking townhome with only the hideous gray half-mourning dress she'd worn that day and a bag or two of her accessories and jewelry from Liverpool. Later, she hoped to retrieve the lavish wardrobe she'd owned as duchess, but in the moment, she had been painfully aware of Beau and Teddy alone downstairs with the duke. She had grabbed a few personal items for herself and a few for Teddy, dashed off a note to Teddy's valet, Mr. Broom, and fled.

Beau had taken her, along with Teddy and Miss Breedlowe, to Henrietta Place straightaway. Elisabeth and Lady Falcondale were pacing the front steps when she arrived. They had practically ripped her from the carriage door and spirited her up the stairs to a beautifully appointed room that Elisabeth explained would be her bedchamber as the new Viscountess of Rainsleigh.

Draped across the bed was the most beautiful gown Emmaline had perhaps ever seen. She reverently had touched the skirts, and layers and layers of diaphanous silk slipped through her fingers. It was a ruby color—not red, not quite pink, but the color of claret in a glass on a summer day. It was vivid and rich, with a smooth bodice trimmed in a corded piping of the same color.

"Lady Frinfrock insisted," Piety Falcondale had told her excitedly. "God knows what she paid to have it made so quickly. She assumes that you've grown weary of the blacks and grays these many months."

Elisabeth had added, "Or rather, she assumes her dear Beau may have grown weary. She dotes on him, which will be your cross to bear, I'm afraid. When she learned of the wedding, her chief concern was that Beau receive a bride who was properly turned out in a gown that he would, er, enjoy."

Emmaline had looked up from the dress. "Do you think he will like it?"

Elisabeth had laughed again. "I think he will like removing it."

And then everyone had laughed, everyone except Emmaline, who could not begin to fathom what she might or might not wear in the nighttime, as she had only just learned of what she would wear in the day.

She had dressed speedily, jumping every time someone came in or out of the room. She could not escape the niggling fear that the Duke of Ticking would storm into the room at any moment and drag her back to his brood. Under normal circumstances, she would have taken care with her appearance, especially her hair, finally unbound and with no hat, but she had been afraid to linger.

When she was dressed, feeling like herself for the first time in nearly two years, the women journeyed with her to Watford.

When they'd arrived at the snug, spare little church, Lady Frinfrock herself, along with her friend, Miss Baker, had met them in the vestibule. Miss Breedlowe had whispered an apology, saying that she'd implored the marchioness not to venture out in the cold for such a brief and informal ceremony, but her plea had fallen on deaf ears. Lady Frinfrock regarded the whole affair with almost proprietary regard, despite the rush. She had studied Emmaline's dress with an eyebrow raised but said nothing. (Jocelyn had informed her that this was very high praise, indeed.) Next, she had produced a hothouse bouquet for her to hold before her like a proper bride.

"Thank you, my lady," Emmaline had whispered reverently, truly humbled. "You've thought of everything. I shall never be able to thank you enough for the gown. It is beautiful."

"You do look far less sallow when removed from the piteous gray," the marchioness had said.

And then Mr. Courtland had appeared from somewhere inside the church and signaled the ladies to take seats. Teddy appeared next, and Mr. Courtland asked Emmaline if she would mind terribly if he walked her down the aisle on one arm while Teddy held her other arm. She nodded, too emotional to speak.

And so Teddy, looking handsome in a new suit, shuffled to her right side and Mr. Courtland offered an arm at her left. She marveled at the lengths to which her friends had gone to free her from the untenable situation in which they'd found themselves. If there had been time, she would have wept in gratitude. But there had not been time. Mr. Courtland suggested that the sooner they were properly married, the safer she and Teddy would be. She'd nodded, and he'd pulled her around the corner of the vestibule. Emmaline had dried her eyes and looked up, seeing first the short, narrow aisle and the small, tidy altar and then...

And then, there he was, tall and handsome in a formal wedding suit, with Joseph and Stoker standing behind him. She hovered in the archway of the door for half a beat, pulling back on Mr. Courtland's arm, just to stare at Beau. Almost as if he felt her gaze, Beau looked up and saw her.

She smiled, their gazes held, and he slowly perused her appearance—ruby dress, hair pulled away from her face but long down her back, flowers, tears she could not blink away. He looked nothing short of dazzled. But his eyes also held impatience and need. Emmaline's breath caught. She too was impatient, and she wondered if the same need was answered in her own eyes.

But then Mr. Courtland was tugging her along, and Beau smiled and cocked that one perfect eyebrow. A quarter hour later, the vicar pronounced them man and wife.

Emmaline was handed up into the Rainsleigh carriage by her husband while her friends and Teddy smiled and waved from the front gate of the church. She settled quickly and turned to wave back, but Beau slammed the carriage door with a *click*. He rapped twice on the ceiling, and the vehicle lurched forward.

"I've had just about all of that I can bear," he said.

She frowned at the closed door. "I thought the ceremony was lovely, in fact." Her frown failed because a pervasive smile had lurked beneath every nonsmile she had endeavored all day. She had even grinned through communion.

"I was thinking that we might suggest a meal together in honor of the…occasion," Emmaline tried, pushing the curtain aside to look out the window. "It's too late in the day for a wedding breakfast, obviously, but it was such a collective effort, wasn't it? It feels almost rude to remove ourselves now."

"No meal," he said, sitting back on the opposite seat. "It's not the slightest bit rude. Come here."

Emmaline dropped the curtain and looked up. "You're not hungry?"

"Yes, I am, in fact. *Quite* hungry. I said, come here."

He was sprawled on the opposite seat, his arms propped slackly right and left, the picture of nonchalant repose. As if he hadn't just been married. As if he wasn't about to make her his wife in earnest. He was so relaxed, in fact, she would doubt his enthusiasm altogether if not for the look of impatient demand in his eyes. He extended his legs as far as the roomy seats would allow, bumping her ankles with his boot.

She wondered about the coachmen and the groom. She wondered about the length of their journey. "But where are we going?" she asked.

He took off his hat and tossed it beside him on the seat. He pulled off his gloves, one finger at a time. Emmaline stared at his hands.

"To bed," he said plainly, casually.

"Now? In the light of day?" Her heartbeat was faster now, racing, despite their relaxed exchange. "Do they know?" She gestured to the window where she'd watched Elisabeth and Miss Breedlowe and both of their brothers wave good-bye.

"Of course they know," he said. "Everyone knows, Duchess, and everyone is thrilled. Me most of all." He patted the seat beside him. "Emma, come *here*."

"Why?" she asked, looking up at him through half-lowered lashes.

He paused a beat, registering that look, and then he said, "Because I wish to tell you what I think of your dress."

She looked down at the ruby dress.

"In the carriage?" Another lowered-lash look.

"*Right here. Right now.*" He reached out and plucked her hand from her lap and yanked.

She allowed it, falling against him. The wall of his chest was rock hard, and his left hand snaked around her waist, locking her to him. She sat on his lap. His muscled thighs were hard through her skirt.

"That's better," he said. Idly, he fingered her hair. She shook her head, and the full weight of it fell around her shoulders. He made a slow hissing sound. He lifted a handful of it, and she felt the cool, weightlessness on her neck.

Suddenly, she wanted all of her hair loose and long and free. Lady Falcondale had plaited two sections away from her face and secured them at her crown with a ruby ribbon. It looked pretty for the wedding, but her hair had always been her secret vanity, and the hats and buns had been a particular punishment these last two years.

While he watched her, she bit off her gloves and reached to untie the ribbon. It skidded down the front of his shirt and the braids dropped to her shoulders.

Slowly, he took up one braid and began reverently unraveling the plait. "You know," he said softly, "the hat you lost in the canal actually washed to shore downstream, and the boys, Ben and Jason, delivered it to me last week. Effective fishing trap, that hat."

"What? No." She laughed.

He nodded once. "They pulled it from the water with two bream skewered on the spines and the body of an eel trapped in the netting on the brim.

"Really?"

"No," he said, "not really."

She laughed, but the carriage hit a bump, and she jostled. His hands left her hair and caught her around the waist. He lowered his head, and she thought he would whisper something more about the hat. She closed her eyes and sank in, but he said nothing. He touched his lips to the area of skin just behind her ear. Emmaline sucked in a breath.

"You were so beautiful, Emma," he murmured. "From the very beginning. Your eyes, so big and bright and earnest, haunted me. When you look at me, I feel as if you see nothing but me."

I do, she thought.

He kissed his way from her neck to her jaw, dragging the roughness of his emerging beard against the soft skin.

"So beautiful," he continued, "even in that hat. Even in the bloody widow's weeds. Did you have any clue how beautiful I thought you were?"

Another nuzzle. He was nearly to her mouth now. She parted her lips, anticipating. Her breath was fast and shallow.

"But when I saw you in this dress," he said, retreating to her ear again, "with color in your face, and light in your eyes, and your hair loose…" He delved his hand into the long trail of her hair and lifted, fitting his fingers around the back of her head, tilting her face up to him. "I thought, never has there ever been a more beautiful woman." His lips returned to the sensitive area behind her ear, and she whimpered.

So close. He'd been so close.

"Do you know what else I thought?" He nuzzled again, following the same path, nearly to her mouth and back. "Do you know?"

Her answer was a whimper.

"I thought, Please, God, let her never bind her hair again. It was a bloody crime, tying it back so tightly, and those hats…"

She laughed, a breathy, distracted laugh, and he shifted so he could see her lips, almost as if he'd forgotten to kiss them. And then he dropped down, finally touching his mouth to hers, sealing them in a hard, slow, open kiss; kissing her as if he would not breathe if he did not.

It was Emmaline, in fact, who did not breathe. She squeezed her eyes shut and clung, sliding her hands up his arms to his massive shoulders. He turned his head, deepening the kiss, and she moaned softly, thrilled by each new closeness. But now she was not close enough, and she could only angle her neck so far.

Beau growled and shifted her, not breaking the kiss. He slid his palm beneath her bottom and scooped her high against him.

"Gather up your skirts," he breathed, dropping his head back.

"Wha—"

"Your skirts," he said to the ceiling of the carriage. "They're in the way." He swallowed. "Bunch them around your waist. Then you can straddle me."

She blinked at him through a haze of desire. *"Here?"*

He turned his head to the side, sucking in breath. "Always."

Shock and modesty were but faint glimmers as she dropped her hands from his shoulders and gathered up the swath of fabric, freeing her legs.

He nuzzled her throat, waiting as she piled handfuls of the ruby silk on the seat. When she was finally free, he lifted her higher, raking his face against the neckline of her gown, and she lifted one gold-slippered foot over his body. She put her hands on his shoulders, and he slid her down his chest, seating her heavily on his lap. Her body was jolted by the sweet sensation of very hard against very soft. She wiggled just a little, unable to not explore the new closeness, and he groaned.

"Hold still." He ground out the words as he clamped his hands on her waist. "Or I will not last."

She puzzled over this, her brain working only enough to understand the source of this new pleasure and repeat it. She wiggled again. He groaned again, louder this time, and closed his mouth over hers.

She was lost then, swept away in a torrent of sensation that erased thought and function. She pulled back only to breathe.

"Careful, Emma," he said, sucking in his own breath. "I can usually be counted on for more control, but you"—He kissed her again, hard and fast—"are like nothing I've ever…" Another kiss. "I've never had to ever…"

But she didn't want to hear about what he may have ever known, and she sank her fingers into his hair, and pulled his lips to hers, and repeated the long, air-robbing kiss.

But now the carriage was turning, rolling perhaps onto a smaller road paved with rounder, bumpier stones. The bounce of the road became a jostle, and Emmaline struggled to keep her balance. But soon she discovered how their bodies absorbed the shock, and she allowed the rhythm of the clipping vehicle to rock them together with its own intermittent *bump-bump-bump*. The sensation erased sight and sound. All she could do was feel.

Beau growled once, lifted her off his body, dropped her on her back on the carriage seat, and fell on top of her, barely breaking the kiss. One moment she was sitting astride his lap, and the next moment she was flat on her back, their legs a tangle against the door.

She tried to laugh, delighted by his strength and ferocity, but he pounced again on her mouth, and she sucked in breath before she was lost again.

He had just located the hem of her gown with his fingers when Emmaline realized the vehicle had lurched to a stop. Next, a rap sounded on the door, two swift knocks, and then retreating footsteps.

Emmaline froze.

"The footmen," she rasped. "I'm...I'm...and you're..."

"Easy, Duchess," he rumbled, allowing them both to catch their breath. He kissed her neck and shoulder. "They would not dare open the door."

Emmaline considered this, wondering *why* they would not dare. Carefully, working hard to separate her brain from the delectable little bites he now nipped on her neck, she asked, "Because...you've asked them not to disturb us?"

"Well, yes," he said, his voice muffled by her skin. "I did ask. But they would never open this carriage door, even if I had not. Not when we've just come from our wedding. En route to our house—well, en route to *a* house." He propped up on his elbows and looked down at her. "You'll be happy to know that I have elected not to bring you home to the boat on Paddington Lock. We've come to Henrietta Place."

"Does this trouble you? I know you do not enjoy your brother's house."

"Ah, but apparently it is *my* house, and that is what bothers me. But he and Elisabeth have not moved away yet. And it is my understanding that you and I will away to New York very soon."

"Yes, we will," she answered, smiling. But her mind returned to the grooms and footmen who loitered outside the carriage but would not open the door. "Rainsleigh?"

"Beau," he whispered, biting her earlobe.

"Beau, do you mean all the servants here also…*know*?"

"If you mean, is the staff aware that I'm halfway to bedding my wife in this closed carriage? Yes, of course they know."

She thought about this. She thought about Elisabeth and Bryson, who would apparently share this house with her, and Miss Breedlowe, who was looking after Teddy tonight. She thought about all the servants she might pass when they left this carriage and walked to…wherever they might go inside the house. Beau had already mentioned the bedchamber. But surely…

She looked at him. "But *everyone* will know that we are…being intimate?"

Beau chuckled and sat up, grabbing her wrists and yanking her up with him. "Yes," he said, "everyone will know. And before you apply your duchess's rule book to whether this may be appropriate or not, let me assure you that I don't care. Although it does happen to be appropriate, considering I just bloody married you. What we're doing and what we shall do, all night long, goes on between every married man and his wife, even these grooms, if they're married, even Lady Frinfrock, when she was married."

Emmaline thought of Lady Frinfrock laid out on the carriage seat and made a noise of distress.

Beau laughed. "The only person who did not carry on in this fashion was your late husband—bloody imbecile—but I thank God for that."

"Why 'thank God'?" she asked. It was a self-serving question, but she wanted to hear him say it. And how much better to enjoy the words now, when he was rumpled and breathless, his eyes the most vivid shade of passion-dipped blue?

"Because that means that you belong only to me, and I have the supreme privilege of introducing you to one of the very best things in life, and then keeping all of your pleasure entirely to myself. Forever. Whether you like it or not."

CHAPTER THIRTY-TWO

"At the risk of saying too much, Emma, I feel compelled to ask you: do you understand what will happen here, in this room, in that bed, in about five minutes' time?"

Beau sat in a chair, pulling off his boots, while Emmaline lounged in a window seat that overlooked the garden, considering a cart of food. She nibbled on a quince. The fruit was halfway to her mouth when he asked this, and she paused, thought about it, and took a bite rather than answer.

Beau smiled. "I only ask because you've said the old duke did not consummate your marriage. And we'll both enjoy ourselves more if no one is…" He searched for a word with less impact than *shocked*. "Taken by surprise."

Of all the beds in which Beau had lain since he was but fourteen years old, he had never been in bed with a virgin. He felt some responsibility, not to mention there was a certain sensuality in explaining it.

Emmaline took another bite.

He prompted her, saying, "Duchess? What did your mother tell you before your marriage to Ticking? Or your friends?" Perhaps it would be easier to discuss what she *did* know.

She swallowed but would not look at him. "I am loath to reveal how little I know, to be honest." She shrugged and glanced at him. "Must we discuss it? May I simply follow along?"

He thought about this. "All right." Not for the first time, he marveled at how her previous husband had resisted her. The carriage ride had been an exercise in exquisitely painful restraint. He could barely keep his eyes off her, even now, and she did little more than perch in the window, fully clothed, eating fruit.

He stood and shrugged from his jacket. He had her full attention, he noticed, and her chewing slowed. The waistcoat came next, and he tugged his shirt from his trousers and jerked it over his head. She stood up. She left the window one step at a time, staring at his chest.

He cleared his throat. "I would be negligent if I did not go over a very few basics." He went to her, and she watched him. The wide-eyed wonder on her face was almost too much to bear.

"Are you...still hungry?" he asked.

She shook her head.

She held a forgotten hunk of bread, and he took it from her.

"Good. Here's what comes next. We will get you out of this dress. You already know this bit from your dip in the canal. Although you may not have enjoyed it quite as much, considering the cold and wet and smell of fish."

Without hesitation, she turned and offered him her back. "Enjoyed it *as much?*"

"If you did not enjoy yourself when I removed the wet dress, then I have a very inflated view of my technique, indeed."

"Well, we know it couldn't be that."

He chuckled and gave the refreshment cart a kick. She watched it roll away, bending her neck and pulling the thick fall of her hair over her left shoulder with deft, efficient hands. His mouth watered in anticipation. A few strands of hair slipped from her shoulder and dropped down her back. He swiped them away, grazing her neck with his fingertips. She took in a small breath.

He cleared his throat. It occurred to him that, in a way, this felt like his first time as well. His eyes kept drifting from the dress to the arch of her neck, the slope of her ear. More hair dropped down her back, and she reached to pull it back. Without thinking, he caught her wrist. "Let me."

He was reminded that he hadn't finished his cautionary explanation. It had seemed so necessary just five minutes ago, but functional thought was rapidly slipping away. He cleared his throat again. "I've been told it may hurt the first time, but, if done correctly, it has the potential to feel very good indeed."

"Very tastefully put, sir," she said.

He paused. Did she *tease*?

He bent to whisper in her ear. "I can explain it in more explicitly specific terms, if you feel it might be useful."

She breathed in. "I cannot say what I find useful."

"If you enjoyed what we did in the carriage, it is…more of the same."

"Oh. The carriage. Yes, that was simply awful."

He smiled. So she would not play the frightened virgin. *All the better.*

When he reached the last fastener at the back of her dress and flicked it open, the slouching bodice drooped and fell.

She made no effort to collect it. It snagged on her petticoats and hung.

The petticoats came next, one tug and two clasps, and then he reached for the strings of her corset. His hands shook. He took a deep breath and pulled.

He asked her, "You're not afraid?"

"No. Am I meant to be?"

Beau's breath hitched at those words, and the languid, heavy desire in his body hardened into an urgent, steely point. He made the indistinguishable sound that could have meant anything, really, and yanked at the corset, jerking the laces free. "You will have to remind me to go slowly, Duchess," he heard himself tell her. My God, was he already short of breath?

"Unless I remind you to go faster," she replied.

Here, Beau paused again, gritting his teeth from another surge of desire. He swallowed and returned to the corset. She wobbled from the force of his pulling, and he mumbled an apology, jerking the last lace free. One slow, steady slide of the silk-and-whalebone panel, and the corset was gone. She sighed in relief.

"Drop the dress, Duchess," he rasped.

She did not hesitate. The ruby silk and petticoats beneath slid to the floor like a puff of smoke.

She turned to him. "Should I be excited or concerned by your proficiency with women's underthings?"

"Double-edged sword, sweetheart," he said.

He sank into a crouch. He ran his hands up her legs until he came to the top of her stockings and slid them down. Next he grabbed the hem of her chemise and tugged it up.

"Raise your arms," he grunted, coming up. The light cotton slid over her head, and he tossed it the way of the corset. He sucked in a breath and took a step back. "I would see you," he said.

When she turned around, she was smiling. This was the second thing he noticed. Or third. First, he devoured the sight of her bare perfection exposed to him. She was...

She was thin, and lithe, and proud.

And mine.

He'd been so focused on taking her that he had not realized how much he wanted to simply *look* at her. The day she'd fallen into the canal, they'd stopped short of her corset and chemise, and he had never recovered from the denial. How had he managed the restraint not to press on to...to *this*?

He dared not speak, dared not even blink. He thought he would never forget every color and texture, every dip and swell, every roundness and hollow. He would see her naked body every time he closed his eyes for the rest of his life.

He must have looked half-mad, because now her smile was an earnest laugh, and the movement spilt her hair over her shoulder, falling down her breasts to her waist. Just like that, he had a new image to never forget.

But now he had looked enough, and his fingers itched to touch her. His body strained against his trousers, and he fumbled for the buttons, desperate to be rid of them.

"Wait," she said, and he went still. *No more waiting*, he pleaded in his head.

She asked, "May I?"

Beau thought in that moment he might well and truly expire. His hands rose out from his sides, and he watched in a lust-filled haze as she reached out to gently pluck the first button from its hole.

"Is this wrong?" She looked up.

He laughed, and swore, and breathed out a long breath he didn't know he'd held. Wordlessly, he watched her pluck the next button, and the next. His body was uncomfortably thick against the wool, and every flutter of her fingers was sweet agony. He dropped his head back and squeezed his eyes shut.

When she finished one row of buttons, she slid her hand to the next. It was perhaps the most exquisite torture he'd ever known.

Her hair fell forward as she worked, grazing his bare chest, blocking the captivating view of her diligent hands. His arms were still outstretched at his sides, frozen where he'd moved them when she stepped up.

He dropped them to clasp her waist. "Enough," he growled, and he hunched down, swept her legs out from under her, and picked her up. She yelped again, and he kissed her, locking in the sound and striding to the bed. She kicked a little, exaggerating the feel of her naked body against his bare chest, and he scooped her harder against him.

When his thighs hit the bed, he broke the kiss and tossed her into the center, sending pillows flying. She'd barely righted herself before he'd peeled off his trousers.

She looked up, eyes bright, hair spilling everywhere, and he could but laugh at the futility of his ridiculous preamble. She required no primer. She was a bloody natural.

He dove into the bed.

CHAPTER THIRTY-THREE

Beau landed with a bounce and caught Emmaline up, rolling them in the same movement. Now she was on top of him, looking down, her hair creating a curtain around their faces. She laughed—laughed out of the sheer, buzzing pleasure of it, out of her love for every part of him, especially the part that would toss her onto the bed and then pounce on top of her. She would never be bored with this man, she knew. After a lifetime of boredom—lessons and rules and greetings and meals and running a house, and on and on it went—finally, she could envision adventure and passion and challenge.

The plans to sell her father's books had been her first taste of purpose and industry, and it had been a heady draught indeed. And now this.

Beau smiled back and then jerked his chin up—the undeniable gesture of *kiss me*. Emmaline laughed again and waited a beat, two beats, reveling in the feel of his rock-hard body beneath her, reveling in the handsomeness of his face. When she finally lowered her mouth to his, she was smiling too broadly to properly manage the kiss, and he rolled them again, landing her beneath him.

Now he lowered his head, kissing her expertly, employing his whole mouth, his tongue, the changing angle of his face. She discovered that a lying-down kiss had an entirely different quality than a standing-up kiss. Longer, more fluid, deeper, hotter. A lying-down kiss allowed unlimited access to so much of him.

But her conscious brain was rapidly sinking into a swirling haze of desire. If she wished to explore his body properly— which she absolutely wished to do—she should do it now, while she could still think.

His body was like an Italian marble statue she'd seen in the British Museum but with warm skin, a sheen of sweat, and a dusting of golden hair. She thought she would never grow tired of touching him.

Even so, there were parts she hadn't touched. She could feel his hardness pressing against her, but their bodies were fused together so tightly she could but slide her hands against the seam where his hip met her thigh.

He broke the kiss and chuckled at her insistent fluttering and snaked a hand down to capture her wrist. "Ah, ah, ah," he warned. "Be careful what you ask for, Duchess. I would recommend that we stay your dizzying exploration for now. I can generally be counted on to last several hours but not tonight." He kissed her. "Not with you. If you touch me, things may come to a very abrupt end."

"But—" she protested.

"Shhh," he soothed. "This only *seems* selfish. I promise, you will enjoy the alternative." And then he shifted a little, falling to the side, and he buried his face in the area behind her ear and trailed the index finger of his right hand from her lips, over her chin, and down her neck. This tickled, and she laughed, but it was a strangled, breathless sort of laugh as her body skittered into a quivering new awareness. Each of her heartbeats became indistinguishable, one from the next.

The riot of pleasure that followed made her alternately writhe and go taut. She called his name or no name at all, simply a wordless sound of assent. Soon the one finger became his entire hand, and then two hands, and she thought she would surely perish from the heart-pounding, thrashing thrill of it.

And all the while, he maintained a slow and steady kiss, sometimes to her mouth, sometimes to her neck. When he fastened his mouth to her breast, she cried out with such enthusiasm, he laughed and clamped a hand over her mouth. She had licked him then, a quick lash of her tongue to the palm of his hand, and he had stopped laughing and replaced his hand with his mouth.

Through it all, she nearly forgot to touch him—nearly. But her ministrations were little more than glancing, floppy half touches and swipes, the occasional grab and hang on. He groaned with each contact, and she loved the power of this. She had the fleeting thought that, thank God they were married so she could have another go, and another, and another.

With no warning, the torrent of sensation became less of discovery and more of a steady, rising need. She began to anticipate exactly what she could expect from the way he touched her—nay, she began to demand it. Crying out, or surging up, or bucking her hips to meet him. Beau answered her pleas by deftly smoothing her out against the mattress and then replacing his hands with his body, rolling them back where they had begun.

Emmaline protested the shift, but then, suddenly, this felt just as good; no, this felt better—this felt *exactly right*—and she raised her hips off the bed to seek out *more* exact rightness, pressing her need to the incredibly hard and urgently attentive body. He groaned. "Yes, Emma. That's right. You have it."

She pressed up, again and again, marveling at how much better this felt, even better than his hands. And then "better" was insufficient; it surged into "necessary," and then "urgent," and then "essential. And then…

Her body was shot through with a surge of culminating pleasure so intense that Emmaline froze. The breath left her lungs, and she blinked up at Beau's face but saw only a bright, hot light. Her body hung there, suspended in the pinnacle of sensation…ten seconds, twenty—she lost sense of time…and then his face swam back into focus, and he smiled down at her.

When the pulsing finally ebbed and she could breathe again, he dropped his face and kissed her once, hard and fast, and gritted out the words, "Thank God."

Then he rose up, planted a knee between her legs and lowered his body down slowly, so slowly she watched the fight for control on his face. She felt the thick invasion of him, and she realized, *Oh, this. Now. Of course.*

She blinked, still trying to recover her wits, but she wanted to be useful; she wanted him to feel the pleasure she had felt, so she endeavored to accommodate. First she spread her legs wider, but that did not seem to help, so she raised her knees. He gasped at this and sank lower, so she raised her knees higher still. She watched him. She wanted to ask, but he seemed wholly focused and disinclined to speak.

Next she burrowed down, feeling for the proper angle. He hissed and squeezed his eyes shut, and she knew she'd found it.

To her own body, the pressure and fullness was new, and tight, and not entirely comfortable, but also it was not unpleasant. She was intrigued by the pressure. She was also intrigued by the look of rapture on his face, but also the strain for control. Working on instinct, she rose up to kiss him. His lips were still, and she kissed him again. This time he caught her mouth, but his body sunk a little deeper, and he ended the kiss on an oath.

Emmaline understood now, and she hooked her heels at his waist, canted her body, and bit down on a wince as he slid all the way. There he remained, entirely still and (if his expression was any indication) totally agonized.

After a moment, she whispered, "But is this…it?"

He opened one eye and looked down at her. "No."

She thought about this. He had been so much more forthcoming before they'd begun. How much more useful that information would be now.

She could but ask. "What will we do next?"

"We will not have a conversation. Typically." He let out a ragged breath and closed his eyes. "Are you in pain, Emma?"

She considered this. "No. Are you?"

"Yes." He dropped his head to her neck and breathed in.

She gasped, not wanting him to hurt. "What can I do?"

"Hold perfectly still. I'm waiting for your body to become accustomed to mine."

This was the wrong thing to say. Disobedience had become second nature in the last year. She wiggled her hips experimentally.

Beau groaned into her neck. *"Emma."*

She smiled and wiggled again, more this time, and he answered with what she would describe as a gentle thrust. This, she found interesting, far more interesting than the stillness or the wiggle, and when she moved again, she copied the movement. A thrust, less gentle but still not forceful.

Beau dragged his face from her neck, grabbing fistfuls of her hair on either side of her head. "May I take this to mean you are ready?" he asked, panting.

"Ready for…?"

He answered her with another thrust, a real one, and she gasped, shocked by the fullness and command and possession of it.

The muscles worked in his neck; his eyes were closed. He held himself in check, still. Emmaline's heart wrenched at his restraint. Taking a deep breath, she answered his thrust with one of her own and said quietly, "More."

His eyes blinked open. "What?"

Another thrust, longer this time. *"More,"* she said on a breath.

"I won't hurt you." He gritted out the words.

"Not hurt," she assured him, and then she realized it was true, and she thrust again without thinking about it, her body moving of its own accord. She closed her eyes, reveling in the first stirrings of another slow burn of sensation.

Beau must have seen the proof on her face because he groaned and dropped his head again, moving his hips—slow at first, and then faster, and then faster still—and Emmaline's own tentative thrusts were caught up with the stronger, harder rhythm of his powerful body. They moved together. His breathing increased, and hers matched it. She felt the urgency building inside her again, and she wanted to pause to understand this entirely new function, but she was too swept up.

She could not stop, and the urgency culminated in another pop of warmth and sizzle and radiating pleasure, somehow better this time.

Her body went taut just as Beau cried out and stiffened, stricken in the same moment. They hung there together, a levitated joining of minds and bodies and hearts.

And then she fell slack, and he did too, and the colors and shapes in the room all swung back into place. She listened to the sound of their labored breathing. He had collapsed on top of her, his head in the crook of her neck. He gathered her up, holding her tightly against him, and she flopped an arm across his back.

When her breathing had almost returned to normal, she said, "Would you be insulted if I found your description of this endeavor to be wholly insufficient?"

He laughed and slowly lifted his head. "Was it? And what, madam, did I leave out?"

"Well, you left nothing *out* certainly," she joked, and he laughed, "but your suggestion, I believe, was that we would *enjoy* it."

"By this do you mean that you did not?"

"I suppose 'enjoy' faintly suggests what I felt. But it's more like I was 'swallowed whole' by it."

He sighed at this, and she could see that she had pleased him.

"Yes, well," he said, his voice going a little hoarse, "we'll get to that."

"Oh, another lesson," she teased. "I do hope you'll go over everything first as if I'm a lily-white maiden, and you were the first man to ever dream it up."

He shouted then, the sound of fake outrage and laughter and—oh how she hoped—*love*. She loved him so much in that moment she felt her heart would burst with it.

But she wouldn't say it now, knowing somehow that it would spoil the moment; and anyway, he'd rolled in the bed, taking her with him, and she absolutely did not want to miss whatever came next.

CHAPTER THIRTY-FOUR

When Beau awakened on the morning after his wedding and blinked at the ceiling of his brother's home, his first thought was, *This might actually succeed.*

He turned and stared at his wife's sleeping face beside him on the pillow. Her slight, delectable body had wedged against him, and she slept unabashedly nude, as he had done.

There was always the chance that she would awaken shy and apologetic, but he would be surprised if this happened. She hadn't been the least bit nervous last night. They'd made love three times, each interlude more intimate and brazen than the last, and she'd betrayed not a moment of hesitation.

And this was why he was hopeful. She'd always tempted him, but he had not known if she could *excite* him. Forever. Until death did they part. He'd married her to free her from the Duke of Ticking. In doing so, he'd refused to dwell of his own freedom and simply…hoped for the best. In fact, he'd been *breathless* to discover the best. How gratifying to discover that their promising preludes were but a fraction of the passion she would eventually offer. She was a minx in bed, playful and open and so enthusiastic. If he had to have a wife, he could think of no better wife to have.

He looked forward, in fact, to *having her* just as soon as possible.

In the meantime, he would ring for coffee and breakfast and task Sewell with locating something fresh for her to wear. As much as Beau resented the responsibility of servants, he could see the advantage when he considered someone else's comfort besides his own.

He'd never thought of anyone else's comfort, of course—if he had, he might not have found the courage to really marry her. But this did not mean that he could not anticipate what she might need or figure out how to get it. He was resigned to learn as he went. And Emma was a self-reliant girl; he would not have married her if she'd been helpless or needy. Best of all, she was perfectly capable of telling him what she needed when she needed it.

He pulled on his trousers and a clean shirt, thinking of her many needs from the night before. When he looked in the mirror to button his shirt, he saw he was smiling.

"But look at you," Emmaline said from the bed. "Fresh clothes, a smile on your face. I think marriage suits you."

Beau turned to her and immediately froze. She was propped up in bed with only the sheet and her long hair to cover her. "Perhaps," he said, crossing to the bed. "The clean clothes were always here. I sleep in this room whenever I stay with my brother. Space is limited, as you might expect, on the boat."

"Your room?" she mused, looking around. "Elisabeth told me yesterday I would inhabit the viscountess's suite after we were married."

He cringed. "Is that what you want? The big rooms upstairs?"

She'd been a duchess before yesterday, and a rich man's daughter before that, he thought. Of course, she would expect nice accommodation and nice things.

She shrugged. "I don't care, really. We'll be sailing for New York soon. I...I should like to share a room with you." She licked her lips and looked away. "If you prefer this room, I don't mind."

Beau breathed more easily. He said, "I prefer my boat, but I will not subject you."

"We would be hard-pressed to fit comfortably inside that terrible boat. You know that when you married me, you took on Teddy too."

"Yes," he said, "I know." He sat on the edge of the bed. "There is a lot we did not discuss before we did this. Where we would live, what our lives would be like."

She giggled. "I'd venture to say we discussed *nothing* before we did this."

He nodded, watching for some disapproval from her. "It was better that way for me. If we said too much, I might not have been able to do it, Duchess."

"I'm not a duchess now," she teased. "Perhaps you should refer to me as Viscountess."

He blinked at her and looked away, not wanting to spoil the pleasant moment. This was another thing they had not discussed. His hated title was now squarely on her shoulders too.

He walked to the window. "I should like to call you Emma," he said, staring down.

"All right," she answered.

"And when we sail for New York, I should like us to be referred to as Mr. and Mrs. Courtland. I—" He stopped, glanced at her, and then started again. "As you know, I use the title as little as possible." Another pause. "Your journey to America appealed to me because nobility matters so much less there."

"Why?"

He looked up. *Why?* The usual reasons sprang to mind. *Because I am lazy and irreverent and disobedient.*

But she deserved more than this, so he said, "Well, in America, success depends almost entirely on one's hard work and talent, not heredity. Naturally, family support and resource—"

"*Not* why is nobility less valued in America," she interrupted. "What I want to know—what I've always wanted to know—is why do you despise the title so much?"

He opened his mouth, ready with another of the many excuses he'd fed Bryson over the years, but she interrupted him again.

"The real reason," she said.

It occurred to him that the very aggressiveness and curiosity that had thrilled him in the dark of night was now skewering him in the light of day. It should have grated, but he could not help but feel a little bit aroused by it, just as he'd been in bed. She challenged him, but not in a way that felt judgmental. Not in a way that hinged on whether she might stay or go. She lay casually naked in his bed. She did not appear to be going anywhere.

He ambled back to the bed and sat beside her, leaning against the headboard and stretching his legs out. "What makes you think I would delude you about it?"

"Not deluded—*evaded*. I have asked you this many times before, and you have always danced around the question."

He considered this. She was too clever for her own good.

She went on. "I've heard you say before that men like the Duke of Ticking abuse the power given to them by the accident of their birth. If you felt so strongly about the political nature of the thing, why not run for the House of Commons?"

"Because the House of *Commons* does not allow bloody viscounts, of course."

"I meant *before* you were a viscount. I assume you felt the same way about the nobility, even then. You could also take a seat in the House of Lords and rally for less power among these land-owning families. You'd be unpopular, but the notion is not unheard of."

He cringed. "I can think of nothing I would rather do *less* than argue in the House of Lords. I'd rather die first."

"But *why?*" she persisted, and he looked down at her. He thought of the great leap of faith she took, marrying him with little or no notice. He thought of her enthusiasm and openness in his arms. He thought of the answer to this question— the real answer, as she'd called it—which he had never shared with another living soul. He should tell her. She deserved to know. More so, he realized he *wanted* her to know.

"I will tell you," he began, "if you drop the sheet."

She squinted at him, clearly disbelieving that he would trade sexual favors for something so earnest. He cocked an eyebrow. "You decide."

"Very well," she said, and she scooted up in bed to sit beside him, leaning against the headboard as he did. The sheet did not follow her up. She sat, gloriously naked, beside him. She waited.

He cleared his throat. "The reason that I despise the title—and all titles—so much is that I was betrayed when I was nineteen years old by five so-called noblemen who should have known better."

"What happened?"

He rolled his shoulders. He took up her hand and stared at their linked fingers. "In my second year at Cambridge, I was invited, along with some other classmates, to the country estate of our mutual friend, Lord Arthur Ellis, who was son and heir to the Earl of Laramie. Have you heard of him? Lord Laramie?"

She shook her head.

"Arthur's father is dead now, and he is the earl."

"The two of you are no longer friends?" she asked.

He scoffed at this. "No. We are not friends. But ten years ago, when I was in school, I felt lucky—indeed, I *was* lucky—to be included in Laramie's circle. He was clever and accomplished. And rich. His allowance was seemingly unlimited, and he shared it generously, buying drinks and girls and even clothes for his friends.

"It was not widely known that Bryson and I were forced to take jobs to finance our own educations, but my close friends knew. Laramie knew. I had no money to spare for holidays or leisure pursuits. My clothes were passable but not fine. I did not travel. But I was...passably charming and able to attract females, and Arthur and his friends seemed to like me very much.

"His parents, the earl and countess, liked me too, despite the notoriety of my own parents, and I was their guest both in London and at their country estate many times. Their holding in Essex is called Hollin Hall, a sprawling estate and lavish manor house. Invitations to their quarterly weeklong parties were highly sought after. I never passed up an opportunity to visit home with Arthur. Bryson loved it when I went. He was ambitious and dazzled by high society, even then.

"And so," he went on, dropping her hand, "at one of these country house parties, Arthur complained to me and our other assembled friends that his mother's guests that week were boring or old or tedious. Furthermore, he convinced us to steal away after dinner to a barn on the property. Claimed to have many fine memories of this structure, as he used to ramble around it as a boy. His plan was to slip out after the meal with a little pudding and a lot of liquor and get roaring drunk, away from the disapproving eyes of his parents and their friends."

Beau shoved out of the bed now, too restless to sit. "I'm sure I don't have to tell you that it took little to convince us. We stole away, taking along enough spirits to require a horse to pull it on a cart."

"Just the two of you?" she asked.

He shook his head. "There were six of us: Arthur, the twin sons of a wealthy baronet from Wales, the son of another earl, the third son of a duke, and me."

"That's quite a distinguished collective."

Beau glanced at her. She'd returned the sheet to her chin, he noticed, covering herself. This was better. It wasn't the sort of story that leant itself to playful barters with naked women.

"And so you stole away to the barn," Emmaline prompted.

Beau nodded and began to pace. It was ridiculous, how clearly he remembered the beginnings of that night. Later, they would become so very drunk that the details were blurred. But he remembered how confident he'd felt among these friends. He was the second son of an impoverished viscount, his family's title was a laughing stock, but he must be very winning and strong, indeed, he'd thought, to run in this crowd.

Beau sighed and soldiered on. "Yes—to the barn. We left a stately home and a lovely meal to sit around, telling off-color jokes, gambling, and drinking, in a drafty barn. For whatever reason, this appealed to us. For the first hour, I'm sure it was quite the lark."

"You…can't remember?"

"Not really. It was all very forgettable, I'm sure. Eventually, boredom overtook us, and we began to dare each other to risk this or that reckless thing to show off. We jumped from the hayloft. We swung from a rope on a hook high in the ceiling. And then we began to toss about the torches we'd brought for light. They were the silly, childish games of overindulged young men who should have known better."

"Oh, no," Emmaline said. She'd drawn her knees up to her chest. If he thought she would allow it, Beau would have left off telling the painful ending with a dismissive, "*And it ended very badly, indeed…*"

But she would not allow it, so he stopped pacing and came to the foot of the bed.

"Anyone can guess what happened next. We were careless with the torches—more than one of them dropped into the hay stores. At first, we barely noticed. Only when a real, honest-to-God fire roared to life, with shooting flames and a heat that burned our eyes, did we realize the danger. The fire spread so quickly and consumed the barn so completely we barely staggered out with our lives. When we cleared the structure, we scattered, sprinting through the hay field, through the gardens of tenants' houses, fleeing into the woods."

"And so a call for help…"

Beau could not look at her. "There was no call. We did not slow down to raise even a warning. Nothing. We ran like inebriated cowards into the forest and let the fire roar. Honestly, I have no real memory of this bit. I remember only the other boys waking me from a drunken sprawl at the edge of a field in the morning. The fire, by then, had burned itself out. Arthur's parents were hysterical, searching for us.

"As we slowly came to in the woods that morning, finally sober, the other boys began to formulate a story we could tell the earl to absolve ourselves from blame. I…I argued against an outright lie. I enjoyed liquor and stupid boyhood larks as much as the next lad, but it felt wrong not to admit that we started the fire. I beseeched the other boys to simply tell the truth to Lord and Lady Laramie."

"I believe you," Emmaline said softly from the bed. "I believe you wanted to tell the truth."

Beau sat on the bed and dropped back into a sprawl. "Oh God, I wish that was the worst of it."

There was a pause. He wondered if he could find the words to say the rest.

Finally, she asked, "Tell me the end."

Beau rolled into a sitting position and propped his elbows on his knees. He stared at the floor. "As we rushed back to the main house that morning, we passed by the barn, which was in ashes, but also the farms of the tenants who worked the Laramie land, tenants who used that barn to shelter and feed their livestock. They were—" He squeezed his eyes shut. "The farmhouses had burned as well. Roofs mostly, but one house had burned to the ground, just as the barn had done. The family that lost their home stood outside when we walked back to the manor house. It was impossible not to see them. They were huddled together in the charred remains of their garden, speaking to the vicar. A doctor was also there, kneeling over a victim who was hidden from our view."

"Oh, no, Beau. Did someone *die?*"

He shook his head. "No—not dead. He was just a boy. One little boy, not six years old, was terribly burned, almost beyond recognition. It's a miracle he lived, but oh—what a difficult life he has now."

"You *know* this boy?"

"Allow me to finish. My friends and I hurried on, whispering again about an excuse. I wouldn't hear of it. I insisted that we take responsibility. As *gentlemen*, I told them." Beau shook his head bitterly. "I suggested that it was our duty. For whatever reason, they eventually agreed. When we showed ourselves to Arthur's parents, we would tell the truth about the fire."

"Good," she said. "Good for you—for convincing them."

"It made no difference," he said, turning back to drop his head in his hands. "It made no bloody difference at all. We did admit what we'd done to the earl, and he bade us return to our rooms without telling a soul. The parents of the other boys were summoned. My parents only made bad situations worse, and I dare not bother Bryson in London with such regrettable news. I told Lord Laramie that my parents were abroad but that I would accept whatever punishment the other boys took.

"When the parents arrived, we were summoned to the earl's library, and—I'll never forget this—the fathers of these boys *worked together* to contrive a story that, for all practical purposes, would free us from all blame with the local magistrate and allow us to return to school without so much as a reprimand. There was no mention made of the lost houses or the burned child. None at all."

"*No*," said Emmaline, shaking her head.

Beau went on, shoving up from the bed again. "Oh, yes. I did not know much at this age, but I knew enough to see the injustice in this. So I—a boy of nineteen years old, barely able to afford to stay in school, the son of a disgraced, bankrupt viscount—dared to contradict them. I stepped forth and respectfully suggested that it was wrong to deny starting the fire, that people's homes had been destroyed, and at least one boy had been horribly burned. *Someone* must be responsible, I told them. We are all responsible, I said."

"And they hushed you up?" Emmaline guessed.

"Well, they asked *who I thought I was* to suggest the moral superlative to them. And then, after discussing it in front of me like I wasn't even there, these great *noble*men changed the bloody story from its being no one's fault to its being entirely *my* fault. They made *me* scapegoat for all of it. They turned *me* over to the magistrate. And they made *me* responsible for the damage to the barn."

"And the houses and the child who was burned?" she guessed again.

He spun back to her, arms outstretched. "Oh, no, these were left entirely untended. Not the houses or the child. The lot of them—these wealthy noblemen, chosen by God to lead us all—left this family to fend for themselves. Including the care for the boy. And a new house. And all of it. They provided nothing."

"Oh, Beau," she said, wrapping the sheet around herself and slipping from the bed. "I can see your agony and regret, but this is not *your* fault."

"Do not say this. It was entirely my fault. It was the fault of all of us. It was not intentional, but it was reckless and indulgent and stupid. And we should have admitted our carelessness and provided restitution for the destruction. Instead, their *noble* parents used their influence to make the problem—"

"Disappear," she finished for him.

"Well, the problem was still very much present. Houses were lost. A boy suffered—he still suffers."

"So what did you do?"

"Lord Laramie threatened to tell my brother that *I'd* done all of it—in his mind, the revised story was now a fact—if I dared suggest to anyone that his son and the other boys were involved. Bryson had worked so hard to see me brought up away from the shadow of our parents' notoriety. I could not bear for him to hear this. It would crush him to know that I had disappointed him in this way. If I could save him from this, I wanted to do it. If I could, somehow I'd manage the magistrate and help the tenants rebuild on my own."

"And that is what you did?" she asked.

He shrugged. "That is what I have been trying to do for the last ten years. I have long since paid back the price of the barn and restored the houses, and I look in on the family in Essex and provide for them whenever I can. But how can I restore the life of a boy who will be forever scarred? How?"

"You cannot," she whispered, "but you can help them in every other way. One repentant man can only do so much."

He nodded. "Yes, I believe this to be true. And the family has been so forgiving and lovely to me, all these years. I have not forgiven myself, but they have, and it has given me sort of a peace. But I can never go along with the notion that *some men* deserve to be treated with undue respect simply because they were born into this family or that. And certainly I can never go along with the notion that *I* should be regarded this way."

Emmaline nodded and took a step toward him. She wanted to reach for him, but she was unsure. He remembered now why he never volunteered this story to anyone.

"I complain about society and the *ton* and their frivolity and pointless customs," he said, "but I don't discuss the fire. It's my own private struggle. I don't expect you to understand, but I will implore you to not, at the very least, flaunt your new title. If you can help it. It is very important to me. I will never be one of them."

"Of course," she said simply. "And I understand."

He studied her. She raised her eyebrows. No excuses for him. No trying to explain it away. Simply, *I understand.*

Maybe he deceived himself, maybe he wanted it too badly, but he felt that in that moment, she *did* understand. He reached out. She padded to him in her sheet, and he tucked her close.

After a moment, she mused, "It's ironic. I married the old Duke of Ticking and earned the title of duchess, yet no one, especially him, believed I really deserved the distinction. I was always the daughter of a tradesman to him. But now I've married you, and you believe *no one* deserves the title."

He pulled her closer. "Irony, indeed. You married two titled men—and for what?"

"Oh," she said, "that is easy to answer. I married Ticking because my parents gave me no choice, and I married you because I fell in love."

CHAPTER THIRTY-FIVE

Beau had neither answered her declaration of love nor denied it. They stood in the middle of the room, locked in an embrace. Soon the embrace was a kiss, and the kiss was like making love standing up. He'd widened his stance and kissed her while slowly unwinding the sheet wrapped around her body. After the last corner unfurled, he'd stepped back and watched with relish as she affected a spin of her own and then stood, naked, before him.

They fell to the bed a moment later, and Beau had allowed her eagerness and love to fade his bitterness of the fire into the background of his mind.

"Do you think," Emmaline asked when they lay, panting, back on their pillows, "that Bryson would mind if we went downstairs for a proper breakfast? I haven't really eaten since I woke up yesterday."

"My brother would be thrilled to have you do whatever you please in this house," Beau said. "You could reschedule breakfast for the middle of the afternoon, as long as we—and by 'we,' I mean 'you'—showed some interest. In his mind, this house and the staff have belonged to me since I was made viscount. He's been waiting for the moment I would do anything so domestic as order breakfast."

"Well, he won't move out now, I hope," she said. "I cannot say how long we'll be in America."

"For once, we actually haven't discussed the future of this house," he said. "You could not know this, but it's not easy to procure a special marriage license in only six days. It was essential that our marriage was legal and binding, and I called on your young lawyer, Mr. Wick, to learn more about your late husband's will. What a tedious document that is. Bryson and I spent hours discovering to whom the late Duke of Ticking left his saddles and golden spittoons. There was no time to speculate on how long we would remain in America."

"You called Mr. Wick?" said Emmaline, amazed at his resourcefulness.

"Charming fellow. Clearly, he's very fond of you."

"He's very fond of the percentage he hopes to earn when I manage to sell the books in New York."

"Bryson's secretary did most of the work. I was determined to extract you without implicating Bryson or his shipyard."

"I would never forgive myself if the Courtlands suffered because of my predicament."

"Really, there was nothing to deconstruct. Our marriage would have been more complicated if the duke had left you any money or property, but…"

Emmaline was braiding her hair, and she paused, turning to him. "Oh, the duke left me nothing."

"This was our conclusion. No provision for you. It's a wonder the new Duke of Ticking did not set you free to go home to Liverpool before he had the bright idea of keeping Teddy close by and stealing his money."

Emmaline nodded. "I remember, clear as day, the conversation in which he discovered our potential to him. I was made a little ill and a little courageous all in the same moment. My gumption took root and began to grow that day, and I began to explore the idea of selling Papa's old books."

"Ha! Your gumption took root while Ticking's greed bloomed. You acquired the far more useful sentiment. You know, Emma, that the duke assumes I am just as greedy, that I have married you for Teddy's money. We have not discussed this, but please tell me that you know I've no interest in the money. It is Teddy's to keep and yours to manage."

"Hmm," mused Emmaline, winking at him. "The life you led on the canal did not suggest an aspirational grab for money. Nothing about you, in fact, suggests you give much thought to money at all. But that does not mean we should not discuss how we will provision ourselves. The duke provided my meals and clothing when I lived under his roof, obviously, but my plan was to live off what is left of the allowance my parents left for Teddy—that is, until I begin to show a profit from the books."

She crossed to the desk by the door and rifled in the drawers until she found ink and pen and paper. "But we should begin making lists and tallies, now that you will travel to New York with us. I had only accounted for Teddy; his valet, Mr. Broom; and me. I shall figure you in." She began to scribble notes to this effect.

"I have my own money, Emma. You needn't feed and clothe me."

"Well, we may pool our resources," she said thoughtfully, "but we do not have to. Will the money you bring be in the form of bank notes? Or English currency? Do you travel with gold, like a pirate? Your brother said the ship's food will be simple but sufficient on the Atlantic crossing, but I will hire a small staff when we get settled in New York. Kitchen help and a few maids. I will do the marketing myself, for a time." She made a note of this on the paper.

"If you help me with the work of distributing the books to the booksellers in New York," she went on, warming to the topic, "which would be lovely, but I do not expect it, mind you—then I believe we may both draw a salary from the money we make. Mr. Wick has made this suggestion. But if you do not wish to work with me, selling the books, you may..."

She could not finish this sentence and looked up, chewing her bottom lip. She stroked her chin with the feather of the pen. "You've already said you will not live as a, er, viscount in New York. But that does not mean..." She turned to him.

The look on his face stopped the question on her lips. He looked stricken. Trapped and tested and a little exhausted. He'd raised his hands to the ceiling and then settled them behind his head, half stretch, half surrender.

"But perhaps," she allowed, "you do not yet know."

He laughed, a hoarse, awkward sound. "Perhaps I do not. Look, Duchess, remember last night, when you asked me to not explain what would happen in bed in terms too precise? When you suggested that you simply might follow along?"

She nodded.

"I should appreciate the same lack of...explanation in these plans of yours."

"You don't want me to explain how we will have money for food and housing? How we will live?"

"No, of course you may explain it. Only please do not look to me for an answer—at least not yet. It has been many years since I was accountable to anyone. Bryson has insisted that I show my face in England once every eighteen months or so, simply to check in, and he's forced me to invest in this or that shipbuilding venture. But other than that, I go and do as I please.

"Raiding brothels for Elisabeth was the longest endeavor in which I'd ever engaged besides my time in the Royal Navy. It is this very…itinerate manner that allows me to sail to America with you without a backward glance—and why not? It does not startle me as it might another man. On the same token, the thought of provisioning and money and drawing a salary? This startles me very much. Do you understand?"

She nodded slowly, trying to balance her own need to sort out their time and money with his very plain request to *not* sort it out.

"You'll forgive my…aggressiveness," she said. "I have not had the freedom to leap first and locate the net on my way down, as you have. I have a brother to provide for. My relationship with my father's board of trustees is tenuous, at best. Ticking complicated everything."

Beau shoved from his chair and crossed to the desk, kneeling before her. "I understand the necessity that compels you. I simply…have never been so compelled. I…I don't know how."

She dropped the pen and placed her hands on his shoulders. "Well, neither do I, but I have been happy to learn," she said, feeling the familiar excitement strumming inside her anew. "I was always going to learn."

"I wonder? Does it make me less of a man to say that I shall...follow along?" He said it like a joke, repeating her words of the night before, but his expression revealed the slightest uncertainty.

"I've not known more of a man than you," she said.

Beau laughed, shoving up. He snatched her discarded dress from the back of a chair and held it out. "Thank God your mother did not allow you to know many men," he said. "But come, let us seek out sustenance before I perish."

She rolled her eyes and shook her head and stooped to retrieve her chemise from the floor.

CHAPTER THIRTY-SIX

Jocelyn Breedlowe rushed from Cavendish Square to Henrietta Place, tugging Teddy Holt behind her. The walkway was dotted with patches of ice, and she skittered and sidestepped, trying to keep them upright.

"Faster, Teddy, that's it," she said in her calmest possible voice. "Faster, if you can bear it."

They slid the last three yards, and she caught the railing with one hand and kept them off the icy steps with the palm of the other. When they reached the door, she pounded, flat-handed, *rap-rap-rap-rap*, until Sewell, finally, admitted them.

"Lord and Lady Rainsleigh?" she gasped, bundling Teddy inside. "Have they come down?"

"In the breakfast room, miss," the butler said cautiously. Jocelyn yanked the door from his hand and slammed it shut, locking the bolt.

"Have Stoker or Joseph called today?" she asked, whipping off her coat and scarf and piling them in Sewell's arms. The boys tended to ramble at night, but they could generally be counted on to return for breakfast.

"In the mews, I believe," he said through the heap of her coat.

Jocelyn thanked God for this small favor. "Take Teddy to them, will you, Mr. Sewell? Tell them not to leave the grounds and not to let Teddy out of their sight."

She did not wait for a response but rushed down the hall. Opening and closing her hands, she repeated the incident in her head. Emmaline would want to know every detail, just as it had happened.

Outside the breakfast room, she paused and took a deep breath. "I beg your pardon, Lady Rainsleigh, Lord Rainsleigh?" She stepped inside.

"Oh, there you are, Jocelyn," said Elisabeth, gesturing to the empty chair beside her. "Come and have your breakfast. But where is Teddy? You must tell Emmaline his reaction to his new room here in Henrietta Place."

The two couples—Elisabeth and Bryson, Emmaline and Rainsleigh—sat around the oval table, smiling at her. Thank God they were all present; Jocelyn would not have to say it twice.

"Something's happened, I'm afraid," she said, coming to stop behind the empty dining chair.

Emmaline shoved immediately to her feet, compelling the gentlemen to also stand. "Teddy," Emma said.

Jocelyn held out a hand. "Teddy is here, and he's well. For the moment. Sewell has taken him to Joseph and Stoker in the mews." She took another deep breath. "But he and I have just raced back from Cavendish Square, and he may well be unsettled."

"Miss Breedlowe, what happened?" asked the viscount carefully, studying her. "Is someone hurt?"

"We were approached in the square by the Duke of Ticking."

"*The duke?*" repeated Emmaline. "In the park? But what did he want?"

"Well," began Jocelyn, cringing, "he was accompanied by a man. A doctor, he claimed. A Dr. Vickery. Of Egham, in Surrey. Apparently, the doctor specializes in...in lunacy and afflictions of the brain."

"Oh God," said Emmaline, closing her eyes.

Jocelyn pressed on. "The duke and this...Dr. Vickery came upon us on a bench. While we sat there—rather, trapped by their proximity—they discussed Teddy at length, discussed him as if neither of us was there. I endeavored to slide away, to lead Teddy over the bench and through the bed of ivy behind us, but they deliberately blocked our progress."

"But what did they want?" asked Elisabeth. "What was this discussion?"

"The duke, it seems, collaborated with the doctor to make some diagnosis of Teddy's mental state."

"Diagnosis?" said Emmaline. "But Teddy is not ill, he is simply...Teddy."

"He referred to Teddy as a 'lunatic,' Emma," Jocelyn said. "He said it again and again, I'm afraid. He would not, in fact, stop saying it."

"*A lunatic?*" cried Emmaline. Her voice cracked, and her husband put a hand on her shoulder.

The viscount said, "You're certain Teddy is here, in this house, at the moment, Miss Breedlowe?"

Jocelyn nodded. "Quite certain. We've just dashed back together. I've assumed he would be safe with Jon Stoker and

Joseph. I thought it best not to relay what happened where he might overhear."

"He is quite safe with the boys," confirmed Mr. Courtland. "And you were right to come to us alone. But please, can you begin from the moment you first saw Ticking?"

This was followed by a chorus of "yes," and "take a drink of water," and "sit down and catch your breath."

Jocelyn refused it all. She rushed to tell them. "Teddy and I breakfasted early and then agreed to walk to Cavendish Square with yesterday's bread to feed the birds. From our place on the bench, I saw the Ticking carriage—the ducal crest is impossible to miss—circle the square once, and then once again, and then a third time. Naturally, this gave me pause. I suggested to Teddy that we return home to escape the cold.

"We had just made the decision to go when the carriage stopped at the nearest corner and the duke himself, accompanied by this doctor, emerged and rushed to us on the bench. The duke greeted me by name and said to the doctor, 'This is the boy. It's him.'"

"But for *what?*" pressed Emmaline, her fists clenched in front of her. "What could Ticking want with a doctor's care for Teddy? We've gone. Teddy and I have gone. He has *nothing* to gain."

"After the duke rattled off a…a list of infractions against Teddy, I excused us and forced our way from them."

"What infractions?" asked Rainsleigh.

"Lies, all of them," said Jocelyn. "That Teddy will not sleep and howls in the night. That we must feed him by hand because he is known to throw his food. That he is prone to undress himself in the middle of the day—"

"*What?*" Emmaline's voice was a tear-choked whisper. The viscount wrapped his arm around her shoulders. She grabbed hold of his arm.

Jocelyn went on. "I told him, 'But this has not been my experience at all with Teddy Holt. Perhaps you are mistaken. Teddy exhibits none of this behavior, none at all. I assist in his care on a weekly basis, and he is a quiet and gentle boy who sleeps and eats and is suitably attired, just like anyone else.'"

"And what did he say?" Elisabeth now rose from her chair.

"He said…" Here, Jocelyn paused, barely able to say the words. "He said, 'Naturally the servants are paid to conceal the boy's episodes.' And then he said something to the effect of…having proof enough to lock Teddy away from 'able-minded people and defenseless children' forever."

Emmaline mouthed *no*, too devastated to voice the word. "But these are *lies*. Teddy is perfectly composed unless he's provoked, and even then he only wishes to be left alone. He is not a bother to anyone. Why would Ticking do this? We were never anything more to him than…than little-known relatives who posed the smallest possible imposition. And my marriage to the late duke bathed the lot of them in money. They live in Portman Square now *because of me*. Why?"

Jocelyn shook her head. "The doctor stood by and studied Teddy with an interest that bordered on salacious. I could not bear the look, and the duke would not hear my protestations. This is when I took Teddy by the hand, and we *ran*. Sewell has just now let us in." She looked at Emmaline. "I'm so sorry, Emma."

The viscountess shook her head mutely, back and forth, back and forth.

Elisabeth reached out and grabbed Jocelyn's hand. "You've done everything exactly right. You handled it far better than I would have done." She looked at the viscountess. "Deep breaths, Emmaline. That's right. Take a moment to be duly outraged, and then let us work out a plan."

Emmaline continued to shake her head. "But why produce a doctor? If what Jocelyn says is true, he's brought this man up from Surrey, just to hound us."

Jocelyn said, "They made no move to apprehend Teddy from me, but there was something about him. I believe that if Teddy had been unattended in the park, they would have snatched him up and taken him."

"Of this I have no doubt, but *why?*" Emmaline repeated, throwing her hands in the air. "Ticking will gain none of Teddy's inheritance, even if he was locked away. Why would he do this?"

Just then, Sewell stepped into the room and said, "His Grace the Duke of Ticking to see you, my lady." All eyes swung to the butler.

"His Grace is here?" asked Bryson Courtland.

"Indeed," said Sewell. "He is accompanied by a man he identified as a doctor and a Runner from Bow Street. Should I tell them…"

He let the sentence trail off and looked first to the viscount, then Emmaline, and then to Mr. Courtland. The authority of the house was uncertain, and even Sewell was lost.

Elisabeth spoke first. "Show them nowhere. They may remain in the entryway. We will attend them there. Thank you, Sewell."

"A Bow Street Runner," repeated Emmaline, starting for the door. "But have they come to *arrest* my brother?" She looked back at her husband who stood, motionless, behind his chair.

She stopped. She held out her hand. "Beau? Will you come?"

The viscount stared at her, hesitating. His gaze dropped to her hand. He did not move.

Oh, no, thought Jocelyn, looking away.

Bryson opened his mouth to speak, but Elisabeth took him by the arm and pulled him from the room.

Emmaline made a strangled noise, the sound of frustration and despair.

The viscount remained unmoving and silent.

Jocelyn closed her eyes, miserable for Emma, worried for Teddy. She slipped from the room. In the hallway, Elisabeth and Mr. Courtland whispered fiercely. She was trapped by silence behind her and rising voices before, and she hovered in between.

At last, Emmaline emerged from the dining room.

Jocelyn looked up.

Thank God, the viscount was at her side.

The five of them exchanged looks but said nothing. In a grim line, they proceeded to the doorway that would admit them to the duke. Ticking's voice could be heard making some proclamation. There were other voices, too—affirmations, a cough.

Mr. Courtland turned to Rainsleigh, but the viscount looked away. Emmaline closed her eyes. Elisabeth and Mr. Courtland exchanged glances, and then his wife gave him a shrug and slight nod. The elder Courtland sighed, adjusted the lapels of his coat, and led them in.

"Here they are," said the Duke of Ticking. He stood beneath the chandelier in the center of the entryway, tapping his gloves against his palm. "You see, sir, how my father's widow seeks refuge among indulgent friends, just as I've said? They harbor her in this opulent house, employing wealth to conceal the lunatic."

"How do you do?" said this man to the Courtlands. He wore the blue jacket of a Bow Street Runner and juggled a pen and packet of papers. Jocelyn had not seen him in the park with the duke and doctor.

Ticking ignored his greeting and continued. "They encourage the reckless, irresponsible care she takes with her brother. And when his temper is too much for her, they work together to disguise the dangers to the innocent and able-minded."

The blue-coated man had begun to scribble notes on paper. "Before we explore danger to the innocent and able-minded, Your Grace, I shall require everyone's name and places of address."

The duke wasn't finished. "But how much does she pay them to assist her with her brother, and for how long can they safely contain him? *These* are the questions one must ask."

Jocelyn turned to her friends. Emmaline had gone white. Her mouth hung open in shock, and Elisabeth took hold of her arm. Mr. Courtland looked from the women to his brother. The viscount's eyes were narrowed, and he looked to be moments from launching himself at the duke.

"I beg your pardon, sir," said Bryson Courtland quickly. "I propose that we begin again." He looked to the man with pen and paper. "If you please, identify yourself, sir." To the duke, he said, "You and I are acquainted, but I should like to know the meaning of this intrusion. By whose leave do you enter this house and spew accusations?"

"By whose leave?" said Ticking. "By the law of this land. Can you not see that I have brought an agent of the magistrate's office in Bow Street? Will you now pretend not to know of the attack on my son?"

Emmaline let out a noise of desperation, but Bryson Courtland spoke again. "I make no pretense, I assure you. And I can see very plainly, Your Grace, but I have not been made privy to who or why or even *what*. I will ask once more. Introduce your colleagues and plainly state your business. You alarm the ladies, you irritate me, and my brother looks to be a heartbeat from launching himself at the lot of you."

"Threaten me, will you?" said the duke. "You have very little room to accuse, sir."

"I will accuse you of interrupting my breakfast, if nothing else. What do you want?"

"Perhaps if you'll allow me, Your Grace," said the man in the blue coat.

"Yes, yes, what are you waiting for?" said the duke. "These people are impervious to reason. Just what you would expect from a family that harbors a lunatic."

Viscount Rainsleigh made a growling noise, but the officer cut him off and introduced himself as Agent Matthew Roe of Bow Street. The other man was identified as Dr. Gene Vickery of Surrey. Mr. Courtland nodded and, in the most measured tone, introduced all of the Courtlands and Jocelyn Breedlowe.

"But what can we do for you, Agent Roe?" he finished.

"Investigation," Mr. Roe replied, gazing down at his papers. "I've the charge of an assault, allegedly perpetrated by one Theodore Holt, aged nineteen. I understand he resides in this house."

"But Theodore Holt is my brother, Teddy," said Emmaline. "And I assure you, he has assaulted no one."

The officer studied her and then made a notation. "So you say. I assure you, Lady...Rainsleigh, is it? Ah, yes, Lady Rainsleigh. I assure you that I have been dispatched by the magistrate in Bow Street to determine just that."

"But assaulted whom?" asked Emmaline.

The officer consulted the papers again. "The Lord Orin Crumbley, son to the Duke of Ticking." He looked up. "But the victim does *not* reside here; is that correct?"

"As I explained in detail to the magistrate"—Ticking gritted out the words—"*my son* is convalescing at home. I've summoned you here because *here* is where the lunatic resides. It is from *here* that you should haul him away. I've brought Dr. Vickery so that he may vouch for the boy's mental vexation. It is to Dr. Vickery's asylum that I hope the law will convey the boy."

Emmaline cried out now and began to quietly sob.

The viscount said, "If you lay one hand on the boy—"

Bryson Courtland cut him off. "So a charge has been filed? May I see it?"

"Yes, of course," said Mr. Roe. "Forgive me. Your copy is here." He extended the paper.

Bryson looked at his brother.

The viscount made no move to take it.

Emmaline began to raise her hand for it, but Mr. Court-land stepped forward, smiled gently to her, and took the papers up.

Mr. Roe went on. "In view of the Duke of Ticking's charge, I will be carrying out a full investigation. I should like to begin with the victim, Your Grace, as is customary. But since *this* was the address you provided, I might as well make myself known to the accused and apprise him of his rights."

"No," said Emmaline tearfully. "No, you might as well not. I am responsible for Theodore Holt, sir, and these accusations are but *lies*. My brother is not a madman. His brain is affected, yes, but it is the brain of a harmless child. He cannot understand legal charges, especially if they are fabricated. The duke terrifies him, and I shall never, *ever* allow him to be examined by this…*doctor*. Furthermore—"

Bryson Courtland cut her off. "I think the less we say, Emmaline, the better. Until you've spoken to legal counsel."

"You see how her friends protect her?" said he duke.

Mr. Courtland ignored him. "The charge is serious but, clearly, false." He waved the papers in the air. "It claims Teddy launched himself at the duke's son, chased him with a fire-place poker, and gouged him in the eye."

"But this is preposterous," said Emmaline.

"Quite," said Mr. Courtland thoughtfully. He looked at the officer. "Is the viscountess required by law to produce her brother at this moment?"

"Yes!" said the duke in the same moment Mr. Roe said, "Not necessarily. As I said, I typically begin an investigation with the victim. I can return to Mr. Holt presently. Likely, I will return several times."

"Very good," said Mr. Courtland. "This will allow the viscountess to explain the situation to the boy. You'll appreciate that this is the first we've heard of the charges against him. The Viscountess of Rainsleigh only departed from the duke's household yesterday, and we knew nothing of his son's injury then." He motioned to Sewell to open the door.

The duke was shaking his head. "We will not wait. The more time passes, the better she may coach the lunatic into respectability." He glared at Mr. Roe. "I bade your office dispatch you *here* so you might witness the boy in his wild, unfettered state. This is the entire purpose of your call, sir. By my word, Dr. Vickery and I just happened upon him in Cavendish Square this morning, and he veritably swung from the treetops. Didn't he, Dr. Vickery?"

"Quite so," confirmed the doctor.

"That is a lie," said Jocelyn, surprising herself. "Teddy and I fed the birds and exchanged not five sentences with His Grace and his…associate. We were—"

She was cut off by the sound of voices down the hallway. Laughter. A boast. A male voice singing two bars of a jig. More laughter.

It was Stoker, Joseph, and Teddy, clattering in from the mews. There was a bark. The viscount's dog. Jocelyn shut her eyes. Why hadn't she bade Sewell to confine the boys outside?

The voices grew nearer, not five feet from the door. More barking.

"Teddy!" Emmaline called frantically.

"Malie," came the answer.

"Teddy, darling, I've just—"

Mr. Courtland cleared his throat loudly, cutting her off. He gave another very slight, very fast jerk of his head. *No.*

Emmaline fell silent, and the three boys walked into the hallway, the dog at their heels.

"Oh, hello," said Joseph on a laugh. "Forgive our intrusion. We weren't aware of callers."

No one spoke, and Joseph and Stoker looked slowly around, taking stock of the hard expressions of the men in the room, the grim faces of the ladies. Joseph studied the duke, and defensiveness crept across his face. He stepped forward with his chest out. Stoker stepped beside him. Peach let out a low, ominous growl.

"Is everything quite all right, sir?" Joseph asked Mr. Courtland carefully.

"You're a good man to ask, Joe," Mr. Courtland said. " 'Tis nothing about which we want to concern Teddy."

Emmaline tried to go to her brother, but her husband held her firm.

Bryson continued. "Mr. Roe, since the opportunity has presented itself, I should like to point out that the...*accused*, Teddy Holt, has just stepped into this room. He's one of these three young men, actually. They are of the same general age, and family friends, all."

The officer studied the boys, and Mr. Courtland continued. "Two of the boys are down from university on holiday. The other is Teddy Holt. I wonder, if you had to guess, could you tell me which of the boys is suspected to be the 'lunatic'?"

"Well, of course he does not look like a lunatic," said the duke.

Mr. Roe considered the three young men and then glanced at the papers in his hand. "I cannot guess, sir. But I warn you—the investigation will not be carried out on speculation."

"Of course not," said Mr. Courtland. "Nor should it. But for your information, Teddy Holt is the young man in the center. My point was to refute the duke's claim that Teddy swings from the treetops, as it were. The truth could not be more opposite. We harbor no madman here."

"Yes, well, that remains to be seen, but I appreciate the introduction. You can be assured that a full investigation will follow, and I will call on this house again and speak to Theodore Holt at some length. In the end, the magistrate will likely decide." He handed his card to Mr. Courtland. "I appreciate your cooperation in the matter. But first, I shall seek out the victim." He raised his eyebrows at the duke. "If you would be so kind, Your Grace."

The duke objected to this, but Bryson nodded to Sewell again, and the door swept open to the January cold. Mr. Roe tucked his paperwork beneath his arm, nodded good-bye, and made his way into the street. Ticking and the doctor followed, calling after him. Jocelyn, along with the two couples and the three boys, were left to stare at the empty doorway. Sewell stepped up to close it with a firm *click*.

For five beats, no one said a word.

Joseph broke the silence. "What's happened?"

"Can we trouble you to keep an especially close eye on Teddy in coming days?" Elisabeth said. "There is some matter with Bow Street and a magistrate. We will explain later, but in the meantime, Teddy can never be left unattended. Can you do this for Lady Rainsleigh, Joseph? Stoker?"

"Yes, ma'am," the young men assured her, looking at each other.

Joseph said to Teddy, "Looks like you're stuck with us now, mate."

Stoker was not so easily put off. "What's been said?"

Elisabeth shook her head. "Not in front of the boy," she said softly. "I will tell you presently. Can you take him to the kitchen for tea, please?"

Stoker hesitated, watching them, but Joseph called to him.

When they were gone, Emmaline said, "I still cannot work out what Ticking has to gain from this. Why do it now?"

Her husband took a wide step back. "He does it because he can. He's a bloody duke, isn't he? His golden goose has been taken away, and this is his revenge. To hell with everybody else. It's unconscionable, yet it happens every bloody day. No one is safe when small, spiteful men have so much power."

He took another step back. And another. His dog heeled at his feet.

Emmaline watched him, her face still white, but he would not look at her.

Mr. Courtland said, "But where was this rebuke when the duke was here? It would have provoked him, but at least you would have contributed to the exchange. You're the ranking member of this family now, Beau. Teddy is your brother-in-law. Had you nothing to say?"

The viscount looked from Mr. Courtland to his wife and back to his brother.

Mr. Courtland tried again. "I have the charges here." He held out the paper. "Take it."

The viscount shook his head and took another step back. And another. His dog barked.

"Beau," called Mr. Courtland. "Do not think of leaving."

Beau Courtland answered him with footsteps. He turned and walked down the hall.

Jocelyn looked down, allowing them a private moment to register his retreat. No one spoke. In the distance, they heard a door open and close.

When she looked up, Emmaline was staring after him down the hall.

Mr. Courtland swore under his breath and crossed to the window.

Emmaline said softly, "Abuse of power is a great struggle for Beau."

"*Struggle* is a great struggle for Beau," Mr. Courtland said.

"He would have fought the duke for me, if it had come to that," she said. "Of this I have no doubt."

"Oh yes, he can fight, can't he? But after the age of fifteen, fewer and fewer of life's challenges are solved with one's fist. I apologize for his behavior, Emmaline. This is the very last thing you need."

She shook her head. "You are not responsible for the Duke of Ticking or for your brother. I will…I will call upon my lawyer." She reached for the charge papers, and he gave them to her. "Beau rescued Teddy from the streets of London twice, something few men could have done. That is help enough for me. I can manage whatever comes next."

She looked at Jocelyn and Elisabeth. "Could I impose on the two of you to accompany me to the office of my lawyer? I would be most grateful for your support. You may help me repeat the details just as they happened. Beau"—she paused and cleared her throat—"will likely not attend me, but I can ask him to mind Teddy with Stoker and Joseph." The women agreed immediately, and Emmaline continued. "Ticking is a duke, but he is not the king. He is not God. He cannot incarcerate an innocent boy just because he feels cheated out of money that was never his." Her voice grew stronger with each pronouncement. After glancing at the charging papers, she excused herself to check on Teddy.

Jocelyn and Elisabeth watched her disappear down the kitchen stairs. They exchanged looks.

"If he fails her…" Mr. Courtland said.

"Do not give up on him yet," Elisabeth said. "He married her, and that is something you never thought he would do."

"Yes," said Bryson grimly. "He married her. And now I pray God that she will not regret it."

CHAPTER THIRTY-SEVEN

Desmond Wick, Emmaline's lawyer, was forced to move two chairs from his reception space to his cramped office to accommodate the three women. Emmaline apologized, but she would have her friends beside her, despite the bother.

Now they sat, shoulder to shoulder, the leg of Emmaline's chair propped onto the bottom rung of Mr. Wick's bookshelf. Emmaline held to the arms of the chair to keep from sliding onto the floor. If Mr. Wick thought it was odd that she'd arrived with two friends instead of her new husband, he gave no indication.

"None of our previous work matters, compared to my brother's safekeeping, Mr. Wick," Emmaline had told him straightaway. "Not the books or America, not Teddy's inheritance, nothing. Can you help me?"

The young lawyer assured her that he would try. Inexperienced but hard-working, Mr. Wick had been the only lawyer willing to take on the exceedingly risky and wholly unorthodox work of setting up Emmaline's book export business behind the back of the Duke of Ticking, and she'd hired him for that reason alone.

By dumb luck or providence (or a little of both), he'd turned out to be proficient and thorough, and best of all, he seemed to actually believe in her dream. At times, Emmaline had been so grateful for Mr. Wick that she strove to succeed in America to reward his loyalty as much as she did for herself and Teddy. Certainly, she would not have won her chance at freedom from the duke without Mr. Wick's discreet research into her late husband's will, the estate of her parents, and the delicate exchanges required to deal with her father's board of trustees.

Now she hoped Mr. Wick could apply this same diligence and cunning to help her fight for Teddy's very life.

"What do you make of the charges, Mr. Wick, and what can I do to counter them?"

"Right," he said, looking up. "I confirmed what I knew of the process as soon as I received your note. It appears that the Duke of Ticking has reported the alleged attack to the magistrate in Bow Street and suggested that Teddy's mental state is to blame. For whatever reason, the duke does not wish to see him jailed so much as locked away in an asylum. The presence of this Dr. Vickery speaks to this."

"Why would he care, if his goal is to spite me?"

"If I had to guess, I'd say he believes he may still have some access to Teddy's inheritance if he controls the boy's future."

"Good Lord," said Emmaline, "he will stop at nothing."

"Regardless, we shall carry on as if this is true," said Wick. "Since we know that Teddy does suffer from mental challenges but is not a threat—and furthermore, we know that he did not lay a finger on the duke's son—we can assume that His Grace's influence and rank have Bow Street hopping to do whatever he suggests. Despite the fairness of the officers on the case, we may also assume that the duke's influence will prevail. I should warn you; this influence may extend to the court as well."

Beside Emmaline, Elisabeth nodded. "Bryson wielded his authority and rank in much the same way before he abdicated the title to Beau. All for the greater good, of course. He was careful not to abuse his power. But I have seen the effect of a nobleman turning up in a government office. Municipal clerks and even supervisors scramble to do his bidding."

"Yes…" mused Mr. Wick, glancing at Emmaline and then away.

The lawyer was thinking of Beau, she knew. In addition to her extreme worry for Teddy, Emmaline swam in an entirely separate pool of dread for her husband. What official and lordly thing would be expected of him during the proceedings?

She'd seen Beau in the mews before they'd departed for Mr. Wick's office. She'd come to say good-bye to Teddy, and her husband had been there too. In low, serious tones, he was explaining the situation to Joseph and Stoker while her brother fed an apple to a horse in the end stall. They had shared several long, heartfelt looks across the stable. From those looks, Emmaline did not doubt his worry for her or his outrage at Ticking. But he had volunteered nothing. Not to join her in the office of Mr. Wick. Not an encouraging word. She told herself this should come as no surprise.

"If the officer decides that the charge has some merit," Mr. Wick was saying, "then he will have little choice but to make an arrest."

Emmaline sucked in a breath. They could not take Teddy from her and lock him in a cell, not even for a day.

"But never do fear," Mr. Wick said. "We will have anticipated this, and I shall go immediately to the magistrate and ask to post bail so that Teddy may remain in your care until a trial." He waved a dismissive hand. "I have every reason to believe this shall be granted. It happens often enough, and Teddy has lived with you, without incident, since the death of your parents. After we post bail and both sides are given time to prepare, all parties shall reconvene for a hearing. The judges chosen to hear the case will be advised by or have personal experience with the types of so-called 'crimes' associated with lunacy or alleged lunacy."

He leaned back in his chair and crossed his arms over his chest. "Of course, I cannot guarantee a good result, but I have every confidence that we will win the day, considering…"

"Considering what?" asked Emmaline.

"Considering the Duke of Ticking appears to have fabricated the entire story. A lie is a lie, isn't it?" He sifted through papers on his desk. "The duke's claim is that Teddy attacked his child, a son, name of Orin?" He looked up. "Can you tell me the approximate age of this child?"

Emmaline ran through a mental role of Ticking's children. "Orin is ten or eleven, I believe."

Mr. Wick made a note of this. "Right. *Not* the heir?"

"Oh, no, there are at least six or seven male children before him."

Mr. Wick made a face but said nothing. "And you've said that you saw young Orin at breakfast the day of your wedding, which was the last day Teddy had direct access to the boy, and Orin appeared entirely unharmed."

"Entirely."

Wick nodded. "Presumably, the duke will present some sort of physical evidence of the attack to the court. Healing bruises...a scabbed-over gash...that sort of thing. Is there any chance that the duke would go so far as to mark the child himself; that is, knock him around a bit, to give the appearance of harm?"

Emmaline thought about this and then shook her head. "I'm doubtful the duchess would allow it. She dotes on her sons. Would he really mark his own child, just to spite me?"

"God knows what these people might do, my lady," sighed Mr. Wick, making another note. "But if the boy arrives in court with no discernible injury, His Grace's charge will rely on the testimony of any witnesses who may have seen the alleged attack, calling on others to corroborate what happened. In this instance, it will be your word—and the word of your own witnesses—against his." Wick sat back in his chair and tossed his pen down.

"But his word is a complete lie," said Emmaline.

"This may be true, but the fact still remains that he's a duke, isn't he? I don't have to tell you what that means." Wick spun in his chair again, staring at the ceiling. "Can you think, Lady Rainsleigh, of whom we might call to testify on Teddy's behalf? Likely, the duke will call members of his family, the household staff, and certainly this doctor. If I had to guess, I'd say they ambushed Miss Breedlowe in the park so that

Dr. Vickery could claim to have 'examined' Teddy without perjuring himself, per se."

Emmaline nodded, thinking of their very small circle of friends. "Well, Miss Breedlowe could testify, of course. And then there is his lifelong valet, Mr. Broom. Also Elisabeth and Mr. Courtland—"

"I should warn you," Mr. Wick cut in, "that any public opposition to the Duke of Ticking by the Courtlands may result in harmful repercussions from the duke. We need only look at the matter before us to see how unpleasant His Grace can be if he feels thwarted."

Elisabeth sat up in her chair. "Please be advised that Bryson and I are *not* afraid of the Duke of Ticking," but Emmaline held out a hand.

"No," she said. "Mr. Wick is correct. I will not risk Bryson and Elisabeth's reputations for this."

"What of the risk to Jocelyn?" Elisabeth protested. "Or Mr. Broom, for that matter? We cannot *all* hide from this person."

"Miss Breedlowe and the valet," cut in Mr. Wick, "have far less to risk than you do, Mrs. Courtland, if you don't mind my saying. It is far less satisfying to bankrupt a valet than it is a shipping magnate such as your husband."

"It's settled," said Emmaline. "We shall build our defense without the testimony of Elisabeth or Bryson. The witnesses shall be me, and the doctor who treated Teddy as a boy in Liverpool...perhaps some other old friends from home, Miss Breedlowe, if I might impose on her, and Mr. Broom."

"Right," Mr. Wick said, spinning his chair right and left. "And what of your new husband, if you don't mind my asking?

To be frank, I believe the most resounding testimony might come from the viscount. Not only is he a man, but he's a titled gentleman. This...*this* is our best chance to face down a duke. Not a caretaker or a valet—or even *you*, for that matter, because you are a woman. If I had to guess, the whole affair will take place in the House of Lords—not the main chamber, of course, but in one of the courts of justice reserved for conflicts among the peerage. Members of Parliament who sit on the committee that regulates lunatic care usually preside over these types of cases, I've learned. Considering the elevated rank of the duke and his colleagues in the Lords, there is chance that, as women, you and Miss Breedlowe would be permitted only the most limited of testimony. But a viscount..." Mr. Wick allowed the sentence to trail off.

Emmaline felt her heart seize up, part by part. Of course, Mr. Wick's assumption should come as no surprise, and she could not argue with the logic. But neither could she commit Beau to set foot in the House of Lords. To testify, even on behalf of Teddy, would be excruciating for him, and she had no idea if he could manage it. The truth was, she'd only known her husband for a month and a half. They'd been married for all of one day. Enough time, she thought, to fall in love, but not enough time to know if he could leave behind his bitterness and anxiety and testify in a court of law—no, not a court of law. The House of Lords.

While Emmaline floundered, Elisabeth leaned forward and laid her gloved hands, side by side, on Mr. Wick's desktop. "He will do it," she said without a hint of doubt.

"Excellent," said Mr. Wick, snatching up his pen. "This is just what I hoped to hear."

Emmaline did not have the heart to challenge Elisabeth's confidence. She did not have the heart to say anything at all.

"Do not worry, Lady Rainsleigh," continued Mr. Wick, newly invigorated. "You and the viscount, along with your fully exonerated brother, will be on the boat to New York City by the end of the month."

CHAPTER THIRTY-EIGHT

Beau stood in Bryson's wine cellar, ten feet beneath the level of the street, staring at the rows of dusty bottles of wine that his brother would never drink. In the corner of the cellar, Bryson studied the labels of two bottles of Bordeaux.

"Why do you own more bottles of priceless wine than you and Elisabeth will ever drink?" Beau asked.

"For the same reason that you drink more cheap bottles than you need. It gives us something to do." Bryson replaced both bottles and turned to scrutinize the opposite rack.

Beau chuckled, wondering what his brother would do if he opened a bottle here and now and drank from the bottle.

"Where is Teddy?" Bryson asked.

"In the garden, breaking the ice off the surface of your goldfish pond. Stoker and Joseph are with him."

"You know the goldfish pond actually belongs to _yo_—"

"Bryson, don't," Beau said on an intake of breath. "I will abandon this house to vagrants before I debate it with you again."

"Fine. We won't debate. But please be advised that Elisabeth and I are moving across town. You're married now; the house belongs to you and your wife. The staff is well trained and can help you along."

"You are aware we are about to sail to America for an undetermined amount of time."

"Then sell the bloody thing. But the house belongs to the viscountcy, and you are the viscount. You've a lady wife now. I've bought a house nearer to Elisabeth's foundation. It's no hardship for us. Elisabeth never loved this house, and I enjoy a new project."

Beau nodded. He hadn't the energy or emotional stamina to argue about something so inconsequential. Not when there were so many more pressing things to say. "I suppose it's all settled, then. Emmaline and I will remain here until we sail for New York. After that...I cannot say."

Bryson walked to the end of the aisle. "If you sell it, the money is yours to do with what you will."

Beau pinched the bridge of his nose. If the topic of conversation was not changed, he would bash a bottle of wine against the wall. "Bryson," he began, "what of the idea of moving up our sail date for New York? What if...Emma and Teddy and I left next week? Or in four days? Or bloody tomorrow?"

Bryson walked back to look at him. Beau continued. "The Duke of Ticking's petty accusations cannot follow us all the way to New York. If we're already meant to go, why linger under his nose, allowing him to torture us?"

"Well, for one," Bryson said, watching him, "the boat is not ready."

"You cannot tell me that you haven't a single ship in your fleet that could see us to New York right away?"

"I *can* tell you this, and I will. I've already shuffled our schedule well into next year, pulling a boat from another route to get her to New York in winter. But the ship needs repair. It cannot make the journey so soon after its last sailing. I've got men working long hours to prepare her, but I cannot, in good conscience, send Emmaline out to sea until it's restored."

Beau could not argue the logic of this. He pulled a bottle of wine from the rack beside him and looked at the label, seeing nothing. "Of course."

"As wearying as it is, I believe the most prudent course of action is to remain in London and take on the Duke of Ticking. Clear the boy's name. Leave so that you may return when you like without fear."

"I'm not afraid of Ticking."

"Well, you're afraid of something."

This was, perhaps, the truest statement Bryson had ever made about him. He was sickeningly, excruciatingly, run-for-your life afraid. Of what? Too many things for him to manage and still sleep at night. His fears tended to pile in his gut until they reached his throat and choked him.

Fear of failing. Failing in general and—this was a new development—fear of losing Emma in particular. Or disappointing her. Or both.

Fear of saying or doing the wrong thing to protect Teddy.

Fear of Emmaline's damnable lists and accounts and questions about provisions.

Fear of the responsibility of this house.

Fear of the responsibility of anyone but himself.

Worst of all, fear of facing down the Duke of Ticking and losing.

Of all the bloody crises to befall them, accusations by a bloody duke who put an innocent boy at risk? What were the odds that the alarming pattern of innocent boys, and dangerous calamity, and bloody members of the nobility would befall him again?

Beau could fight, he could sail, he could rescue women and children from captivity and peril. But he could *not* go toe to toe with pompous, overeducated, underreasoned lordlings who'd been told since birth that they mattered more than anybody else. He could not. He'd tried it before and failed.

How ironic that this was the one heroic deed that his new wife required. His beautiful, clever, forgiving, courageous wife. He could embody many roles as savior for her, but he could not embody this. Not without becoming a laughingstock and losing her brother to the horrors of a bloody asylum in the process.

Beau took a deep breath and looked at his brother. He would expect an answer. He always expected an answer.

"I am afraid of failing her," Beau said. The situation seemed too bleak, for once, to joke.

"The only way you can fail her is by running away."

"Not if I remain and make her situation worse." This reply took no thought. When he tried to envision how or when they might confront the duke, he only saw himself saying the *wrong bloody thing*. Repeatedly.

But he would not misspeak if he was not available to talk.

"My God, Beau," said Bryson, "please tell me you are not considering leaving her to face this alone."

Beau opened his mouth to tell him he didn't know what he considered, but they heard footsteps on the cellar stairs, and they turned to see Emmaline bustle down.

"Beau?" she called. "Are you there?"

"Yes, here." He glanced at his brother. Bryson stared back with a look that said, *Don't you dare.* Beau looked away.

"Careful on the stairs," he called, reaching for her.

Emma appeared, smiling sadly when she saw him. He took her hand to help her down from the top step, and she fell against him. "Sewell said I'd find you here."

Beau scooped her up, reveling in the feel of her against his body. He'd wanted to hold her all day.

"Where is Teddy?" she asked against his chest.

Bryson answered this, clipping up the staircase behind them. "In the garden with Stoker and Joseph. I was just going to look in on them. Did the lawyer offer any hope?"

"Some," she said. "He is very resourceful. Elisabeth will tell you."

"Of this, I have no doubt," he said, and he disappeared up the stairs, leaving Beau alone with his wife.

"I'm sorry, Emma." As much as he'd wanted to hold her, he'd wanted to say *this.*

"Sorry for..."

"Abandoning you to this madness."

"I'm sorry that you married a woman with so many...complications."

He kissed the top of her head. "Do not apologize. You are falsely accused. Or Teddy is. Ticking has victimized you both. Typically, victims are my specialty, just...not this type."

She chuckled. "I refuse to think of us as victims, but now I must ask. What type is not *your* type?"

"The kind that does not need to be rescued but rather"—he searched for the correct word—"needs an advocate."

"Stop. What I really need now is your support," she said, snuggling into him. "I managed the meeting with Mr. Wick quite well on my own. But it's ridiculous how quickly one becomes accustomed to friends and…lovers." She chuckled.

"*Lover*," he corrected. "Just the one, I hope."

"The only one," she whispered, and he dropped his lips to her neck and kissed her behind the ear. He had the irrational wish that the door to the cellar would slam shut, and lock, and they could safely be held beneath the earth for four or five hours. Or days.

"Would you like to hear what Mr. Wick said?" she asked.

No, he thought, but he sighed heavily and said, "All right."

The story that followed was long and detailed, not the thematic summary for which he'd hoped. She drifted from his arms as she spoke, walking up and down aisles of the cellar, gesturing and exclaiming. He learned of the asylum, and the way the investigation would go, the threat of Teddy being taken into custody, and the importance of money for bail so he could remain in her care until a proper hearing. It was much of what he had expected until she got to the very end.

"Mr. Wick believes that we'd do very well to have you, my husband and a viscount, make some testimony before the court."

Beau's skin went cold. He reached for the rack of wine beside him, trying to keep his face neutral.

Emmaline glanced at him warily but continued to walk and talk. "I made no promises. Of course I would speak to you first. But that's not the worst of it, unfortunately."

Beau followed her nervous prowl around the cellar. The moment she'd uttered the phrase "*as my husband and a viscount, make some testimony,*" he'd felt himself begin to pull away.

"The worst part, I'm afraid, is that the hearing itself will likely occur in the House of Lords." Another glance she could not hold. "Not in the main chambers but in a small courtroom reserved for the conflicts among peers, particularly if they involve a parliamentary committee. In this case, the judges will be members of the Lords who serve on the Royal Commission for Lunacy Care." She stopped walking and looked at him, really looked at him. "I know this is not what you wanted to hear."

Beau wondered how he could hear anything over the roar of blood in his ears. He felt, rather than heard, the *clink, clink, clink* of wine bottles rattling beside him. His hand on the top rung had started to shake.

"Beau?" Emmaline asked, taking a step toward him.

He wanted to tell her that he was a poor choice for this, that his nerves and resentment and bloody life's journey around the world instead of around the Britain's leisure class would sabotage him.

He wanted to tell her that he would stammer, or sneer, or laugh in their faces and tell them all to go to hell. At least this would be a complete and fully formed thought, unlike anything official or meaningful he was meant to say.

Unlike anything remotely beneficial for Teddy.

He wanted to tell her that he would be nineteen again, facing off with five noblemen who listened politely and then assured him that he was well and rightly mad if he thought he could convince them of anything but exoneration for their sons.

But these arguments sounded weak and peevish and unsubstantiated, even to his own rapidly panicking mind, and he was not sure he could stand the indignity of her assurances.

His fear was irrational; he knew this. He was a man, just like any other, and he could certainly stand up in a court for the purpose of saving the life of a sweet and innocent soul. He could grit out the words that needed to be said.

And yet, what if he could not? He had not been able to convince Lord Laramie ten years ago, and, for good reason, he'd tried nothing of the sort since then.

Honestly, he could not say whether he could try it now.

Even for her. This woman who now looked at him with anxious, tear-bright eyes. The woman with whom he suspected very strongly he was falling into the thing everyone called love.

Especially for her, he could not promise to do it.

If he did not try, he would not fail.

Beau released the shuddering wine rack and said, "I was thinking of taking Teddy out of the crush of London to Wiltshire, to our family estate, Rossmore Court, until you are in need of him for the hearing."

She took another step toward him. "You're going to Wiltshire?"

"We cannot rely on Stoker and Joseph to look after Teddy forever. They are due back in school. And you are busy preparing for the journey to New York and mounting a defense against the duke in bloody Parliament. Jocelyn has duties at Elisabeth's foundation. She's been useful with Teddy, but now that I'm no longer leading the raids, she'll be needed more than ever."

"You're *going* to Wiltshire?" Emmaline repeated.

Beau would have laughed if he were not suffering from such debilitating cowardice. She looked as if she might take up one of Bryon's priceless bottles of wine and hurl it at his head.

"Just until he's needed for the hearing. I'll take Mr. Broom to help me. You know that I can keep him safe, and the atmosphere in the country is relaxed and slow—a nice change after he's been shifted from the dower house, to the ducal townhome, and now here."

"That logic would be sound if you weren't proposing to move him yet again. *To Wiltshire.* Should I take this to mean that you will *not* testify in your role as viscount at Teddy's hearing?" She would not look away from his face.

"No," he made himself say.

"*No*, you won't testify, or *no*, you will?"

"I don't know," he snapped. "I warned you, Emmaline. I warned my brother, I warned all of you. I am not capable of…of…" How could he make her see without showing her the parts of himself he hated the most?

"Of what?" she demanded. "Don't be cryptic and dismissive, not now."

"You're right," he shot back. "You. Deserve. More. I've said it from the very first. You deserve a proper husband who can take on the world. When I say I am not capable, I mean I am not capable of looking after for you." He strode past her and put his boot on the first step of the staircase.

"That," she said, spinning around, "is a horrible thing to say. I don't require looking after. I've learned that about myself in the last year. What I need is a partner. And I think we are brilliant together. And I think you should testify for my brother, even if you are afraid."

Beau began to climb the stairs. "You are the one who takes things on, sweetheart, even when you are afraid. Not me. It's why you took on the Duke of Ticking, and look where that's gotten you."

He regretted the words, even as he said them, but he did not want to be followed.

"Stop talking!" she called up after him. "Do not say another word. You make it more difficult to forgive you, the more you say!"

It was only a matter of time for that, sweetheart, Beau thought, rounding the top of the stairs, but he was careful to take her advice and *stop talking.*

CHAPTER THIRTY-NINE

By the time Beau left with Teddy, his dog, and Mr. Broom for Wiltshire, Emmaline had come to terms with his departure. She did not like it, but she was prepared for it on an intellectual level. Her heart, of course, could never be prepared.

Beau had been forced to linger two days to await Mr. Roe's interrogation of Teddy. Teddy had endured this brilliantly, answering the questions he could understand and sitting in calm silence for the questions he did not. Mr. Wick was invaluable as his advocate and intermediary. Best of all, the young lawyer argued to allow Teddy to remain in the care of Emmaline and Beau until the time of the trial, and the magistrate agreed.

In many ways, sending Teddy away with Beau felt like the best course. Teddy had been traumatized by the suggestion that he had attacked anyone, especially the duke's son Orin, the only of the duke's many children that Teddy had actually enjoyed. He had backed slowly into the corner of the drawing room when Mr. Roe had gone, covering his ears and shutting his eyes. It had taken a half hour to coax him from the wall, and only the promise of a ride on Beau's horse to the countryside had done it.

So perhaps Wiltshire was best, Emmaline thought. Best for Teddy but hell for her. The loss of her husband, so soon after she'd married him, felt like a physical crack in her heart that bled loneliness into her chest. The fact that she was also angry and confused did little to diffuse this heartsickness.

After their fight in the wine cellar, he'd returned to the Paddington Lock to sleep in his boat rather than join her in the room they'd shared for all of one night. By the end of the week, he'd collected Teddy and gone. They'd passed those days with few words between them. She was angry; he was…inscrutable. (Although if Emmaline had to guess, she would say he was angry too.) He'd not foreseen this when he'd asked to marry her—solicitors and hearings and facing a duke in parliamentary court. To make matters worse, his brother, Bryson, was furious at his desertion. Likely, Beau felt as if he'd disappointed everyone.

The irony was, she could understand if his past failures, or his present resentment, or the unnamed…*whatever it was* prevented him from testifying for Teddy.

If he could not do it, so be it. She loved him too much to hold that particular weakness, whatever the source, against him. God knew she harbored every manner of weakness for nearly her whole life. Only in the last two years, when she'd been given no other choice, had she found courage and the spirit to fight.

Perhaps Beau would, one day, learn to deal with Important Men about Serious Matters or perhaps he would not, but she would love him just as much, regardless.

What troubled her was his inability to discuss it with her and his neck-breaking flight from her side.

She might not need him to testify, but she certainly needed him to hold her at night when she could not sleep for fear. She needed him to listen to her recount the progress that she made, building their defense, with Mr. Wick. Simply put, she needed *him*.

And this—this need and his abandonment—would be the first thing she discussed with him when he returned Teddy for his hearing.

If he returned.

As it now stood, she had no idea whether he intended to carry on as her husband after the hearing came and went, or return to the canal, or sail to New York or Timbuktu.

And perhaps that was the most infuriating bit of all. The *not knowing*. It was painfully similar to other times when she'd been made to guess where he was and if he would come for her. She had enough problems without trying to understand the vague evasiveness of Beau Courtland.

And so it was with a mix of heartsickness, frustration, and sheer exasperation that she greeted her husband two weeks later, when the date for the hearing rolled around, and Beau and Teddy returned to London. Due to storms off the channel, the carriage had arrived close to midnight, barely managing the icy roads at a slow lurch. Teddy had fallen asleep in the carriage, and Beau had carried him to his room and tucked him into bed while Emmaline watched from the doorway.

Her husband looked more haggard than ever she had seen him—even more haggard than when she'd first called on his boat and discovered him unconscious.

To her great frustration, his wrung-out condition served to suppress her planned list of questions and concerns. He'd ridden through a storm to deliver her brother to her. Would she harangue him as soon as he walked through the door?

"I've missed you," she heard herself say instead. Teddy was finally asleep, and he met her in the dark hallway.

He grabbed her up and crushed her to his chest with such force the embrace was half of a hug and half an effort to keep the two of them from tipping over. They stood for five, maybe even ten minutes in the hallway outside Teddy's room and simply held each other. He inhaled the scent of her skin and rubbed his beard against her hair. She allowed the solid, muscled strength of him to shore her up.

Not enough, she'd said in her brain, but she could not bring herself to say the words. The truth was, in that moment, it felt very much like enough. It felt like all she'd ever wanted.

"Will you come to bed?" she heard herself ask.

He pulled away and stared at her. "Emma," he began, sounding confused, "you cannot mean to allow me to—"

"It's not for you." She sighed, realizing that she meant this.

And so they had gone to bed, and he had made love to her with such ardent, passionate, tender feeling she had wept from the futility of all they had missed while he had been away. She had fallen into the first peaceful sleep she'd had since the night of her wedding. She dreamed of Liverpool, and her parents before they had drowned, and New York City.

But when she awakened in the morning, her husband was gone.

B eau slipped from Emmaline's bed just before sunrise, dressed quietly, and crept down the stairs. Peach followed silently behind him. The street outside the house was swathed in the icy murk of frozen fog. He turned up the collar of his coat and hunkered down against the cold.

"Rainsleigh?"

Beau went still, reacting to the name he still thought of as his brother's.

He turned with exaggerated slowness, squinting into the mist of Lady Frinfrock's front garden.

"Lady Frinfrock?" he whispered. It was five o'clock in the morning.

"Yes, of course," came the reply. "Who else would be standing in my garden, calling your name before dawn?"

"What are you doing out of bed? Does Miss Breedlowe know you are out in the cold?"

"I don't live or die by Miss Breedlowe's command. If she does not approve of the hours I keep, she wisely does not impose her judgment on me. I enjoy the sunrise on icy winter mornings, if you must know. What excuse have you?"

Beau shrugged. "Running away from home, I suppose." He had not bargained on trading Emmaline's questions for the marchioness's.

"Again?" she asked.

Beau looked right and left down the hazy street. The chambermaids and kitchen staff would be up soon, readying their houses for the day, but now the silence of nighttime reigned. He ambled to the black iron spears of her garden gate.

"Have you brought the boy back for his day in court?" she asked.

"I have. He does not understand the hearing, but we have talked about what it may be like and how he must behave."

"And have you talked about how you must behave?"

The question took him by surprise. Either his short marriage had softened his instincts, or he was still half-asleep. He opened his mouth to answer but closed it and looked at the sky. He squeezed his eyes shut. The answer, of course, was *no*.

"Did you know, Beauregard, that everyone is granted by God with certain gifts?"

He stifled a groan. The last thing he needed in this moment was a lecture on the gifts from God.

The marchioness went on. "For example, I was granted the gift of cultivating the earth with beautiful vegetation and of sharing my sage counsel with people who need it most. That is to say, sharing it with everyone."

"And I give the appearance of someone who may need this sage counsel, do I?"

"Well, you are not a vegetable in need of cultivation. It is common knowledge that you are quite skilled in cultivating, all on your own."

He smirked.

She continued. "But you are handsome and charming, dashing and brave, aren't you? You are in possession of what some might call a large heart but with a champion's eye for the smallest among us. These are *your* gifts, a very rare and—dare I say—beguiling combination indeed."

"Er, thank you." Beau had never heard her say so many positive things in one sentence.

"But did you know, we all have other skills, and qualities, and traits that we may not classify as 'gifts' but that can still be called upon to get the job done? We must work harder at these."

"*My lady*," he cut in wearily. It was obvious, what she intended, and he was too old to be lectured.

"For some reason," she went on, "you believe that you cannot represent your family or your marriage or even this dear, daft boy who relies on you, because you've convinced yourself that you've no aptitude for this sort of thing. In this, my dear boy, you are mistaken."

"No," he said, irritated now, "I'm not mistaken. I *don't* have the aptitude, and I—"

"Oh, *not* mistaken about having no aptitude. Of course you do not. It's clear to me that you may be very average, indeed, at the task of testifying in parliamentary court. There'll be no harlots to rescue or lost simpletons to find inside those moldering halls. It will be precisely what you fear: stodgy, self-important men, preconceived notions about right from wrong, and entitlement. Of this is not what I speak. You believe you *cannot do it* because it does not come easily to you. But you *can* do it. It *can* be done. It's not *impossible*. It simply takes more work. Time and preparation and care. Not every useful skill comes naturally to most people, Beauregard. In the end, you may do passably well or you may do dreadfully. It depends on how hard you are willing, finally, to try, doesn't it? But regardless, it will get the job done."

"You think I cannot appear in court because I don't want to make the effort?" he asked.

"I think you cannot appear because you are *too afraid* to make the effort. You won't allow yourself to be less than perfect. It's a silly fear, really, and I won't allow it. Not from you. Only someone as blessed as you...with your myriad other dashing skills...would even consider it. Did you know most poor souls struggle with everything they do? We cannot all be perfect, can we? Not all the time. Sometimes we have to settling for being *adequate* at one or two endeavors. Sometimes we have to simply stay the course despite our inadequacies and simply say that we've turned up to give it a go."

When he had no answer for this, she went on. "You won't be surprised to learn that the very skills that aren't second nature frequently turn out to be the most worth your while. Like finding the courage to marry your wife, perhaps. And protecting your brother-in-law. And defeating the pompous Duke of Ticking at his own game."

"But how can you know?" asked Beau. "What if I cannot do it?"

"Don't be absurd. Of course you can do it. I've just said you could, and I'm never wrong. It's another of my gifts. Have you not heard a word? It takes effort. So give it the effort it deserves and then do the best you can. Perhaps you will win, perhaps you will not, but at least you have not run away."

Beau laughed bitterly. "But this is what I'm trying. I've...I've written this testimony, but what I really want to do is bolt. I am afraid. What if my failure costs me Emma or harms her brother? I cannot eat for this fear. I cannot sleep. I'm only in the street now going over and over the remarks in my head."

"Oh, lovely! A rehearsal." The marchioness clapped her hands together. "See, you're doing the hard work already. But you must allow me to hear these remarks. I am an incredibly diligent critic, and, believe it or not, I have one or two insights about the Duke of Ticking and his family that might prove useful. You'll have to leave your mangy animal outside, of course. But it shall be worth it. I knew the elder duke—what a lecherous toad of a man he was. I'm so glad you've risen to the occasion. After marriage to him, your poor wife has suffered enough."

Your poor wife has suffered enough.

Beau watched the marchioness's small, oval profile limp through the fog to her front door, confident that he would follow her.

Your poor wife has suffered enough.

This was certainly true, he realized. Perhaps everything she had said was true. Testifying for her brother suddenly seemed less about Beau's fear, and Beau's failure, and Beau's virulent resentment of the men who would judge him, and entirely about the woman he now realized he loved with all of his heart.

If there was suffering to be done, it was *his* turn to do it.

The marchioness had just heaved open her own heavy door when Beau admitted himself to her garden and clipped up the steps behind her.

"I must ask, my lady, given the many gifts that come easy in life to us both: what is one of the *challenges* that you face?"

"Oh," sighed the marchioness, stumping into her house, "what a silly question, and I cannot believe you cannot see it for yourself. But not everyone notices, I dare say. For better or for worse, I…am *not tall*."

CHAPTER FORTY

At nine o'clock in the morning of the next day, standing just outside the courtroom that would hear their fate, Emmaline learned that the tribunal of judges would *not* have time to hear the remarks she had prepared to plead her case for her brother's freedom. The court docket lagged woefully behind, Mr. Wick told her, a carry-over from an extensive trial the week before. Emmaline and Miss Breedlowe would only speak as part of their expected testimony as witnesses—simple answers to the lawyers' questions. This, Mr. Wick said, was customary procedure and all the court could permit. There would be no allowance for the additional personal appeal that Emmaline had prepared.

Emmaline had been warned by Mr. Wick to expect this, but tears still clogged her throat when he knelt beside her chair in the hallway and delivered this news. What a bloody waste. She had painstakingly written three heartfelt pages of memorized remarks—barely a quarter hour of the judges' time—and she was convinced that, despite whatever lie or surprise attack the duke might hurl, this personal appeal would have an impact on their decision. And now they would not hear her.

"I'm sorry, my lady," said Mr. Wick. "We discussed the probability of this, you'll remember. It was certainly worth a try, but they were not likely to hear more from any woman than her expected testimony on the stand."

Emmaline had nodded and wiped away her tears, not wanting Teddy or Jocelyn or Mr. Broom to see her and lose heart. Mr. Wick had worked endless hours to build their defense, and she was confident that he would do everything in his power to serve her brother. Even if he did look nearly as young as Teddy in his white wig and black robe.

"They will be ready for us in about five minutes' time, my lady," Mr. Wick went on. "Do you have everything you need? Are you ready?"

Like a fool, Emmaline looked at the doorway to the street once more, checking for Beau. She saw only clerks and parliamentary regulars coming and going. Even if he came, she reminded herself, what good could he possibly do now? He had not practiced the answers to Mr. Wick's examination. He had not been coached on what to expect from the examination of Ticking's lawyers. He would not even be here to stand beside her when the verdict was read. She'd awakened to find him gone, with no word. That was proof enough. He'd delivered her brother and vanished. She was on her own with Jocelyn and Mr. Broom. Even Teddy's old doctor from Liverpool had declined to appear, citing fear of opposing the Duke of Ticking in a court of law. He'd supplied a copy of Teddy's medical records, which showed no history of violence, but that was all. The few other old friends from Liverpool to whom she reached out refused to come for the same reasons. At least Beau was not alone in his unwillingness to cross a bloody duke, she thought. It would seem that everyone in England was afraid of Ticking but her and Mr. Wick.

At nine thirty, they were ushered inside the small courtroom, a chamber upholstered so thickly with crimson velvet it reminded Emmaline of the inside of a butchered animal. The Duke of Ticking, accompanied by a knot of solicitors, the doctor Jocelyn had seen in the park, and the alleged victim, young Lord Orin, were already seated proudly on the opposite side of the aisle. Behind him sat a row of blue-coated officers from Bow Street. The duke glanced scornfully at Emma when she entered, and then away. Less regard, she thought, than he would pay a servant.

Before the tribunal of judges entered the chamber, Emmaline leaned to Mr. Wick and whispered, "How long has the duke been in the courtroom? I did not see him arrive."

"Oh, he's only just come," said Mr. Wick. "Because he's a member of the House of Lords, he and his party may come and go by way of a private door"—he pointed to a small door at the side of the room—"without using the public hallway."

Emmaline absorbed this, allowing herself the tiniest bit of early panic. What a buffoon Ticking had seemed to her until now. He'd been oblivious, all those months, to the elaborate plans she had concocted, with very little effort, from her father's old dream. But also, he'd been effectively penniless, as had been his father before him. Meanwhile, Emmaline had sailed into the ducal household with finer clothes and jewelry, with better-dressed servants, and a generally grander way of life. Her dowry had paid their debts and restored their property and bought beef for supper. She'd actually felt a little sorry for them before she had known better.

But not now.

Now she knew the duke's influence bought so much more than her father's money ever had. Emmaline looked around. Now all she had was an untried lawyer, a female caretaker, and an old valet. And the side of right.

With only these and a quick prayer, Emmaline followed the bailiff's call to order and took up Teddy's hand, trying to keep calm and positive for his sake.

The court proceedings went along much as Mr. Wick had explained to her. The duke's solicitors made their case by calling witnesses, including young Lord Orin, whose claim was that Teddy had chased him around the room with the fireplace poker and then tackled him, hauled him to the kitchen, and shoved him, bodily, into the cold oven and threatened to cook him. In doing so, he had gouged his right eye.

When Emmaline thought of the hours that she and Mr. Wick had devoted to speculation about what, exactly, the details of the attack might be, she wanted to laugh. Never in a million years could they have dreamed up this. She had trouble schooling the expression on her face to hide how incredibly bizarre—and false—the notion sounded.

But Ticking's legal team sallied forth with officers who testified to signs of struggle near the oven, to gashes in the wall from fireplace poker blows that landed in the plaster instead of on Orin's entirely unharmed body. Dr. Vickery spoke at length about the lifetime he had studied ailments such as Teddy's, wherein madness lurked, inert, inside the unpredictably placid brain of a simpleton, only to erupt without warning and pose grave danger to unsuspecting family members and an able-minded general public.

After that, it was Mr. Wick's turn, and he called Emmaline, Jocelyn, and Mr. Broom before the judges. Although she would not be allowed to appeal to the tribunal with her memorized remarks, they would hear her answers to Mr. Wick's examination and the cross-examination of the duke's lawyers. She was determined to convey as much conviction and truth into her answers as possible.

Despite his inexperience, Mr. Wick skillfully established the timeline of her and Teddy's departure from the Duke of Ticking's house for good, which left no window of opportunity for this fire poker and oven assault. He further described Teddy's calm and nonviolent general nature, his history of good health, and glaring lack of previous conflict.

Teddy took the stand for Mr. Wick a mere five minutes. And when the duke's solicitors cross-examined him, he sat silently in his chair and did not speak. But he was not violent, and he was not aggressive, and he looked rather pitiful, in fact, slumped in the seat, hammered by questions that he did not understand. Throughout it all, he looked at Emmaline, and she smiled and nodded back encouragingly with tears in her eyes.

After the expected questions from cross-examinations and a closing argument by both sides, Emmaline studied the faces of the judges, trying to guess how they might rule. Before they could adjourn, one of the duke's solicitors stood up across the aisle.

"I beg your pardon, my lords," said the man. "If it pleases your lordships and this court, His Grace the Duke of Ticking would like to impart a brief personal account of his experience with the accused and his history with the boy's family, including his former stepmother, Emmaline Courtland, nee Crumbley, nee Holt." This progression of names, blatantly devoid of Emmaline's two titles, was said with equal notes of tedium and accusation.

Emmaline spun in her seat, looking at Mr. Wick. The young solicitor leapt up to object, citing the judge's denial of Emmaline's request for the same opportunity.

But Mr. Wick was overruled with no explanation, and the Duke of Ticking was invited to take the stand.

The diatribe that followed was almost too much for Emmaline to bear. Indeed, Jocelyn extended a cool hand and laid it gently on Emmaline's wrist to keep her from leaping up and shouting, *liar!* Beside her, Mr. Wick scribbled furious notes, hoping for a rebuttal, but Emmaline knew that no such fairness would come. This was Ticking's parting shot, designed to overshadow all of the fictional (and, in fact, outrageous) evidence, the vague testimonies, and the odious doctor. It was a show of his most princely, most erudite, most arrogant-yet-gracious self; an effort to demonstrate a distinct line between *them*—meaning her merchant family, her father's salacious books, and her brother's propensity for unaccountable violence and her mercenary marriages—and *us.* The dukes. Their fragile ducal sons. The ancient families. The established. The moral. The educated. The reasonable. The good.

When he was finished, he thanked the judges, he thanked the Commission for Lunacy Care, he thanked the brave Runners of Bow Street, and he thanked God. And then he sat proudly down and closed his eyes as if in prayer.

Emmaline watched this performance, blinked twice, and then drew breath to say something...anything...to counter the slander and injustice of it all. Jocelyn's hand on her wrist increased in pressure. Mr. Wick snapped his head to her, his pleading eyes wide—*do not say a word*—but she did not care. Some fair and equal opposition must be said.

"I beg your pardon, my lords," said a voice from the doorway. The secret, special doorway, just for peers of the realm.

Emmaline closed her mouth. She went completely still in her velvety red seat. Her heart, formerly beating like a wild, maddened thing, missed two beats and hung, suspended in her chest.

Emmaline knew that voice.

Emmaline *loved* that voice.

She spun in her chair, staring, mouth agape, at her husband.

"Many apologies for my tardiness," said Beau Courtland from the private door. "I was detained by matter of national commerce. I'm in the process of exporting a shipment of English literature to America, and this trade embargo with President Jefferson has me running half-mad."

This what with whom has him doing what? thought Emmaline.

Emmaline felt as if she'd been magically transported to another courtroom where someone *else* had prepared night and day for the hearing on which her brother's very life hinged, and strangers that she did not know enacted all the parts.

The bailiff trotted over to Beau, they whispered an exchange, and then the bailiff intoned, "The Viscount Rainsleigh."

The judges exchanged whispers and motioned him forth. Beau strode confidently to the desk behind which Emmaline and Teddy and Mr. Wick were seated, and he leaned down and whispered a few words to Mr. Wick.

The solicitor had the courtesy to cast an alarmed, defensive look to Emmaline, but then he cleared his throat and addressed the judges, asking if they might hear Lord Rainsleigh's remarks in defense of his brother-in-law, Theodore Holt, in the same way they had entertained the Duke of Ticking's.

Emmaline was so shocked by his very presence she forgot to be shocked that the judges allowed it.

She gaped at her husband, who looked so tall and impeccably dressed in a dark suit and gloves, with a proper hat tucked beneath his arm. She had never seen him so well turned out, even for their wedding. He was cleanly shaven, with his hair stylishly slicked back. A creamy cravat billowed almost to his jawline.

In the moment before he turned and took the stand, she stopped looking at his person and stared him in the eye. He paused, looking back, and she realized he was waiting for her to look at him.

He could not speak to her, of course, but she could discern the meaning with his eyes. She read contrition, and fear, and *love*, plain as day, in their blue depths.

She blinked twice, trying to understand the jumble of emotions so clearly identified in that look, and he raised one perfect eyebrow. She was suddenly shot through with the same damnable reaction she always had whenever he raised his eyebrow at her: hopefulness, and love, and toe-curling thrill.

But now he was taking his place before the judges, setting down his hat, pulling off his gloves. Emmaline watched him closely, and she wondered if anyone else could see his hands shake. Or the small muscle twitch in his jaw. But when she looked in his eyes, she saw only blue-eyed charm come to life.

No, she decided, no one knew. But *she* knew, and the bitterness and frustration that had banded around her heart these last two weeks began to loosen, thread by thread, as he surpassed his fear in front of all of these people.

"My lords," Beau said, "I extend my gratitude to you for permission to testify out of turn. Your time, I know is, precious, and a young man's life will be forever changed by the decisions you make here today.

"If you would indulge me, I should like to begin by telling you the brief story of the way I came to know my lady wife and her brother. My own family, quite at their wit's end, introduced us with the hope of my personal improvement. I had newly inherited, and, as a second son who never imagined he'd see the title or lands on his shoulders, I was in dire need of refinement. The mean habits on which I skated along as an officer in the Royal Navy would never do in London society, you see. And so my brother actually charged Lady Rainsleigh—then the Dowager Duchess of Ticking—with refining my pathetic manners. Lady Rainsleigh, who was raised the daughter of one of Liverpool's finest families and herself a dowager duchess, was the perfect candidate to school me. She volunteered in the charity pursuits of my sister-in-law, you see, and under the hopeful eyes of my brother and his wife, Lady Rainsleigh rose to the challenge of taking me in hand."

A ripple of laughter followed this statement. Emmaline looked around the room in disbelief.

"At the time, I was a confirmed bachelor, focused on renovating my boat and looking in on the viscountcy if I had the time. But Emmaline...Emmaline's natural beauty and charm was difficult to resist. My interest in refinement began to rise with amazing speed." Another chuckle. "Before long, we exhausted my ability to learn any more on the topic of good manners, and I was forced to show my hand. She was nearly two years gone in mourning her late husband by this time, and I began to court her. The courtship was not a long one, I'll be the first to admit. When we realized the fervor of our attraction, I knew at once we must wed. I obtained a special license and married her earlier this month at a little church in Watford, with her brother and my family looking on. She is..."

Here, Beau paused, turned in his seat, and looked Emmaline square in the eye, "The love of my life."

He looked back to the room. "I will not deny it. I relate this sappy tale of requited love because I managed to hear a little of the Duke of Ticking's remarks from the hallway. Forgive me for listening through the door, but I did not wish to interrupt. And now that I've heard his appeal, I worry that I would be remiss if I did not question the incredibly bitter, slanderous tone of His Grace's history with Emmaline and her brother, because my history has been so very opposite."

After that, Emmaline's hearing went a little bit off because her throat had closed, and her eyes had filled, and her own pulse pounded too loudly in her ears. From what she could make out, Beau spoke eloquently of Teddy—both of his time with him in London and their days alone with Mr. Broom in Wiltshire. He called up Teddy's love of birds and horses, of fish and books. He spoke of the loneliness Teddy felt when he was away from his sister and the grief he still knew over the death of his parents.

At the mention of Mama and Papa, even Jocelyn pulled her hand from Emmaline's wrist so that she too might wipe the tears from her eyes.

Next, Beau alluded to Emmaline's and Teddy's parents, the joy they brought to thousands of readers and the commerce they generated with the brisk sales of their books. Walking the fine line between suggestion and slander, he mentioned that Teddy's inheritance may have, at one time, seemed available to the Duke of Ticking, but when Emmaline married out of the family, that availability vanished.

Was it possible, Beau asked, that this change in fortune resulted in the duke's need for some revenge?

After that, Beau devoted two spare two sentences to Emmaline's marriage at the age of nineteen to the bankrupt elder duke, adding that Beau himself was heavily invested in the shipping empire of his brother and had no interest in the inheritance of the mentally challenged brother of his new wife.

By the end, Beau revealed more of his signature dash and swagger, and Emmaline found herself helplessly consumed. She felt a love so complete, she worried for the future of her own helpless heart.

"I cannot deny that I stand here today, in part, because I love my wife," he said in closing. "You will concede that jewelry and furs only go so far. But there is no gift quite like public defense of one's brother-in-law in a court of law." He cleared his throat suggestively, and the courtroom chuckled again.

"But I've also come because I am a man who loves my country. A decorated veteran of the war with France, I've also sailed the globe and shown the face of Britain to countries far and wide. But the England I've shown the world is *not* a country that steals innocent young men like Teddy Holt from their loving families and incarcerates them with unfamiliar doctors in Surrey.

"The England that I have shown knows compassion and the value of a family who looks after its own. It is a country whose wise courts can make the distinction between a lunatic and a simple boy who wishes to live a simple life. In other words, it knows the distinction between a lie and the truth.

"Yes, I have seen many things in this great, wide world of ours, my lords, but I have never seen a woman more devoted to her brother, nor have I seen a young man—afflicted though he may be—more gentle and trusting, peaceful and calm."

After the final word rang out, he waited a beat, and then he rose, collected his hat and gloves, and made his way to an empty seat in the audience. Emmaline could not prevent herself from turning and watching him go. He dropped in a chair next to an officer, balanced his hat on his knee, and blew out a long, exhausting breath. When he saw her looking at him, he cocked one elegant eyebrow.

Emmaline's traitorous heart did a flip, and she turned around.

CHAPTER FORTY-ONE

The judges deliberated only ten minutes before they returned, and the bailiff read the ruling: "Innocent on all accounts and free to return home with his family."

Emmaline barely managed to contain a scream before she leapt into Teddy's arms and held him to her. "You did so well, Teddy!" she whispered through her tears. "You did so very well! And now we may go. Would you like to go home and prepare for our journey? Are you ready to sail on the big boat to America? The Duke of Ticking cannot stand in our way anymore. Shall we go, you and I? Like we planned?"

"Beau?" asked Teddy, clinging to her.

Emmaline pulled away. "Yes, did you see him? He was very brave and very important. How proud we are to have him speak on our behalf."

Now Mr. Wick wanted to shake her hand. But even more so, he wanted to shake the hand of Lord Rainsleigh, who...stood directly behind them.

She released Teddy and stared up at him. "Mr. Wick seems eager to thank you," she said carefully, allowing Mr. Wick to jostle her aside for a handshake.

"I will shake the hand of Mr. Wick and anyone else after I have had a word with you," Beau said, leaning to be heard over the crowd. "Can I pull you away for a moment?"

Emmaline blinked. "All right," she said, gesturing to Mr. Broom to stay with Teddy because Jocelyn was nowhere to be found.

She followed him into the hall, and he led her to a far, shadowy corner beneath an elaborately mounted coat of arms.

"I was late, Emma, and I'm sorry."

She was not sure what she expected to hear, but it was not this. "Yes, well, you dashed in in the nick of time and made up for it, didn't you?"

"I believe the judges would have ruled on behalf of Teddy regardless."

"You did not see their faces after Ticking's lofty speech."

"Regardless. It was cruel and unfair to keep you wondering, and I…I wanted you to know that I'll not do it again."

She laughed at this; she couldn't help it.

"What's so funny?" he asked, smiling down. He was so breathtakingly handsome when he smiled.

"Let us aim to not be late 'for *once*,' shall we, before you vow to 'never do it again.'"

"Oh, darling," he said, taking her hand and pressing it to his mouth. "Your days of wondering are no more. I've said I shall not be late, but what I mean is, you'll not wonder about my affections, or my devotion, or even *where the bloody hell I am*, ever again. Not as long as I draw breath. I will be at your side. I love you, Emma. I have loved you for so damn long. I just did not know what to call it."

"But this is your problem," she said, but she laughed, and she raised up on her toes and tilted her head, offering her lips. "I've said it all along. You're too painfully specific. And it makes you uncomfortable. It makes everyone uncomfortable. If only you'd tried to tell me something like, 'This feeling is pleasant. I like pleasantness. I shall pursue this feeling,' then we would have known."

"I know I should like to pursue pleasantness right now," he said, and he kissed her.

Emmaline gobbled up his kiss, and the next, and the next.

When she opened her eyes, she noticed Miss Breedlowe, walking near the door to the street. She leaned back. "But that looks like Miss Breedlowe hurrying out. She cannot go; we've ridden together in the Rainsleigh carriage. But wait. Who is that with her?"

Emmaline let out a little gasp. "Is that *Lady Frinfrock?*" She looked at Beau. "Why would the marchioness come to our hearing?"

Beau shrugged and looked across the gleaming floor of the wide hall. The departing form of the marchioness stumped with her cane out the door. "I cannot say for sure. But I'm glad she did. How else would I have known about the special door?"

When the Holt-Courtland party and their dog, Peach, reached New York Harbor in March 1814, the Eastern Seaboard of America was in the throes of its coldest, snowiest spring on record.

The freezing temperatures and sunless days were a trial for a family that had always considered themselves impervious to inclement weather (they were English, after all), but the real challenge was transporting Emmaline's books in the deep snow. Even so, Emmaline insisted that the books be put up for sale immediately. They could not wait for spring if they wished to have money to live. And what season, she told them, was better for selling books than the cold, dark, bleak months of an endless winter.

No one worked longer hours in the bitter cold than Beau. He learned the streets and alleys of New York, ferreted out the hardiest and most motivated of day laborers, and drove their wagons of books through the frozen sludge to every shop and newsmonger, from upstate New York to New Jersey.

While Beau provided the product, Emmaline charmed shopkeepers, convincing them to display the books alongside winter hats, firewood, and other staples of winter.

Their work did not go unrewarded. Listless, confined Americans, idle for months by the cold, devoured the books. Sales of Holt's Fireside Adventures far exceeded her wildest expectations, and Emmaline was able to write to Mr. Wick as early as May of that same year.

> *Please begin negotiations with the Holt board of trustees for subsequent titles. Demand is overwhelming. Simply put, we need more books. In the meantime, I have begun talks with a handful of aspiring writers about commissioning original novels. The Americans are cleverer than one would expect. Words cannot express my excitement over the prospect of acquiring an original work to be published by a New York branch of Holt Publishing. Please find attached a bank note for your role in the launch of the American arm of this company...*

The modern, densely populated nature of New York also allowed Emmaline to discover a special school for Teddy, one that allowed him to indulge his love of books and birds every day with other adult students like him. It was difficult to know what Teddy enjoyed more, weekdays spent at school or Sundays spent at home with Beau and Emmaline.

Of all the expatriated Holts and Courtlands, Beau flourished and enjoyed New York perhaps most of all. He loved the wild, sleepless pulse of the city, the vibrant mix of people from all over the world, and perhaps best, he loved *not* living on a moldering houseboat to escape the expectations of his title and rank.

The expectations of most Americans, he found, extended to minding one's own business, delivering on one's promise of books or rent or hard work, and simple survival. Every day was a challenge, and he relished it. Succeed in commerce and get along in the swirling morass of cultures and populations—this was what mattered in America. Beau thrived. Even his dog was happy.

At Emmaline's suggestion, he sold the Henrietta Place town house in London and hired a capable steward to oversee the estate in Wiltshire. He attended other stray business of the viscountcy through the post, declining every invitation and selling off any interest that became a burden.

His brother, he knew, would never understand his ambivalence or detachment, but Bryson's frequent letters were cheerful and well-wishing, with more questions about Emmaline and Teddy and their life in New York than anything he left behind in England. Bryson signed every letter the same way.

Nothing is half as clever or diverting since you've gone. We miss you all. When are you coming home?

"When *are* we coming home?" Beau asked Emma one night, after reading his brother's letter aloud. They'd been in New York two years, sold thousands of books, and the following spring would see the release of the first original Holt's Fireside Adventure acquired by Emmaline.

"I cannot say," she replied. "In many ways, it feels like we're already there."

"Already home, you mean to say?"

She smiled and reached across the bed to take his hand. "It's no boat on Paddington Lock, I know, but it feels correct in many ways."

"I was going to say," he said, dropping his brother's letter, "exactly the same thing. But then again, you were always home to me." And then he scooped his wife into his arms and kissed her as he always had, even from the very beginning…

As if he were coming home.

ACKNOWLEDGMENTS

One for the Rogue is the third of three books originally released all in the same year, and my family, including my mom and dad, sister, in-laws, husband, children, friends, and even my dogs tolerated a lot of absenteeism on my part, both of mind and body, to make this year happen, plus hours of shop talk. I am forever grateful for their support and encouragement. I would also like to thank the real-life inspiration for Teddy Holt, my friend Kyle and his inner circle, all so dear to me, for the joy and resiliency they bring to their bright corner of Houston, Texas, and everywhere they go.

Discover Bryson and Elisabeth's unconventional
happy ever after in

THE VIRGIN AND THE VISCOUNT

The Virgin

Lady Elisabeth Hamilton-Baythes has a painful secret. At fifteen, she was abducted by highwaymen and sold to a brothel. But two days later, she was rescued by a young lord, a man she's never forgotten. Now, she's devoted herself to save other innocents from a similar fate.

The Viscount

Bryson Courtland, Viscount Rainsleigh, never breaks the rules. Well, once, but that was a long time ago. He's finally escaped his unhappy past to become one of the wealthiest noblemen in Britain. The final thing he needs to complete his ideal life? A perfectly proper wife.

The Unraveling

When Bryson and Elisabeth meet, he sees only a flawless candidate for his future wife. But a distant memory calls to him every time he's with her. Elisabeth knows she's not the wife Bryson needs, and he is the only person who has the power to reveal her secret. But neither can resist the devastating pull of attraction, and as the truth comes to light, they must discover that an improper love is the truest of all.

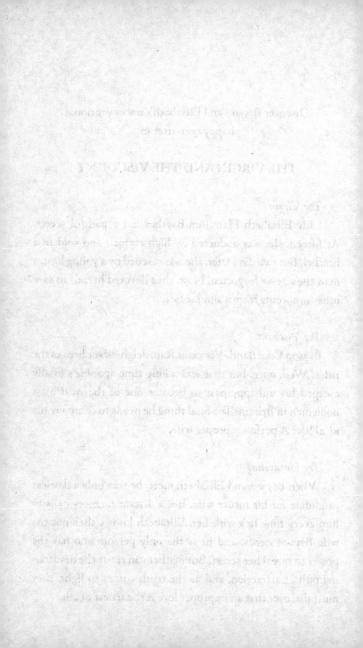

And travel back to Henrietta Street to
discover the joys of

THE EARL NEXT DOOR

American heiress Piety Grey is on the run. Suddenly in London and facing the renovation of a crumbling townhouse, she's determined to make a new life for herself—anything is better than returning to New York City, where a cruel mother and horrid betrothal await her. The last thing she needs is a dark, tempting earl inciting her at every turn...

Trevor Rheese, the Earl of Falcondale, isn't interested in being a good neighbor. After fifteen years of familial obligation, he's finally free. But when the disarmingly beautiful Piety bursts through his wall—and into his life—his newfound freedom is threatened...even as his curiosity is piqued.

Once Piety's family arrives in London, Falcondale suddenly finds himself in the midst of a mock courtship to protect the seductive woman who's turned his world upside down. It's all for show—or at least it should be. But if Falcondale isn't careful, he may find a very real "happily ever after" with the woman of his dreams...

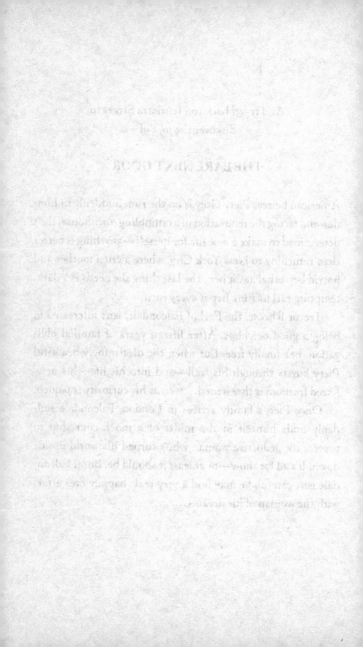

CHARIS MICHAELS believes a romance novel is a very long, exciting answer to the question: "So, how did you two meet?" She loves to answer this question with different characters, each time she writes a book. Prior to writing romance, she studied journalism at Texas A&M and managed PR for a trade association. She has also worked as a tour guide at Disney World, harvested peaches on her family's farm, and entertained children as the "Story Godmother" at birthday parties. She has lived in Texas, Florida, and London, England. She now makes her home in the Washington, DC, metro area.

Discover great authors, exclusive offers, and more at hc.com.

Give in to your Impulses . . .
Continue reading for excerpts from
our newest Avon Impulse books.
Available now wherever e-books are sold.

ALONG CAME LOVE
by *Tracey Livesay*

WHEN A MARQUESS
LOVES A WOMAN
THE SEASON'S ORIGINAL SERIES
by *Vivienne Lorret*

An Excerpt from

ALONG CAME LOVE

By Tracey Livesay

When free-spirited India Shaw finds herself
in trouble, she must rely on the one man she
never planned to see again—her baby's father.

Michael Black's cellphone vibrated against his chest and he pulled it from his inner pocket. The caller ID showed an unfamiliar number with "San Francisco, CA" beneath it, but no other identifying information.

His brows converged in the middle of his forehead. It was probably a wrong number. And yet his finger hovered and then pressed the green button.

"Hello?"

"Mike."

He straightened. Her voice stroked his hedonistic hotspots. The tingle caused by every whispered declaration, every lingering caress, hit him all at once.

"Indi."

"Long time, no hear."

Her forced gaiety jarred him loose from her vocal web and allowed his brain to function. Why had she left? Where had she been? What did she want? Why was she calling?

"I know I'm probably the last person you want to talk to and I understand, considering how I ended things and I—"

He remembered this about her, the stream of talking on an endless loop. His favorite remedy? A cock-stirring, toe curling kiss.

"Indi, spit it out."

A thick silence, and then—

"Can you post bail for me? I've been arrested for burglary."

Well *that* happened.

The door to the precinct closed behind Indi. Exhaustion weighed her down, leaving her head throbbing and her sight unfocused. She shivered, her cable knit sweater offering inadequate insulation from the chill.

If she had a bucket list, she could confidently check off this experience: get yourself arrested in an unfamiliar city. It hadn't been anything like *Orange is the New Black*—Thank God!—but she had met some interesting women while she'd been booked and processed. Turns out, her unstable living situations and various relocations equipped her with the unique skill set needed to survive the city's holding cell.

But she didn't do bucket lists. They were created for people who scurried through life afraid to take chances, regretting their caution when faced with their mortality. Indi's life *was* a bucket list. Hence, her current predicament.

"Where's Ryan?"

The brusque voice wrapped itself around her heart and squeezed. She stilled and her breath went on strike.

Those words. That tone. This situation. It wasn't how she'd pictured their reunion.

Though their best friends were married to one another, careful planning on her part would've given her several years to let time and distance erode the memories and allow them to communicate without her recalling the way he'd made her body quake with ecstasy. She'd be cool, look polished, and possess the proper grace to put them both at ease.

That had been the fantasy BN—Before Nugget. Now she'd settle for an encounter where she didn't look and smell like a cat lady's ashtray, and she possessed something other than an unplanned pregnancy and a felony charge.

Despite his harsh tone, the man leaning against the metallic silver Porsche Panamera—new; the last time she'd seen him, he'd been driving a Jaguar—was as gorgeous, as powerful, and as autocratic as the luxury sedan he drove. He'd tamed his blond curls—what a shame—into a sleek mass that shone beneath the street lamps and his body looked trim and powerful in a dark tailored suit and crisp white collared shirt without a tie. He could've been waiting for his date to a society gala and not standing in the street in front of the sheriff's office after midnight, waiting for the state judicial system's newest enrollee.

Indi hefted her backpack onto her shoulder, ignored the dips, swerves, and inversions occurring in her belly, and slowly descended the concrete steps. "He's finishing up the paperwork."

She'd forgotten how big he was. She was a tad taller than average and she knew from experience her eyes would be level with his chin, a chin now covered in downy blond fuzz. Experience also taught her the stubble would be a delicious abrasion against her skin.

"Do you have anything to say to me?"

She blinked. She had much to say to him. But here? Now?

She'd hated calling him. Truthfully, she would've hated calling anyone in this situation. Would rather have stayed behind bars and figured a way out of this mess. But this wasn't about her personal preferences. She needed to make decisions in Nugget's best interests. And *that* meant doing what was necessary to ensure she spent as little time in jail as possible.

She hadn't seen Mike in three months, since she'd awakened to see his face softened in sleep. Terrified of the feelings budding to life within her, she'd stealthily gathered up her belongings and left without looking back. And despite her behavior, when she'd called, he'd shown up. He deserved many things from her, starting with gratitude.

But did he have to be an arrogant ass about it?

She balled a fist in the folds of her skirt. "What else would you like me to say?"

He pushed away from the sex-mobile. "How about 'Thank you for canceling your plans and coming to get me'?"

Crap. She'd pulled him away from something. Or someone.

It was none of her business. She'd given up any say in who he spent time with the night she'd walked away.

"How in the hell did you get arrested for burglary?"

She swiped at the allegation. "Those are trumped up charges."

"So you didn't do it?"

"Of course not. I mean, breaking and entering makes you think of a cat burglar or someone in a ski mask robbing the place. That's not how it happened."

Mike narrowed his eyes and subjected her to his self-righteous stare. "Then why don't you tell me what happened."

An Excerpt from

WHEN A MARQUESS LOVES A WOMAN
The Season's Original Series
By Vivienne Lorret

Five years have passed since the Max Harwick
shared a scandalous kiss with Lady Juliet, only to
have her marry someone else. He's never forgiven
her . . . but he's never stopped loving her either.

Some days Lady Juliet Granworth wanted to fling open the nearest window sash and scream.

And it was all the Marquess of Thayne's fault.

"*Good evening, Saunders.*" A familiar baritone called from the foyer and drifted in through the open parlor door. *Max.*

Drat it all! He was a veritable devil. Only she didn't have to *speak* his name but simply *think* it for him to appear. She should have known better than to allow her thoughts to roam without a leash to tug them back to heel.

"I did not realize Lord Thayne would be attending dinner this evening," Zinnia said, her spine rigid as she perched on the edge of her cushion and darted a quick, concerned glance toward Juliet.

Marjorie looked to the open door, her brows knitted. "I did not realize it either. He said that he was attending—"

"Lord Fernwold's," Max supplied as he strode into the room, his dark blue coat parting to reveal a gray waistcoat and fitted blue trousers. He paused long enough to bow his dark head in greeting—at least to his mother and Zinnia. To Juliet, he offered no more than perfunctory scrutiny before heading to the sideboard, where a collection of crystal decanters waited. "The guests were turned away at the door. His lordship's mother is suffering a fever."

Juliet felt the flesh of her eyelids pucker slightly, her lashes drawing together. It was as close as she could come to glaring at him while still leaving her countenance unmoved. The last thing she wanted was for him, or anyone, to know how much his slight bothered her.

Marjorie tutted. "Again? Agnes seemed quite hale this afternoon in the park. Suspiciously, this has happened thrice before on the evenings of her daughter-in-law's parties. I tell you, Max, I would never do such a thing to your bride."

Max turned and ambled toward them, the stems of three sherry glasses in one large hand and a whiskey in the other. He stopped at the settee first, offering one to his mother and another to Zinnia. "Nor would you need to, for I would never marry a woman who would tolerate the manipulation." Then he moved around the table and extended a glass to Juliet, lowering his voice as he made one final comment. "Nor one whose slippers trod only the easiest path."

She scoffed. If marriage to Lord Granworth had been easy, then she would hate to know the alternative.

"I should not care for sherry this evening," Juliet said. And in retaliation against Max's rudeness, she reached out and curled her fingers around his whiskey.

Their fingers collided before she slipped the glass free. If she hadn't taken him off guard, he might have held fast. As it was, he opened his hand instantly as if scalded by her touch. But she knew that wasn't true because the heat of his skin nearly blistered her. The shock of it left the underside of her fingers prickly and somewhat raw.

To soothe it, she swirled the cool, golden liquor in the glass. Then, before lifting it to her lips, she met his gaze. His irises were a mixture of earthy brown and cloud gray. Years ago, those eyes were friendly and welcoming but now had turned cold, like puddles reflecting a winter sky. And because it pleased her to think of his eyes as mud puddles, that was what she thought of when she took a sip. Unfortunately, she didn't particularly care for whiskey and fought to hide a shudder as the sour liquid coated her tongue.

Max mocked her with a salute of his dainty goblet and tossed back the sherry in one swallow. Then the corner of his mouth flicked up in a smirk.

She knew that mouth intimately—the firm warm pressure of those lips, the exciting scrape of his teeth, the mesmeric skill of his tongue . . .

Unbidden warmth simmered beneath her skin as she recalled the kiss that had ruined her life. And for five years, she'd paid a dire price for one single transgression—a regretful and demeaning marriage, the sudden deaths of her parents, and the loss of everyone she held dear.

By comparison, returning to London to reclaim her life as a respected widow should have been simple. And it would have been if Max hadn't interfered.

Why did he have to hinder her fresh start?

Of course, she knew the answer. She'd wounded his ego years ago, and her return only served as a reminder. He didn't want her living four doors down from his mother—or likely within forty miles of him.